THE LEVEL UP

PART 2

LUXURY KING

LOCK DOWN PUBLICATIONS AND CA$H PRESENTS

Lock Down Publications

P.O. Box 944

Stockbridge, GA 30281

www.lockdownpublications.com

Like our page on Facebook: Lock Down Publications

www.facebook.com/lockdownpublications.ldp

STAY CONNECTED WITH US!

Text **LOCKDOWN** to 22828 to stay up-to-date with new releases, sneak peaks, contests and more…

Like our page on Facebook:
Lock Down Publications

Join Lock Down Publications/The New Era Reading Group

Visit our website:
www.lockdownpublications.com

Follow us on Instagram:
Lock Down Publications

Email Us: We want to hear from you!

CHAPTER 1

The 2015 Grammy Awards

"Winner for best rap album is," the lady presenting the award opened the envelope in her hand, "Presidential Peso!" She read from the card.

Everyone in attendance stood and clapped for Peso, who was dressed in an all-white Tom Ford suit. He took his daughter, Mya, by her arm then turned to his girlfriend, Princess. "Come on, Queen. Come share this moment with us." Peso then looked back to his little brother, Shoota, and right-hand man, Hitta. "Y'all pull up too. I want my family up there with me." He led the way to the stage.

Peso stepped on stage and gladly accepted his fifth award for the night. He cleared his throat before speaking. "Five for five at the Grammys; I'm extremely blessed," he said, not able to hold back his smile. Tears of joy began to form in his eyes. He let one fall freely. "Only if you people in this building knew what me and my family had to endure to get here. Only if y'all knew all the losses we had to take to get this one win. I remember being in prison, looking at a life sentence, still telling myself every single day that I was gonna win a Grammy. This didn't happen by mistake. It was manifested. The power of manifestation is real. To the young boys and girls out there watching this, chase your dreams, put what you want into the universe, and work hard for it, and that's what will appear in front of you."

MEANWHILE IN CONEY ISLAND

Flee cruised down Mermaid Avenue in his brand-new AMG Mercedes Benz. Hitta had put him in the race, and he'd been winning ever since. He pulled up in front of the liquor store, hopped out of his Benz, and walked inside. The place was a bit crowded, so he waited in line. To kill some time, Flee pulled out his iPhone and scrolled down his Instagram timeline. A huge smile was plastered on his face when he saw a picture of Peso holding several Grammy awards. He double tapped the picture to like it; just when he was about to post a comment, someone lightly tapped him on the shoulder.

Flee turned around and locked eyes with one of the most beautiful women he had ever seen. "Excuse me, handsome, you gon play in your phone all day, or are you gonna step up and order something? Cause I got things to do," said the beauty before him. The girl was a spitting image of the singer, Cassie. They could really pass for twins.

"Pardon me, love. Y'all can skip me," Flee said and stepped to the side, so the Cassie lookalike and her girls could pass him. She twisted her face up playfully.

"You don't even look old enough to buy liquor," she teased.

Flee leaned in close enough to kiss her neck. "I'm not old enough. Keep that between us though," he whispered.

The girl looked Flee up and down, and her panties instantly became moist. Not only did he seem to be the perfect gentleman, but he was handsome with a smile that was breathtaking. The 14-karat gold Cuban link looked too heavy to be on his neck, but it was his bust down Rolex that screamed for attention with all the Rolex diamonds dancing on its face. He was sporting a Balmain jean suit. The Fendi belt that was around his waist was pointless because his jeans were sagging. On his feet were a pair of Air Jordan Retro 3s.

In this new era, one would think that Flee was in the fraud lane, but this chick knew better. His swag didn't scream scammer. He had dope boy written all over him. He was most definitely her type. She gave him the "you can get it look" then stepped past him. "Your secret is safe with me," the girl flirted a little. Her attention was now on the man behind the counter. It was now Flee's turn to eye her up and down. He got a view of her perfectly round bottom. "Can I get your big bottle of Patron?" She looked back just in time to catch Flee staring at her butt. "Stop staring," she teased. "But what you drinking, handsome? It's on me."

Flee stepped up to the counter. "Mr. James, what's going on?" He greeted the owner.

"Wassup, Flee? You getting your regular, or are you gonna get something small since the lady is treating?" Mr. James asked.

"You can get me my regular." He dug in his pocket, but she stopped him.

"I told you it's on me." She handed the man behind the glass her credit card, or at least what he thought was her credit card.

After paying for both bottles, she handed Flee a bag, and

they walked out of the store with her home girls behind them. "Good looking, big spender," Flee teased.

"You got jokes, huh?" She smiled. "Don't thank me. Thank the card god." She winked at him and walked away with her friends.

"Ayo!" Flee called out, walking toward her.

"My name is not Ayo!" she shouted back in a feisty tone but stopped for him. "Wassup, handsome?"

"I'm not gonna lie, shawdy. You fire." He bit down on his bottom lip while giving her the once over. "You deserve to be on the arm of a nigga like me," he said with just a little bit of arrogance.

"Is that so?" She blushed. "I don't even think you are old enough for me. I'm not tryna go to jail," she said playfully.

"What's age to a nigga that has all this experience?" he shot back without missing a beat. "Here." He tried to hand her his phone, but she declined.

"What you giving me your phone for?" She smiled.

"So, you can put your number in it." He smiled back.

"I'm not gonna lie. My life is complicated right now," she claimed.

"So let me make it less complicated. I promise you won't regret it. Let a nigga just get one date."

"A promise is a comfort to a fool. You better impress me. Give me your phone."

Flee handed her his phone, and she stored her number in it then handed it back to him. "It's saved under Lexi. You have my number and my name now, so what's yours?"

"They call me Flee."

CHAPTER 2

Los Angeles, California

Hitta sat on the foot of the king-sized bed, smoking a blunt. He'd just watched his best friend's dreams come true a few hours ago. Seeing Peso accept those Grammys made Hitta feel like he'd won the awards also. He was truly happy for Peso.

VRRRRRRRM! VRRRRRRRRM! VRRRRRRRRM! His iPhone vibrated. He looked down and saw Peso's name across the screen. He slid his thumb across the screen and answered the FaceTime call. Peso's smiling face popped up on the screen. "Wassup, brozay?" Hitta said while smiling also.

"We up, my brother," Peso replied. He was still not able to hold back his smile. Truth was he couldn't believe that he'd just won five Grammy awards. He hadn't come down off his high yet, and he probably never would.

"I can't lie, bro, I'm extremely proud of you. All that hard work you put in has finally paid off."

"Nah, all that work *we* put in has finally paid off," Peso

corrected him. "You been with me every step of the way. To be honest, none of this shit would even be possible without you, bro. Thank you," he added, expressing his gratitude.

"No need for the thank you. We brothers. Everything I've done, I know you would do for me twice over. We all we got."

"And we all we need. What's good with Ash?"

Hitta and his lady were not on the best of terms right now. She hadn't said a word to him since being released from Rikers Island yesterday. Even though she was innocent, she was still held without bail. The D.A. was hoping that she would give them something on Hitta, but she stayed solid like the rider that she was.

"She still ain't say shit to me, bro. I fucked up for real this time. I don't think I ever seen her this upset before," Hitta admitted.

"So go holla at her and make that right. This is Ashley we talking about, Hitta. That woman worships you. We done fell on way tougher times than this one. Sis been here with us through some shit. She's a lil hurt right now, but without a doubt, she really loves you wholeheartedly, and a love like Ashley's ain't just walking away. She wouldn't even be here with you if it was over."

"Nigga, she came here for you," Hitta chuckled.

"That may be true, but she's going to bed with you. Nigga, stop being stubborn and go talk to ya wife. Fix that, Hitta. I was just checkin in tho. I love you, bro. I'll hit you in the a.m."

"Love you more, my nigga. Kiss my god daughter for me."

"I got you, bro." The call ended.

Hitta dropped his phone on the bed and headed to the bathroom. Just as he was about to enter, Ashley opened the door, wearing nothing but a towel. "I was coming to join you, baby girl," he said softly.

"Go join that bitch that you were on that date with." Ashley pushed him out of her way and stormed off. Hitta didn't chase her. Instead, he just entered the bathroom and stripped down.

Hitta stood under the steaming hot shower water in deep thought. First, he had his home situation with Ashley, who was upset because he was out with another woman. He couldn't wrap his head around why she was so upset. It was only an innocent dinner, nothing more. Then, there was this situation with Rolex Rich, who was trying to have him killed behind what was somewhat a lie.

Things were just so bittersweet at the moment because even with all the drama going in in his life, his best friend was really living out his dreams.

Hitta finally turned the water off. Grabbing a towel off of the rack, he dried his body thoroughly before wrapping the towel around his waist. When he opened the bathroom door, the sight before his eyes shocked him. Ashley stood there with his Glock .45 aimed at him.

"What are you doing, Ash?" A look of confusion was plastered on his face.

Ashley had tears running down her face. She was extremely hurt at the moment and wasn't thinking clearly. Still, she held the Glock steady. Hitta didn't want to try her because he knew firsthand that Ashley was just as good with a firearm as he was. On top of that, she was mad enough to shoot him.

He humbly submitted by putting his hands up. "Baby girl, chill," he pleaded.

"'Baby girl, chill?'" she repeated in disgust with a look of death bleeding from her eyes. "Nigga, ain't no fucking chill!" she barked. "You think shit is a game, Amir? You toying with my heart? *You think we need a marriage certificate to solidify this shit!*" she screamed.

"Ash, calm down, Ma."

"Ain't no calm down, nigga!" she barked. "All the shit we been through, all of your secrets that I hold dear to my heart, and you think you just gon leave me for some bougie Hollywood bitch?"

Hitta took one step closer, and Ashley cocked the gun back, putting a round in the chamber. "Move again and I swear on my mother's life I will empty this clip."

"Ash, just hear me out please," he begged.

"Hear you out." She laughed demonically. "What is it to hear, Amir? I'm sitting in jail for you, and you out here on dates. That was a slap in my face. How do you think I felt when my man's face pops up on TMZ with another bitch? I always tell you, Amir, be respectful and keep shit out my face, but you had to play me in front of the world." She began to break down. She could no longer conceal the bottled-up pain she was feeling.

Hitta slowly pulled her into his arms and held her tight. She was sobbing loudly, and her body was shaking uncontrollably. Hitta had never seen her like this. "It's okay to cry, baby girl. Let it out. I ain't going nowhere, Ma. I would never leave you," he assured her.

"So, why embarrass me like you did, Amir?"

"I didn't mean to, baby girl. You know you mean the world to me. Going on dates ain't even my style. I stopped her man from beating on her, and she wanted to repay me. That's all it was. Nothing more, nothing less. I wasn't tryna play you,

Ma. You're my everything, Ashley. We in this shit forever. I love you." He hugged her tight and planted a kiss on her forehead.

CHAPTER 3

Metropolitan Detention Center
Brooklyn

Rolex Rich sat back on his bunk with his eyes glued to the screen of his contraband iPhone. He was currently watching an episode of the hit TV show, *Power*. "Boy, I tell you, that nigga, 50, knows how to keep his hand in the pot. When the rap game changed, he switched to film, and that shit is really working for him," he said to his cellmate, who also had his eyes glued to a contraband iPhone, but he wasn't watching *Power*. He spent his time monitoring the stock market.

"Hustlers always going to be able to eat, and that nigga, 50, is a hustler. That *Power* shit is official. He got the whole world hooked on that shit," Jet Black replied.

"Black, roll something up, nigga. I'm about to go holla at the old man about those nacho bowls." Rolex Rich tucked his phone inside the slit of his mattress. "Hold that down for me."

Rolex Rich exited his cell and walked four cells down. Just as he went to knock on the door, someone called out his name. He looked back to see that a dude that he didn't know nor talk to was the one calling him. Out of respect for the man, he made a U-turn.

"Wassup?" Rolex Rich said dryly.

"Pardon me, I know we don't know each other, but I was wondering if..." The man didn't even get to finish his sentence. Another man snuck up behind Rolex Rich and slid a size eleven surgery scalpel across his face. Blood began to spill out of the wound like water coming out of a faucet. Rolex Rich was shocked for a second, but the reality of what had just happened set in fast, and something inside of him snapped.

He quickly turned around and lunged toward the young kid who'd just gave him a buck fifty across his face. He grabbed the kid by the neck and headbutted him. Blood was now all over both of their faces. Rolex Rich wasn't the only one bleeding though. The headbutt split the kid's head open. He then followed up with a fast right hook that landed directly on the kid's chin. His legs became wobbly. Rich threw another blow that knocked him down. Now, Rich was standing over him. The kid looked upward, and him and Rich locked eyes upside down. Rich badly wanted to punch him again but decided against it. "Get the fuck off my unit!" he barked and walked directly to his cell.

The unit was so quiet that you could hear an ant fart. The officer peeked out of the bubble. The sudden silence alarmed her. She saw the blood all over the floor, then she saw the young kid with blood on him. "Oh, hell no, who whipped yo ass?" she clowned. "Step off the unit. Recall!" she announced. "Everybody to ya cells now!" She then hit the pin on her walkie talkie to get an emergency response team on deck.

———

HITTA SAT in the driver's seat of a tinted-up Mercedes Benz. In the car with him was three of his favorite young niggas in the world, Shoota, Heat, and Caine. The four of them had been sitting in this same parking spot for the past hour. "It's lit. There them niggas go right there," Shoota said, alerting his comrades. He cocked back his FNH handgun and slammed a bullet into the chamber.

Shoota, Heat, and Caine all exited the Benz and crept across the street to where their targets stood. They caught the four men by surprise when they popped up with their guns brandished. The men were very much startled, bodyguard included. They all remained calm as the three men gave their orders.

"Y'all know what the fuck this is. Take all those jewels off," Shoota demanded.

The men quickly began to relieve themselves of all jewelry and cash. Caine quickly snatched the bodyguard's gun and smacked him across the face with it. He then walked over to Richie Rich, who was scared to death but did a great job at hiding it, and smacked him across the face with the gun also. *BOOM!* He fired a shot into the head of the bodyguard. The shot killed him before he even hit the floor. The three of them took off running to the Mercedes.

TWENTY-FIVE MINUTES Later

After the little mission, the four of them made it back to the hood safely. They were now sitting in one of their many honeycomb hideouts, or bando as the young generation called it. Hitta was sitting on the loveseat, rolling a blunt.

Heat was busy pouring Lean into a bottle of Sprite. Shoota scrolled down his Instagram timeline while listening to Caine rant about the mission they'd just went on. Caine was on ten right now as he spoke. "Big Homie, you should've let me park all them niggas," he said. all hyper, while pacing back-and-forth. He had way too much energy. The Molly he popped on the car ride back only made him more hyper.

"Caine, sit ya lil nut ass down," Hitta said playfully. "All you wanna do is shoot shit. Ya lil crazy ass don't like pussy? I never see you with no hoes," he teased.

"I learned from you, big homie." Caine flashed a smile. "And hell yeah, I like pussy, nigga. Don't be tryna play me. I fuck more hoes than all y'all niggas," he shot back, and the four of them rolled over in laughter.

"Yo, Hitta, what we doing with all this money and jewelry?" Heat asked.

"That's all y'all. Do what y'all want with it. That lil mission was personal," Hitta replied.

Vrrrrrrrm! Vrrrrrrrrm! Vrrrrrrrrrm! The sound of Hitta's phone vibrating caused him to look at the screen. He saw it was an unknown caller, but he still answered. "Yo, who this?"

"You sure this is what you want? You sending ya lil flunkies at me? I should have killed his ass," the caller said with anger. The caller was none other than Rolex Rich. "And you playing family games? If y'all would've touched my son, I would've..."

"You would've never did shit." Hitta cut him off. "You ain't here to protect them, Rich. I could make shit real hard for you. You drew first blood when you had Breeze hit. I ain't ask for the smoke, old man. You did," he added.

"Fuck you, Hitta," Rolex Rich said before ending the call.

. . .

MEANWHILE

Peso was in the studio; he paced the floor with a lit blunt in his hand. A one-of-a-kind instrumental spilled from the speakers. The studio was filled with a few of his homies and home girls. Plenty of liquor, even more weed, and a bunch of firearms were displayed on the tables.

Peso bopped his head to the beat while taking long pulls from the blunt. "Yo, Lee, play that back one more time," he said to his longtime engineer.

One would think he would be distracted with all that was going on in the studio right then, but he was not. It seemed like Peso was in the room all by himself because he was extremely focused. The only words he'd said in the past thirty minutes were, "Lee, play that back."

His iPhone vibrated, and a huge smile was plastered on his face when he saw Princess' name on the screen. "Yo, Lee, you can break. I'mma take this call real quick," Peso said while making his way to the door.

Peso exited Studio A and walked to Studio B, which was empty. "Hey, King," Princess smiled when Peso's face popped up on her screen.

"Wassup, Queen, how you feeling?" he replied.

"Horny," she admitted.

"Oh, yeah?"

"Yes, Daddy. I miss you so much," she whined.

"I miss you more, my love. What you wearing? Lemme see something."

Princess lifted the phone, so Peso could get a good view of her naked body. "Oh, you on some naked shit. I'm on my way now," he said.

"No, I know you working, Daddy. I don't wanna be self-ish, but I badly need some dick," she admitted.

"I tell you what. How about you come to the studio, so I can knock these tracks down and knock ya walls down?" he chuckled.

"Yass, Daddy, talk that shit. I'm on my way now," she said before blowing him a kiss and ending the call.

CHAPTER 4

Marlboro Houses

Reem was a member of the Blood Gang Organization. He was top ranked and was the youngest nation leader on the entire East Coast. His name rang bells from the Brooklyn streets to California. Not only did he have a huge following on the outside, but his following in the prison system was much larger. This young man was known in every prison across the nation. He was a legend in his own right.

For the past twenty-one days, Reem and his set had been at war with another Blood set that was ran by his former mentor, B-Gunnz. The two of them had it out on a personal level, and things hadn't been the same since. B-Gunnz happened to be one of the most powerful and respected Bloods to ever walk the streets and prisons of New York. Reem murdered his brother, who was an informant, and the two of them had been at war ever since. By B-Gunnz being in prison and Reem being free, he was losing the war by a landslide.

Here Reem sat behind the steering wheel of a candy apple red 7 series BMW. In the passenger seat sat his most trusted comrade, Sho-Tyme. The two of them were cruising through the hood with no set destination, just riding and smoking. "The homie, 2- Gunnz, called me today and said the fool, B-Gunnz, is waving the white flag," Reem said.

"So that means we standing down?" Sho-Tyme asked.

"Yeah, we gon focus on this money. B-Gunnz knows that as long as I'm free, he can't win this war. We have the upper hand. We are able to touch everyone close to him, and there is nothing he can do," Reem answered with a smile.

"Pull over right here by the liquor store," Sho-Tyme said when he noticed three dudes standing in front of the liquor store. One of the three owed Sho-Tyme a hefty debt and had been ducking him.

Sho-Tyme dashed out of the passenger seat with a quickness Reem had never seen before. The dude who owed the debt went by the name of Wiz. He was a Rollin 60's Crip. "What's poppin, Wiz?" Sho-Tyme greeted, catching him by surprise.

"Oh, shit, Sho-Tyme. What's good with you, cuz?" Wiz replied.

When his eyes landed on the FNH handgun that Sho-Tyme had brandished at his waist, they stretched wide open in fear. "Come on, cuz, put the strap up, man. You know I got that paper for you. I just been outta town for a minute." He lied with a straight face. Truth was, he had been sold all of the coke that Sho-Tyme gave him on consignment. He'd just been ducking him because he took the profits from the flip and flipped it again. He flipped the profit three times to be exact.

Wiz dug in his pocket and pulled out a huge bankroll.

"This six bands ($6,000) right here, cuz." He handed the money to Sho-Tyme.

"Nigga, stop calling me cuz. You know I don't like that shit," Sho-Tyme replied back, annoyed. "And six bands? Nigga, you three grand short." Sho-Tyme was becoming more annoyed by the second.

"That's all I got on me right now. Gimmie about sixty minutes and I'll be forwarding it to you. You still on deck?"

"Yeah, I just got a fresh batch."

"I'll bring the other three stacks when I re-up. Is that cool?"

"Yeah, man, but have mine or be mine." Sho-Tyme turned and walked back to the car.

The minute the passenger door closed, Reem pulled off. "You a funny nigga, Sho," he chuckled.

"Why you say that, skrap?"

"You been dying for a reason to fuck Wiz over ever since y'all had that fight in high school. You front the nigga work, hoping he fucks up ya money, so you can have a reason to shoot him." Reem laughed a little harder while shaking his head.

"Stop thinking you know me, skrap." Sho-Tyme laughed also.

"Nigga, you my brother. I prolly know you better than you know ya self. On the real tho, Blood, that nigga, Wiz, knows how to get a bag. They got a nice flow on their side of the projects; we can use Wiz to move our work in the Crip community. Always remember this, Blood, your network is your net worth." Reem put him on game.

Like a sponge, Sho-Tyme soaked up every bit of game Reem dropped on him. "Instead of tryna knock the nigga off behind some old high school vendetta, use the nigga for his worth. T-Top and them niggas doing big numbers. They flushing kilos like clockwork. We need them niggas moving our work, but the only way we can get them on board is through ya man, Wiz. We on money time, beloved, fuck all that other shit. Let's look at the bigger picture."

"Say no more, skrap." Sho-Tyme nodded in approval.

CHAPTER 5

Days Later

Peso was in the studio, but at that moment, he wasn't writing or recording a track. He sat on the sofa with his head back and his eyes closed. Between his legs, on her knees, was Tia Savage, the chart topping, multi-platinum selling, Grammy winning mega-pop star. She was giving Peso some mind-blowing oral sex. "Damn, Tia, slow down," Peso moaned while running his hand through her hair.

Studio A's door opened, and in walked Mariah, the mother of Peso's daughter, who was also his manager. "Tyler, what the hell are you doing?" she said, catching Peso and Tia off guard.

Peso quickly jumped up and grabbed his pants. "What the fuck, Mariah? Why you just walking in without knocking? You playing ya self," he said with a hint of anger.

"No, nigga, you playing ya self. I'm telling Princess," Mariah shot back and tried to storm off, but Peso grabbed her by the arm.

"Mariah, you better not do that." He then turned to Tia Savage. "My bad, Tee, I'll hit you later."

"Okay, hunny, hit my line." She smiled and exited the studio.

Peso turned to Mariah. "You really gon tell on me, baby momma?" he questioned seriously.

"You really a thot, Tyler." Mariah laughed. "Princess is a good girl, Ty. You need to get it together. I'm only here right now because you have an interview with the Breakfast Club in about an hour. I also wanted to show you something that caught my eye," she said and went inside of her Chanel purse and pulled out her iPhone. She located the viral video on Instagram, pressed play, and handed it to Peso. "What the fuck is that, Tyler?"

Peso watched the video of him beating on a man and pulling a gun out on him in IHOP. He just shook his head. "You tryna throw ya future away, Ty? All this shit you worked so hard to obtain, you tryna lose it all behind some silly shit?" she said with a clear attitude.

"Mariah, that video is old; some nigga that Princess used to fuck with pulled up being disrespectful. I tried to keep my cool, but I lost it. Dude wouldn't let up," Peso explained.

"You pulling out guns in public places and shit," she said in disgust. "How many times you wanna leave Mya? That girl worships you. Get ya shit together, bro."

"Mariah, I just told you that was old. I ain't going nowhere. You gon keep going crazy, or are we gonna head to this interview?" Peso now had a smile on his face. He did this whenever Mariah was upset with him. Just like so many other women, Mariah could never resist his smile. Peso usually charmed his way out of everything. He'd been this way since a kid.

"Nigga, don't be tryna smile like you cute." Mariah rolled her eyes playfully. "I catch you cheating on ya lady, and you over here smiling like shit funny. Get ya life, Tyler. Clean yaself up and meet me outside."

MEANWHILE
Downtown Brooklyn 225 Cadman Plaza...
Breeze stood there in front of the federal court building. He was just released from custody fifteen minutes ago. All charges against him were dismissed due to a dirty cop admitting to pocketing some of the money that Breeze was arrested for on a voice recording.

Besides the pain in his upper back from being stabbed six days prior, Breeze was feeling great. He was extremely happy to have obtained his freedom once again.

"Aye, Breeze, I'll give you a call in a few days to start that civil suit. I just need you to stand clear of anything illegal. You just beat the Feds, so they gon be on ya ass," said his attorney, Kenneth Rich.

"I got you, man. I'mma be out the way," Breeze promised.

"You need a ride? I spoke with ya lady, and she said she couldn't take off of work."

"Nah, just let me use ya phone."

The attorney handed Breeze his phone, and he quickly dialed Hitta's number to let him know that he had been released. Hitta promised to be at the court building in twenty-five minutes. Breeze handed the attorney his phone back. "My brother on his way to come scoop me. Thanks, Kenny."

AT POWER105.1 RADIO Station

"Peace to the planet. I'm Charlamagne tha God."

"I'm Angela Yee."

"D.J. Envy."

"And we are the Breakfast Club!" the hosts said in unison.

Charlamagne took the floor. "Today, we have a special guest in the building, my guy, Presidential Peso. No, let me correct myself, Grammy award winning Presidential Peso," he introduced. "Peace and blessings, brother. How you feeling, man?" he said to Peso.

"I'm blessed, man, extremely grateful," Peso replied humbly.

"So, how does it all feel, man? The success and everything?" D.J. Envy asked.

"To be honest, it still kind of feels like a dream. Some days, it doesn't even feel real to me," he replied.

"People think your success came overnight. Some don't know you been doing this for a minute," said Charlamagne.

"Overnight?" Peso chuckled. "Nah, I been doing this for a minute. It took a whole lot to get where I'm at today. Check YouTube. I most definitely put the work in. I been racking up millions of views since I dropped my first video. I just had a setback with the law and had to sit down for a minute, but I'm back," he added.

"Before moving forward, we must address the elephant in the room. There is a viral video floating around of you beating up some guy and pulling out a gun in an IHOP," said Angela Yee.

"Of me?" Peso laughed. "I never said that was me in that video. That's all allegations. We just gon leave it at that. I rather change topics."

"Sources say that video was old. Do you think it was posted to destroy you?" D.J. Envy asked.

"They can't destroy God's plan. Can we move to another topic tho? Respectfully."

"Let's talk about this new single you just released with Swagger B. It's on top of the charts right now. Y'all got the streets in a frenzy with this one," Charlamagne said.

"We had the streets in a frenzy with the last one." Peso bragged a little.

"True. You and Swagger B both come from Brooklyn. Did y'all know each other before rap, or did the label link the two of you together?" D.J. Envy asked.

"Nah, we met one night in the studio and just clicked. The relationship wasn't forced; it happened organically. That's my dawg. He's one of the dudes I actually rock with in the industry."

BACK IN BROOKLYN

Hitta pulled up in front of the Shake Shack in his Ferrari, and Breeze hopped in the passenger seat. "Gorilla stack 62!" Breeze saluted while greeting Hitta with the UGF handshake.

"No keys, push to start!" Hitta replied. "What's the word tho, bro? How the fuck you got Brown on tape?" Hitta asked.

"The second he pulled me over, I put my phone on audio record and locked my screen," Breeze explained. "With the type of history we got with that pig, I would never trust him. What made ya man, Rolex Rich. line me up tho?"

"Pardon me for that, bro. You know I would never put you in harm's way. That nigga on some fuck shit. We fell out over some nut shit. You know how I rock tho. We most definitely up on the score board. I'm pretty sure you heard about the lil rap nigga," Hitta smiled.

"And the bodyguard," Breeze laughed. "You know I got

word. I put my young boys from the Stuy on him. Hopefully they touched him already."

"I gotta shoot to Brownsville real quick. You gon ride with me?"

"Yeah."

BACK AT POWER 105.1

"On the single, *No Faking,* you and Swagger B talk about rappers lying in their music, wearing fake jewelry, and frontin in cars and houses they don't own. I take that as you do none of the above?" said Charlamagne.

Peso couldn't help but laugh. "Yo, Charlamagne, I swear you ask some of the funniest questions. But hell no, I can't be lying to the people."

"So, you never wore fake jewelry?" Angela Yee asked.

"I can't be wearing no fake shines. I got sensitive skin," Peso chuckled. "For the record tho, I touched my first million at seventeen. I did come in the rap game with a Mercedes, a Porsche, and a Ferrari all paid for. I copped my first Rolex at seventeen and bought my moms, may she rest in peace, a house before I ever signed a deal. I always been about my paper." He bragged a little.

"People are always bringing up your past. Does it bother you?" Charlamagne asked.

"Nah, because without my past, I wouldn't be who I am or where I am today."

CHAPTER 6

Tilden

BROWNSVILLE, BROOKLYN

Hitta's Ferrari pulled up on the outside of the projects. Today was a nice day, so even though the clock hadn't even hit noon yet, a lot of people were outside.

Onlookers stared at the beautiful automobile in awe. Some people noticed Hitta and began to pull their phones out and take pictures. Hitta still didn't believe that he had celebrity status, so he didn't get why people snapped pictures of him everywhere he went. He was not the rapper Peso was. But to the world, Hitta wasn't just Hitta, one of the UGF founders. He was Hitta, best friend of five-time Grammy award winning, multi-platinum selling, superstar Presidential Peso and one of the founders and owners of Luxury Records. Even though Hitta didn't think so, he was really a big deal.

Hitta led the way through the projects. He and Breeze walked into one of the buildings and rode the elevator up to the top floor. When they made it to the rooftop, they were greeted by twelve other members of the UGF's Brooklyn chapter.

Big-Tyme, who was one of the shot callers for the Brooklyn chapter, took the floor instantly. "Now that bro is here, let's get down to business. Last night, one of our traps got hit. The family took a hefty loss. My gut tells me it was an inside job, and my gut is usually always right. Besides myself and X-Rilla, who is still in a coma, only Barn, Murk, and Juice have access to that spot."

Each man he named shot him a look of pure hatred because they were being singled out, and they knew Hitta would not take this lightly. No one wanted to be accused of being a thief.

Big-Tyme was livid right now. Sixteen kilos of pure Columbian cocaine had gone missing on his watch. The only thing on his mind right now was murder.

"Do any of you have anything to say to the family?" Hitta finally chimed in. When everyone remained quiet, Hitta let out a small, demonic chuckle. Breeze knew this chuckle all too well. Hitta was about to snap at any minute now. His blood was beginning to boil. "I asked you niggas a fuckin question!" he barked and brandished a .44 Bulldog. "Somebody better say something, or I'mma start parking shit on this roof. I'm not at all playing about my money."

"I been OT, bro. I got back two hours ago." Murk was the first one to speak. Hitta turned to Big-Tyme. "Can you vouch for that?" he asked.

"Yeah, he was outta town, but that don't mean shit. All these niggas is suspect!" Big-Tyme spit.

"Fuck you tryna say?" Murk stepped toward him and brandished a Glock .22.

"I ain't tryna say shit, nigga. I'm saying exactly what the

fuck I said. All you niggas is suspect. You better back the fuck back with that gun before I knock ya punk ass out," Big-Tyme said, not at all backing down.

Hitta stood between the two of them. "Y'all niggas chill the fuck out. We gon' get to the bottom of this, and when we do, it will be hell to pay. That's on the gang!" he declared.

As the little standoff was going on between Big-Tyme and Murk, a homie by the name of Juice had his eyes glued to the screen of his cell phone as he sent a text message. In one swift motion, Hitta snatched the iPhone from his hand. "What the fuck is so important that you disrespecting family time while we having a shootout (meeting)? You bigger than this family now, Juice?"

"Pardon me, ape. I ain't mean no disrespect," Juice replied.

Fact of the matter was, right then, Juice was scared to death. He was praying that Hitta didn't go through his phone.

"Right now, we on family time. Don't disrespect this family again; whatever dirty ass bitch you texting can wait," Hitta said. Just when he was about to give the phone back, he picked up on his comrade's nervousness. "Fuck you moving all suspect for?" he asked.

"Nah, bro, I ain't moving suspect. I'm good," Juice lied.

Something inside of Hitta told him to go through the phone, so he did. Juice was praying that Hitta didn't stumble across his secret. An instant look of relief plastered across Juice's face when Hitta handed him back his phone. Without hesitation, Hitta upped his .44 Bulldog and aimed it at Juice's face.

BOC! A single shot removed a huge chunk of it before his body even hit the floor. Hitta then stood over him and fired two more shots into his already dead body.

Hitta bent down and grabbed Juice's phone. He tossed it to Big-Tyme. "Go get my shit, nigga!" he said sternly. "This monkey ass nigga stole from us, right up under ya nose. Tighten the fuck up, B.T., for real. Until X-Rilla is back with us, Shoota will be holding down his spot for the Brooklyn chapter." He then looked back at Big-Tyme. "Those niggas behind that message better be dead in the next twenty-four hours." He now looked to Breeze. "We off this, bro."

Days Later

Flee looked at himself in the mirror and smiled. He was in total approval of his appearance right now. "Damn, I did this," he said to himself while admiring his attire. That day, he sported a fresh Fendi outfit and a pair of high-top Fendi sneakers. The solid gold Cuban link on his neck weighed three hundred fifty grams. An iced-out pendant that said FLEE in script weighed another two hundred fifty grams. The chain was complemented by an eighteen -karat gold Rolex that had Rolex diamonds in its bezel.

Today was somewhat of a special day for Flee. This day on the calendar marked exactly seven months he had been free. Thanks to Hitta and Peso, his life had changed drastically. As promised, everything that touched their hood went through the hands of Flee first. With cocaine prices at $38-$40 per gram, Flee was sitting on a goldmine because he had each kilo on consignment for $30,000. At this number, he was able to supply the little fishes and big fishes in the drug game. The dealers who paid $40 per gram bought in small quantities, five grams here, ten grams there. The dealers copping kilos paid $36 per gram, giving him a minimum score of $6,000 off each kilo. He had by far the best numbers in the city. With all of the networking he did while locked up, his arm stretched pretty far. Flee even had people coming from upstate New York to purchase coke from him.

Today wasn't about business for Flee. This day was all pleasure for him. He finally got to link up with the beautiful female he'd met a few weeks ago. She called him earlier today and told him that she was free. Flee could barely hold his excitement. He canceled his original plans and agreed to pick her up around 7 p.m.

Flee's Mercedes Benz pulled up in front of a building in the Crown Heights section of Brooklyn. A few dudes stood around smoking weed, drinking liquor, and having meaningless conversation.

Flee hopped out of the driver's seat and sat on the hood of the car. He then pulled out his phone and sent Lexi a text, letting her know that he was outside waiting for her.

The dudes loitering in front of the building stole glances at Flee, wondering who he was and what he was doing on their block. Some flashed looks of envy while others flashed looks of admiration. Flee paid them no mind and charged it all to the game.

Several minutes later, Lexi walked out of the building looking like something straight out of a magazine. Not the ratchet hood magazines that the inmates went crazy for in prison. Nah, Lexi was looking more like a model from a smooth magazine. She was sporting an all-white, soft denim jean suit, a pink belly shirt that showed off her flat tummy and belly ring, a pink belt, and a pair of white and pink low-top sneakers. An oversized purse was slung over her shoulder, and a pair of oversized shades covered her eyes. Every single part of her outfit was Fendi.

"Oh, hell no, you copying me," she teased.

"Nah, love, you just got dressed. I been had this fit on," he smiled. "Plus, my name Flee, so it's only right I rock the Fs," he replied and pulled her in his arms for a hug. This kind of shocked Lexi.

"Comfortable, I see?" she said in his ear.

"You mine already," he replied with confidence.

Flee then opened the passenger side door for her. "Shit, you opening doors. I just might be yours. So far so good, youngin. Keep up the good work," she teased.

As Flee hopped in the driver's seat, he noticed one of the dudes standing in front of the building shoot Lexi a funny look then ice grilled him. Flee just shook his head and smiled.

"Who that fat nigga in front of ya building?" Flee asked when he entered the car.

"That's K.B. Why? Wassup?" Lexi asked.

"I don't like the way boy looked at you," he replied and pulled off.

CHAPTER 7

Same Day

Hitta stepped off of the elevator and into Peso's penthouse. He was furious right now. Exactly seven minutes ago, he received a call from his connect telling him that the two of them could no longer do business due to his beef with Rolex Rich.

Peso was sitting in the living room with Princess and Mya. The three of them had been bonding all day. Currently, Princess was presenting her business proposal to Peso. He and Mya were all ears; both loved the idea of her cosmetic line. "Can I model the lip gloss, so my picture can be all over the world?" Mya said with the biggest smile.

"Of course you can, sweetie," Princess replied.

Mya looked up and saw Hitta. She quickly ran over to him and jumped in his arms. "Uncle Mir!" she screamed.

"Hey, pretty girl. How are you?" Hitta hugged her tightly and planted a kiss on her forehead.

"I'm okay. Me, my daddy, and Princess are spending time together because he is about to go on tour," Mya explained.

"So, I'm messing up y'all family time, pretty girl?"

"No, because you are family too. Plus, you are the best uncle in the whole wide world." Mya put on her prettiest smile. This little girl was Hitta's soft spot. Every time he saw her, he got baby fever.

"Thank you, pretty girl. You are the best niece in the whole wide world." He hugged her once more before walking over to Princess and Peso. He greeted Peso with the UGF handshake then turned to Princess. "Wassup, sis? How you feeling?" he greeted.

"I'm good, bro, can't complain. How's Ashley?"

\"She's good. Her ass finally let me out the doghouse," he chuckled. "Can I borrow my brother real quick? I won't be long. I promise."

"No problem. I'll take Mya in the back with me, so y'all can talk."

Once Mya and Princess were out of the living room, Peso sparked a blunt that he had sitting in the ashtray. "What's the vibes, bro?" he asked while taking a long pull from the blunt.

"More money, more problems. Big said it best, my nigga," Hitta replied. Peso reached out and passed him the blunt. Hitta took a deep pull. "This nigga, Rolex Rich, cut the faucet off on us, bro," he vented.

"Cut the faucet off?" Peso asked, confused.

"Yeah, bitch ass nigga told the plug not to do business with me. Juan talking about he can't supply me anymore until I settle my differences with Rich. That shit got me tight right now, bro. This nigga just hit niggas where it hurt, right in my pockets."

"You should have been prepared for that. That's light tho. We can always get another plug."

"Yeah, but not one who's the leader of a Columbian cartel.

You don't just stumble across niggas like Juan Calle-Serna every day."

"Maybe it's time you say fuck the streets and focus on this legit paper. Dope ain't the only way to eat. You ain't pressed for no paper. We rich, Hitta. Shit, you probably richer than me, and I'm the rapper," Peso chuckled. His comment put a smile on Hitta's face.

"Nigga, knock it off. You up like a duck," Hitta replied, and they both laughed. "For real tho, I got our whole nation depending on me to feed them. I gotta do something."

"How much work you got left?"

"About eighty joints, but we both know how fast them shits gon fly. I'm thinking about going to see Jamie and getting back on that heroin wave. We touched our first mill off that dog food."

"Jamie? What Jamie?" Peso was really confused now. The only Jamie he knew was the Panamanian drug lord, Jamie Estrada, the old connect who they met through Matt Murda.

"Jamie Estrada, nigga. What other Jamie you know, beloved?"

"Nigga, Jamie Estrada is super loyal to Matt Murda. Even through death he gon stand with that nigga, bro. Murda was like his son."

"You might be right, but what do I have to lose right now? Besides, shooting niggas and robbing dope is all a nigga knows." A smile popped across Hitta's face as he thought of the old days when the Murda Team controlled the heroin trade in the Brooklyn streets. "That Black Rose stamp made history in the streets," he added.

"Nah, nigga, we made history in them streets," Peso smiled. "Speaking of Matt Murda, his body was never recovered with Brown's. That shit ain't sitting right with me, bro," Peso said in a more serious tone.

"You think he alive?" Hitta asked.

"I was right on that nigga, bro, point blank range," Peso reminded him.

"I know, nigga. I was there with you," Hitta chuckled. "Maybe the cops just covering their tracks. Fuck that nigga tho."

MEANWHILE

Flee was dropping Lexi off after the two of them enjoyed the day together. They dined at a place called The Brooklyn Wine Yard, then Flee drove to Coney Island where the two of them walked the boardwalk and talked about everything under the sun, from their childhoods to their future plans. The two of them had made a real connection. Neither of them wanted this night to end, but Lexi had to get home to her four-year-old son.

The two of them sat doubled parked in Flee's Benz in front of Lexi's building. "I really enjoyed myself today, handsome. You iight for a young boy," she teased.

"You ain't never gonna get over my age, are you?" Flee asked.

"You ain't the average twenty-year-old tho. I can tell you come from really good stock. Whoever raised you really did a great job. You been around some real niggas."

"Check you out, talking like you some old head. You only got me by four years, Queen."

Hearing Flee address her as queen really made her smile. He was earning points by the minute and didn't even know it. "I'm old enough to legally buy liquor and you not." She continued to tease him. "I don't want this night to end," she admitted. "But my sister had my son all day. I don't wanna o'd because next time she might not watch him." She looked at Flee, who was just staring at her. "What?" she asked.

"Nothing, I just want you so fucking bad," he replied.

His comment caused her to blush. "Yeah, maybe it's best this night does end because if you keep giving me that look, I'mma put this wet on ya young ass. Gimme hug." She leaned in and wrapped her arms around his neck. "Goodnight, handsome."

"Let me get ya door for you," he said and hopped out of the driver's seat. He walked over to the passenger's side and opened the door for her. "Such a gentleman," she smiled. "You better call me when you get home too."

"Shit, I'll call you as soon as I get in the car." He pulled her into his embrace and hugged her once more. His hands slid down her lower back to her butt.

"You think you so smooth. You just wanted to feel my fatty," she smiled. "Goodnight, handsome." Lexi leaned in and kissed him on the cheek. She then turned and walked away.

Flee stood there and got the perfect view of her perfectly round bottom. Lexi put an extra switch in her walk because she knew Flee was watching her.

The dude, whose name Lexi said was K.B., popped up in the building lobby. This gave Flee the feeling that he'd been watching them the entire time. The dude opened the lobby door for Lexi. She turned back to Flee. "Make sure you call me."

"I gotchu, Queen," he assured her.

When Lexi was no longer in sight, Flee hopped back in his car. He had a weird feeling about something. His gut told him that something wasn't right. He pulled out his iPhone and called Lexi.

"You miss me already, Papi?" She picked up on the first ring.

"I really do though," he admitted. "Just making sure you got in the crib safe, Queen. I'll hit you when I get home."

BOOM! Flee heard a loud bang from Lexi's end of the phone. "Yo, Lexi!" he called out, but she didn't answer. He just heard a bunch of commotion in the background. He quickly reached in his glove box and pulled out his Compact 9-millimeter before hopping out of the car. He ran to the building entrance, but the door was locked. He rang a bunch of different buzzers until someone buzzed him in.

Now inside of the building, he was confused because he didn't know what door or floor Lexi lived on. The building only had four floors, so her apartment shouldn't be too hard to find. He heard loud noises coming from the second floor, so he sprinted up the stairs and followed the noise.

Soon as he made it to the second floor, an apartment door flew open, and K.B. came running out with a duffle bag slung over his shoulder and a handgun in his right hand.

He saw Flee and quickly tried to up his strap, but Flee beat him to it and fired two shots from his .9mm. Both bullets crashed into K.B.'s chest. The impact sent him crashing into the wall. *BOC!*

Flee fired another shot, and a slug landed directly between his eyes. He looked up to see Lexi standing in the doorway of her apartment with her son and sister. "Y'all gotta come on. I'm not letting y'all stay here." He picked up the duffle bag and grabbed Lexi by the hand.

CHAPTER 8

The Next Day

Middletown, **New York**

Hitta pulled up to the gated entrance of the beautiful mansion. This beautiful home belonged to the Panamanian drug-lord, Jamie Estrada. Hitta hadn't been here in years, but the place was still as beautiful as he remembered. "Excuse me, sir, are you lost?" Hitta was asked by the armed guard.

"Nah, I'm here to see Mr. Estrada," he replied.

"Is he expecting you?" the guard asked.

"Listen, man, just tell him that Hitta is here to see him," Hitta replied, becoming more annoyed by the minute. The guard stepped back into the booth and placed a call. A minute later, the gate opened, and Hitta pulled his Ferrari into the driveway.

Standing out front, puffing on a Cuban cigar, was Jamie Estrada's righthand man and bodyguard, Poncho. The man was all smiles when Hitta hopped out of the Ferrari. Even though it had been a long while since the two men last saw each other, Poncho remembered him. "Well, if it isn't my good friend, Hitta," Poncho greeted him.

"In the flesh." Hitta opened his arms and smiled.

"Long time no see. How's life treating you, my friend?"

"It's been too long, but life has been treating me well," Poncho smiled. "I'm surprised your partner in crime isn't here with you. How is Peso these days?"

"He's good. Bro is on tour at the moment."

Poncho put out his cigar and led the way inside of the mansion. When they made it to Jamie Estrada's office, he was sitting behind his desk, puffing on a cigar. He was accompanied by his younger brother, Peto, and Matt Murda's brother-in-law, Rah-Rah. "Hitta, what's going on, old friend? What brings you here to see me?" Mr. Estrada got up from his seat and shook Hitta's hand. "Peto, you remember Hitta, right?" he asked his brother.

"How can I forget a man like Hitta?" Peto replied. "How have you been, old friend?"

"Everything is healthy. Life is good," Hitta replied and looked to Rah-Rah. "Rah, what's the word?" he greeted.

"Ain't shit," Rah-Rah replied dryly. Truth was, Rah-Rah didn't know how to feel about Hitta due to his beef with Matt Murda. Rah-Rah had a massive amount of respect for Hitta, but his loyalty would always be to Matt Murda.

"Jamie, I'm not about to sit here and waste ya time. You know I ain't the type of man who beats around the bush. I have a problem, a very big problem," Hitta said.

"What's the problem, old friend?"

"I got plenty of money to spend, but I don't have a plug with the type of quality or quantity that you possess. We have history. Me and the guys have made you a lot of money back when everything was good. I was hoping we could pick up where we left off and get back to doing business."

Mr. Estrada didn't speak right away. He seemed to be in deep thought. Truth was, he was trying to find the right words to say to Hitta. "Hitta, I have a huge amount of respect for you," he claimed. "But you know that Matt was like a son to me, and I can't go behind his back and do business with you knowing that you two have an issue that was never resolved. That would be an act of disloyalty. I'm sorry, old friend, but I do not operate on the system of disloyalty."

"Overstood but thank you for your time." Hitta turned to leave.

"Hitta, hold up a minute." Peto stopped him.

Peto happened to really like Hitta. He had always been his favorite member of the Murda Team. There was something about the young man that always made him stand out from the rest of the group. Truth be told, Peto didn't have the same bond with Matt Murda that his brother had, so he didn't have the same amount of loyalty to him. Just like back in the day, Peto still saw a fire in Hitta's eyes that he had never seen in another man.

"How much product can you handle?" Peto asked.

"Peto, what the hell are you doing?" Jamie chimed in.

"I'm saving our business. That's what I'm doing. You and I both know that our business is in dire need of someone like Hitta. Now, like I was saying, Hitta," Peto dismissed his brother, "how much product can you handle, and how soon can you be ready for it?"

"No handouts, Peto. I have two million in cash right now inside my car. How soon can you fill my order?" Hitta replied, and Peto just smiled.

. . .

CONEY ISLAND

Flee laid back on his California king sized bed, blowing smoke clouds up to the ceiling. Every few seconds, he looked over to his left where Lexi slept peacefully, looking as beautiful as ever. After the incident that took place last night, Flee made Lexi, her son, and little sister come stay with him. Going back to her apartment was currently not an option. They both knew that the police were still snooping around, looking for answers about K.B.'s dead body.

Flee would usually be running the streets, but for some reason, he didn't want to move from Lexi's side. He slowly slid out of the bed, trying not to wake her. "Flee," she called out softly. The sound of her voice let Flee know that his attempt to not wake her had failed.

"Yes, love," he answered.

"Thank you so much," she replied sincerely.

"No thank you needed, Ma. You good." He laid back down on the bed so that he was face to face with her. "You in good hands now, Lex. You, your son, and your sister. Y'all can kick it here for as ever long as y'all need to," he said sincerely.

Lexi stared into his eyes. She was becoming weaker for this young man by the second. He just killed to protect her and her family, and he hadn't even known her for that long. His actions spoke volumes to her. She couldn't help but fall for this man. "Your building doesn't have any cameras, right?" he asked.

"No, none at all," she replied. "Where is Fresh and Manny?"

"They in the living room, sleep; the duffle bags you had is

under the bed."

VRRRRRRRM! VRRRRRRRM! VRRRRRRRRM!
Flee's phone vibrated on the nightstand. He reached over to grab it and saw Hitta's name on the screen. Sliding his finger across the screen, he answered immediately. "What's the word, gang?"

"Ain't shit, my boy. I'm in the hood. We gon have a lil shootout (meeting) at 3 o'clock. It's imperative, all good news tho. Meet us at Ne-Ne spot."

"Say less, I'll be there. Everything healthy tho?"

"Super healthy, gang. See you in a minute, Gorilla stack 62."

"No keys, push to start." Flee ended the call.

CHAPTER 9

Lincoln Houses
Harlem, New York
Same Day...

It was a beautiful day out today. The sun was shining and so was Hitta. He was in a great mood at the moment. Things couldn't be better for him right now.

He hopped out of his Ferrari, dressed to impress, and as usual, his neck and wrist were on freeze. He was not on his side of town, but he was very much comfortable here. Bystanders stared at him, wondering where they knew him from, trying to figure out if the man was an actor, rapper, or athlete. All they knew was close to a million dollars was standing outside of the projects all alone.

Hitta pulled his iPhone out and placed a call. "Yo, gang, I'm outside. Pop out," he said when the man he was calling picked up.

Less than five minutes later, the man Hitta was here to see came walking out of the projects. RobLo, a member of the UGF and one of Hitta's childhood friends, who moved from

Brooklyn years ago, had just came home from doing a federal probation violation. Hitta was here to drop him off a care package.

"Ceaser's home!" Rob-Lo saluted while greeting Hitta with the signature UGF handshake.

"Call the national guards." Hitta saluted back in UGF lingo. "Welcome back, gang. The streets missed you, my boy," he added.

"I'm happy to be back and off them papers. A nigga finally got his freedom back for real, for real."

"Trust, bro, I know the feeling. Shit is real sturdy for the home team tho. You still got a line for that dog food (heroin)?" Hitta asked.

"Nigga, this Harlem. I'mma always have a line."

"Bet, so in a few days, I'mma have somebody come pull up on you and drop something in ya lap. Shit gon be like back in the day. Grade A shit. My word," he promised.

A huge smile popped up on Rob-Lo's face. It had been a very long time since he last had some grade A heroin on the market. Hitta was bringing him back to life right now and didn't even know it. "Shit about to be litty out here, ape," Rob-Lo said while rubbing his hands together.

"Trust me, bro, I know. Grab that bag out the passenger's seat. It's a ten pack ($10,000) in there for you. Go get yaself cleaned up. I'll hit you in a few days."

FIFTY MINUTES Later

Hitta still had a little bit of time to kill before he had to meet with the guys. He glided down Mermaid Avenue in his Ferrari, blasting Peso's new mixtape, *Paroled 2 the Trap Vol.2*. The sound of Peso's voice could be heard over the wind that was blowing heavily due to the windows being rolled down. "Talk about the times when I ain't have shit. Now with all this jewelry on, I'm lookin' like a lick." Hitta grabbed his chains with his free hand while rapping along. "She was frontin last year, now she want the dick, but I never been the type to fuck a last year bitch, haaaaa! That's like rockin last year shit. You should've let me hit it last year, bitch."

The sound of his phone ringing made him lower the music. A smile was plastered on his face when he saw Nautica's name across his screen. He let the phone ring for another ten seconds then answered. "Wassup, lovely?" he greeted rather smoothly.

"I see you don't know me anymore, huh?" Nautica replied.

"Trust me, it's not that. You know I got a lady. Going to dinner with you last time had a nigga all over TMZ and shit," he chuckled. "My lady seen that shit and had a fit. She put a nigga right in the doghouse," he admitted.

"I'm sorry. I didn't mean to cause any confusion in ya relationship. The dinner was only a thank you for helping me," she claimed.

"You good, love. How you been tho? How's that Hollywood life treating you?"

"Lonely," she admitted.

"So, you really done with boy, huh?"

"Hell yeah, I'm done with him. I deserve so much better. Plus, I got my eyes on something new, but he's scared of me," she laughed.

"Sneak dissing? You know I got a lady, Nauti," he replied. Only if he could see her face right now. She was blushing super hard. She really loved when he called her that.

"How about we all go on a date?"

"Don't play cause we will take you up on that offer and have you fall in love with both of us. Don't make me call ya bluff, love," Hitta challenged.

MEANWHILE

Peso paced the floor of his hotel suite. He was beyond pissed at the moment. In about forty minutes, he had a photo shoot, and the stylist that Mariah hired had picked out a bunch of outfits that Peso would never wear. "Are you shittin me right now? I'm not wearing none of this bullshit, Riah. Look at this," he said while holding up one of the shirts. "Shawdy must think she dressing one of those pop artists. I'm dressing myself."

"Why are you being so stubborn? We don't have time for this, Tyler. Just wear the damn outfits!" she barked. Mariah was pissed off as well. She hated the fact that she dropped the ball by hiring this stylist. When she saw the things that the girl picked out, she just knew that Peso would never wear any of them. But right now, they didn't have time for debating over what he was going to wear because they were running out of time.

"I don't care if you get mad, Riah. This is ya fault. You better call that lady now and tell her that her services are no longer needed. I'll meet you in the lobby. Good thing I'mma fly nigga and keep good drip on standby. Shawdy tried to have a nigga dressin' like Young Thug. That's my nigga, but I ain't wearing no man skirt. I don't follow trends. I make them," Peso chuckled.

Mariah just rolled her eyes at him and headed for the door. "Baby momma," Peso called out.

"What, Tyler?" Mariah replied with attitude.

"Thank you for not snitchin' on me to Princess."

"Fuck you, Ty! I did it for her, not you. She's a good girl, and I didn't want to see her hurt. That's honestly the reason I didn't say anything to her," she replied and walked out.

BACK IN CONEY ISLAND

The time was now 2:45 p.m. Flee had just finished getting dressed. He entered the living room where Lexi, Fresh, and little Manny sat on the sofa, watching a movie. "I gotta run out real quick. Y'all good here tho," Flee said.

"We don't gotta worry about no bitch poppin' up, do we?" Lexi replied sarcastically.

"You just gotta say some slick shit, right?" Flee chuckled. "For the record, y'all the first females to ever step foot in this crib. Bitches either get a short stay in the telly or they get fucked in my car. It's plenty of food in here. The washcloths and towels are in the closet by the bathroom. Everything brand new," he said and headed for the door.

"Flee!" Lexi called out while jumping up from the sofa. Flee turned to face her. "Gimme hug before you go and please be safe out there," she said while hugging him tightly. Truth was, she didn't want to let him go. Everything felt so right in his arms, and she felt a sense of security that she hadn't felt since her brother died. After what took place last night, she knew that sooner or later, she would let Flee all the way in.

When Flee made it to the spot, Hitta was already there along with the UGF shot callers. Reem and Melly were in attendance also. "I'mma get straight to the point of this lil shootout (meeting)." Hitta took the floor. "I just lost the plug we had supplying us with the coke, but when one door closes, another always opens. I got plugged back in with some fire

47

dog food (heroin). Anybody who know me knows me and my niggas changed the dope game years ago; like we really made history. I touched my first million in the dope game. We about to take shit to a whole new level.

"You niggas thought y'all was eating good off that coke. Y'all about to get full off this dope shit. By a show of hands, how many of y'all nigga sold dope before?"

Flee, Shoota, and Kavali were the only ones who raised their hands. "Well, this shit is simple because the dope we got is so fuckin' good it's gon sell itself. Let me break this shit down to y'all. Selling dope ain't like crack or coke. Dope fiends need their medicine to function. Without it, they will get sick. You niggas have access to the best dope in the whole New York state." Hitta paused for a second to open the shoe box he had sitting on the table. Inside of the sneaker box sat several bricks of dope packaged in glassine bags and neatly wrapped in newspaper. He removed one brick which consisted of fifty bags of heroin. "This right here is a brick," he said while holding it up. "A brick is five bundles, fifty bags. Each bag goes for ten dollars on the streets.

"Ten bags is one bundle. Hitting the ground running, bag for bag, or bundle for bundle, you gon make $500 off each brick, but we ain't on that type of time. We on some real boss shit. We gon be selling bricks wholesale because the dope game is all about the quick flip. A brick wholesale going for anywhere between $225-$275, depending on who you getting it from and the quality of the dope. I'mma be frontin' bricks to y'all at $190 per brick. Y'all gon front them to ya ground runners at $275 per brick. If y'all got niggas with cash on deck, y'all charge them $250 per brick. Remember, dope is all about the faster flip. Y'all gon be moving through ten thousand bricks in a matter of days. Trust me." He looked at his team and smiled. He saw the hunger in all of their eyes. "These bricks that I'm about to give y'all are samples. In forty-eight hours, everyone will be situated. Do not sell these bricks. Pass them out. Greed will get us nowhere. The stamp on our bags will say untouchable. Niggas gon be dying to get they hands on this shit. We gon have the town looking like the eighties. Mark my words. Any questions?"

"On my side, the old heads got that dope shit in a head-lock. Everything be moving through them," said a dude by the name of Premo.

"Make them niggas fall in line. Give them a chance to get on board with the movement, pass them a few samples. If they don't jack it, then eliminate the niggas, bro. Simple," Hitta replied coldly. "Whoever ain't with us is against us. This shootout is now concluded."

CHAPTER 10

Matt Murda's eyes popped open. His throat was very dry; he felt like he had been eating sand. He tried to move, but his body was too weak. He looked around in a confused state. It was mainly because he was hooked up at a bunch of machines, but he wasn't in a hospital room. He saw Fatimah, his wife, in the corner of the room, sleeping on a small sofa. "Baby," he said in a raspy whisper. "Baby," he whispered again after trying to clear his throat.

Fatimah heard his voice and thought that her mind was playing tricks on her. She looked over and saw Matt Murda trying to move, and she jumped off the sofa instantly. "Oh, my God, Matt, you're awake!" she screamed. Tears of joy fell from her eyes. Words couldn't explain how happy she was at the moment.

"Water," Matt Murda said in another raspy whisper.

"Okay, baby. I'mma go get you some water and the doctor," Fatimah said before running out of the room. "Jamie! Jamie! Matt is awake!" she screamed.

Matt Murda was shot by Peso months ago, and he had

been in a coma ever since. Everyone thought he was dead, but Matt Murda was very much alive.

Two minutes later, Fatimah walked back into the room with Jamie Estrada and a doctor. "Matt, I knew you wouldn't die on us," Jamie said with a smile. Matt Murda was the closest thing Jamie had to a son. The news of Murda's near-death experience had crushed him. Jamie was happy that Matt pulled through.

Fatimah poured a cup of water and was about to put it to Matt's lips, but the doctor stopped her. "No, Fatimah, he can't drink like that just yet. You have to give him the water like this." The doctor dipped a brand-new sponge into the pitcher of water and rubbed it on his lips. "Lick your lips, Matt," she ordered. They repeated this process several times.

Meanwhile in Atlanta

"ATL, I love y'all!" Peso screamed out to his fans before walking off stage. This was another sold out arena. The place was packed, and the crowd was going crazy. Peso just set the stage on fire, but the highlight of the show was when Hitta and Reem surprised him by showing up and performing with him. They gave Peso more motivation. The crowd really enjoyed the energy.

When Peso made it backstage, Mariah was standing there, waiting for him, along with a very pretty, brown skinned chick who Peso didn't know. Not only was she drop dead gorgeous, but her body was amazing also. She was very curvy. "I did my thang, baby momma?" Peso asked while wiping the sweat from his face with a towel.

"You always do ya thang. The crowd loved the energy when Hitta and Reem walked on stage. They had it litty,"

Mariah replied. "This is my new artist I was telling you about, Kiyanne Quick," she introduced. "Those were her tracks that I played for you," she added. Peso extended his hand to Kiyanne, who accepted the handshake with a smile. She really wanted to jump up and down right now, but she kept her composure. This was really a dream come true for her. Peso was her favorite artist. She had been a fan of his since he was an underground rapper. He was also her celebrity crush.

"I heard some of ya tracks. You really got some heat, shawdy. Like you are really, really dope. Keep grindin' and trust me, that hard work gonna pay off. I'mma make ya journey a lil easier for you tho, sis. I want you to open up for me when I perform in the garden," Peso said.

"Oh, my God! Are you serious?" Kiyanne could no longer hold back her excitement. "Like, I'm not even big enough to perform in Madison Square Garden."

"Of course I'm serious. I wouldn't play like that. You gon be a star. Watch. All you gotta do is promise me you gon set that stage on fire."

"Trust and believe, I'mma make you proud," she smiled.

"Say less. Let's take a pic real quick for the gram." Peso stopped one of the arena security guards and got him to take a picture of him, Mariah, and Kiyanne.

After the show, Peso headed to the studio while his entourage hit up one of Atlanta's most popular strip clubs. Peso would usually be right with them, but these days, he'd become a lab rat, meaning all he did was work. Peso found his fun in recording music and shooting videos.

A young Atlanta producer by the name of Twizzy Beatz pulled up to the studio for a session with Peso. He was the hottest new producer out, and he was currently unsigned. Not only was Twizzy the hottest producer on the hip hop scene, but he was also the weed connect out here in the A.

Peso had Hitta and Reem with him in the studio. Twizzy Beatz walked in by his lonely. "Presidential Peso, what's the vibes, kid?" he greeted Peso with some dap.

"Ain't shit, Twizzy. What's the word, my boy? Tell me you got some gas with you. Me and the bros got some money to spend. Everybody told me you the man to get next to for that designer," Peso replied.

"Fasho. You know ya boy keeps that fiii," Twizzy said with a southern drawl as he removed the Goyard bag from his back. He opened it and pulled out a pound of weed that was dressed in a fancy vacuum sealed bag with a colorful label on it.

"Ayo, Twizzy, these my brothers right here, Hitta and Reem," Peso introduced, and Twizzy dapped both men.

Twizzy then passed the pound of weed to Peso, who opened the vacuumed sealed bag and smelled the bud. "This shit smells like it came from a bakery," Peso said with a smile. "This is it right here." He passed the bag to Hitta.

"That's called Cookie right there. Some people saying it's the best weed in the world. That shit gas, but I had better flavors to be honest. I'm the only nigga in the A with this. If a nigga got it, he got it from me," Twizzy bragged. "Mane, that shit go for fitty-six hunnit ($5,600) a plate, but that right there is a gift from me to y'all. Welcome to the A."

BROOKLYN

Flee was moving around the town, collecting money from his workers. The dope Hitta told him to pass out as samples had put the streets in a frenzy. Ever since then, he had hit the ground running. His phone had been ringing nonstop. Everybody he knew was trying to get their hands on the Untouchable brand. After his final pick up, Flee headed up to his apartment.

When he walked through the door, Fresh was in the kitchen cooking. "That shit smell good, sis. What you cooking up?" Flee asked.

"Baked chicken, rice and beans, spinach, cornbread, and Lexi made some banana pudding for dessert. The food will be ready in about twenty minutes," Fresh replied.

"Say less, I'mma go roll up real quick. Where Lexi and Manny?"

"They in ya room. Before you go back there, let me holla at you."

"Wassup? Talk to me."

"I really just wanna thank you for holding us down that day. What you did really means a lot to me and my sister. I owe you my life, bro. Just know I would do anything for you. We family now," Fresh said sincerely.

"No thank you needed. Real niggas do real shit. I'mma keep it a stack with you, Fresh. The minute I seen Lexi, I just knew that I would do anything for her. When we went on that date and we vibed the way we did, I told myself that I wasn't letting her go," he admitted. Fresh just smiled.

"Lexi really likes you. Since y'all met, all she talked about was you. My sister never does that. She has a hard time letting new people in. On the real, you remind me so much of my brother who got killed last year. You a real nigga, Flee. Don't change."

"If I was to change, then I wouldn't be who I am." He winked at her then headed out of the kitchen.

When Flee entered his bedroom, Lexi was sitting on his

bed with her laptop and two machines Flee had never seen before. Right now, Lexi was in her zone. She was currently making a bunch of cloned credit cards while Manny slept peacefully. "All work, no play, huh?" Flee asked with a smile. He loved the fact that Lexi was not just beauty, but she had brains also.

"You know I gotta get back focused. I don't wanna go back to that apartment. I never wanna think about that night again. On Thursday, I'mma go check out this condo I seen online, then I'mma go get the rest of my things from that apartment," she replied.

"Damn, Queen, you in a rush to get away from a nigga?"

"Not at all, but I know you need ya space. I ain't tryna crowd you."

"You ain't crowding me, Ma. I really want you here. I was just getting used to having a family. I really enjoy having y'all around," he admitted. Fresh knocked on the door before peeking in.

"The food is ready. Y'all come eat. I'mma let Manny sleep with me tonight, so y'all can have some alone time. Lord knows Lexi needs some dick," Fresh teased her sister.

"Fuck you, bitch," Lexi shot back playfully.

"Nah, bitch. Don't fuck me, fuck Flee."

ATLANTA

After a long, productive studio session, Peso and the fellas were exiting the building when an all-black Suburban pulled up with a masked man hanging out of the window with a Draco in his hands. "Peso, get down!" Twizzy Beatz yelled and pushed Peso down to the ground. The gunman let off a series of shots from his Draco, and all four men took cover behind a nearby car. Hitta snatched his .45 ACP off his waist and returned fire.

BOC! BOC! BOC! BOC!

Reem did the same, running in the street, letting his .40 cal bark. *BLOC! BLOC! BLOC!* Sirens could be heard approaching. Hitta ran over to Peso and Twizzy. "Y'all good?" he asked.

"Yeah, I'm straight, but Twizzy hit," Peso replied. "Twizzy, hang in there, gang. We gon get you to a hospital." The sound of sirens was getting closer.

"Yo, Peso, tell the bros they gotta go. Both them niggas got hot guns on them. We don't need them getting cased up," Twizzy said.

"Yo, Hitta, y'all niggas gotta slide."

"Bro, you know damn well I ain't leaving you," Hitta replied.

"Nigga, I don't need y'all getting locked up. The boys coming, bro. I'mma be iight. Y'all niggas got smoking guns on y'all, bro. Be smart."

Hitta and Reem hated to leave Peso behind, but they both knew that he was right. If they sat around, they would end up in jail. So, they jumped in the rental that they came in and pulled off.

Twizzy was in pain, but the shot wasn't gonna kill him. It was only a flesh wound. The bullet went in and out. If Twizzy didn't push Peso to the ground, it would have been him who was shot. Twizzy had just saved Peso's life.

CHAPTER 11

Matt Murda was in the gym of Jamie Estrada's mansion with the physical therapist. Being in a coma for months had his body kind of weak. At first, he could barely walk, but now, he was back like he never left. The only thing that wasn't working was his memory. He had partial memory loss. Matt Murda couldn't remember any of the events that led up to him being shot.

Fatimah stood outside of the gym, watching Matt exercise through the glass window. Jamie walked up and placed a hand on her shoulder. "He's a very strong young man," he said softly.

"I'm just so grateful that he is awake," she replied.

"Hitta's presence woke him up. Matt must have felt him."

"Wait, Amir was here?" Fatimah was now confused.

"Yes, he came here trying to get back in business with the family. I respectfully declined, but that didn't stop Peto from working with him. My brother is so damn stubborn at times." Jamie shook his head. "Not too long after Hitta left, you came and told me that Matt was awake," he added.

"Jamie, I don't wanna tell Matt about his beef with Hitta because I know he will not stop until one of them is dead. However, I don't want to keep if from him because it makes me feel like I'm being disloyal," she admitted.

"You won't be being disloyal. You will be being a wife that's desperately trying to save her husband from his self. God gave Matt another chance at life. What we need to do is sit down with Hitta and Peso, so we can think of a solution to this problem."

PESO CAME STROLLING out of JFK International Airport. He was all smiles when he saw Princess and Mya there waiting on him. "Daddy!" Mya screamed and ran over to Peso and jumped in his arms. Peso picked her up and spun her around in a circle then smothered her with kisses.

"I missed you so much, baby girl. Did you miss me?"

"Of course I missed you, Daddy," Mya said and put on her most beautiful smile.

Peso and Mya walked over to Princess, who was standing in front of Peso's snow-white Bentley GT. A huge smile was plastered on both of their faces when they locked eyes with each other. Peso approached his lady and pulled her into his arms. "Damn, I missed you so much," he said before kissing her lips. "How you feeling, Ma?" he asked.

"Much better now that you are home. I hope you are hungry cause me and Mya wanna take you on a date," she smiled.

"Hell yeah, I'm starving like Marvin," Peso replied.

"Daddy, who's Marvin?" Mya asked.

"A very hungry man," he replied, and he and Princess

burst out laughing. "I'mma drive, Queen," Peso said and opened the passenger side door for her.

"Nah, King, I got it. You had a long flight. Today is all about you so sit back and relax." The three of them hopped in the Bentley and took off.

After a good meal at Peter Luger's, Peso's favorite steak-house, they headed to the spa. Now, they were entering their downtown Manhattan penthouse. Mya was asleep, so Peso carried her into her bedroom.

When Peso walked back into the living room, Princess was just sitting on the sofa, staring at him. "What's wrong, Queen?" he asked.

"Take a seat, babe. We need to talk," Princess replied. The look in her eyes let Peso know that it was something serious. He took a seat next to her, and she placed her feet in his lap. Peso began to rub them.

"Talk to me, Queen."

"Don't you think it's time for you to hire some security? Tyler, you are not some underground rapper. You are the biggest name in hip hop right now. We not trying to lose you, Ty," she vented.

"Where is all this coming from, Ma?"

"I read the blogs. There were back-to-back attempts on your life, Ty. The one in Atlanta when the producer was shot, I figured that may be a coincidence, wrong place wrong time. Then the tour bus gets shot in North Carolina. That's when I knew someone was gunning for you. I know you a gangsta and all, but you have that pretty little girl in there to live for, and you also have me. We don't need anything happening to you, King." Princess now had tears rolling down her cheeks. Peso kissed her tear-stained face before gently using his thumbs to wipe away her tears.

"Stop crying, Queen. I ain't going nowhere," Peso said before kissing her lips. He slowly began to remove her clothes. "Ty, stop. We are talking," she pleaded.

"I've been gone for two whole months. I'm tryna talk to this pussy."

METROPOLITAN DETENTION CENTER (Brooklyn)

Rolex Rich entered the facility's visiting room with extreme confidence. All eyes were on him as he walked over to the table where his two sons sat waiting for him. He hadn't seen Lil Rich or Ray in person for quite some time now. He only saw them on FaceTime calls from his contraband iPhone.

Rolex Rich greeted them both with tight bear hugs. "Damn, Pops, you getting big as hell," said Lil Rich.

"I'm trying," Rolex Rich replied modestly. "So, what do I owe the pleasure of this visit? You two ain't been up here in months. What y'all need?" he added.

"Why we gotta need something in order to come see you?" Ray replied defensively.

"Cause that's the only time y'all come up here. By the way, you been playing like shit, Ray. Your team was not supposed to get bumped the first round in the playoffs."

"Playing like shit?" Ray chuckled. "Pops, are you shitting me, or are you shitting yaself? I averaged 31.7 points, 11.6 assists, and 10.2 rebounds. To add spice to that, I shot ninety-seven percent from the free throw line, seventy-one percent from the field, and fifty-three percent from three. The team didn't lose because of me. I was putting on," he replied with arrogance.

"That's true, but in game seven, you didn't show up in the fourth quarter. You folded when your team needed you. Ray, you let that bum, who was guarding you, hold you to six points. How is it that the leader of the team didn't show up in crunch time?"

"I had a lot going on that day. My head wasn't completely in the game," Ray claimed.

"Let me guess. You trippin' over Nautica and Hitta, right? Fuck Nautica. You are Raymond fucking Royal. There isn't a woman out there that you can't pull."

"He ain't pulling another Nautica Taylor," Lil Rich teased.

"Fuck you, bro," Ray shot back, and the three of them shared a laugh. Rolex Rich turned his attention to Lil Rich.

"I'mma say this one time and one time only, Rich. Stick to that rap shit and running the label. Let me handle the street shit. Them niggas you sending at Hitta and Peso are rookies. Those niggas are moving real sloppy. How the fuck they miss twice? In Atlanta, they hit a fuckin' innocent bystander. Twizzy Beatz is a producer, a damn good producer at that."

"He with the ops, so he will get treated like the ops. That nigga ain't a innocent bystander. A friend of my enemy is an enemy. Every time we see those niggas, it's on sight," Lil Rich replied.

Rolex Rich just shot his son an icy glare. "Richie, I'mma act like you ain't just say that stupid ass shit to me. You sound like one of these studio gangstas. Knock it the fuck off before you end up in a cell next to me. If one of them goofy ass niggas get locked up, they are not gonna hesitate to trade your future for their's. Tighten the fuck up. Focus on music, focus on being Richie Rich, the president of Royalty Records, our family empire. All that other shit, let go. I got a plan for Hitta and Peso. Fall back. Do I make myself clear?" he asked, looking his youngest son in his eyes.

"Yes, Pops, I got you," he replied.

"Good. Now that we off of that, I want you to sign the producer kid, Twizzy Beatz."

Meanwhile at Peso's Penthouse

Hitta stepped off of the elevator and into Peso's penthouse. He held a huge army duffle bag in his grip. Peso and Princess were on the sofa, wrapped up in a blanket. Their clothes were all over the living room. Prior to Hitta pulling up, the two of them had a long overdue sex session. "Damn, did I come at a bad time?" Hitta joked. "Y'all was in here making a baby?" he teased.

"We sure was," Princess said with a smile. "You good tho. We done now." Princess kissed Peso on the lips before exiting the living room wrapped in a blanket.

Peso hopped up from the sofa, dressed in nothing but a pair of Calvin Klein boxer briefs. Tattoos covered his entire upper body. "I ain't gon hold you, bro. Ya shit up right now. No freaky," Hitta said while squeezing Peso's bicep. Peso flexed his muscles.

"A lil pushups and pullups ain't never hurt the body," Peso replied with a smile. "I'm tryna catch up to you tho, beloved. What's the word? Talk to me," he added.

Hitta unzipped the duffle bag that he came with. "Money, my brother. Money is the word." Inside of the duffle bag sat a bunch of neatly stacked one-hundred-dollar bills wrapped in rubber bands.

"What's this for?" Peso asked.

"That's ya half of the last flip. I went to see Jamie Estrada, and he refused to do business wit me, but his brother, Peto, wasn't jackin' that, so we plugged back in to that raw heroin we was getting back in our Murda Team days," Hitta explained. "We getting it at forty-five bands ($45,000) a joint. I took a mil from you and a mil from me, so we went in two million strong. The apes got shit on lock right now, bro. The streets in a frenzy. We got shit looking like 2009 again," he continued.

Hitta had a huge smile plastered across his face. He lived for the thrill. Making money gave him a rush, but the bigger rush came from seeing how he was changing the lives of the people around him and bringing life back to the dope game that people once thought was dead. These days, it seemed like the scammers had taken over and were the only ones making money. Hitta wasn't at all feeling that, so he gave the drug game life again. You could now see dope traffic on damn near every street in New York City. "We seeing $190,000 of each joint, so once this flip is over, we split exactly $8,550,000. Not bad for niggas who made it out the trenches, huh?"

"Not bad at all," Peso replied with less excitement. He had a few things that he wanted to get off of his chest, but he didn't want to sound like he was preaching. However, he had never been the type to bite his tongue, so he spoke his peace. "Let me ask you something, bro. How much money is enough? Nigga, we rich already. Ain't like you trappin' for the money. We got a label that's doing very well. We own half of a luxury car dealership, the management company is doing great, the real estate is up and jumping, and on top of that, Nike is tryna cut us a check. We are more than good, gang. We don't gotta sell dope no more, Hitta. Dope ain't the only way to eat, my nigga."

"I feel you, bro, but those are your dreams. Yeah, we rich, ain't no hiding that, but I wanna be wealthy. I'm talking generational wealth. Fuck us. I wanna make sure our kids and grandkids are good in the future. I want all generations to come in our family to be secured. Feel me?"

"I most definitely feel you on that, but you can do that on some legit shit, bro. It don't gotta come from selling dope. The Feds can take all that shit from us when shit hits the fan. The Feds can't touch this legal paper. I'm not preaching nothing. I'm just giving you the game because you my brother, and I love you. We still got diamonds that we ain't even touch. After this flip, fallback, bro, and let me show you what this legal paper hittin' for. Let me put you on to this crypto currency and this stock market shit. We can be legal billionaires and never have to worry about the Feds taking shit from us. Once again, I'm not preaching. I just really want the best for you, bro," Peso said sincerely.

"I tell you what, bro. Give me a year. Whatever I don't have in the next twelve months, I won't have at all. Speaking of those diamonds, what you tryna do with them?"

"We not at all pressed for no paper, just save them for a rainy day."

The two of them sat around for about another hour or so, smoking blunts and listening to some of Peso's unreleased music.

Two Hours Later

Ashley's CLS Mercedes Benz floated along the Belt Parkway. The sound of Meek Mill, Nicki Minaj, and Chris Brown's, *All Eyes on You,* track poured from the speakers. Hitta sat in the passenger's seat with the seat reclined, puffing on a stuffed Backwood filled with a potent weed strand called Cereal Milk. He reached out to pass the blunt to Ashley, but she declined. "Too strong, baby girl?" he asked.

"Nah, I'm just high already," she laughed. "You literally smoke every five minutes. I'm hungry. Can we go to Nathans? I badly want some frog legs and cheese fries," she added.

"Yeah, let's make this stop to the block first. I gotta go meet the young boys real quick. I won't be long. I promise."

Ashley exited the Belt Parkway on Cropsey Avenue, drove a few blocks, then made the turn on Neptune Avenue. An unmarked police car came out of nowhere and hit the signal for Ashley to pull over. "Fuck," Hitta mumbled while spraying some smell good in the car to kill the weed smell.

"Babe, where ya gun?" Ashley asked.

"It's in the stash box. We straight." Hitta rolled down the window as the detective approached. "What's the problem, Officer?" he asked.

"Amir Moore, we have an I-Card out for you, so step out of the car. You know the drill," the detective replied.

"An I-Card for what?"

"That's above my pay grade. If you not guilty of nothing, you will be out in no time. Now are we gonna do this the easy way or the hard way?"

Hitta turned to Ashley. "Baby girl, call the lawyer," he said before getting out of the car and letting the detective cuff him.

Meanwhile in Gravesend Houses

Shoota and Heat pulled into the middle parking lot of the projects. The two of them had been out of town in Vermont. The place was a dope dealer's dream. The two of them had ran through two thousand bricks of Untouchable in just three days.

Shoota met a chick while on tour with Peso, and she

plugged him into the town. This was history repeating itself because, years ago, Vermont was a place that Peso took over. He ran three different towns, Burlington, Bennington, and Winooski.

Both men hopped out of the rented Dodge Charger, holding Gucci bookbags filled with cash. They entered building 3201 and took the elevator up to the seventh floor. When they entered the apartment, they were hit by a huge cloud of smoke. Caine was sitting in the living room with two females from around the way, smoking and drinking.

Caine passed Shoota a blunt while greeting him and Heat with the UGF handshake. "My guys finally back. What's shakin'? How shit looking OT?" Caine asked in a hyper tone. One thing about Caine was he always had a lot of energy, except when he was off the lean. Today, he hadn't sipped any syrup. He was just smoking weed and drinking Hennessey.

"You know the vibes, bro. Pull up to the back room so we can chop it up." Shoota turned to the two females. "Y'all excuse us for a minute. We gotta holla at bro real quick. Matter fact, here, take this bud." He dropped a Ziploc filled with Gelato #9 on the glass table. He then dropped two packs of Backwoods.

Once in the back room, Shoota and Heat both began pouring stacks of money from their bookbags onto the bed. Caine's eyes lit up like a Christmas tree. "Damn, gang, shit lit out there like that?" he asked with a huge smile on his face. Even though he didn't go with them, he was extremely happy to see his friends winning.

"Facts, bro. All straight cash too. I'm talking $100 a bundle. I know you love the hood, but you can't sit out on the next trip," Heat said.

"Nigga, that's a milly in cash on that bed, gang." Shoota pushed Caine on top of the money.

"That's what a mil feels like, my boy," he added, and they all laughed.

Caine got up and walked to the closet. He grabbed a Gucci bookbag identical to the ones Shoota and Heat had and dumped a bunch of rubber band stacks on the floor. "That's three hundred racks ($300,000) cold cash right there. After I give Hitta his $190,000, I got $110,000 for myself. Y'all ain't the only niggas eatin'," he smiled.

That was what they both loved about Caine. He didn't have a drop of hate in his blood. He didn't care if they made more money than him. He was no pocket watcher. Caine was happy that all of them were leveling up. "We give Hitta $380,000; me and Heat split $620,000." Shoota added up the number like a mathematician. "And since you the bro, I'mma toss you $50K," he added.

"I'mma toss you a fifty pack too," said Heat. Caine was now confused. He didn't see why both of them were passing him fifty thousand apiece for no reason.

"What y'all niggas passing me fifty racks for? It ain't my birthday," he said with a confused look on his face.

"We passing you the bread, so you won't be too far behind us. Now, you got 210K on top of what you already have in the stash," Shoota explained. Hearing this put a huge smile on Caine's face.

"I really love y'all niggas with all my heart, gang. You two niggas been taking care of me forever."

"Because we brothers, and brothers take care of each other. We all we got, gang," Heat replied.

"And we all we need," Shoota joined in.

"I o'd appreciate y'all niggas, man. Call Hitta and see

where he at. In the meantime, let's go fuck on these thotties and smoke some gas."

Heat pulled out his phone and called Hitta but didn't get an answer. After the first failed attempt, he tried two more times and got the same results. "That nigga ain't picking up."

"He prolly moving around. Trust and believe, big bro gon hit back," Shoota said while leading the way to the living room.

CHAPTER 12

60th Precinct Brooklyn Coney Island
Same Day

Hitta sat inside of the interrogation room, bored out of his mind. He had been sitting in this same spot for over an hour already. When he told the detectives that he wanted to use his right to remain silent, both of them stormed out of the room, pissed off. Hitta just laughed when the detective's pale white face turned bright red from anger.

The door opened, and two men dressed in black suits entered the interrogation room, one African American and the other Caucasian. "Well, well, well, we finally get to meet you, Mr. Moore, or should I call you Hitta?" the Black guy spoke.

"You can call me Amir," Hitta replied dryly. "Who you niggas supposed to be, the men in black?"

"Very funny, shithead. I didn't know you were into comedy. Let me properly introduce myself. I'm Special Agent Jackson, and that's my partner, Special Agent Tibbs." The Black guy introduced himself and his partner.

"Agents? What the hell y'all want with me? We all know I'm completely legit."

"That's what all drug dealing murderers say when they start cleaning money through record labels. All you street punks are the same. You ain't legit, nigger," Agent Tibbs finally spoke.

"Ain't no need for the name calling, sir. I'm no drug dealer or murderer, so please don't disrespect me by putting false titles next to my name," Hitta replied calmly. "Respectfully, don't ever refer to me or any other Black man as a nigger. Black men are kings, you fuckin Nazi," he added while turning to the Black agent. "Brother, you should be ashamed of yaself. That badge don't make you a white man. I ain't tryna kick it with y'all tho. If you clowns got anything to say, contact my attorney. Whatever y'all gotta say, I use my right to remain silent."

"We just wanna ask you some questions about Detective Brown."

"Like I said, talk to my attorney. He'll be here any minute."

"You think you're some type of gangsta?" Agent Jackson barked, slamming his fist down on the desk. This caused Hitta to roll over in laughter.

"Laugh now, cry later," Agent Tibbs said while removing a quarter from his pocket. He did a coin toss, and it landed on tails directly in front of Hitta. "You see that bird?" He pointed to the quarter. "Remember it because when we take you down, this bird is all you gonna see," he added with a smile before he and his partner left the interrogation room.

Twenty minutes later, Hitta exited the precinct. After briefly talking to his lawyer, he walked over to Ashley. She hugged him tightly. "Everything alright?" she asked.

"They on my body right now. The Feds were in there tryna question me," he explained while opening the driver's side door for Ashley before hopping in the passenger's seat. That never got old to her. No matter how gangsta Hitta was in the streets, he was always a gentleman when it came to her.

"What are they saying, babe?" Ashley questioned.

"I ain't let them say shit. I used my right to remain silent. They did try to ask me about that dirty cop that killed Relo tho. Other than that, I ain't let them say shit else. Where my phone at, baby girl?"

"Right here," Ashley replied and handed him his phone. "Heat was blowing ya line up," she added.

"That means him and Shoota came back from OT. Drive to the yard real quick. I don't know why you ain't pull off yet. Got me sitting in front of this hot ass precinct. This shit making me itch and shit," he chuckled.

Ashley just ignored him. While Hitta was in the precinct, Heat wasn't the only one calling his phone. He received two calls from someone whose phone number was stored under a boat emoji. If her assumption was correct, the boat was code for Nautica. "Before I pull off, Amir, let me ask you something. Depending on how you answer my question, that will determine if I'm gonna drive or not because I might end up in jail for fucking you up." She began to remove her earrings from her ears. "Do you still be talking to that actress bitch? Or did you get rid of her number?"

"Ashley, please get away from this precinct."

"If you don't answer my question, I'mma punch you right in your shit."

"Baby girl, I didn't delete her number. It's still saved in my phone," he admitted. "I never called her. Shawdy hit my line from time to time just to check on me. It be all innocent tho. I never linked her or made plans to link her. After seeing how much I hurt you, that made me tighten up. Ain't no bitch in the world worth losing you, Ash."

Ashley cut her eyes at him. This was something she did when she thought he was lying. Hitta looked her in the eyes. "Ashley, I'm not lying. That's word to Rico," he said.

Hearing Hitta swear on his fallen comrade let Ashley know that he was telling the truth because this was something he never did. "You really feeling that bitch, huh, Amir?" Ashley asked with a smile on her face. Hitta was confused now. The sudden change in her mood had him spooked. He felt like she was up to something. He knew firsthand how crazy Ashley could get.

"Baby girl, get me from in front of this precinct please and put ya earrings back in. You starting to look like a lil boy," he joked.

"Never could I look like a boy, nigga. Fuck you, Amir," she laughed. "But don't change the subject, nigga. Answer my question. You really feeling that bitch, huh? You don't gotta front. I'm not gon get mad," she claimed. "Like who wouldn't be feeling Nautica Taylor? She is a bad bitch."

"She's iight," Hitta smiled. "She ain't fuckin' with my baby tho." He reached out and stroked her face. His comment caused her to blush.

"Let's make a deal, Daddy," Ashley said seriously. "If you wanna fuck her, we gon fuck her together."

Hitta looked at her like she was crazy. He thought she was trying to set him up. He just shook his head.

"What?" she smiled. "I'm dead ass serious. Hit that bitch and let her know this dick comes with stipulations," she added before pulling off.

. . .

MINUTES LATER AT GRAVESEND HOUSES. A.K.A. The Yard

Ashely pulled into the middle parking lot. Hitta opened the stash box and removed his Glock .45 and Ashley's .380 bodyguard. He tucked his gun in his waistband and slid Ashley's gun in her purse. "Babe, you gonna call her?" Ashley asked.

Hitta didn't respond. He just exited the car, and Ashley did the same. "We gonna finish this conversation at home cause I see you all in gangsta mode right now," she teased as they entered the building.

Together, they rode the elevator up to the seventh floor. Hitta pulled out a single key and opened the door to apartment 7A. When they walked inside, Hitta couldn't help but laugh at the sight of his young niggas. Shoota stood in front of a chick, getting head, while Caine hit her from the back, doggy style. On the other couch, Heat was sitting down while another chick had both feet planted on the couch, bouncing up and down. "Oh, my God!" Ashley said while covering her eyes and quickly walking to the backroom.

"When y'all niggas done, I'll be in the back, gang," Hitta said while grabbing a pack of Backwoods off of the glass table.

MEANWHILE

Peso sat in the studio, working on a new project. Thick clouds of smoke filled the room, and a pungent aroma of marijuana seeped all throughout the building. The potent weed could literally be smelled from outside.

Plenty bottles of liquor were on the tables along with a bunch of candy, mainly Airheads and Mike and Ikes. These things were a must when Peso was recording. This was the only time he ate candy.

Several UGF members and several of Peso's day one homies sat around drinking, smoking, and enjoying the company of the females that were there. Peso's personal engineer was doing his thing while Kiyanne Quick was in the booth, laying down her verse to Peso's new track, *Leveled Up*.

Peso also flew Twizzy Beatz in from Atlanta. The two of them had finally found time to chop it up. "Yo, Twizzy, thanks again, my nigga." Peso thanked him for what seemed like the millionth time.

"You don't gotta thank me, bruh. We people. You solid, my nigga. I appreciate the gratitude tho," Twizzy replied.

"Nigga, you took a bullet for me," Peso reminded him.

"Real niggas do real things. You don't owe me nothing tho, bruh. When I was on my way up here, I bumped into the boy, Richie Rich, and his mom. They tryna sign a nigga."

"Oh, word? What you told them?"

"You know I'm doing the independent thing, but if the money and paperwork right, I told them we prolly can do something," Twizzy admitted.

"Fuck them, Twizz. The money and paperwork right on this side. I'm pulling Luxury from this label real soon, and I got plans on being the biggest independent label in hip hop. I need you on my team. I'll give you a million-dollar advance and give you full creative control of your music and release dates. No slave deal. Come sign with me, my boy."

"Say word."

"Word," Peso replied and reached his hand out. Twizzy gladly accepted the handshake. "So, it's official?" Peso asked,

"Fasho," Twizzy replied.

"What you think about home girl?" Peso asked, referring to Kiyanne.

"She the truth. Lil buddy can sing her ass off, and she can rap. You ain't sign her yet?" Twizzy asked just as Kiyanne was exiting the booth. "Shawdy go hard in the paint, bruh."

"You talking about me?" Kiyanne smiled, showing her pearly white teeth.

"Yeah, we talking about you. What you think about signing to my label? You can be the first lady," Peso said.

"Honestly, that would be a dream come true, but you would have to talk to my manager tho. I'm not cutting her out of any deals," she replied honestly.

Peso admired her loyalty to Mariah. Her comment just showed a lot about her character. People like Kiyanne were hard to come by. Peso just smiled at her. "Mariah is already on board. By the way, I am the co-owner of that management company." Peso handed Lee his iPhone. "Let's put the world on to this power move and let them know y'all officially with the winning team." He picked up his Goyard bag and pulled out two jewelry boxes. Peso was prepared for this moment; he'd purchased both Kiyanne and Twizzy iced out Cuban links with custom Luxury pendants.

Lee started up the Instagram live video. "It's ya boy, Presidential Peso, a.k.a. Mr. Luxury himself. I got some news for y'all. Let me introduce the first lady of Luxury Records, the beautiful Kiyanne Quick." He handed her one of the jewelry boxes. Kiyanne opened it and took out the bust down Cuban link and pendant. She placed it on her neck with a smile.

"I'm holding back tears right now," she said, not able to hold back her excitement.

"Introduce yaself, first lady," Peso encouraged her.

"It's the pretty brown mami, Kiyanne Quick. Luxury baybee."

"What, y'all thought we was finished?" Peso said into the camera. "Nah, we ain't done yet. Y'all know I had to get the hottest new producer in the industry right now, my man a hunnit grand, Twizzy Beatz," he added while handing Twizzy the other jewelry box.

Twizzy opened the jewelry box and removed the bust down Cuban link and placed it on his neck. "It's ya boy, Twizzy Beatz da fireman. You heard it here first, Luxury Gang. From New York to the A, we don't play."

"With that being said, we got a bunch of heat on the way. Stay tuned in."

CHAPTER 13

Weeks Later

Flee pulled up in front of Queensboro Correctional Facility. He was there to pick up his righthand man, Gat, who'd just finished serving a three-year sentence for a gun charge. Flee and Gat had been best friends since they were running around with snotty noses. The two of them were more like brothers than anything. Gat was older than Flee by one year.

The sound of Flee's iPhone ringing snapped him out of his thoughts. He slid his thumb across the screen to answer the FaceTime call from Lexi. "Wassup, Ma? I see you finally up," Flee greeted when Lexi's face popped up on the screen.

"I opened my eyes and didn't see you next to me, Papi," Lexi whined. "Where are you, Pa?"

"I told you last night that I had to go pick up my brother. He should be getting released any minute now," Flee reminded her.

"Oh, yeah, I forgot. I'm sorry, Pa. I wasn't pressing you. Me and Manny just wanted to take you out for breakfast."

"How about we do lunch?"

"Sounds good to me. Just call me when you on ya way home."

"I gotchu, Ma," Flee replied and ended the call.

Gat came strolling out of the prison. Flee sat back and watched his every move, just to see how long it would take for Gat to see him. After watching Gat look around for another two minutes, Flee decided to call out to him. "Yo, fat boy, over here!" he yelled from the driver's seat of his Benz. Flee jumped out and met Gat in the middle of the street. The two of them embraced each other with a bear hug. "My fuckin' boy, welcome home," Flee said. He was happy to have his closest comrade home.

Gat was a chubby Puerto Rican kid with long, silky hair. He was known in the streets for his knuckle check and pistol play. He was a wild young nigga who was also about his paper.

"This you right here?" Gat pointed to the Mercedes Benz.

"Yeah, this lil shit mine, bro," Flee replied modestly.

"This lil shit," Gat mimicked Flee. "Knock it off, baby boy. You out here doing big shit. Hold up, nigga. You got a Rollie on? That's what the fuck I'm talking about. My niggas got the town litty," Gat said, all smiles.

They hopped inside of the Benz, and Flee pulled off. Once they made it to the highway, Flee sparked a blunt and passed it to Gat. "Ayo, bro, the big homie, Peso, really got the rap game in a frenzy. Big bro all over the T.V.," Gat said while inhaling the potent weed smoke. The second he exhaled, he started to cough uncontrollably.

"Aye, take it easy, holmes." Flee mimicked Hector from the movie, *Friday*. "That's gas right there, bro. You been gone a minute. Slow down." Flee chuckled. "But yeah, Peso really on. He ain't on no Hollywood shit either. Bro the same nigga he's always been. He be pulling up, tryna take niggas out the hood and shit. You wanna call him? I know he gon be super hype to hear from you. When he see you home, he gon be o'd happy."

"We gon hit bro when we settle in. What you got going on out here, bro? You scammin'?

"Gat, you know me better than that. My lil hunny fuck with the pieces tho. I'mma always be a dope boy. You know I'm trapper of the year," Flee smiled.

"Let's not forget you got some jackboy in you," Gat replied, and they both shared a laugh.

"On the real tho, Gat, niggas got that raw dope again. Shit looking like '09 out here. Remember when Matt Murda came home and had that plug on the dog food? Shit looking like that right now, gangsta! We got the best dope around. It's a ten all over the land, gang. The squad up-up right now, Gat."

"Shit, I can tell," Gat smiled like a kid in the candy store. He could barely hold back his excitement. One thing Gat knew for sure was if his team was on, then he was on.

"So, what you wanna do now that you home, bro? What's ya plans?" Flee asked.

"Bro, I'm just tryna get in where I fit in. A nigga tryna run it up, but I don't wanna move too fast. Feel me? I'mma sit back and watch how shit moving out here. Before I make a move, I gotta get back familiar with the streets," Gat replied.

"Shit way different. Ain't no need to rush. You came home to some real paper. Me and the gang been putting money to the side for you since we been in position. Me, Shoota, Heat, and Caine all had a lil kitty put up for you. That shit don't even include what Hitta and Peso gon set you out with. You sturdy, bro. That's on my gangsta," he promised.

. . .

Twenty Minutes Later

Flee pulled into the parking lot of his apartment complex. He and Gat both exited his Benz and headed toward the building. When they entered Flee's apartment, Fresh was in the living room, punching up some pieces (cloned credit cards). "Yo, Fresh, this my brother, Gat, I was telling you about. Gat, this Fresh," Flee introduced them.

"Sup," Fresh replied, never taking her eyes off of the laptop and machines.

"That's the sis. She valid, bro. Just super in her zone right now. Come on. Ya shit is in my room, gang," Flee said, leading the way to his bedroom. They walked in and found Lexi in the mirror, flat ironing her hair, while little Manny laid on the bed, playing a game on her iPad. Flee kissed Lexi then introduced her to Gat.

"Nah, I thought you was Cassie for a minute," Gat said through a laugh. "That's really your twin," he added.

"Nigga, I'm badder than Cassie," Lexi replied, turning to Flee. "Right, Papi?"

"You know that shit," Flee said and kissed her again. He then walked to the closet and pulled out a Goyard bag. "This a care package from me and Lexi. She put ten bands in there, so that's $60,000 altogether. All those bags over there are yours. Fresh swiped all of ya clothes and sneakers. The sneakers are stacked up in the closet out there by the door," Flee explained.

"I really appreciate y'all, gang. No funny shit. Lexi and Fresh don't even know me and they showing up like this. What y'all just did for me means a lot." Gat turned to Lexi. "Thank you, sis. I fuck wit you, no cap. Anything you and ya sister need, I got y'all," he added sincerely.

"That's light, Gat. That ain't about nothing. You Flee's brother, so that makes you family. We just tryna make sure you sturdy out here. Now go wash that jail shit off of you and throw on a good fit. We all about to do a family lunch."

"Hold up before you go hop in the splash." Flee grabbed a jewelry box off of his dresser and handed it to Gat. Gat opened it and admired the three hundred fifty-gram bust down Cuban link with a three-hundred-gram UGF pendant flooded with diamonds.

"This why you my boy," Gat smiled.

"Welcome to the level up," Flee replied with a smile.

MEANWHILE AT PESO'S Penthouse

"Oh, my God!" Princess screamed from the bedroom. "Tyler, come here!" she called out for Peso. She was so happy right now, and she couldn't hide her excitement. Tears of joy slid down her face.

"Wassup, Queen?" Peso entered the bedroom. He took a look at Princess, who was jumping up and down with tears in her eyes and smiled. He knew why she was so happy because he played a part in her happiness.

"Baby, I'm a millionaire, like I'm really rich," she said happily.

"You been rich, my love. Look who ya man is," he replied with just a little bit of arrogance.

"That's your money, King. I'm not talking about your coins. I'm talking about my cosmetic line. Sales are crazy right now, bae. I already pulled in four million. Thank you so much for investing in me. I can pay you back your money now that you put up to make this possible, and I can also give you back the million dollars that you anonymously spent. You are not low, nigga." She playfully rolled her eyes.

"I don't know what you talking about," Peso claimed.

"You know exactly what I'm talking about. Don't lie, Ty. I'm giving you that money back. I appreciate you trying to make sure things went right, but you didn't have to do that. I wanted to know what it feels like to get a win on my own. You already invested, so you helped with that, but you didn't have to help with sales too. Let me learn from experience, King."

"Babe, I gave you a boost. That's all. You did catch a win on your own. Yeah, I spent a mil to help ya business grow, but, Queen, look at the bright side. You pulled in three mil on top of that. That wasn't my hard work, baby girl. That was yours. I don't want no money back. I just really want to see you win. If you want to help me, just help someone else who's stuck at the bottom," Peso replied and pulled her close to him. They looked into each other's eyes for what seemed like eternity.

"Thank you so much for investing in me, Ty. I wasn't trying to come off as ungrateful or like I'm nagging, I just don't want you to feel like you have to carry me. I'm an asset to your life, babe. I bring things to the table also," she said.

"I know you do, P. That's why you are still in my corner. You don't have to thank me for nothing that I do for you. Just giving me your love and loyalty shows your gratitude. Princess, you gon be my wife one day. There is nothing I won't do to see you happy." He planted a kiss on her forehead and wiped her tears with his thumbs.

"These are happy tears, King. You don't have to wipe them. Let them flow," she smiled before kissing his lips. "You are a great man, Tyler Carter. Every blessing that comes your way, you deserve it. How can I ever repay you for being so good to me?" she added.

"Just continue to be you, keep loving me, keep supporting me, stay loyal, continue to be good to Mya, keep cooking those bombs ass meals, and giving me that mind blowing sex. You know, regular shit." He winked at her.

"That's easy, King."

"Oh, yeah, I want a few babies too. Our first set has to be twins tho," he smiled.

"Twins?"

"Yeah, that would prove to me that you are my soulmate."

"You think you so smooth. I do want twins tho. How about we start working on them right now?" Princess replied with seduction all in her tone before passionately kissing his lips.

The sound of Peso's phone ringing interrupted their little session. Both of them looked at the screen and saw Mariah's name. Princess grabbed the phone and answered it. "Riah, you are so being a soccer goalie right now," Princess said playfully.

"A soccer goalie?" Mariah asked. She was super confused.

"Yeah, bitch, a cock blocker," Princess replied, and she and Mariah both fell out laughing. Even Peso was cracking up. This was one of the many things that he loved about Princess.

"Fuck you, bitch. I ain't no cock blocker," Mariah joked. "I'm calling with good news. I will only be a minute. Put the phone on speaker," she added.

Princess hit a button on the screen to put the call on speaker. "You on speaker, Riah."

"*GQ* magazine just contacted me, and they want y'all two to be on the front cover with a full interview. Y'all with it?"

"Of course we are. Set it up," said Peso. "Sounds like we need to do some celebrating, but right now, we about to do some grown people stuff. I love you, baby momma."

"Love you too, baby daddy. Later, Princess." Mariah ended the call.

CHAPTER 14

Marlboro Houses

It was a beautiful day today. The sun was shining, kids were out playing, and the ladies were walking around showing off plenty of skin. Summer wasn't even here yet, and it was eighty-three degrees.

Reem pulled up to the projects in his brand-new, candy-apple red Maserati Tourismo. He paid $140,000 cash for this car, and to him, it was worth every single dollar that he'd spent. Reem loved the crack game, but the dope game had been treating him way better. In all of his years of drug dealing, he had never seen money coming in so fast. His situation had changed drastically. He and his team were eating on a whole new level.

He hopped out of the driver's seat and walked through the projects like the hood celebrity that he was. Today, he was dressed in a white Givenchy shirt, white Balmain jeans, with a red Fendi belt holding his pants up. On his feet, he rocked a white and red pair of Christian Louboutin sneakers with the spikes. Today, he was light on the jewelry, just a yellow-gold three hundred fifty-gram Cuban link with a Jesus piece and a Yacht Master II Rolex.

Reem pulled out his iPhone and called his homie, Young World, who picked up on the first ring.

"Reem, what's poppin, Bloody?" Young World greeted.

"Us, never them. Where you at, beloved?"

"I'm up top by the corner store."

"Say less, gang, I'll view you in a minute," Reem said and ended the call.

While walking through the projects, Reem bumped into an old head named Doggy. Now, this OG was by far one of the most ruthless killers in the whole New York City. He was also the uncle of Reem's childhood friend, Bricks, who he murdered for siding against him in the war with B-Gunnz. "What it do, Reem?" Doggy greeted him with a fist bump.

"Same fight, different round. What's good with you, Uncle Dog?" Reem replied.

"I'm fair for a square. I see you shining, nephew. Put a nigga on the payroll of something. I heard you got this killer herron." Doggy mispronounced the word heroin. "When you started moving that dog food? Ya lane is crack. You done switched over?"

"Unk, you know my lane is whatever lane I choose. You know I'm one of those multi-talented niggas," Reem chuckled.

"Shit, I can tell. On another note, I'mma shoot it straight to you, Reem. You like a nephew to me, and I love you," he said, looking Reem in the eyes. "Some very disturbing news came across my desk, nephew. You know I ain't the one for politics, but this shit came across me on more than one occasion," he claimed.

"Talk to me, Unk," Reem replied.

"The streets saying that you the one who hit Bricks. You either a cold-blooded killer or a slithery ass snake because you came to the funeral and hugged my sister and mom. Say it ain't so, nephew. Please tell me you didn't back door your comrade on some sucker shit."

"Hell no, Dog. How the hell you gon ask me some nut shit like that? Bricks was like my brother. We came from the sandbox together. Went to war and slept on floors together. I been out here dropping shit for the homie. I been the only nigga out here standing on business," Reem lied with a straight face.

"I'mma give you the benefit of a doubt. Don't let me find out you lying to me, or I will come for you and every single person you love. Nobody would be exempt. You of all people know how I get down. From one gangsta to another, I respect you, Reem, but if you killed my nephew, I will murder ya mom, aunt, sister, and that ugly ass dog," Doggy spit before walking off.

"I gotta bump this old nigga," Reem said to himself.

Reem made it to the corner store where Young World stood, waiting for him. The two greeted each other with the signature Blood handshake. "What's poppin', skrap?"

"We poppin', gang. That five poppin'," Young World replied.

Young World was a dark-skinned cat who stood about 5'9". He sported a tapered dark ceaser with 360 waves. He was a funny, easygoing dude who always had a smile on his face. The wise knew not to take his kindness for a weakness. Young World was always down to put in some work, but he was a cool motherfucker.

"Shit looking real right for the home team, Blood. That

shit I copped from you got shit jumping. When you gon bring that number down tho?" Young World questioned.

"When the plug brings the number down for me. World, you my day one. I wouldn't slut you out, skrap. You know me way better than that," Reem replied truthfully. "I'm giving you a better number than everybody else I'm serving because you my brother. I charge you $220 a brick. I only make $30 off you because I pay $190. That's on my gangsta," he swore. "I'm charging everybody else anywhere from $240 to $270 a brick. Ask around, beloved."

"Yo, who the fuck is this walking toward us with that big ass hoodie on? It's eighty degrees, bro. Shit look suspect as fuck." Young World pointed out. Reem looked to his left and saw the person who Young World was talking about. Reem knew the walk from anywhere. The man with the oversized hoodie on was Doggy.

Once Doggy stepped in the middle of the street, he brandished two huge, dusty ass .44 revolvers. Reem peeped the play. "World, get down." Reem pulled his comrade down for cover.

BOOM! BOOM! BOOM! BOOM! Doggy let his cannons off. Reem now regretted leaving his gun in his car.

Young World quickly pulled his .9mm from his waist and fired three shots at Doggy. The shots didn't hit anything, but they forced Doggy to take cover behind a nearby car and gave Reem time to take off.

BOOM! BOOM! BOOM! Doggy continued to fire. He still wasn't hitting his target; the cars along the sidewalk weren't so lucky. Doggy chased behind Reem and Young World like a trained military vet. *BOC! BOC! BOC!* Young World sent three more shots in Doggy's direction. Sirens could be heard nearby and forced Doggy to abort his mission and run in the opposite direction from Reem and Young World.

MEANWHILE IN THE **Bronx**

Santana, one of the UGF shot callers, sat inside of a White Castle, eating an order of chicken rings. Across from him sat Premo, who was one of the shot callers for the Queens chapter. He was stuffing his face with the restaurant's signature burger. "Yo, Santana, I'mma keep it funky with you, ape. I don't like the number that Hitta charging us. Bro treating niggas like workers," Premo claimed. "Like how we go from getting birds to getting packaged dope? That shit wocky, ape, for real. Nigga charging us $190 a brick. I be letting mine go for $250, so I be making $60 dollars off each joint. I know he pulling in way more than that, bro."

"Nigga, you pocket watching? That's some real clown shit," Santana replied in disgust. "Bro doing the right thing, and you over here complaining. That nigga don't owe none of us shit. You don't even pay for shit upfront. He's passing it to you on the arm. Go to bro with some bread, and I bet you the nigga drop the price. You on some real Bozo shit right now."

"He ain't dropping no price, bro. That nigga using us," Premo claimed.

"Using us? You sound like a straight bitch right now. You ungrateful ass nigga, you just pulled up in a brand-new Audi A8 with 100K worth of jewelry on. It's niggas like you that divide families. I'mma act like we never had this conversation. Get ya shit together, Premo, before I help you get ya shit together. You lucky I don't knock ya fucking head off right now," Santana said and got up from his seat and exited the White Castle.

Hearing the things that he'd just heard from Premo had him livid. Santana was by far one of the UGF's most loyal and trusted members. He'd been around since the beginning. He was one of the first five members who helped Hitta and Peso pave the way in the trenches. When things got crazy behind those prison walls and the UGF was beefing with all the other gangs, Santana was frontline. The three of them had put in a lot of work together, and now, the three of them were all free, doing everything they planned while in prison but on a whole new level. Santana pulled out his iPhone and shot both Hitta and Peso a text message.

MEANWHILE IN BINGHAMTON, New York
A.K.A. The Twilight Zone

Breeze had just finished making drop offs to his workers. Ever since his brief stay in the Feds, he'd been very lowkey. He spent most of his days with his lady, Amina, just enjoying the luxuries of being free. That didn't slow up his money in any way at all because good dope sold itself. The shooters loved it, the sniffers loved it, and every hustler in and out of town was trying to get a hold of it.

Breeze didn't deal with too many people outside of his team. He served a small number of hustlers. An exclusive club of men. A secret society was what he liked to call it. He parked his 7 series BMW in front of a two-family house on Fayette Street. On the first floor of the building was one of his many trap houses, and on the second floor was one of his many lady friends named Daisy.

He walked up to the second floor and knocked on the door. Seconds later, an attractive Hispanic chick with red hair opened the door. "Omg, I missed you, Breeze." Daisy greeted him with a hug.

"I missed you too. Where Loopy at? I been hitting his phone for hours," Breeze asked as he stepped inside of the apartment.

Loopy was Daisy's younger brother. He and Breeze were real close. Breeze headed straight to Daisy's bedroom and took a seat on the bed. "I just tried to call him too and got no answer. He was just here earlier," Daisy informed.

Breeze's iPhone rang, and Loopy's name popped up on the screen. Breeze answered the call instantly. "Talk about it, baby boy."

"What's crackin', big bro?" Loopy greeted. "I know you been blowing my line up. Pardon me, bro. I was handling some important shit. Where you at tho? I'm about to walk in the crib now."

"I'm already here," Breeze replied and ended the call.

The minute Breeze hung up with Loopy, his phone rang again. He didn't recognize the 215-area code, but he still picked up. "Yo, who this?"

"It's the bul, Eighty," the caller replied. Eighty was Breeze's comrade from Philly who he met in the Feds. When Rolex Rich sent an old gangster to stab Breeze, Eighty came to his rescue. That secured their bond. Eighty was a solid dude. The moment the two of them became cellmates, they clicked.

"Eighty, my guy. What's shakin'? You home?"

"Nah, bul, I got about ninety-three days left. These nut ass crackers sent me all the way to Yahzoo, Mississippi. These niggas be drawn down here, man, I swear, but it is a sweet spot. A real sweet spot," Eighty claimed.

Breeze was cracking up right now. Eighty's Philly dialogue always gave Breeze a good laugh. Eighty caught on to the fact that Breeze was laughing at him. "Why ya nut ass over there laughing?" Eighty laughed also. "Bul, you over there on some nut shit."

"You know I always get a good laugh hearing ya lingo, gang. But damn, they sent you all the way to Mississippi? That's nasty work. You Gucci tho, right?"

"Yeah, everything player on my end. I got that $2,500 you put on my books too. I appreciate you, bul," Eighty said sincerely.

"That ain't about nothing, my guy. You saying that spot you in sweet. Why you don't got a situation?" Breeze was asking him why he didn't have a cell phone.

"I'm short. I ain't tryna get caught up. What you got going on out there? How's freedom treating you?"

"Everything is super healthy. I'm just taking it light. A nigga waiting on you to touch down. I'll fuck around and put you in a Benz or something," Breeze claimed.

"Nigga, you drawn. Yo ass ain't doing the pussy like that," Eighty teased.

"Only big boy shit on my end, bro. Watch and see. You held a nigga down, bro. That makes you family, and where I'm from, family takes care of each other," Breeze replied sincerely.

"That's love, but you don't owe me shit. We locked in. Let me finish talking to my jawn before this shit cut off. Save her number so you know it's me calling. I'll shoot back at you in a few weeks. Stay dangerous out there, gangsta."

"Always, my guy," Breeze replied and ended the call.

Daisy walked back into her bedroom just as Breeze got off

of the phone. "You in here chattin' with one of your chicken heads?" she said playfully. "My brother here."

"Nah, that was one of the guys. Where those two sneaker boxes I gave you tho?"

"They in the closet. You want them?"

"Bring them to Loopy's room." Breeze got up from the bed and walked out of the bedroom.

Breeze entered Loopy's bedroom. Loopy was sitting there with another young dude who Breeze didn't really know. The two of them were smoking weed and listening to G Herbo's new mixtape. "What's craccin', big bro?" Loopy greeted.

"Ain't shit. Lemme chop it up with you on the solo tip real quick," Breeze replied.

Daisy entered the room with two sneaker boxes and sat them on the dresser. "Gimmie some weed," she said to Loopy, who tossed her a Ziploc filled with OG.

"Don't o'd on shit, Daisy." Loopy turned to his man. "Smoke, let me holla at big bro real quick."

Once Daisy and Smoke exited the room, Breeze got down to business. He opened both sneaker boxes. They were filled corner to corner with bricks of Untouchable. Each box held fifty bricks. "Shit about to change for you, baby boy. Niggas are gonna start hating, so keep ya circle tight.

"Only an exclusive group of men have access to this dope on a wholesale level. You are now a part of that exclusive group of men. This is a hunnit bricks. Ya price is $240 a brick." Breeze looked Loopy in the eyes and saw the hunger. Loopy had been asking Breeze to put him on for the longest; now, he was finally getting a shot. "This is just a test run. Show me that you can move this hunnit, and the floodgates are open. You can hit ya niggas at $270 a brick and score a $30 profit off of each joint, or you can hit outsiders at $290 and score $50 off each joint. Shit, you can even hit the ground and maximize your profit by selling that shit to the fiends bag for bag. The choice is yours, gang. You are on the money train now."

"Say no more, big bro." Loopy accepted the dope with a smile and great intentions.

CHAPTER 15

Staten Island, New York

Peso and Princess sat at the dining room table in Princess' mother's house along with her mom, little sister, and best friend. Together, they ate a huge dinner that Ms. Vivian had prepared for them. Peso was full as a bull, but the baked mac and cheese was so good that he had to have more. "Queen, can you get me some more baked mac please?" Peso whispered to Princess.

Princess laughed at Peso because he was always acting shy around her mom. She decided to play a little game with him. "You gotta ask Mommy," she replied out loud.

"Ask Mommy what?" Ms. Vivian said.

"Tyler wants more mac and cheese."

"Tyler better get his ass up and go get it," Ms. Vivian replied and got a laugh out of everyone. "You acting all shy," she added.

"Bro, you family. No need to be shy. We all know that every time Mommy makes baked mac, you eat half of the pan," Imani teased.

"I am not shy," Peso defended himself. "Queen, you really not gonna get it for me?" he whined playfully.

"Nope, you heard Mommy. You gotta get up and get it yourself," Princess continued to tease.

"Say that when you want your feet rubbed." Peso got up from the table and kissed Princess on the forehead.

"Okay, babe, you win." Princess got up also.

"Too late, I'm already up."

Together, Peso and Princess walked into the kitchen. As Princess made his plate of baked mac and cheese, Peso was in his phone, scrolling down his Instagram newsfeed. He saw that over one million people had tagged him in a post. He clicked the video, and there was a young man who didn't look a day over sixteen years old spitting bars. Peso clicked on the kid's Instagram page and followed him. The fact that the kid had 550K active followers showed Peso that he knew how to market himself.

"Here, King." Princess handed him a plate of mac and cheese.

"Thank you, my love." He kissed her lips.

In between bites of the baked mac and cheese, Peso was watching the young rapper's latest video. The kid went by the name Baby Buccs, and from looking at the pictures and videos, Peso could tell that the kid was a Crip from Brownsville, Brooklyn. Peso commented on the trailer to the kid's latest video.

He put several fire emojis. Minutes later, Baby Buccs replied to Peso's comment.

"Good Looking, Cig Cro,"- Baby Buccs 83rd.

Peso read the comment and smiled. Peso's assumption was correct. Baby Buccs was a member of the Crip gang. He purposely spelled big and bro with the letter C.

Presidential Peso_UGF: No question. Keep grinding, lil homie, and the game gon be yours.

Baby Buccs_83rd: This really you, gang?

Presidential Peso_UGF: Facts! Check this out tho. I got this track that I need you on. You tryna work?

Baby Buccs_83rd: Hell yeah, just give me the date, time, and location.

Presidential Peso_UGF: I'll pull up on you now. DM the location.

Baby Buccs_83rd: You cappin'. I'm in Brownsville houses tho.

Presidential Peso_UGF: Ain't no cap in my rap, gang. Say less tho.

Peso finished up his baked mac and cheese then slid his feet back into his Balenciaga runners. "Where you going, King?" Princess asked.

"Gotta ride to Brooklyn real quick. This young boy I seen on the Gram got the internet going crazy. I wanna sign him. I'll be back to pick you up in a couple of hours," he replied and walked over to Ms. Vivian and kissed her cheek. "Thank you, Mom. As always, the food was amazing."

"You welcome, son. Be careful out there," she replied.

"Later, Imani. Later, Tamara."

"Be safe, bro," they both replied.

"Tyler, you don't need to be out there like that. It's dangerous. You are not just some regular dude," Princess whined.

"Yes, I am a regular dude, and the streets ain't more dangerous than me," he winked.

"Ty, I'm not joking, I'm serious. We had this talk already."

"I'm good, babe," he assured her before kissing her lips. "I love you, and I'll be back in a lil bit."

"I love you more. Be careful out there."

FORTY-FIVE MINUTES Later

Peso was walking through the Brownsville houses with a bunch of jewelry on and a Glock .45 on his waist. The weather was beautiful on this Sunday night. A bunch of people were outside, and a huge dice game was going on. Peso walked over to the dice game. "What's in the bank?" he asked.

Currently, all eyes were on him. People couldn't believe what they were seeing. They looked at Peso in total surprise. "Oh, shit, it's Presidential Peso!" someone said out loud, and a bunch of people started pulling out their phones and recording.

"Y'all know where I can find Baby Buccs?" he asked the people in the crowd.

"That's my brother. What you want with him?" a pretty dark-skinned chick asked.

"I wanna change his life. Call lil bro for me and tell him I said pop out," Peso smiled.

No more than five minutes later, Baby Buccs came walking up. He stood no taller than 5'6". "Nah, you really pulled up to my hood," Baby Buccs smiled. "No security or nothing. You don't even got ya team with you. I see you ain't just rapping," he added.

"What I need security for, lil homie? Ya projects ain't no different from mine. I came from the trenches. It's savages everywhere, bro," Peso replied while giving Baby Buccs dap. "Take a ride with me real quick, so we can chop it up."

Baby Buccs turned to his sister. "Neefa, he wants me to take a ride with him."

"So why you still standing here? Boy, you better take that ride," she smiled. She was so excited for her little brother. She knew that after this moment, his life was going to change and so was hers.

"Come on, sis. You can pull up too," Peso said.

When the three of them made it to Peso's Bentley GT that was parked on the outside of the projects, Baby Buccs was in awe. "This shit is beautiful," he said while admiring the automobile.

"Good looking. You know how to drive?" Peso asked.

"Hell yeah. I ain't got no license tho," Baby Buccs replied.

"So, what you waiting for? Hop in and drive her." Peso walked over to the passenger's side and got in. Baby Buccs hopped in the driver's seat, and his sister hopped in the back.

"Yo, this shit looks even better on the inside." Baby Buccs admired the interior.

"Don't even trip. Soon, you gon be pushing one of these. All you gotta do is put the work in. Y'all smoke?" he asked, pulling out a vacuum sealed bag of Gelato.

"Yeah, we smoke," Baby Buccs replied.

"Here, sis, twist something up." Peso handed Neefa the weed and a pack of Backwoods.

Baby Buccs was cruising all around Brownsville in a Bentley. This was really a dream come true for him. "How old are you, Buccs?" Peso asked.

"I'm about to be seventeen next month," Baby Buccs replied.

"You got talent, lil homie, real talent," Peso admitted. Neefa passed Peso the blunt as he spoke.

"You really think so?"

"I wouldn't be here if I didn't." Peso took a pull from the blunt then turned back to Neefa. "What you think, sis? Bro got bars?" he asked.

"He's iight," Neefa replied playfully. "Nah, lil bro got some fire," she admitted.

"On the real tho, I'm tryna sign you to my label. That's why I'm here. The only problem is you not eighteen yet, so we gotta go through ya parents."

"My dad ain't around, and my mom's running around somewhere getting high," Baby Buccs admitted shamefully. "All I got is my sister."

"Now you got me, lil homie. Don't count ya mom out tho. No matter how much drugs she uses, that woman is your queen, bro. My mom got high also, so I know what it's like. I remember when me and my lil brother ain't have shit to eat. Those are the days that made me great tho. I never gave up on my mom. I loved her through all of her imperfections. My love for her is what made her get clean." He passed Baby Buccs the blunt. "By changing ya situation, you can save ya mom, feed ya niggas, and take care of ya sister. You can put all of ya people in positions to make millions. How old are you, Neefa?"

"I'm twenty-three," she replied.

"Perfect. Do you have a problem with lil bro signing to my label?"

"Not if you gon treat him right," she replied.

"My label is built off of family. Signing to me makes y'all family, and I always take care of mine. I would do anything for my family, including kill, die, lie, and take ya deepest secrets to the grave with me," Peso said sincerely.

"You wanna sign to him, bro?" Neefa asked Baby Buccs.

"Hell yeah," Baby Buccs replied with a smile.

"Say less. Take my number and we gon link in a few days."

After exchanging numbers, they parked, smoked another blunt, and Peso left with promises of coming back.

CHAPTER 16

Coney Island, Brooklyn

Summer was finally here. Everything was going smoothly for the Untouchable Gorilla Family. Money was coming in full speed. The connect was happy, and so was the team. Well, everyone except Premo, who was one of the shot callers for the Queens chapter.

Not too long ago, Santana, who was one of Hitta and Peso's most trusted comrades, sent both of them a text with some very disturbing news. Not only was Premo back biting his brothers, but word had also got out that he was trying to start his own branch off of the UGF called Untouchable Gorilla Empire. This dude even created his own stamp. He was putting the Untouchable brand of heroin in different bags.

Hitta had finally got around to addressing Premo's disloyalty. He called a small shootout. In attendance, you had Flee, Shoota, Heat, Santana, and Gat. They had been waiting for Premo for over an hour already. The six of them stood on a rooftop, smoking blunts and sipping D'ussé.

Premo finally arrived. He walked on the rooftop, smiling ear to ear. He reached his hand out to greet Santana with the UGF handshake, but Santana left him hanging. Premo reached out to Hitta, who did the same. "What's the word, ape?" Premo asked, confused.

"You tell me," Hitta replied dryly. "The family ain't been good to you? You ain't eating enough? You questioning how I run my shit? Niggas changed ya life, Premo, and you running around on some ungrateful shit. You a real fuck boy," he added.

Premo looked straight to Santana. If looks could kill, Santana would be dead already. "Fuck you grillin' me for, nigga?" Santana gripped his .357 firmly.

"Santana, stand down, gang. Let's hear the homie out," Hitta smiled. "Speak ya peace, Premo."

"Ape, it wasn't even like that. Santana took what I was saying the wrong way. I appreciate all you and Peso do for the family. All I was saying was the number is a lil too high. I wasn't on no goofy shit," Premo claimed.

Santana just laughed. "This nigga is a bozo," he said out loud.

"The number too high? Are you shitting me? Nigga, you getting dope on the arm. You ain't coming with no money on the wood. From the looks of shit, you ain't hurting. You got two new whips, you living in a luxury condo, you got a shit-load of jewelry, and you stay in some designer shit.

"My nigga, you got a fuckin' Patek Phillipe on ya wrist," Hitta chuckled. "I'mma tell you what tho. Premo, your services are no longer needed. You are no longer a member of this family, and that Gorilla Empire shit you got niggas on ya side jackin, it's a dub. Who the fuck even sanctioned that?"

"Hitta, we got history. Don't do me like this, bro," Premo pleaded.

"Nigga, our history ain't mean shit when you was plotting against the family. You pocket watching ass nigga. Niggas help ya bum ass level up, and you being ungrateful. Ya bum ass got rich off of me and my niggas' blood, sweat, and tears, and you just spit in our faces. You know what? Nigga, strip." Hitta brandished his .44 Bulldog.

"Strip?" Premo asked, confused.

"Yeah, nigga, take all those shines off and empty ya pockets. Give all that shit to Gat. Baby bro just touched down."

"Come on, Hitta. Don't do this, bro. We go back way too far."

"I know. That's why I ain't gon kill you. Now take all that shit off. Don't make me say it again. Matter fact, since you wanna hesitate, take everything off —_clothes, sneakers, socks, boxers, everything, nigga. Get naked."

Premo knew firsthand how dangerous Hitta was, so he slowly started removing his clothes. He now had tears forming in his eyes. "Now this nigga wanna cry," Santana teased. "And all this time, I thought this nigga was a fuckin gorilla. Boy a monkey," he continued.

Premo now stood there on the rooftop, naked. Gat had all of his money and jewelry. Even though he didn't need it, he took it anyway. Who in their right mind would turn down a Patek Phillipe?

"When you get out the hospital, let B-Boy know that he has seventy-two hours to check in, or we gonna assume that he's against us," Hitta said.

"When I get out the hospital?" Premo was super confused right now.

"Yeah, nigga, when you get out the hospital." Hitta turned to Gat. "Give this nigga a 50/50."

"A 50/50?" Gat was now confused.

"Yeah, bro, a 50/50 percent chance of living," Hitta smiled.

Gat quickly brandished his blue steel .38 and shot Premo in the stomach.

Meanwhile in MDC Brooklyn

Rolex Rich covered his cell window and pulled out his contraband iPhone. He placed a FaceTime call to his nephew, Nico, who was his deceased brother's only son.

Nico was a wild young dude from the Soundview projects in the Bronx. He just recently got acquitted on a triple homicide, and he was back on the streets doing what he did best, which was knocking off dudes for the right price. Nico was a hired gunman.

After a few rings, Nico's face popped up on the screen. "What's blazin, Unk?" Nico greeted Rich, talking in a lingo that he didn't understand. Nico was a high ranked member of the notorious Sex Money Murda Blood set.

"What's blazin?" Rich chuckled. "What ever happened to just saying wassup? You young niggas be losing me," he laughed a little harder.

"Knock it off, Unk," Nico laughed also. "What's good tho? How you holding up?"

"Everything is healthy. What you got going on out there? How ya pockets looking?"

"Shit Gucci over here. I could always be better tho," Nico admitted.

"I got a lil situation for you, but I need it done asap," Rolex Rich explained.

"Talk to me. Wassup?" Nico was all ears now. He knew that his uncle paid well.

"You was locked up with a nigga name Hitta, right?"

"Light skin, pretty boy nigga with braids from Coney Island?"

"Yeah, that's him. His number has been called. I got 150K for you."

"You gotta get somebody else to do that, Unk. Hitta is my comrade. The homie got busy with me up north when them Spanish niggas was on my ass. He saved my life. That's fam right there," Nico explained.

"Nigga, I'm ya blood family. Fuck that nigga. I got a million cash for you," Rolex Rich desperately offered.

"I just told you that you gonna have to get someone else for that job. I got rules that I live by, and I won't break them for you or nobody else. There ain't a price that can make me compromise my integrity."

"You can't be serious right now. I'm ya blood, Nico. You siding with my enemy over me? Ya pops gotta be turning over in his grave right now. I'm ya blood."

"Yeah, we blood, but that shit don't make us family. It only means that we related. We ain't really been family since my pops died," Nico replied harshly. "You sitting on millions. Ya family living in a big ass mansion while I'm in the trenches. I just came home from fighting a triple homicide. You ain't put that big shot lawyer on my case. I spanked that shit with a legal aid attorney. Miss me with that blood shit. This the only time you know me, Rich. For all I know, you could be tryna set me up to trade my freedom for yours."

Everything that Nico had just said was true except for him

trading his freedom for Nico's. That was something he would never do. That fact that Nico would even think that had just broken his heart. In that moment, Rolex Rich was livid. "You know what, lil nigga? Suck my dick," was all he could say.

"Hurd you," Nico laughed. "I don't do no phone thuggin, nigga. You know my body," Nico added and ended the call.

CHAPTER 17

Piscataway, New Jersey

Peso pulled into the spiral driveway of a beautiful mansion. Princess sat in the passenger's seat with a blindfold over her eyes. "King, are we here yet?" she asked impatiently. Princess wanted badly to snatch the blindfold off but didn't want to ruin the surprise. One thing she had learned about Peso over the years was that his surprises were always over the top.

Peso quickly parked the car in the driveway and hopped out. He quickly ran over to the passenger's side and opened the door for Princess. "Yes, we are here, Queen," he said while helping her out of the car. He then removed the blindfold from her eyes.

Princess instantly started crying tears of joy. The outside of the home was beautiful, and she could only imagine what the inside looked like. Peso didn't half step when he purchased this mansion. The place was 32,000 square feet. It had thirteen bedrooms, eleven and a half bathrooms, a twelve-car garage, a movie theater, a recording studio, a library, a music lounge, an award room, a gym, a NBA regulation basketball court crowned by a twenty-one square foot skylight, three offices, six master walk-in closets, an indoor and outdoor pool, a hot tub, a spa, and so much more.

"Let's take a tour," Peso said with a dazzling smile.

One Hour Later

Peso and Princess laid on the floor of their new huge master walk-in closet, which was attached to the master bedroom. The white carpet that was designed by Fendi was so comfortable that neither of them wanted to get up. What started out as a tour around the mansion ended up being a wonderful sex session in the walk-in closet.

Princess laid on top of Peso with her head on his chest, while he ran his fingers through her long, pretty hair. "Tyler, I love you so much. Thank you for being so good to me," Princess said sincerely.

"No thank you needed. You really one of the best things that has ever happened to me. Without you, I prolly wouldn't even be so great. Your love has helped me beat these demons that's attached to my soul. I should be the one thanking you," he replied and planted a kiss on her forehead.

"How about we just thank each other?" Princess began to kiss on his neck then slowly made her way down.

Meanwhile in Middletown, New York...

After his daily workout and a hot shower, Matt Murda was beat. It took a while to regain his strength after waking up out of the coma, but right now, he felt better than ever. He lounged on the sofa, eating a plate of oxtails, rice and peas, with a fresh cup of carrot juice. Timah sat next to him with her eyes glued to the screen of her laptop. "Baby, why Hitta and Peso ain't come check me yet? Them niggas ain't fucking with me or something?" Matt Murda asked with a straight face. Ever since Matt Murda woke up from the coma, he'd been dealing with temporary memory loss. He wasn't aware of the beef he had with his two old friends.

Timah had been dying for this war amongst them to be over ever since it started. She didn't even want to bring it up. She really felt like God was giving Matt a fresh start. "Babe, you heard me?" Matt Murda asked, snapping Timah out of her thoughts.

"You know Peso is a big superstar now. Him and Hitta are on tour right now," Timah lied. Truth was, she didn't know where Peso and Hitta were. She was just not ready to tell Matt that his friends were no longer his friends.

"That's wassup. Peso always been super nice with that rap shit. I remember when Rico used to play his shit for me over the phone when I was locked up. Call them niggas and let them know that I'm back," he said while getting up from the sofa. "Matt Murda is back in full effect." He did a little dance before walking to the kitchen.

Seeing a smile on her husband's face really made her happy. Knowing that at any day, his happiness could be crushed by the news that he didn't really have any friends besides her, Rah Rah, Gangsta, and Jamie really hurt her heart. She refused to remind Matt of all the past bloodshed. So, she came up with an idea that could possibly put an end to all the madness. She was just praying that it worked.

SOUNDVIEW PROJECTS BRONX, New York

Hitta stood in the heart of Soundview projects. A few hours ago, he received a call from his comrade, Nico, telling him that it was imperative the two of them link up. Hitta wasted no time jumping in his brand new CLS Mercedes Benz Drophead coupe and hitting the road. He snatched up his homie, Melly, for the ride.

They stood there with Nico and a few of his homies, sipping Hennessy, passing blunts around, and watching the dice game that was going on. Hitta and Nico stepped off to the side, so they could speak in private. "Yo, gang, I don't know what type of static you got with my uncle, but the nigga called and tried to get me to push it on you. He offered a nice bag too. The nigga sounded desperate," Nico chuckled. "Went from offering a hunnit racks to offering a whole million," he added.

"Ya uncle?" Hitta asked, confused.

"Rolex Rich, nigga, you forgot?" Nico reminded him. "That nigga really desperate, bro. He was practically begging me, bro."

"You ain't take the bag?" Hitta discreetly gripped his Glock .17.

"Loyalty doesn't have a price tag, Hitta. You really my comrade. I owe you my life for saving me that day, beloved. I wouldn't be standing here right now if you ain't come to the rescue. No amount of money could get me to trade in our friendship. You don't gotta be on alert, bro. My hood is your hood," Nico said sincerely. "The red carpet is rolled out for you and ya man. This my shit. Pick a bitch, they all eyeing you when they walk past. You safe, bro. I ain't tryna rock you to sleep. That's on my gangsta. You my brother, skrap. We bonded by this thang called loyalty," he said sincerely. "Besides, I know how you rock, skrap. If I was gon take you out, I wouldn't have let y'all get out of the car." He looked Hitta dead in the eyes.

Hitta's stare matched his. "The day a nigga catch me, he gon have to earn it. I'm taking a few niggas with me. The only way a nigga could catch me slippin is if it comes from a nigga that I love and trust. The fact of the matter is I don't love and trust too many people. What part of this story are you leaving out? Rolex Rich is ya blood family, and I'm a nigga you met in jail. Why are you siding with me over ya uncle?"

"I ain't leaving nothing out. That's on my two guns," Nico swore. This was something all members of Sex Money Murda said to let people know that they were being truthful. "Let's just say when my pops died, Rich said fuck me and my moms. You of all niggas know that blood doesn't make a person family. It just makes them ya relative. You ain't just some nigga I met in jail, Hitta. You my family," Nico said sincerely. "I owe you my life, bro. It ain't no snake in my blood at all," he added.

"Don't feel no way about me having my guard up. A nigga could never be too sure these days. A nigga in my position can't afford to slip up. I gotta stay dangerous and on point at all times. I done left too many bloodstains on these New York pavements. Since you kept it a buck with a nigga and ain't try to snake me out, I'mma put you in position to make that mil that Rich offered you. Later tonight, you are gon get a shipment of the best heroin around. My shit is a ten all around the globe. I'mma hit you with a thousand bricks at $190 per joint. How that sound?"

"Like a motherfuckin plan," Nico smiled.

"Say less, my nigga, but on another note, me and the family having a big cookout on my side Friday. You and ya guys pull up. Shit gon be lit."

CHAPTER 18

Coney Island. Kaiser Park

It was Friday night, and everybody who was somebody was at the UGF cookout in Kaiser Park. They were giving away free food, free liquor, and free weed. They were even doing a huge raffle where the first place winner received 50K in cash, second place winner received 25K in cash, and third place winner received 10K in cash.

Peso was dressed to impress, and as always, he had on enough jewelry to feed a small town. He had been signing autographs and taking pictures since he arrived at Kaiser Park. This routine never got old to him. Being in his hood, he thought he would get the day off today because everybody knew him, but the people would not let up. They were treating him like royalty.

"Ayo, Peso!" Gat called out. He was holding a bottle of Ace of Spades in his hand. "Take this picture with me for the gram, big bro," he smiled.

Peso walked over and posed for the picture. "What's the word, my boy?" he greeted Gat with the UGF handshake.

"Welcome home. I know you happy to be back," Peso said with a smile. "You done touched down at the right time," he added.

"Most definitely did. It's a movie out here. It feels good to be back around the family; I got that bag you sent me. I appreciate the love, gang. No funny shit," Gat said sincerely.

"That ain't bout nothing, bro. You day one family. Anything I could do to make life easier for you, I'mma do it. I heard you been on ya rap shit. You gon take it serious, or are you gonna horseplay and waste ya talent?"

"I been getting my bars up a little," Gat replied modestly.

"So, when you gon jump in the booth with me? You just came home, Gat. Shit is way different now. You don't gotta risk ya life to eat anymore. You can hit the road with me and get some of this show money. This rap money is lovely," Peso smiled.

"I can tell. I'm wit whatever. Just connect the dots, bro. I'm putting my lil mixtape together now. Once I record a few more songs, I'll be ready to hit the road."

"Nigga, in two days, I'mma come scoop you, and you gon record ya whole mixtape with no distractions. I ain't taking no for an answer. Let's walk to the store real quick. I need some condoms," Peso said while leading the way to the corner store.

The two of them stepped inside of the corner store, and the owner hopped over and embraced Peso with a hug. His name was Saba, and he'd been the owner of the store since Peso was a kid. "Tyler, my friend, how are you?" the man asked, all smiles.

"I'm blessed, my brother, I'm blessed," Peso replied with a smile. It was always good to see Saba. Peso really loved this guy. Saba had saved Peso's life years ago when he was shot for the first time. He also saved Peso's little brother, Shoota's, life when he was shot. On both occasions, the man didn't wait for an ambulance. He drove them to the hospital himself. He was like their guardian angel.

"How's the family?" Peso asked.

"Everyone is well, Alhamdulillah," Saba smiled. "I'm so proud of you, brother. I always knew that you would make it. Since you were a little troublemaker, I always knew that you had the potential to be great. I always kept you and your brother in my duwah (prayer)."

"I appreciate that, brother. If you didn't find me that night, I prolly wouldn't even be here today. I owe you my life. Anything I can do for you and ya family, I'm here," Peso said sincerely.

"You don't owe me anything. My son is always listening to your music."

"That's love. Wassup with Asuad? Tell him I send my love and let him know when I go back on tour, he is more than welcome to join me."

"Asuad is fine, and I will let him know, inshallah (God willing). What can I get for you?"

"A box of Backwoods and a box of Magnums." Peso pulled out a huge bankroll from his pocket. "Put your money away. I will take care of the fee today," Saba said.

Peso placed the entire bankroll on top of the counter. It was a total of $20,000. "Keep this, Saba. It's for all the times you fed me and my brother. I won't take no for an answer. You saved my life. There is nothing I can do to repay you, but I'm in a position to help make life easier for all of those around me. In about two days, I will have somebody deliver 100K to you," Peso promised. "I know you may not need the money, but it's the least I could do after all you done for me and my brother over the years."

"My friend, I can't take your money."

"Yes, you can because it's plenty more where this came from. When I was ten years old and my mom was out here getting high every single night, you gave me and my brother free food. I would always ask you why were you helping us. Do you remember what you said?"

Saba nodded his head up and down. Tears were now building up in his eyes. "I told you that when Allah blesses you, you have to bless other people," Saba replied.

"Exactly. I'm blessed, so I'm blessing plenty of people. Please accept the money.

"Tyler, you still have a heart of gold. Let's take a picture before you go."

After taking the picture, Peso said his goodbyes to Saba and got ready to walk out of the store. As him and Gat were leaving, four honeys were entering. "Oh, shit, Peso, wassup?" one of the females greeted him. Her name was Toya, and she was Peso's childhood friend. Peso greeted her with a bear hug.

"Damn, sis, long time no see. I missed you."

"I missed you too, bro. I'm so proud of you. My mom always asking about you," she replied.

"Tell Mommy I send my love. Y'all pulling up to the cookout?"

"Yeah, shit looking lit over there."

"Bet, pull up and smoke one with ya boy," Peso said before turning to the other three females. "Sup, y'all?" He hugged them all one by one. He put his attention on Solita. She was the prettiest one out of the group. Peso had a crush on her back in the day, but she would always front on him because she dated older dudes.

"Damn, Peso, you looking all good and shit. When you gon gimmie some of this?" she asked while grabbing his dick.

"Never, cause when I wanted to give it to you, you ain't want it," he replied.

"Always wanted it, but ya lil cocky ass ain't chase hard enough. You fell back after the first curve," she smiled.

"Why would I chase something that I watched so many dudes have? You know that ain't my style. Plus, you told me that in order for me to hit it, I had to have Bentley money. Now I own a Bentley and don't even want the box no more. See how the tables turn." Peso turned to Toya. "Meet us in the park, sis."

"Fuck you, Peso!" Solita barked.

"You wish you could, but I don't fuck bitches who wear last year's Gucci," he laughed, and he and Gat walked away. Gat was dying laughing. He was literally in tears.

"Big bro, you a fool."

"Nah, she a fool. Look how the tables turn. Watch that Suburban over there. That shit look suspect," Peso replied, putting Gat on point.

Meanwhile

A black Suburban pulled up in front of the corner store just as Peso and Gat were crossing the street. The men inside of this SUV had been watching the two of them ever since they walked inside of the store. Inside of the Suburban sat Premo and three of his young hitters from 40 Projects in Queens.

After Hitta humiliated him and gave Gat the order to shoot

him, Premo had vowed to get some payback. Just as Peso and Gat made it to the entrance of Kaiser Park, Premo and two other men hopped out of the SUV with semi-automatic weapons brandished. They were caught by surprise when both Peso and Gat spun around and opened fire.

Premo got low to prevent being hit, but one of his men wasn't so lucky. A slug from Peso's .45 ACP crashed into his chest and sent him down to the pavement. Premo fired back but didn't hit anyone.

Out of nowhere, Hitta and several members of the UGF ran toward the action, opening fire on Premo and his crew. Premo backpedaled quickly toward the Suburban while letting off his cannon. An all-out gun battle was in effect. Premo and his men were in no way prepared for this. He hopped inside of the SUV, leaving his men behind. Only one of them was lucky enough to make it back in the Suburban with him. The driver recklessly peeled off.

CHAPTER 19

Same Night

After a full fledge gun battle, Hitta headed home. Nobody in his crew got hit, which was a blessing. Too bad he couldn't say the same for the dudes who came with Premo.

Hitta stepped off of the elevator and into his penthouse. The sound of Dej Loaf's *Me, You, and Hennessy* seeped through the speakers. The sound of the music let Hitta know that Ashley had made it home before him. He kicked off his spikey Christian Louboutin red bottoms and walked to his bedroom.

The sight before him caught him completely off guard. Ashely was laying on her back with a naked female between her legs, eating her out. There was a bottle of Hennessy on the dresser. Hitta walked over and grabbed it. He took a long swig from the bottle. Not once did he take his eyes off of Ashley and the woman between her legs. The Molly that he popped a few hours ago had him charged.

Ashely opened her eyes and smiled when she saw Hitta. She instantly blushed when the two of them locked eyes. "You gonna join us, Daddy?" Ashley asked. Hearing Ashley speak caused the female, who was feasting between her legs, to take a break. When she turned around and looked at Hitta, he was in complete shock. Seeing Nautica Taylor in his bed with his lady caught him off guard.

When Hitta didn't answer Ashley's question about having a threesome with Nautica, she went in his phone and got Nautica's phone number. After weeks of texting and FaceTime calls, she convinced Nautica to come to New York, so they could surprise Hitta with the time of his life. "You gon stand there and drink, or are you gonna come join us?" Nautica asked with a smile. She was dying to finally feel Hitta inside of her.

"Y'all finish what y'all doing. I'm about to hop in the shower real quick. Don't let me fuck the wave up," Hitta replied while coming out of his clothes.

Meanwhile in Peso's Mansion

Peso had Princess on all fours, pounding her doggy style. "Mmm-mmm this dick feels so good, Daddy," Princess moaned. Hearing her sexy moans only made Peso fuck her harder. The Molly he popped with Hitta and the guys hours ago, had brought a different animal out of him.

He watched his dick slide in and out of her pussy. Princess was so wet that her juices were running down her thighs. Her pussy made noises as he stroked. "You hear that pussy talking to me, Queen?" he asked.

"Yes, Daddy, I hear this pussy talking to you. Ohhh, fuck, I'm cumming again!" Princess screamed. "Daddy, please don't stop. Please keep fucking me like this," she begged.

"Whose pussy is this?"

"It's yours, Daddy. This pussy is yours."

Tamara was standing in the doorway, paralyzed. The sight of Peso pounding on Princess from the back was driving her crazy. She was drunk and horny. Hearing the way Princess was screaming had led her up here to the bedroom door. She and Princess had several drinks before Peso came home an hour ago, and the liquor had really kicked in.

Tamara rubbed on her clit as she watched them. When Peso took his dick out of Princess and she started to suck him off, Tamara rubbed her pussy a little faster. The sight of Princess bent over with her huge ass in the air while she sucked Peso off sent Tamara into a frenzy. "Fuck this," Tamara mumbled to herself and entered the bedroom. She walked behind Princess and started eating her out from the back.

Back at Hitta's Penthouse

Hitta laid on his back while Ashley rode his face and Nautica rode his dick. The two of them were kissing while Hitta pleased them both. Several minutes later, they switched positions. Hitta now had Ashley bent over doggy style. He was slow stroking her long and hard while she ate Nautica's pussy. The sight of these two beautiful women had Hitta ready to explode. He pounded harder while smacking Ashely on the ass. Ashley's body began to shake uncontrollably, letting Hitta know that she had reached her climax. Hitta pulled out of Ashley's box, and Nautica crawled over to him and sucked Ashley's cum and juices off of his dick.

Meanwhile in Flee's Apartment

Flee had Lexi laid on the bed with her legs pushed all the way to her shoulders while he ate her pussy. He was eating her like she was his final meal. "Oh, my God, Papi. I can't take it no more. Please fuck me," Lexi begged. Flee paid her no mind. Her pleas only excited him. "Fuck me now, Papi, please." She continued to beg while playing with her breasts and biting on her bottom lip.

Flee was eating her so good that she literally had tears rolling down her cheeks. Lexi's body began to shake as she reached her climax. After she came, Flee came up and kissed her lips while sliding his dick inside of her wet box. The second he entered her, she began to cum again. "Flee, Papi, what are you doing to me?" she cried. "Papi, put a condom on," she added.

Since the two of them had been together, they had always used protection when having sex. Tonight was different. Flee wasn't trying to hear none of that. He wanted Lexi to know that she belonged to him. "Fuck that condom shit, Lex. You my bitch, right? This pussy belongs to me, right?" he demanded to know while slamming into her harder and harder with each thrust.

"Yes, Papi! I'm your bitch!" she screamed.

"So, tell me this pussy belongs to me," he growled.

"This pussy belongs to you."

Flee pulled out of Lexi and turned her around. He entered her from the back. He started off fucking her slow, but the way Lexi was throwing her ass back let Flee know that she wanted to be handled. He grabbed a handful of her hair and pounded her harder. You could hear slapping sounds from their skin touching. "That's right, Papi. You know how I like it. Fuck me harder," Lexi ordered.

"You gon cum on this dick, Ma?"

"Yes, I'mma cum on it."

"What you gon do after you cum on this dick?"

"I'mma suck it off," Lexi replied while throwing her ass back harder. She peeked over her shoulder at him. "Cum for me, Pa," she added.

He pushed her face to the pillow while gripping her waist with his other hand. With each stroke, her nice, soft, round ass moved like a tidal wave. Without warning, Flee splashed his seed deep inside of her. Just as promised, Lexi grabbed his tool and sucked him clean.

CHAPTER 20

Hitta left Ashley and Nautica in bed and headed to the dealership. He pulled off of the lot in a milk white Rolls Royce Wraith and was now pulling into the spiral driveway of Peso's beautiful new mansion. "Damn, this shit different," he said to himself while admiring the home. "My boy really knows how to stunt," he smiled while hopping out of the Wraith.

He pulled out his iPhone and called Peso, who answered on the first ring. "What's the word, brobro?" Peso greeted.

"I'm outside ya casa, gang. I can't lie, big homie, this shit is a dope dealer's dream. You living life for real," Hitta replied.

"Nah, gang, we living life. Mi casa, su casa," Peso chuckled. "I'm coming down now. You think you like the outside, wait until you see the interior."

"I can only imagine what the inside looks like. You a natural born stunna. Now hurry ya ass up and come let me in," Hitta chuckled and ended the call.

Exactly two minutes later, Peso opened the door sporting a

white and gold Versace robe and a pair of white and gold Versace slippers. When he saw the Rolls Royce Wraith, he quickly ran over to it. "Nah, big homie, you ain't cop the Wraith. This is what I like to see. You really that nigga, bro." He opened the driver's door and took a look at the car's interior. "Yo, this shit really got stars in the roof." Peso was like a kid in a toy store right now. Hitta just smiled as he watched his best friend.

"I'm glad you like this shit because we both know that white ain't my color," Hitta grinned. "This shit fit you more," he added.

"Say word?" Peso said in shock.

"Word. That's all you, big homie. Happy birthday, my brother. I wanted to be the first to get you a gift, no homo. I love you, my brother."

Peso bear hugged Hitta and lifted him off of his feet. "I love you more, big bro. They really don't make niggas like you no more."

"Nah, they don't make niggas like us no more, gang," Hitta corrected him.

"I got some bad news tho." Peso's facial expression instantly went sad.

"What happened?"

"You wasn't the first person to get me a gift." Peso smiled while thinking about what took place in his bedroom last night. "Princess beat you to the punch, gang."

"What she got you, bro?"

"A gentleman never tells," he smiled. "I'mma just say that the shit was mind blowing," he grinned.

"Sound like she done let another female in y'all bed," Hitta smiled. "Let me drip you down to what happened to me last night when I went home. Fuck all that gentleman never tells shit. I walked in my crib last night, and Ashley and Nautica in my bed getting nasty. I don't know how it happened, but it happened. A nigga about to have two wives."

"You cappin, bro," Peso said.

"When have you ever known me to cap? That's on the set," Hitta replied.

The two of them entered the mansion, and Hitta instantly fell in love with the place. He smiled when he saw the huge gold picture frames that held pictures of their fallen comrades. Hitta walked over to the picture of Peso's mom. He kissed two fingers and placed them on the picture. "I miss you, Momma," he said then walked over to the picture of Relo and Rico, two of their truest comrades who they lost along the way. "Not a day goes by that I don't miss you niggas, man," he said sadly. Then, he walked over to a huge picture of their fallen comrade, TK, a true street legend. "Without you, there would be no me. TK, you taught me everything I know about the streets. You a real street legend, bro." A lone tear fell down his face. Peso stood next to him, and tears fell freely from his eyes.

"Never know the love without feeling the pain," he said.

"Come on, bro. Let me finish showing you around,"

When they made it to the indoor gym with the NBA regulation size basketball court, Hitta grabbed one of the basketballs off of the rack and began to dribble. "You still can't fuck with me, my boy," Hitta challenged.

"Is that a call out? Cause you know those are mandatory," Peso replied.

"Take it how you wanna take it," Hitta said and pulled a three-point shot from about thirty feet. The ball went in, all net. He looked to Peso. "Suit up," he challenged.

. . .

MEANWHILE IN BROOKLYN

Reem glided down the Brooklyn streets in his Maserati. In the passenger's seat sat his little homie, Lucci. Out of all the young boys on the set, Lucci happened to be Reem's favorite.

Lucci was a seventeen-year-old young man who had been on the set since he was about thirteen years old. He really idolized Reem; he felt blessed to even be in the presence of his big homie. Not too many got the privilege to kick it with Reem on the one-on-one tip.

Reem pulled over in front of the corner store, and he and Lucci hopped out and walked inside. Lucci got a soda, and Reem got a pack of Backwoods. When the two of them exited the store, Lucci asked if he could drive, and Reem gave him the okay.

Ten minutes later, the two of them were parked on the outside of Marlboro projects in the tinted-up Maserati, passing a blunt of Gorilla Glue back-and-forth. Lucci sat in the driver's seat, all ears, as Reem dropped jewels on him. "Lucci, Blood ain't all about being a gangsta, and being a gangsta ain't all about putting in work and doing a bunch of destructive shit to destroy the community. You feel me?" Reem looked over to Lucci, who nodded his head in agreement. Reem let his words sink in before he continued. "Blood is about honor, strength, loyalty, integrity, love, and uplifting our hood. Uplifting our brothers and sisters. Blood is a part of our culture. It's our way of life.

"When people see Blood, they are supposed to see beauty because Blood is beautiful," he paused and took a long pull from the blunt before passing it back to Lucci. "We destroyed our own culture, baby bro. It was us who took the beauty away, so it's on us to make it beautiful again. As *damus,* we supposed to strengthen our communities, but instead, we destroying it. Gangstas take care of their families. Gangstas are smart. Malcom X was a gangsta, Huey P. Newton was a gangsta, Assata Shakur was a gangsta. I can go on all day with that list, Blood, but you catch my drip," he smiled. "Niggas that's running around broke, just killing for no reason, ain't gangsta, bro. Those niggas stupid. Lucci, you a smart young nigga. That's why I fucks with you so heavy. I don't let dumb niggas around me. I got a plan for you, baby bro. You gon be the golden child. I got a hunnit racks ($100,000) for you to go to college and make something of yourself, something ya mom can be proud of. I ain't gon have you stuck here so you can self-destruct. We need more business owners, Black lawyers, doctors, and politicians that come from where we come from. Feel me?"

"Yeah, I feel you, big bro. I'mma stay focused," Lucci promised as he passed Reem back the blunt.

A run-down Nissan Altima pulled up on the driver's side of Reem's Maserati. The passenger's side window rolled down, and a huge, dusty .44 long hung out of the window. "Lucci, get down!" Reem screamed, but it was too late. Shots were already fired. *BOOM! BOOM! BOOM! BOOM!* Reem tried to shield Lucci's body with his own.

The Altima peeled off recklessly. When the gunfire stopped, Reem moved his body from on top of Lucci's. What he saw before his eyes crippled him. Lucci sat motionless in the driver's seat. Every piece of life had left his body. Reem broke down in tears. "No!" he screamed.

SAME DAY

Flee stepped out of his building, feeling like a million bucks. Today was a regular day, but he was feeling great, extra great. He was sporting a sky blue and yellow Givenchy shirt with a pair of faded Amiri jeans, which he used a yellow Fendi belt to hold up. On his feet were a pair of sky blue, yellow, and white Fendi sneakers.

Flee wasn't calm with his jewelry today. Both Cuban links on his neck were bust down with diamonds. The bust down Cartier watch and bracelet only complemented his chains. He jumped in his brand-new Mercedes coupe and glided down Mermaid Avenue. He made a stop on 28th Street and walked inside of the chicken spot. "Aye, let me get an order of popcorn chicken with cheese fries, two center breasts on the side, and a Sprite. I'mma be out front." He placed his order then walked outside to his car. He leaned in through the window to turn the music up. Peso's latest mixtape, *PAROLED TO THE TRAP VOL.2*, bled through the speakers. "Money all around me, I don't fuck wit no broke niggas. Bands on bands on bands, this shit came from dope dealing. Who the fuck said trapping was dead? I'm a drug dealer's hope, nigga. The plug blowin up my line. He said he got a new load with him," Flee rapped along.

A black-on-black Range Rover pulled up in front of Crown Fried Chicken, and two older dudes from around the way hopped out. Flee was very familiar with the driver, but he didn't quite know the other guy. The driver's name was Prince, and he was the face behind the "Worldwide" dope stamp.

That brand of heroin had the streets on smash until the "Untouchable" stamp hit the market.

Both men approached Flee. "What's good, young buck?" Prince extended his hand for a pound, and Flee gave him dap.

"What's the word, OG?"

"Ain't much going on with me, just about to grab some eats real quick. Can me and you rap for a second?" Prince said then turned to his man. "Aye, Goon, order me a gyro and some fries while I rap with the young king real quick." Prince sent Goon away to kill any tension that may be lingering in the air.

"Speak ya peace," Flee said once the other man walked off.

"You know the streets talk, and the word around the streets is you the man to see about that Untouchable stamp. Y'all niggas making a lot of noise back there," Prince said while eyeing Flee's jewelry.

"Oh, word?" Flee asked sarcastically.

"Word." Prince cracked a smile. "I'm tryna be a part of what you got going on. How can I get in on the situation? I'mma keep it all the way real with you, Flee. You slowing my bread up. However, I won't take it personal as long as I can get involved in what you got going on. War won't benefit neither one of us."

Flee listened to the old head speak and smiled. This wasn't a good smile though. He felt that Prince had just made a slight threat toward him. "Take it personal?" Flee chuckled. "Sounds like you just made a threat, OG. Check this out tho. You can't be a part of nothing that I got going on. I don't fuck with you. We from two different eras, and we from two different sides. As far as me slowing ya paper up, that's what I'm here for. You the competition. Well, you were the competition, but those days are long gone," Flee smiled. "If you wanna get in the race, you gon have to get some better dope cause that bullshit you got ain't cutting it, champ. Now pardon yourself. I gotta go get my food," he added before walking off.

After paying for his food, Flee exited the chicken spot. "You be cool, old head," he said while hopping in his Mercedes.

"You sure you wanna do this, Flee?" Prince asked.

"I'm positive," Flee replied harshly. Flee then restarted the song and turned the volume all the way up.

"Money all around me, I don't fuck with no broke niggas. Bands on bands on bands, this shit came from dope dealing. Who the fuck said trappin' was dead? I'm a drug dealer's hope, nigga. The plug blowing up my line. He said he got a new load with 'em."

Flee peeled off just as Peso finished the hook. He knew Prince was a problem that he had to get rid of quick, and he intended to do just that.

CHAPTER 21

Same Day

Peso and Hitta were on their third one on one game of basketball. They had both won one game apiece. Right now, the score was 9 to 9, and the first one to eleven points won the game.

Hitta dribbled the ball as Peso guarded him closely. He faked right then went left and pulled an eleven-foot jumper. *SWISH!* The ball dropped in all net. "You better guard up," Hitta taunted. "That's game point, baby boy," he added.

Peso just smiled. He checked Hitta the ball, and Hitta dribbled the ball a little. Peso was in his defensive stance. He reached for the ball, and Hitta hit him with a swift crossover then pulled a step back three pointer. The ball rolled off of the rim, and Peso grabbed the rebound. He quickly cleared the ball at the free throw line. Hitta forced him left. Peso faked a jump shot, which caused Hitta to jump a little. Peso took advantage of this opportunity and ran to the basket and laid the ball in.

"That's point up. What we doing?" Peso asked.

"You know what we doing, nigga. Next point win. Ain't shit change," Hitta replied and checked the ball. He gave Peso a little room at the three-point line.

"You know this shit water, bro. You giving me way too much room," Peso said and let it fly from the top of the key. *SWISH!* The ball fell in, all net. "Game time." Peso walked over to Hitta and gave him dap. "Good game, bro," Peso said.

"That was definitely a good run. I'm a lil rusty. I'll get you next time," Hitta said with a smile. "I had to let you get that last one cause we in ya crib," he claimed. "I ain't gon take it light on the next one," he added.

"Nigga, stop it. You was playing ya heart out. Truth is, you still can't fuck with me," Peso teased. "We ain't do that in a long time tho. Let's go get some food. Princess in there making pizza burgers and mozzarella sticks. Bro, she make them shits just like my moms," he added.

The two of them entered the kitchen where Princess and Tamara were making lunch. "Sup, y'all?" Hitta greeted them both before reaching his hand inside of the fresh batch of mozzarella sticks. Princess smacked his hand.

"We not gon do that, bro. Wash them hands."

"Damn, sis. I'm just tryna get one." Hitta put his hands up as if he was surrendering.

"You can get however many you want after you wash those hands. Now, how many pizza burgers do you want?"

"I'll take three," Hitta replied.

"What about you, King?" She turned to Peso.

"You can give me three too, Queen," Peso replied while walking behind her and wrapping his hands around her waist.

GRAVESEND HOUSES

When Flee made it back to his block, he pulled out his phone and called Gat, who picked up on the first ring. "Yo, gang," Gat greeted.

"What's the vibes? Where you at?" Flee asked.

"I'm in the yard by the flagpole. Pull up."

"Say that. I'll be there in a minute," Flee replied and ended the call.

Flee pulled into the parking lot exactly two minutes later. He jumped out of his Mercedes and greeted each of his comrades with the UGF handshake. Standing at the flagpole with Gat was Shoota, Heat, and Caine. Flee opened his tray of food, and all of them helped their selves to the popcorn chicken and fries. Gat even grabbed one of the center breasts. "Ya fat ass just had to grab a whole chicken," Flee teased.

"You know I'm a O.F.N.," Gat said with a smile.

"What the fuck is an O.F.N.?" Heat asked.

"An official fat nigga," Gat replied, and they all rolled over in laughter.

"This nigga silly," Flee said, cracking up. "On a more serious note, I just had a lil run in with the old head, Prince, at the chicken spot a few minutes ago," he explained.

"What boy chattin about?" Shoota asked.

"Nigga talking about he tryna be a part of our situation. He also saying that we slowing up his paper," Flee chuckled. "Y'all know I wasn't going for none of that tho."

"Speaking of the devil. This Range pulling in the parking lot right now," Shoota said, putting everybody on point.

Prince pulled into the parking lot and hopped out of the driver's seat of his Range Rover. An older dude from the projects by the name of Poe hopped out of the passenger's seat. Poe had watched all these young men grow up. Being that he was from their projects, Prince thought it would be a good idea to approach them with someone they all had in common. Poe was a good dude, who was well respected in the hood. He also happened to be Prince's first cousin.

"Yo, Flee, let me holla at you, baby boy," Poe called out.

Flee walked from the flagpole into the parking lot. All four of his comrades were right behind him.

"Damn, young niggas, I come in peace," Poe smiled. "Can we chop it up in private?" he asked Flee.

"Anything you gotta say to me, you can say in front of gang. We don't do that secret shit," Flee replied.

"Okay, cool. This my cousin, Prince. I know y'all all familiar with him. He's a legend out here in Coney."

"Nah, we ain't heard of boy, but I'm pretty sure he heard of us and how we shaking the streets up," said Caine.

"Listen, lil bro, we came to talk business," Prince finally chimed in.

"First and foremost, don't ever lil bro me, and we ain't got no business to discuss with you. Y'all old niggas need to pack it the fuck up," Caine replied.

Prince just chuckled. "Flee, let's come to some type of agreement. We can sit down like men and come up with a solution that's beneficial for all of us. We can make each other a whole lot of money," he claimed.

"All money ain't good money. Ain't shit to figure out tho. I told you what it was earlier. Plus, you heard what bro just said. It's time for y'all old niggas to pack it up. You rich already, Prince. You need to retire. Staying in the game is only gon make us crash, and me and my niggas coming full speed," Flee said while gripping his .380 Keltek.

"Y'all may wanna reconsider," Prince replied in a threatening manner.

All five men brandished their pistols. The bystanders

standing around began to scatter. "Reconsider?" Flee laughed. "Nah, both of you niggas better burn it the fuck up before y'all be a double homicide on this beautiful summer day," Flee said, meaning every single word. "Poe, you played ya self. You of all niggas know how we coming, and you bringing outsiders back here tryna play mediator and shit."

"Baby boy, we all just tryna eat. You know I ain't on no bullshit."

"Well, since y'all tryna eat, eat a dick," Gat chimed in.

"Y'all got it. Come on, Poe," Prince sad as he backpedaled to his Range Rover. Both men hopped in, and Prince pulled out of the parking lot.

"We spinnin that nigga's block. I'mma go change and grab a bigger strap. I'll meet y'all right here in twenty minutes, and if Poe come back over here, we bumpin' him too." Flee hopped in his Mercedes and recklessly peeled off.

When Flee pulled up into the parking lot in front of his building, he saw Lexi walking out with little Manny. "Flee!" Manny screamed when he saw him exiting his car. Lexi let Manny's hand go, and he ran over to Flee, who picked him up.

"Wassup, lil man?" Flee spun the little boy around in a full circle.

"Stop, I'm gonna be dizzy," Manny giggled.

Flee put him down and greeted Lexi with a kiss on her lips. "Where you going, Ma? And what's wrong?" Flee asked, sensing that her vibe was off.

"Manny's dad came home, so I'mma go drop him off real quick, so they can spend some time together," Lexi replied.

"I thought boy had twenty in the Feds."

"Turns out that he just came home on an appeal."

"That's wassup. Don't look so sad tho, Queen. You should be happy for him."

"I am. I just don't want the headache and drama that comes with him being home," she claimed.

"Don't stress ya self," Flee said and pulled her into his arms. "Go drop little man off, and when you come back, the two of us could go out and spend some quality time together. How that sound?"

"Like a plan." She kissed his lips. "Later, Papi."

"Later, Ma, drive safe."

"Later, Flee!" Manny shouted.

"Later, lil man."

Back at Peso's Mansion

After a good lunch, both Peso and Hitta were stuffed. The two of them sat in the home theater, passing a blunt back-and-forth. Princess had left out to drop Tamara at the airport, so it was just the two of them.

Peso's iPhone vibrated. He looked at the screen and didn't recognize the number, but he still picked up. "Yo, who this?" he answered.

"It's ya uncle," the caller replied. The second he heard the caller's voice, he knew exactly who it was. Not only was the man Peso's favorite uncle, but he was also the dad of Peso's closest relative outside of his little brother. "Oh, shit, Uncle Smooth, what's the vibes?" Peso said.

"Same shit, different day. Euro wanted me to call and ask you if you in town. They about to read his verdict in a few hours," his uncle explained.

"Say less. I'm on my way," Peso promised.

"Cool. I'll see you in a minute, nephew," he replied and ended the call.

Peso looked at his Richard Millie to check the time, then he looked to Hitta. "They about to read Euro's verdict in a few hours. You tryna pull up wit me?"

"Hell yeah. You know I gotta support my boy. I just pray he gets acquitted," Hitta replied.

Hours Later

Peso and Hitta entered Brooklyn Supreme Court. The last time the two of them were in this building, they were on trial for several murders, firearm charges, and drug charges. They hated being here, but they wanted Euro to know that he had some support.

The two of them entered the courtroom just as the court officers were bringing Euro out. Euro Carter was Peso's first cousin. He was incarcerated for exactly five years, fighting two murders that he did not commit. Euro was a very good dude, a real pretty boy who was on his way to the NBA until he was shot several times. A bullet to the leg ended his basketball career.

Euro looked over to Peso and Hitta and smiled. Today, he was dressed in a navy-blue Tom Ford suit. His long, silky hair was pulled back into a ponytail. The ponytail was complemented by a fresh taper. A pair of eighteen-karat gold Cartier frames sat on his face. His demeanor was cool as usual.

"All rise!" the judge ordered.

After the normal introductions, the judge allowed a member of the jury to read the verdict. An African American man stood up and began to read the verdict out loud. "Count one, murder in the second degree, the jury finds Mr. Euro

Carter not guilty. On count two, murder in the second degree, the jury finds Mr. Euro Carter not guilty. On count three, criminal possession of a weapon in the second degree, the jury finds Mr. Euro Carter not guilty."

The courtroom was now in a frenzy. Everyone was excited, jumping up and down and celebrating. No one in attendance could hide their excitement. Euro turned to his lawyer and hugged him tightly while expressing his gratitude. "Order in the court!" The judge banged his gavel.

CHAPTER 22

Gravesend Houses A.K.A. the Yard

It was pouring down raining, but that didn't stop the traffic of dope fiends that were walking through, trying to get their hands on that Untouchable. Caine played the building lobby, making sale after sale. The sound of his iPhone ringing caught his attention. He pulled the phone from his pocket and looked at the screen. He saw that it was Heat calling, so he picked up instantly.

"What's the word, brozay? Where you at?" Heat asked the minute Caine picked up.

"I'm right here in front of the Buck-Wild building," Caine replied.

"Copy. Stay right there. I'm on my way across the street. I'm standing on the terrace. That nigga, Poe, just pulled up. He's sitting in his car, right in back of the building. We gon park this nigga."

"Stay where you at, my boy. I got him," Caine said and ended the call.

Caine quickly used his key to open one of the many mailboxes and pulled out a .357 Magnum and tucked it in his waistband. He then pulled his hoodie over his head and tightened the strings before exiting the building. When he made it to the back of the building, just like Heat said, Poe was sitting inside of his car. Caine brandished the .357 and crept up on the driver's side window.

BOOM! BOOM! BOOM! BOOM! BOOM! He pumped five shots into Poe's body and took off running back the way he came.

Meanwhile On Mermaid Avenue

The tinted-out, rented Dodge Charger SRT cruised down the avenue at a moderate pace. Behind the wheel was Flee; Gat sat in the passenger's seat. The two of them had been lowkey tailing Prince's Range Rover for about two blocks.

Flee made sure to keep a nice distance between them and the Range Rover. The light ahead on 30th and Mermaid turned from yellow to red. "It's now or never," Flee said to Gat while clutching the P90 Ruger on his lap. Gat's weapon of choice was a .44 Bulldog.

Flee pulled up right beside the Range Rover and rolled the window down. Gat was already hanging out the passenger's side window. They both fired their weapons like professional hitmen. The windows of the Range Rover shattered before Prince sped off recklessly. Several shots from both guns had hit Prince. Seconds later, he lost control of the wheel and crashed into several parked cars. Flee hopped out of the driver's seat of the Dodge and trotted over to the Range Rover.

BOC! BOC! BOC! BOC! He pumped four slugs into

Prince's body before sprinting back to the Dodge and peeling off.

Minutes later, they'd made it back to the block safe and sound. Flee parked the car on 31st and Bayview Avenue on the outside of Kaiser Park where there were no cameras. Both men hopped out, crossed the street, and entered the projects. The rain was still coming down heavily, so they didn't look suspect walking through the projects with hoods on their heads.

When they made it to the other side of the projects, they cut through the parking lot that took them across the street to the Sea-Rise apartment complex. They noticed that in back of one of the buildings, there was a crime scene. The area was blocked off with yellow tape, and a bunch of ambulances and police were on the scene.

"It looks like somebody got parked," Gat said.

"I pray it wasn't none of the guys," Flee replied. "I'mma go change real quick. I'll hit ya line when I'm poppin back out," he added.

"Say that. I'mma go do the same. Just hit me." The two men dapped each other up and went in separate directions.

Flee speedwalked to his building. The minute he made it to his crib and stuck the key in his door, his cell phone rang. He ignored the call and stepped inside of his apartment. To his surprise, Lexi and Fresh were both out and about.

He walked straight to his bedroom and saw that both Lexi and her son's belongings were gone. A piece of paper on his bed caught his eye. He picked it up, and it read:

Flee, you came into my life and gave me a sense of happiness that I had never felt before. Every minute I spent with you, I felt so loved, appreciated, and safe. Thank you for just being so great to me, Manny, and Fresh. You are a great man.

In another life, I would have married you. If circumstances were different, I could see myself spending the rest of my life with you, but this ain't no fairytale. I must accept the harsh reality. I will forever be in debt to you for what you did for me and my family. However, you and I cannot be together. When we first met, I told you that my life was complicated. You deserve so much more than I can give you at the moment. As you know, Manny's dad is home, so we gonna work on being a family. My son deserves that. I'm so sorry, Flee, but me and this man have so much history. I will forever cherish the moments you and I have shared tho.

Love, Lexi

Flee sat there in total confusion. He didn't have a clue what went wrong. Him and Lexi were just great. He pulled out his iPhone and tried to call her, but the number was no longer in service. He sat on the edge of his bed in deep thought. He replayed last night's sex session that he and Lexi had. She fucked him like she was saying goodbye. "Damn, I should have seen this shit coming," he said to himself.

Flee got up from his bed, stripped down to his boxers, and headed for the shower. Just when he walked into the bathroom, he heard the apartment door open. He exited the bathroom, thinking that it was Lexi who'd just walked through the door, but it was Fresh. "Hey, bro," Fresh greeted him with a smile.

"Sup?" he replied dryly.

"What's wrong? Why the long face?"

Flee walked to the bedroom and came back out with the letter that Lexi had left and handed it to Fresh. "This bitch is bugging the fuck out," Fresh said after reading the letter. She then pulled out her phone and called Lexi, only to get the same result that Flee had just gotten moments earlier. "No, this bitch did not change her number. Let me check her Instagram and Facebook."

"Don't bother," Flee said.

"You want me to leave?"

"Why would you ask me some nut shit like that? You ain't do nothing wrong. Shit ain't gon change between me and you, sis. Stay for as long as you need to," Flee replied and headed to the bathroom to take his shower.

CHAPTER 23

Peso glided through the Brooklyn streets in his brand-new Rolls Royce Wraith. In the passenger's seat sat his first cousin, Euro Carter, who was just acquitted on a double homicide. The two of them had always been very close, more like brothers than cousins. Peso had just taken him shopping and blew well over 80K getting him situated. This didn't include the Presidential Rolex and custom Cuban link with the UGF pendant flooded in diamonds that Peso copped for him.

"Talk to me, cuzzo. What you tryna get into now that you home? You know I got a spot for you in my camp. You don't gotta go back to working in Footlocker. My label pays way better," Peso teased Euro, who was a manager in Footlocker before his incarceration.

Euro laughed at his cousin's joke. Little did Peso know, his days of being the good guy were over. Sitting on Rikers Island for almost five years had turned him into a whole different person. He had no plan on working a nine to five ever again. "Peso, I'm not the same nigga I was before the bid. My mind is different. My heart is black, cuzzo. I done seen and been through too much in the last five years. Shit really turned me cold. The whole experience traumatized me," he admitted. "You know firsthand what comes with sitting on that island. I got unfinished business in these streets tho. I got locked up for murders that my so-called righthand man did, and he left me for dead, stole my money, and tried to rape my bitch. My fiancée left me high and dry on my bid after the first three months. Shit has been crazy. Working in Footlocker is out of the question.

"I'mma finish up this shit with Rocko, then I'mma pass the bar and start my own law firm. You know I was in school before I got locked up. The good thing is while I was on the island, I had a lil cell phone, so I was able to finish up school online."

"That's wassup, cuzzo. Anything I can do to help, I'm here. Just let me know," Peso replied.

"I was on the island running it up and made a nice piece of change. Ain't no money like jail money," Euro chuckled. "I got two hunnit racks ($200,000) right now, cold cash. I been hearing UGF got the best dope in the city, a ten all over the land. I need in on that, cuzzo."

"Nah, you don't need in on that, Euro. Look around. I'm rich, so that means we all rich. You free. Let's just enjoy life. I would be devastated if something happened to you out here, man. I done lost too many niggas I love," Peso said sincerely. "I can always drop a bag on Rocko and get him out the way. You know I got niggas who will kill and die for me," he added.

"Nah, this is personal. That nigga been my best friend since the second grade, and he crossed me. I gotta be the one to make him pay. All the shit I did for that nigga, and he betrayed me. I was there through all of the bids and all of the beefs in the streets. I been nothing but a true friend. We both know that disloyalty is unforgivable. The sooner I kill this nigga, the sooner I can start my law firm. Hearing my name buzzing in the streets will bring him out. You gon plug me in or not? It's money to be made."

"As bad as I wanna say no right now, I can't. I understand where you coming from. I'mma patch you all the way in. I don't touch no work these days. I'm strictly legit now. Hitta takes care of all that. He will get you situated. It's $100K in that bookbag. That's all you. Anything you need, just call me. I'm here, bro. You know that. Please be careful out here. It's a jungle in these streets."

"And I'm a fuckin' Gorilla," Euro replied with a smile.

MEANWHILE IN MARLBORO Houses

Reem knocked on the door of Lucci's mother's apartment. A beautiful woman, who appeared to be in her early thirties, answered the door. She could pass for Pam in the TV show, *Martin*. "Good evening, Miss Jones. My name is Reem. You may not know m…"

"I know who you are," she cut him off. "Cut that Miss Jones crap out. Call me April. Come in." She stepped to the side, and Reem entered, holding a big Bloomingdale's shopping bag in his hand.

An instant wave of sadness hit Reem when he saw all of the pictures of Lucci hanging up in the living room. "He was my only son," April said sadly.

"I know that nothing I say can bring your son back, but I'm truly sorry for your loss," Reem said sincerely. He looked into April's sad eyes, and his heart got heavy. "That bullet was meant for me," Reem admitted. "If I didn't let him drive, he would still be here. But when he asked me, I couldn't deny him. The smile on his face when he was driving that Maserati was priceless. I loved your son like a little brother. He was my lil homie." Reem could no longer hold back his tears. He let them fall freely. "Lucci, I mean Mario, was a good kid. He wasn't like the rest of the little homies running around here. That's why I kept him away from the streets as much as I could. I made sure he went to school every day and stayed focused. I kept money in his pocket, so he wouldn't run around robbing people or selling drugs. No matter what I did to save him, I failed because he still died because of me," he cried harder. "It took everything in me to come up here and face you. I didn't wanna come here, but I couldn't just hide like some coward," he sobbed.

April hugged him tightly, which caught him off guard. He was expecting her to hate him. Truth was, she couldn't hate Reem because she knew all of the things Reem had done to keep her son on the right path. Her son worshipped him. This woman never respected gangs until she saw how much of a positive impact it had on her son. She knew gangs were not good, but she also knew that they weren't all bad either. She knew that gangs such as Blood was started for a good cause, just like the Black Panther Party. A while back, she was cleaning her son's room and stumbled across some of the paperwork Reem gave her son. She sat up for hours reading it, and it helped her get a better understanding.

"Reem, don't blame yourself. God called him home. This isn't your fault. I know your intentions were always good when it came to my son. I wasn't only his mother. I was his best friend. Mario never kept anything from me. I know all about the bond the two of you shared. He looked up to you. All I ask is that you find that bastard that murdered my baby and make his family feel the same exact pain we are feeling. For every bullet he put in my son, I want two bullets in him," she vented.

"You have my word on that. No one is exempt from the pain I'm going to bring. For every tear we shed, blood will spill. I will not let up until that nigga is dead. I have to get going." Reem picked up the Bloomingdale's shopping bag he came with and handed it to her. "This is a hunnit racks ($100,000). I had it put up for Mario to get up out of here and go to college," he said sadly. "It should be more than enough to cover funeral expenses. Anything else you need, don't hesitate to ask. If I got it, so do you. I always make sure that my family is straight. The next time I come here, the man who murdered your son will be dead," Reem promised before exiting the apartment.

Reem made it to the lobby where a lot of Lucci's peers were lighting candles and signing a huge picture board with his face on it. Reem badly wanted to sign it but refused to do so because Lucci's killer was still alive.

Reem walked two buildings over and headed inside of his aunt's apartment. He walked straight to his old bedroom and opened the closet. He pulled out an old toy chest and opened it. He removed a dusty .357 Python and looked at it with a smile. This gun held sentimental value. Doggy gave this gun to Reem when he was just thirteen years old. This was the same gun that he used to murder the man who murdered his dad. Now, he would use this same gun to murder the man who gave it to him.

Meanwhile at the W Hotel

Peso entered the hotel lobby, trying to look as normal as

possible. He casually walked to the elevator and stepped inside. The female who was working behind the desk stared at him but didn't say anything. As the door closed, Peso was trying to figure out where he knew the female from, but he couldn't remember.

When he made it to the penthouse suite on the top floor, Roxy was just getting out of the shower. She had a long flight in from Paris. Even though she was tired, she still had more than enough energy for a great sex session with Peso. "Wassup, light skin?" he greeted her with a hug.

"I missed you so much," she claimed while hugging him back.

"Oh, yeah? How much?"

"Let me show you," Roxy replied and dropped to her knees.

In Brooklyn

Princess had just picked up her sister, Imani, from a baby shower, and now they were about to go have drinks. Princess' phone rang, and she answered without looking at the screen. "Hello."

"Princess, you at my job right now?" the caller asked anxiously.

"Who is this?" Princess asked, finally looking at the screen of her iPhone.

The caller was a female named Tania, who was her cousin's girlfriend. "Bitch, I know you didn't delete my number," the caller replied playfully. "It's Tania," she added.

"No, bitch, I got a new phone. I couldn't get into my iCloud, so I had to reset it, and why would I be at ya job if ya slutty ass work in the W Hotel?" Princess chuckled.

"I'm only asking because I just seen Peso walk in here a lil while ago."

"What Peso? My Peso?"

"Yes, bitch, your Peso. I thought you was with him."

"Listen, I got five bands if you can find out what room he's in and get me the key."

"I'll get you that for free. Lemme do my homework. I'll have everything for you by the time you get here."

"Say no more. I owe you big for this one, bitch." Princess ended the call. She looked over to her sister. "I think Ty is cheating on me. That was Tania. She said that Ty is at her job right now. I'mma drop you off cause if I get locked up, I'mma need you to bail me out. I'mma put hands on Tyler and whoever the bitch is that he's with."

"Drop me off? You must be drunk. I'm coming with you," Imani replied.

"Cool, but you staying in the car, no debating."

BACK IN MARLBORO Houses

Reem had been standing in the same spot for over an hour already. He was currently in the hallway of Doggy's brother's apartment building. Just when he was ready to abort the mission, the apartment door opened. Reem brandished the .357 Python and pushed the man back inside. "Who the fuck else is in here?" Reem asked.

"My son and nephew in the back room," the man replied.

Reem forced the man to the back room and was met by two men sitting on the bed, playing a game of *NBA 2K*. One of the men happened to be the brother of Bricks. He was also a Blood member, but he belonged to a different set. Reem caught both men by surprise. "Yo, Reem, what's banging, Blood? What's all this about?" Brick's brother asked.

"Where the fuck can I find Doggy? I'm only gon ask one time."

"I don't know," the man claimed.

BOC! Reem fired a single shot, hitting the man in the head, killing him instantly. "That was the wrong answer. If y'all don't wanna end up like Beezo over there, I suggest y'all tell me where I can find Doggy."

"He been laying low in the Gravesend projects in Coney Island. He got a bitch over there. That's all I know," the man claimed.

Reem didn't waste any time giving the next two men headshots before making his escape.

BACK AT THE W Hotel

Princess took the elevator to the top floor penthouse suite and quietly entered. Moaning could be heard coming from the suite's master bedroom. The sound of "her man" pleasing another woman crushed her. Princess badly wanted to turn around and leave but decided not to. She slid open the double doors and saw super model, Roxy Royal, on top of Peso, riding him like her life depended on it. The two of them were so caught up in their sex session that neither of them noticed that Princess was watching them.

After two minutes of watching, Princess ran over and snatched Roxy by her hair. "You dirty bitch!" she barked while dragging her off of Peso, who quickly jumped off the bed and grabbed Princess.

"Baby girl, chill."

Princess was punching Roxy like she was a MMA fighter.

"'Baby girl, chill?'" Princess laughed demonically as she punched Roxy once more. "Nigga, don't fuckin touch me. You wanna be in here cheating with this ho," she said while punching her some more.

"Princess, that's enough!" Peso barked, getting his lady's attention. This shocked Princess because he'd never raised his voice at her since the two of them had been together. She was now in tears, but she still gripped Roxy's hair firmly.

"Tyler, are you serious right now? Like you really taking up for this bitch. You tryna save her, and you in here fuckin' this ho without a condom. You must love her, Tyler." Princess finally let go of Roxy, who got up and ran into the bathroom, locking the door behind her. "That's why you tryna save her, because you love her, right?" she cried.

"How you gonna ask me some shit like that, Queen? I'm only stopping you because I fucked up, not her. I'm the one you should be mad at. I'm sorry, P. I fucked up," he said while trying to pull her in his embrace.

Princess threw several punches, and one landed directly on top of Peso's right eye. He quickly grabbed her and held her tight. "I love you to death, P, but let that be the last time you punch me like that," he said seriously.

"Let me go!" Princess barked.

"You gon chill?"

"Yes, just let me go please," she begged. Peso let her go, and Princess slapped fire out of him before storming out of the suite.

CHAPTER 24

Same Night

Reem pulled into one of the parking lots of the Gravesend Houses in Coney Island. He tried calling both Hitta and Peso but got no answer on every attempt. With no other option, he called Peso's little brother, Shoota, who picked up on the second ring. "Yo, Reem, what's the word, big bro?"

"Ain't shit. What's poppin', gang? I'm on ya side. You around?" Reem replied.

"Yeah, I'm on deck. Where you at?"

"I'm in the parking lot by the flagpole in the red Camaro."

"Say that. I'm pulling up on you right now," Shoota said and ended the call.

Reem pulled out a pack of Newport shorts from his pocket and lit one up. He'd quit smoking cigarettes over a year ago, but since losing Lucci, he had been smoking them nonstop.

Shoota walked up to the Camaro and knocked on the passenger's seat window. Reem hit the locks, and Shoota hopped in. "What's the word?" Shoota greeted Reem with some dap.

"I can't call it, bro," Reem said dryly.

"Everything healthy, big bro?" Shoota asked, sensing Reem's off demeanor.

"I ain't even gon hold you, bro. Shit all fucked up right now. I'm looking for this old head name Doggy from my side. I got word that boy been laying low over here. He touched someone dear to my heart, bro. I gotta get next to boy. You ever heard of him?" Reem asked with sadness plastered all over his face.

Shoota had never seen Reem like this. He was so used to him running around on demon time, but today, he saw the pain written all over his face. Shoota had lost people close to him as well, so he knew the pain Reem was feeling right now. "I got a line on the old nigga, big bro. He be selling me chops (guns) and buying dope off me," Shoota admitted. "The nigga just hit me like twenty minutes ago. I'm supposed to meet him in building 15. We can rock him right now."

"Nah, this is personal, bro. Just get me next to boy and I'll take it from there," Reem replied.

"Nigga, you my family. I ain't tryna hear that personal shit. You sitting here hurting is hurting me, nigga. I'mma make the call," Shoota replied while pulling his iPhone from his pocket and placing a call.

Reem's trigger finger was itching as he listened to Shoota talk to Doggy. He was so close to killing this man that he could actually taste it. Shoota ended the call and turned to Reem. "How you wanna do this? The nigga is coming from the store right now. He wants me to meet him at the building. We can park him on his way from the store, or we can drop him in the building. Either way, this nigga is outta here tonight," Shoota promised.

"We gon let him go in the building. That way, less attention is on us," Reem said, firmly gripping the .357 Python while sliding out of the driver's seat.

Shoota led the way to building 15, and the two of them entered through the back exit to avoid the camera that was in the lobby. The two of them took the stairs to the third floor. "Yo, bro, wait on this side. When you hear me talking to him, just pop out," Shoota said.

He walked to the elevator and pulled out his phone. He strolled down his Instagram timeline just to kill time. Minutes later, the elevator doors opened, and Doggy stepped off. A huge smile popped on his face when he saw Shoota. "My favorite young nigga, Shoota," he said with a smile. "What's good, youngin?" he greeted Shoota with a fist bump.

"Same shit, OG. What you needed?"

"Let me get a brick." He handed Shoota a bunch of wrinkled up bills, and in return, Shoota handed him a brick of heroin, which equaled to five bundles or fifty dime bags. "Good thing I seen you now cause I was about to slide for a day or two, and them fools across town got straight trash. You, my nigga, got that fire. This shit right here came straight from the dope God." Doggy laughed at his own joke. He was so caught up in running his mouth that he never even noticed Reem step from around the corner.

"Turn around, Dog. I ain't gon shoot you in ya back," Reem said calmly.

The sound of Reem's voice sent a chill down Doggy's spine. He shot Shoota an icy glare. "Damn, Shoota, you gave this nigga the drop on me? After all the guns I done put in these projects," he said in disbelief.

"Reem is my family, nigga, and where I'm from, we put family above all." Shoota brandished a brand-new chrome

.9mm with a pearl handle. He purchased this gun from Doggy two days ago.

Doggy just shook his head and turned to face Reem. He chuckled when he saw the .357 Python in Reem's hand. "Ain't this about a bitch. I gave you that Python when you was still pissing in the bed. On top of that, I sold that nine to Shoota like two days ago. This is really a dirty game." Doggy shook his head.

"This is why you never sell a gun because the gun you sell can be the same gun to kill you. Tell that bitch ass nigga, Bricks, that I send my love," Reem smiled.

BOOM! BOOM! BOOM! BOOM! BOOM! Reem pumped five shots into Doggy's body. Shoota then stood over him and filled him with five more slugs. This was simply overkill.

SAME NIGHT

Peso had left Roxy in the penthouse suite. He was now driving around, looking for Princess. He had called everyone, including her mom, but no one had heard from her. When he made it home, there was no sign of her. The fact that she hadn't packed her things was a good sign, and it gave Peso some hope.

He cruised the streets in his snow white 600 Benz, smoking blunts back-to-back. Peso was furious right now. He really didn't want to lose Princess. He tried calling her phone again, and it went straight to voicemail. "Fuck!" he barked. He was really a complete wreck right now. At the moment, he couldn't even think straight. Instead of keeping his anger bottled in, he called his righthand man, Hitta.

"What's the word, big homie?" Hitta picked up after the first ring.

"Can't call it, bro. Where you at right now?"

"I just got in the crib with Ash and Nauti. Why you sound like something wrong? You good, bro?" Hitta asked, picking up on his vibe.

"Yeah, I'm sturdy, bro. You the man tho, big homie. Life is really great over there," Peso chuckled. "My nigga got two women who actually know about each other," he teased.

"If that's what you want to call it." Hitta cracked a smile. "Don't try to igg my question. You good over there or not?"

"Nah, bro. I'm all fucked up over here. Princess caught me with Roxy. Like really caught us dead in the act. Princess beat fire out that girl, bro," Peso said sadly. "I fucked up, gang. I think she left. You of all niggas know I ain't no tender dick nigga, bro, but shawdy got my soul, Hitta," he admitted.

Hitta had never known Peso to stress over a female other than his first love, Kendra. When the two of them broke up years ago, Peso was crushed. Something about him had changed since then. Peso would never admit it, but he had never been the same since losing Kendra. His heart became colder. Then, he met Princess and was able to love again.

"She just needs time to cool down, bro. She's upset right now. Princess loves you. It's gonna take more than a friendly fuck to break up what y'all built. Don't trip, just give her a minute to herself. What she seen is a lot to take in, bro. Let her breathe. Don't crowd her. You fucked up, accept that. Allow her to be upset," Hitta replied. "Matter fact, pull up to the crib and smoke one with ya boy. I got some things I wanna run by you anyway."

"I ain't gonna bring my bad vibes over there. I'mma just go to the studio for a few. You know we gotta be in Atlanta for the BET Awards Sunday. You still pulling up, right?"

"I wouldn't miss it for nothing in the world. Like I said, the door is open if you wanna pull up," Hitta reminded him.

"I already know. Enjoy ya ladies tho. I'mma hit the booth. See you in the morning, gang. I love you."

"I love you more, just hit me."

The minute Peso hung up the phone, he got a call from Mariah telling him that she needed to speak with him asap. He sped through traffic and made it to her condo in twenty minutes flat.

When he stepped off of the elevator, Mariah was sitting on the sofa, having a glass of wine. Her eyes were currently glued to the screen of her MacBook. "Wassup, baby momma?" he greeted her.

"Nothing much. I really need to talk to you tho. Have a seat. Would you like a glass of wine?" she offered.

"Wine?" Peso chuckled. "Ya bougie ass know damn well I ain't drinking no wine. I'mma open that bottle of Remy tho," he said and walked to the minibar and grabbed the bottle of Remy Martin VSOP. He didn't bother getting a glass. He just opened the bottle and took a huge gulp before walking over to the sofa where Mariah was sitting with the bottle in his hand.

"Wassup, Riah? What you needed to holla at me about?"

"Tyler, are you crazy or just plain stupid? Princess deserves better than what you are currently giving her. That girl loves you and our daughter. Nigga, you better tighten the fuck up," Mariah said.

"Damn, she told you?" Peso replied, shaking his head.

"Yeah, she told me, dummy. If you don't get ya shit together, that girl gon leave ya nut ass. You really gonna be sick if you lose her. Why you gotta be out here sticking ya dick in everything when you got a good woman at home? I don't get you, Ty. I really don't." Mariah rolled her eyes.

This was one thing that Peso loved about Mariah. She wasn't some bitter ass baby mother. She truly wanted the best for him. All she wanted was to see him happy, even if it was not with her. Here she was, calling him over at one in the morning to talk to him about how much he needed to get his shit together.

"Riah, I can't lie. I fucked up. I'm not even gonna sit here and try and make no excuses for that. I just pray she doesn't leave me. I don't even know where she's at right now," he sadly admitted.

"Tyler, that girl is not leaving; she loves you way too much. Ya nut ass is the only person that doesn't see it. Princess could have been anywhere in the world right now, but she's in the room with our daughter. She called me and asked if she could come lay with Mya. That's a good woman. She could have went out to the club or hit up one of her old niggas and got a revenge fuck, but she didn't. Don't take advantage of her love, Ty. She is the one for you."

"She's in the bed with Mya right now?" Peso's face lit up. He was really ready to run in his daughter's room, but he kept his composure.

"Yes, they are sleeping. Do not go in there and wake them. Let me ask you something. How would you feel if Princess was to cheat on you?"

"I would have been sick. I prolly would have killed her and the nigga she was cheating with," he admitted.

"So, why do something to her that you wouldn't want done to you? That's selfish."

"Riah, these bitches don't mean shit to me. I fucked up. I can stand on that. I'm a man. Sometimes I lack self-control when it comes to women. It's easy to turn down three or four, but I got millions of women throwing pussy at me on a daily basis. It gets hard sometimes," he claimed.

"I don't wanna hear none of that bullshit!" she barked. "Get the hell out my face, Tyler. Be careful with that woman's heart," Mariah said and got up from the sofa and headed to her bedroom.

Peso sat around for another thirty minutes, drinking and smoking. He then got up and walked to his daughter's bedroom to find her and Princess sleeping so peacefully. He turned off the TV before walking over to Mya and placing a kiss on her forehead. Then, he slid in the bed behind Princess.

CHAPTER 25

Next Day

When Peso woke up, the clock read 1 p.m. To his surprise, no one was home. He grabbed his phone off of the dresser and called Princess, but she sent him to voicemail. He then dialed Mya's number, who picked up instantly. "Hi, Daddy," she said in an excited tone.

"Hey, pretty girl, where are you?"

"Me, Mommy, and Princess are out doing girl stuff. Do you want me to give one of them the phone?"

"Yes. Let me speak to Princess please."

"What do you want, Tyler?" Princess asked. He could hear that she was still upset with him.

"I'm sorry, P. I fuck…'"

"I don't wanna hear it," she cut him off. "You are interrupting our girls' days out. I will talk to when I feel I'm ready to. Don't force it. It's only gonna push me away. I'm upset, and I'm hurt. Just give me some space please," she added before ending the call.

Peso just shook his head and smiled. "It could be worse," he said to himself.

He took a shower before heading out to see his jeweler. Tomorrow wasn't only the BET Awards; it was also his birthday. So, he decided to treat himself to something new and get something for Mya and Princess.

Two hours later, Peso was walking into the barbershop in his hood. The place wasn't crowded, and everybody greeted him with love when he entered. He took a few pictures then hopped in one of the empty chairs. "Yo, Melly, take a lil off the top and tape me up," he said to the barber.

Melly, the co-owner of Cut Close barbershop, had been cutting Peso's hair since he was a kid. The two of them had a very good relationship. Melly had watched Peso come up in the streets. He watched him go from a boy to a man. "That last mixtape you dropped was heat. That shit a classic, my nigga, no cap," Melly complimented.

"Good looking, my nigga. You know I gotta give the streets what they been looking for. It's only right. I'm the voice for the niggas in the trenches that don't have a voice," Peso replied.

"When you gon do something with Meek? The streets waiting on that," said X, the other owner of the shop. He was two chairs down, cutting someone's hair.

"That's already in the works," he smiled, "Look out for my performance at the BET Awards. Shit gon be a movie. Y'all may wanna tune in."

"Who in ya top five right now?" X asked.

"Top five?" Peso chuckled. "You know I don't do none of that. My top five is me. I fuck with a few niggas tho, but I won't put them in no bracket. Feel me?"

"So, who you fuck wit?"

"The same niggas I been fucking with —_Meek, Yo Gotti, Ross, Future, Fab, Hov, Jeezy, Weezy, and Nipsey Hussle. I like the boy, Durk, as well. But I fuck with Drizzy and J. Cole too."

MEANWHILE AT HITTA'S Condo

"Yo, Ash, what time is our flight?" Hitta called out to Ashley from the bedroom.

"7 p.m.," Ashley replied while entering the bedroom.

"Cool, that means I still got time."

"Time for what?"

"I gotta go to the hood and pick Flee up."

"Peso is already out there. See if he would pick him up," Ashley suggested.

"Good idea," Hitta replied while grabbing his iPhone off of the bed. He placed a FaceTime call to Peso.

"Yurrrr!" Peso greeted when his face popped up on Hitta's screen.

"You sound better than you did yesterday. That means you and wifey made up, huh?"

"Nah, she still not fucking with me, but she ain't leave a nigga. The whole time I'm looking for her, she's at Mariah crib, laying in the bed with Mya."

"She's a real one, bro. You must keep her. What's the word tho? Where you at?"

"I just left the barbershop. I'm about to spin through the block real quick to find Shoota."

"Copy, snatch Flee for me while you over there."

"I gotchu, gang. I'mma hit you when I link him. I love you, my boy."

"I love you more. Be safe out there." Hitta ended the call.

BACK IN CONEY ISLAND

Flee had just walked out of his grandmother's apartment. She lived in the next building from him. This was where he tucked all of his money away. His old bedroom was his stash spot.

When Hitta called Flee and told him that they were going to the BET Awards, the news made his day. He'd been a little down since Lexi left him, so this getaway was much needed. He pulled out his phone and called Fresh to let her know that he was going to be out of town for a few days. He also called Gat and told him to hold things down in his absence.

Just when Flee was about to click on Gat's number, his phone rang. Shoota's name popped up on the screen. "What's the vibes, gang?" Flee answered.

"Ain't shit, my boy. Caine just got locked," Shoota informed him.

"For what? I just seen bro."

"Attempted murder. That nigga, Poe, pulled through. The streets saying the old head made it too. Shit about to get real ugly, my nigga."

Hearing that Prince survived had Flee fucked up because he'd jumped out of the car and put four extra slugs in him at point blank range. He just shook his head. "I got whatever lil bro needs for his bail. If you wanna come snatch the bread from me now, pull up. Peso is about to come get me in a minute. You flying out too, right?"

"Nah, I'mma fall back. Tell bro give my ticket to Gat. He just came home, let bro go enjoy himself. I'mma play the trenches. Me and Heat got the bail situated. Y'all niggas enjoy the trip. I was just letting you know what was up."

"Copy. Y'all be safe. Love you, gang."

"Love you more." Shoota ended the call.

CHAPTER 26

BET Awards

Peso had just set the stage on fire with his performance moments ago at the BET Awards. The crowd really loved him. Tonight, he was nominated for three awards, so far, he had already won two of them. After changing his clothes, Peso headed back to his seat. In attendance with him, you had his daughter, Mya, Princess, Mariah, Hitta, Ashley, Nautica, Flee, and Gat.

Peso was trying to have a good time, but the fact that Princess still hadn't said a word to him was eating away at his heart. He was silently praying that he won the next award because he had a trick up his sleeve. He was so caught up in his thoughts that he didn't hear the host call his name for the winner of the best new artist award. "Presidential Peso, don't tell me yo ass done left already," the comedian presenting the award joked.

"Ayo, bro, that's you," Flee said, snapping him out of his thoughts.

Peso stood from his seat. His entire outfit was Balenciaga,

and he was heavy on the jewelry today. He grabbed Mya's hand before turning to Princess. "Come on, Queen. I got a surprise for you," he smiled while reaching his other hand out to take hers. For the first time since he was caught cheating, Princess had a smile on her face. Together, the three of them walked to the stage hand in hand where Peso gladly accepted his third award for the night.

"First and foremost, I wanna thank God and my fans. Without God and without my fans, I wouldn't be who I am today. I won several Grammy awards, but in my opinion, nothing holds more weight than the BET Awards. I remember watching this same exact award show as a kid, telling myself that I was gonna make it up to this stage one day. I've been manifesting this exact moment for many years. Not only did I win all three awards that I got nominated for, but I won them on my birthday. I'm extremely blessed."

"Happy birthday, Peso!" the crowd chanted.

"Thank y'all so much," he smiled. "I don't wanna keep y'all for too long, but I have to do this because this beautiful woman standing up here with me deserves the best. She's a Black woman who rocks," he added while facing Princess, getting down on one knee, and opening the jewelry box that contained the biggest diamond that Princess had ever seen.

Princess was ecstatic. She couldn't hold back her excitement. "You are not doing this right now, Ty." Her body began to shake as tears fell down her face. "Do you know what you're doing right now?" she asked.

"Yes. Now, Princess Carter, will you marry me?"

"Yes, Tyler. Yes, I will marry you," she cried.

"She said yes, BET."

. . .

MEANWHILE IN MARLBORO **Houses**

Reem had just purchased a white candle from the corner store. He was now walking to Lucci's building. It was a beautiful summer night, so plenty of people were outside. In front of the building, there was a bunch of little homies sitting around, smoking, and drinking. He greeted them all one by one with the signature Blood handshake before entering the lobby.

Today, he could finally sign the huge picture board with Lucci's face on it. He couldn't bring himself to do it before because the man responsible for Lucci's death was still alive. He grabbed the marker that was taped to the wall and signed his name before lighting the candle. "I love you, Lucci. Now you can finally rest in peace, skrap," he said while staring at the picture of his little homie.

Reem took the elevator up to Lucci's mom's floor and knocked on the door. April answered the door with a smile. She jumped in Reem's arms and hugged him tightly. "Thank you so much, Reem," she said sincerely.

"No thank you needed. Wassup, Miss April, how you feeling?" he replied while entering the apartment.

"Boy, stop that Miss April shit. I am not that much older than you, boy." She pushed him playfully.

"I am a man of my word, so Lucci can rest in peace now. I know it won't take our pain away, but at least we ain't the only people hurting."

"Absolutely. Are you gonna stay and have a drink with me?"

"Only if I can smoke in here."

"You sure can." April got up and walked to the kitchen. Seconds later, she returned with a bottle of Hennessy and two glasses. "Would you like ice or nah?"

"Nah, that's for the boys. Men drink Henny straight," he smiled. "Can I turn the TV on?"

"Do your thing. The remote is right there." She pointed to the glass table in the middle of the living room.

Reem grabbed the remote and turned the TV on. BET was replaying the award show from earlier. He turned it on just in time to catch Peso's performance. Reem watched his friend with a smile. The smile got wider when he saw Hitta, Flee, and Gat on stage performing with him. So much had been going on with Reem that he didn't even realize today was Peso's birthday. He pulled out his iPhone and placed a FaceTime call to his comrade.

Peso picked up instantly. "Reem, what's the vibes?"

"Happy birthday, my brother."

"You late, nigga. It's past twelve," Peso chuckled. "Good looking tho, gang. Where the fuck you been at tho?" he added.

"Shit been kinda brazy out here, but we will talk about that in person. I turned the TV on just now and seen y'all turning up. Can't lie, my boy. That shit made my day."

"That means you ain't seen the main event yet. I proposed to Princess. Ya boy about to be a married man," Peso said with a smile.

"Nah, not pretty boy Peso," Reem teased.

"Yeah, nigga, pretty boy Peso. It's time for ya boy to grow up tho. A nigga been a player since junior high. You know me, Reem. What you dealing with tho?"

"Ain't much. About to roll one, sip on this Henny, and watch the rest of the awards. I was just sending you some birthday love, my brother. Hit me when you back on these sides. I love you, my boy."

"I love you more, gang. Stay dangerous."

"Always, my boy." The call ended, and Reem put his phone down. He looked over to April. "Pardon myself. I forgot today was my bra's birthday," he apologized.

"You straight. Ain't like we on a date," April teased.

For the next hour or so, the two of them sat around drinking, smoking, and talking. Reem was twisted. He could barely get up from the sofa. "It's late, April. I'mma slide," Reem said.

"What if I don't want you to leave?"

"What you mean?"

"What I mean is, I've been sitting in this apartment all depressed and shit. I'm tired of stressing every minute. I'm enjoying ya company, and I don't want you to leave. Can you please stay? Unless you have somewhere important to be right now, you don't need to be walking around like this. You are an important man with enemies. You don't need to be slipping."

Her last statement caught Reem off guard, and it showed on his face. The facial expression he made caused April to laugh. "What, you thought I was some square ass bitch?" she said with a smile.

Meanwhile in Coney Island

Shoota and Heat had just left the bail bondsman. The judge set Caine's bail at $150,000, so they only had to pay $15,000 because they found a bails bondman where the fee was ten percent. Shoota pushed his Maserati down the Belt Parkway. Both he and Heat had a lot on their minds. The bail bondsman promised to have Caine out by the morning. The two of them were just trying to kill time right now. "You heard from Lil Ricky and them?" Heat asked.

"Yeah, bro just text me not too long ago. They made it out there safe," Shoota replied.

Lil Ricky was one of their workers, who they put in charge of their Vermont operations. "Oh, shit, that nigga, Power, called earlier for two hundred bricks," Shoota reminded him.

"Nigga, we both know Power ain't coppin from nobody but us," Heat chuckled. "I'mma call him now and let him know that we on the way. After that, let's shoot to the Bronx and check the ape, Santana."

Twenty minutes later, Shoota's Maserati pulled up in front of a small townhouse. He pulled out his iPhone and clicked on one of his many apps. After pressing a code in the app, the dashboard popped open. Inside of the compartment was a Footlocker bag that contained the two hundred bricks that Power ordered. The stashbox could hold up to two thousand bricks and two handguns. The app for the stashbox was created by a white boy who Peso went to school with. Peso felt the app would be a success, so he invested and had made his investment back twice already.

Shoota and Heat approached the townhouse, and Heat rang the doorbell. A minute later, Power opened the door, shirtless, with a big blunt hanging from his mouth. Power was an older dude who was a major player in the dope game until the Feds sat him down for nine years.

These days, Power was just trying to survive. He was no longer purchasing kilos like he once was, but he wasn't doing too bad. His townhouse was paid for, and so was his 7series BMW. His pockets weren't really hurting either, but what he was doing now was small time compared to what he was doing back in his day. "What it is, my boys?" Power let them inside the townhouse with a huge smile on his face. He was so happy that they didn't stand him up because he had already missed a nice chunk of change waiting on them. He didn't want to go another second without dope. "Y'all wanna hit this gas?" He offered them the blunt.

"Nah, big dawg, we kinda in a rush," Shoota declined. He handed Power the Footlocker bag. "That's the two hunnit you ordered," he added.

"Square bizness. That's why I love fucking with y'all niggas, man. Y'all always doing the right thing," Power smiled. "Where is that lil crazy nigga who's always with y'all?"

They both laughed, knowing that he was talking about Caine. Everybody who knew them addressed Caine as the lil crazy nigga. Truth was, Caine loved that title. "He got locked the other day. We just posted his bail, so he'll be back in a minute," Heat replied.

"Hope everything works out for the youngin. I like the lil crazy nigga. Let me go get that cheese for y'all," he said and walked to his bedroom.

Seconds later, he returned with a huge bankroll that was wrapped in rubber bands and handed it to Shoota. "That's $55,000. It's all there. Five ten band stacks and one five band stack. I missed a lot of money today," he complained.

"You ain't miss no paper, nigga. You on the winning team, big bro. Ya clients still waiting on you. Trust me. They ain't willing to settle on that bullshit them other niggas selling. One thing I know for sure is everybody wants the Untouchable. It's an exclusive brand," Heat said with a smile.

When they made it back to Shoota's Maserati, he did the same routine to get the stashbox open, and he placed the money inside. He and Heat would split $17,000, and the remaining $38,000 went to Hitta. They charged Power $275 per brick, and they both put up one hundred bricks apiece for the sale. After securing the money, Shoota pulled out his phone and called Santana.

MEANWHILE IN SOUTH BRONX

"Booking on the interstate, I'm bailing with them bricks, cooking with the flour, hit me if you need the fish. Bottom of the ninth, choppas loaded. That's the ball game. Pussy, you a target, and I barely ever miss. Fuck up out my dope house, get the fuck up out my dope house." Santana glided down Boston Road in his brand-new 5550 Mercedes Benz blasting Chinx Drugs' track, *Dope House.*

He rapped along as he swerved through traffic. Today was a good day for Santana. He'd just sold his last four hundred bricks of Untouchable. Now, he was ready to just lay back for the night and have some much-needed fun. The sound of his phone ringing caused him to turn the music down. A smile plastered across his face when he saw Shoota's name on his screen. "Shoota, what's good, ape?"

"Ain't shit, big bro. What you fucking with?"

"I'm about to snatch a few of the apes, and we gon shoot to ya side and hit up one of them strip clubs," Santana said.

"Which one? Lust?"

"Yeah, I believe so."

"Me and Heat was about to pull up on you, but since you headed this way, that's even better. Hit my line once you get to Brooklyn and we gon hit Lust together."

"Say less. Gorilla stack 62," Santana saluted.

"No keys, push to start," Shoota replied.

CHAPTER 27

Atlanta, GA

It was now 2 a.m., and Peso was just walking inside of his hotel suite. Mya was with her mom, so Princess was there alone. She still hadn't said a word to Peso, even after saying yes to his marriage proposal.

Princess was laying across the bed when Peso walked in. As always, she was dressed in some sexy lingerie. The sight of her beautiful skin all oiled up was breathtaking. Dej Loaf's soft voice bled from the speakers. "You still acting light skin, Ma?" Peso asked with a smile. His charm usually worked but not today. Princess refused to let him off the hook easily.

"You still fucking bitches raw, Pa?" she replied back.

Peso just ignored her smart comment and took a seat on the foot of the bed. He grabbed her right foot and began to massage it. Princess didn't stop him. "Baby girl, I fucked up. I fucked up bad, and I can't make any excuses for what I did. You can ignore me if you want, but yo ass gon listen to what I have to say," Peso said sternly.

Princess just cut her eyes at him. He caught the look she

gave him, but he continued. "I love you, Princess, and I can't see myself living without you. After my daughter, you are the best thing that has ever happened to me. This may sound corny as fuck, but I'mma say it anyway because it's the truth. Princess, before I met you, I loved you. I say that because for so many years, I pictured you in my mind. I wrote a list to the universe giving all the qualities that I wanted my soulmate to have. I didn't ask for a particular person, just particular qualities. I swear on my mother's grave that you have every single quality that I wrote down on that paper. It's like the universe made you just for me, Ma," Peso paused and looked into her eyes. He leaned in to wipe the tear that was falling, but Princess slapped his hand.

"That was corny as fuck, Tyler," she laughed. "And knowing you, ya ass probably think that was some smooth shit. You gotta come better than that," she laughed harder. "It was kind of cute tho, but I know you could think of some better shit to say."

"I could, but I ain't trying to run no game. What we have ain't no game. I hold you sacred to my heart. You know how I feel about you, P," he replied sadly.

"How do you feel about the other bitch?"

"It ain't no feelings when it comes to her. I mean, she a cool chick, but my heart belongs to you. Roxy was more of a bucket list fuck. A fantasy fulfiller. I always wanted to fuck her, so I fucked her. Nothing more, nothing less. I met both of y'all around the same time, but I chose to be with you. She ain't got nothing on you, P." He leaned in and stroked her face. "My mom even said you were the one for me. Whenever I didn't listen to her, shit went wrong, so I took her advice on this love shit. I don't just wanna come home to you. I wanna share my life with you. Princess, you're smart, ambitious, independent, loyal, caring, bossy, swaggy, you got spunk, you funny, sexy, ya body is perfect, ya smile is breathtaking, you love basketball and rap music. Princess, I can go on all day. You get the picture."

"No, I don't. Keep going." She blushed.

"I ain't even mention that you got some pretty ass feet, you a great cook, the sex is always amazing, you good with Mya, you just got it all together. I never meant to hurt you, P. I was thinking with my dick. I was being dumb and selfish. I never once took a minute to think about how you would feel —or how I would feel if you did some shit like that to me," he admitted "I will do better tho. Anything I gotta do, I will do," he added.

"You better. Don't let these hoes be the reason you lose half of everything." She held up her left hand and showed her huge engagement ring.

"You can have it all, Queen. You the woman of my dreams. All this shit will mean nothing without you. Shit, half of it belongs to you anyway cause you been my muse since I met you. You motivate me to make great music; you motivate me to go beyond my creative capacity."

"It's gonna take more than you sticking ya dick in some tramp for me to give up on you. I love you, Tyler, but you disappointed me. Why cheat when I give you everything you want at home? I just gave you a threesome with my best friend. Was that not enough for you?" she asked.

"That was more than enough," Peso smiled, replaying the night in his head.

"So, why cheat, Ty?"

"I don't even know, P. I can't make up no excuse, babe. I fucked up, and I will do anything I have to do to make this right. Let me ask you something tho. What made you give me a threesome with Tamara? That shit don't feel weird?"

"No, it doesn't feel weird. Like I told you when we first met, me and Tamara tried being together when we were teens, but both decided that we weren't really lesbians. We were just experimenting with each other. Me and her have been best friends since we were in first grade, so she knows everything about me. She also knows that I wanted to have my first threesome with her and the man I plan to spend the rest of my life with. You and Tamara are gonna be in my life forever, so why not enjoy it to the fullest?" she smiled then quickly got serious again. "Tyler Carter, I'm so in love with you. Please don't take advantage of my love. Loving you doesn't make me stupid or weak, so don't take my love for a weakness. Loving you gives me so much life. Ever since you came into my life, you been making me feel like I can fly. I feel like a superhero whenever I'm next to you. I'm so in love with you," she smiled again. "How can I not be?

"You are the smartest man I ever met. You are very talented, funny, considerate, unselfish. You swaggy as fuck, you're a leader, a momma's boy, a great dad, and the list may never stop because you show me more and more every day. It's so many layers to you, Ty, plus you cute or whatever," she laughed.

"Princess, I ain't meet you by no mistake. Destiny brought us together. You are really my soulmate. It's so real that you don't even have to change your last name. You are already a Carter," he chuckled.

"You swear you so smooth," she blushed. "On the real tho, it's time you meet my dad, Ty. I will arrange it when we get back. I'mma go take a bubble bath."

"Can I wash you up?"

"That's a dub, baby boy. You are still in the doghouse," she replied while getting up from the bed.

"Damn, I can't get none for my birthday?"

"Your birthday is over. Look at the clock. It's past twelve," were her last words before heading to take her bath.

Lust Gentlemen's Club Brooklyn, New York

The place was packed; there was barely any room to stand. Shoota, Heat, Santana, Wopo, and two other members of the UGF stepped in the spot, looking like money. Bottle girls and strippers were on them the minute they walked in.

The group of men were led to the V.I.P. where bottles of Ace were delivered to them with sparkles. Shoota scanned the club and smiled at the sight of all the beautiful women in attendance. Not only were the strippers and bottle girls looking good, but the female patrons in the building, who were standing around, making it rain on the dancers, were looking even better. These days, the females played the strip clubs just as much as men.

Santana handpicked a few dancers to join them in V.I.P. to get their party started. Shoota stopped one of the bottle girls. "Yo, shawdy, take this hundo." He handed her a hundred-dollar bill. "You see them four baddies over there?" He pointed to a group of females making it rain on some dancers. The bottle girl nodded her head. "Tell them to come join me and my niggas. Bring them a bottle of Ace also," he said, handing her the rest of the hundred-dollar bills in his hand.

"I gotchu, cutie," the bottle girl promised before walking off.

The fellas were turning up with the dancers that were in their section. Shoota was too busy watching the females he sent the bottle to to have any real fun. "Yo, Shoota, here." Wopo reached out and passed him a blunt. Just as Shoota took a pull, the ladies he sent the bottle to approached the V.I.P. section. They were all dressed in designer from head to toe with jewelry that you would usually see on men. The Cuban links and bust down Rolexes only added to their swag.

"What's the vibes? Y'all sending invites and shit. I hope y'all worth the company because we don't fuck with lames," said the leader of the female pack. She was the one who Shoota had been eyeing. The chick stood about five foot four inches, and she had a dark brown skin tone. Home girl was slim but very curvy. The soft denim Fendi pantsuit that she was rocking hugged her petite frame perfectly. She sported no shirt under the soft denim jacket, just a Fendi bikini top. Tonight, she was showing off her flat tummy and belly ring. The short haircut she was rocking gave her the swagger of Detroit rapper, Dej Loaf. This chick was most definitely Shoota's speed. "I sent the invite, love, and it definitely ain't no lames over here," Shoota said smoothly. "I just figured you ladies wanted to be in the presence of some real niggas," he smiled.

"What claims to be real is almost always fake," the Dej Loaf lookalike replied slyly.

"That was real cute," Shoota chuckled. "Get to know a nigga and find out if I'm faking. My name is Shoota by the way." He extended his hand. The chick accepted his handshake.

"Lanie," she introduced herself.

"Ya home girls are already having fun with the guys. You should sit ya fine ass down and get comfortable. You with me now." His words bled arrogance, but truth was, he was just confident.

"Cocky, are we?"

"Baby girl, there is a fine line between cocky and confident. You smoke or nah?"

"Nah, I sip a little bit tho."

THIRTY-FIVE MINUTES Later

Santana had his eyes glued on the other side of the club. He was watching Premo, a former UGF shot caller, who was currently making it rain on two of the dancers. Many members of the family wanted him dead, but nobody wanted him out the way as badly as Santana. "Yo, Shoota!" Santana called out.

"What's the vibes, ape?" Shoota replied.

"There go that nigga, Premo, over there," he informed his comrade. Shoota looked over and saw Premo looking like he was having the time of his life.

"Say less. We gon lay on that nigga, bro. He's outta here tonight," Shoota promised.

The commotion on the other side of the club snatched their attention. Premo's crew and another group of men were exchanging words. Out of nowhere, Premo smashed a bottle on some guy's head, and all hell broke loose.

Shoota tapped Heat and signaled for him and the rest of the crew to follow him. They made it out of the club, along with their new lady friends, without incident. "What y'all doing? We going out to breakfast?" one of the females asked.

"IHOP on Church?" Lanie suggested.

"Yeah, we can do that. Where y'all parked at?" Shoota asked.

"Right down the block," Lanie replied.

"Perfect cause we parked over there too."

The fellas let the ladies walk in front of them, so they could chop it up in private. They wanted to come up with a plan to kill Premo and still go to breakfast with the ladies. "Premo is out of here tonight, no matter what. So, how we doing this?" Santana was first to speak.

"I'mma go with you, and the bros gonna follow the hoes to IHOP. We gon be right behind y'all," Shoota said.

"You sure?" Heat asked. Deep down inside, he really wanted to go on the mission also, but he didn't debate with his comrades.

"Positive. That way if anything goes wrong, we have an alibi. Here, take my keys." Shoota handed Heat his car keys, and he and Santana walked across the street to Santana's Benz.

Minutes later, the females pulled off, and Heat followed them. Shoota and Santana were circling the block, looking for Premo's car. "That's his shit right there." Shoota pointed out the Audi A8. "That's definitely his cause I can see them niggas walking down the block right now. How you wanna do this, gang?" he added.

"Don't matter to me. We can wait until he gets in his car and box him in, or we can jump out now. Boy can't outrun thirty shots," Santana laughed while pulling his Sig Sauer with a ladder (thirty shot clip) from under the seat. He then pulled out a 9mm, also with a ladder attached to it, and handed it to Shoota.

"This shit nice, ape." Shoota admired the chrome 9mm.

"That's Wopo's shit. It's brand new too."

"Not after this movie we are about to make. These niggas getting closer. Let's bump this nigga, bro."

"Here, put this on." Santana handed him a King Kong

mask while sliding another one on his face. Both men hopped out of the Benz and crept toward Premo's Audi.

Premo was opening the driver's side door of his A8. He'd had way too much to drink tonight, so he was moving very slowly. He looked up and saw two masked gunman holding handguns with extended clips hanging out of them. "Yo, it's a hit!" he yelled out to his crew, but it was already too late. Both gunmen started letting off. *BOC! BOC! BOC!*

The impact from the shells sent Premo crashing into the Audi. Another series of shots went off, and more bullets ate through his flesh, knocking him down. Both gunmen stood over him and fired until he was lifeless.

CHAPTER 28

It was a beautiful Tuesday afternoon. Flee had just walked inside of his apartment. "Yo, Fresh!" he called out. Fresh didn't respond, but the running shower water indicated that she was here. Flee dropped his bags and headed to the kitchen to grab a bottle of water from the refrigerator. He then walked to his bedroom.

Once inside of his room, he kicked his sneakers off and took a seat on his bed. He rolled and sparked a blunt. The minute the blunt was lit, Fresh walked out of the bathroom, wrapped in a towel. "I came out right in time. Pass that splif, bro," she said with a smile. Flee passed her the blunt. "How was ya trip? I see Peso's fine ass get down on one knee and propose in front of the whole world."

"Yeah, bro ready to tie the knot. It's crazy because I always thought he would be the last one to ever get married. Peso ain't never been no one woman type of man, but Princess is the one for him tho. She makes him a better man. The trip was cool tho. I had a lil fun," he said while reaching out to get the blunt back from Fresh, who plopped down on his king-sized mattress. "Come on, sis. You getting my bed all wet and shit," he complained.

"Trust me, you haven't seen wet," Fresh replied boldly. Flee heard what she said loud and clear but didn't even respond to the comment. He thought she was trying to test him. He instantly changed the subject.

"Wassup, you haven't heard form Lexi?" he asked.

"Nope, and I really don't care to hear from her. She put a nigga before me, something we both promised each other that we would never do. She got that dusty ass nigga controlling her. That's my sister, and I love her, but I can't fuck with her no more," she claimed.

Flee just shook his head. Lexi going ghost had hurt both of them. He could see the sadness in her eyes. Fresh and Flee locked eyes with each other. "Let me take your mind off of her. Let me help you stop thinking about her." She took the blunt away from Flee and placed it in the ashtray. She then stood up in front of him and let her towel fall to the floor.

Fresh looked just like her sister in the face, but she had Lexi beat in the body department, hands down. Fresh was thick as fuck —perfect sized breasts, flat tummy, and a whole lot of ass. The tattoos all over her body made her look even sexier. She straddled Flee and kissed his lips. "Fresh, we buggin. This ain't right." He put up his weakest protest.

"Sshhh." She kissed his lips again. "She betrayed us, Flee. Just fuck me one time pleeeeassse," she begged.

MEANWHILE IN QUEENS

"Come on, Flee. Please pick up," Lexi mumbled to herself as she listened to the phone ring out. When his voicemail picked up for the third straight time, Lexi began to cry.

At the current moment, Lexi was being held hostage in someone's basement. It turned out that her son's father didn't really come home on an appeal. He lied to her. Truth was, he testified in someone's trial to get a time reduction from the Feds. His actions had led to his baby momma and son being tied up. The dudes couldn't catch Swift, so they settled for Lexi and little Manny. They felt that grabbing them up would bring Swift out of hiding. "Let me guess, that nigga ain't pick up, right?" one of the kidnappers asked.

He was the leader of the two men who'd grabbed her and Manny. His name was Hood, and he was a well-known gunslinger throughout the Brooklyn streets. "I been stopped calling Swift. That was someone else," Lexi admitted. "Hood, I can get you the money, just let me go. I don't have anything to do with the shit Swift got going on. I'm not even with that nigga. I ain't know nothing about him snitching or running off with ya work. He told me he came home on an appeal."

"Home on an appeal?" Hood laughed as if Lexi had just said a Kevin Hart joke. "Man, that nigga was a star witness on my brother trial. Here, read this." He handed her a stack of papers. "Those are the trial transcripts. His testimony starts on page six. That nigga deaded me on some bricks then got locked up for some shit and told on my brother. Now, the nigga riding around Brooklyn in a Bentley like shit sweet. Call that nigga again. I'm starting to get impatient. Don't call nobody else. Call him!" he said sternly.

Lexi tried to call Swift one more time, and surprisingly, this time, he answered. "Yo, I'm busy right now, Lexi," Swift said into the phone.

"Nigga, stop whatever you doing and come get me and Manny. Hood kidnapped us. He wants the money you owe him plus fifty bands on top of that. Or he's going to kill us," she cried.

"Hood ain't gon kill shit. That nigga is a bitch. Where you at, Lexi?"

"I don't know. I'm in somebody's basement. Just give him the money, Swift."

"Bitch, I ain't giving him shit. You better call that pretty boy nigga you was fucking with while I was locked up. I don't give a fuck about ya thot ass," he laughed in her ear. This situation was comical to Swift. He really thought this was funny; he was entertained by all of this.

"Don't do it for me, do it for your son," she cried harder.

"Don't cry, Lexi. I'mma murder that pussy nigga for touching my son, but I ain't paying no hunnit racks ($100,000). I can always make another son. You and that little bastard can rest in peace. Now stop calling me. I got shit to do." He ended the call.

Lexi sadly looked up at Hood. The call was on speaker, so he heard it all. Truth was, right in this moment, he felt bad for her and her son, but he had come way too far to turn back. He did not snatch her up and risk his freedom to come up empty-handed. "That's one foul nigga. I feel for you, shawdy. I really do. But I want my money. You better call whoever you gotta call. Time is no longer on your side."

CONEY ISLAND

Shoota and Caine were cruising with no set destination. Last night, Caine was released on $150,000 bail. He was just happy to be free. "Yo, good looking for coming to get me, gang." He thanked Shoota for what seemed like the hundredth time.

"Bro, you don't gotta keep thanking me. We family, bro. I know you would have did the same for me. What they was talking about tho?" Shoota replied.

"That nigga, Poe, ain't die," Caine said while shaking his head in disappointment. "I thought I parked that nigga. I gotta get his ass before he tries to take the stand on me."

"You think the nigga telling?"

"He has to be, bro, cause how else would the boys know to grab me?"

"Only time will tell. Shit gonna be alright tho. Crazy thing is, the nigga, Prince, pulled through too. He got hit the same day as Poe. Word is the old nigga dropped a bag on Flee. The war is on. The torch is lit, so we all gotta stay on point," Shoota said. "We gon pull up on Flee in a minute. Let's go get some eats real quick," he added while pulling up in front of Golden Crust.

The place wasn't at all crowded when they entered, so they headed straight to the counter. "Can I get a small order of oxtails, rice, and peas?" Shoota ordered then turned to Caine. "What you eating, bro?" he asked.

"Just get me an order of jerk chicken. I'mma step out and smoke a cig real quick," Caine replied while walking back out of the restaurant.

Seven minutes later, Shoota exited the Golden Crust. "Yo, let's go get a bottle real quick. That couple of days in the system got a nigga ready to get drunk," Caine said to Shoota and led the way across the street to the liquor store.

As the two of them entered the liquor store, Goon was paying for his bottle. Goon was an old head who rolled with Prince. He ice grilled both of them as he exited. "We ain't with the face fighting, old head. That's the type of shit that'll get you knocked out." Caine stepped toward him.

"What, lil nigga? I will smack the shit out of ya lil ass," Goon threatened.

"You wouldn't slap ass in a strip club, nigga. You bluffing. I ain't with the talking, my nigga," Caine replied and threw a quick right hook that Goon never saw coming. Shoota quickly followed up with a few punches of his own.

Goon was a big dude. He stood about six foot two and weighed at least two hundred forty pounds solid. He was trying his best to intimidate the young men, but as he could now see, these young niggas weren't easily intimidated.

SEA-RISE APARTMENT COMPLEX

The sound of Flee's phone vibrating woke him up. He looked over to Fresh, who was sleeping peacefully, and shook his head. The two of them had crossed the line. What they'd just done, neither of them could take back. He blamed Lexi for all of this. Had she not just up and left, none of this would have happened.

He grabbed his phone and looked at the screen. He didn't know this number, but he picked up anyway. "Yo, who this?" he answered.

"Flee, it's Lexi. Please don't hang up. I need you right now," she cried.

"You need me?" Flee chuckled. "Bitch, you trippin. You left me for another nigga; now, you talking about you need me."

"Flee, just hear me out please," she begged. "Me and Manny got kidnapped. These guys want a h…" Before she could finish her sentence, the phone was snatched from her hand.

"Yo, listen up," a male voice said from the other end of

the phone. "I need a hunnit bands ($100,000) in the next hour, or her and this lil nigga is dead," the man said.

"What type of games y'all playing?"

"Games?" the man chuckled. "This ain't no game, homie. Do I have to let my lil homies gangbang this lil pretty bitch in front of her son to show you that this ain't no game?"

"Hold on, fam, you don't even gotta do all that. I got the money. Where do you want me to bring it to? Just don't hurt them."

"Now we talking. Gateway Mall in two hours. Don't be late and don't call no police."

"You don't gotta worry about no police. I'm a street nigga."

"Pussy, I ain't tryna hear none of that shit. Like I said, you got two hours," the man said and ended the call.

BACK DOWN THE Ave

Shoota and Caine had been jumping Goon for the past five minutes. He'd been fighting like the beast that he was, but he was no match for these two young men.

Today was a beautiful summer day, so Mermaid Avenue was packed. Some bystanders watched while others recorded. They were beating the shit out of Goon, but he would not let up. The fight started inside of the liquor store; now, they were in the middle of the street, holding up traffic. Cars and dollar cabs honked their horns.

Goon was now out of breath, throwing lazy punches. He threw one at Shoota, who ducked, scooped him below the knee, and body slammed him on his back. He and Caine were now stomping him out. A few dudes, who worked in the nearby barbershop, ran out and pulled the two young men off of Goon.

CHAPTER 29

Gateway Mall, Brooklyn

It was now pouring down raining. Flee pulled into the parking lot of the outdoor mall with Fresh in the passenger's seat. His vibrating phone caught his attention, and he instantly answered the call. "I'm here in front of Target," he said.

"Cool. Now go inside and walk to the electronic department. My lil man gon be there with the little boy. You give him the money, and he will give you the boy. Once I see you ain't on no funny shit, you can get the bitch back. Deal?" said the caller.

"Yeah, man, whatever you say." Flee exited his car and walked inside of Target. He headed straight to the electronic department. He spotted Manny holding the hand of a teenage boy. Manny noticed him and screamed. "Flee!" he yelled out with a smile.

"Wassup, lil soldier, you okay?" Flee asked while hugging him. He quickly scanned Manny's body for any bruises. Once he saw that Manny was alright, he handed the teenage boy the shopping bag. "It's all there," he claimed.

"Go to the black Altima in the parking lot," the teen said and quickly walked off.

Flee picked Manny up and quickly walked out of the Target. He dropped Manny to Fresh, who was still sitting in the car, and quickly scanned the lot for the black Altima. He located it and ran over to it instantly. He looked in the car and didn't see Lexi. Just when he was ready to give up, his phone rang. He picked up instantly. "Don't give up so easy, champ. Ya bitch is in the trunk," the man said. Flee hung up instantly and ran back to the car. He popped the trunk and found Lexi curled up, wearing nothing but a bra and panties, while holding a stack of papers.

MEANWHILE

Peso and Princess cruised the New York streets in Peso's milky white Rolls Royce Wraith. They finished up their photoshoot for *GQ* magazine. Together, they would bless the cover and share an eight-page layout and interview. "Queen, you gonna be my date tonight for Swagger B's album release party?" Peso, who was driving, turned to Princess, who he caught lowkey recording him. He couldn't help but smile at his lady, who was madly in love with him. "Why you sneaky recording me, creep?" he teased while playfully blocking his face with his hand.

"Don't try to hide now, Daddy. The whole world already know you mine." Princess flashed her huge engagement ring into the camera for her six million Instagram followers to see. "Of course I'll be your date tonight, but you have to let me be your stylist for the event. Can I dress you tonight, Daddy?" she asked.

"My love, I will do anything to have you on my arm," he answered with a smile.

"Y'all heard it here first. I will be his stylist tonight for Swagger B's album release party." She smiled into the camera before ending the Instagram live video. Peso's iPhone rang.

"P, get that for me," he said to Princess.

"It's Hitta FaceTiming you," she replied while answering the call. Hitta's face instantly popped up on the screen.

"Wassup, sis? Where my boy at?" Hitta greeted her. Princess put the camera on Peso, so Hitta could see that he was driving.

"Gorilla Stack 62!" Peso saluted while keeping his eyes on the road.

"No keys, push to start!" Hitta replied. "I know you driving, so I'mma be quick. Timah just hit me. She wants us to link her asap. She says it's imperative. Miss Grace having a cookout in Kaiser. We can pull up there if you want."

"Bet. I'll see you there," Peso replied.

TWENTY-THREE MINUTES Later

Peso pulled his Wraith up alongside Kaiser Park. He quickly hopped out and walked over to the passenger's side and opened the door for Princess. He took her by the hand and helped her exit. All eyes were on the two of them as they walked through the park hand in hand. People instantly began running up to Peso, asking for pictures.

After pleasing the people, the couple walked over to the cookout Miss Grace was having. Miss Grace, who was Timah's mom, stood behind the grill, doing her thing. As always, she was the life of the party. Peso and Princess walked toward her. The second she noticed Peso, a huge smile was plastered on her face. "Oh, my Lord, if it isn't my super-star." Miss Grace happily greeted him with a hug and a kiss on his cheek.

"Hey, Auntie Grace. How you been?" Peso was all smiles. He really loved this woman. She had always been good to him.

"I'm fine, baby. Now introduce me to the beautiful young lady who got the ring. She is a lucky girl."

"Nah, Auntie Grace, I'm the lucky one," he replied humbly. "But this is my fiancée, Princess."

"How are you, beautiful?" Miss Grace hugged Princess. "You must be a bad girl, getting this little horny ass nigga to put a ring on it," she laughed at her own joke. "Tyler was a straight up horn dog," she teased. "I'm happy he found his better half. You are a beautiful woman," she added.

"Thank you," Princess blushed.

"Y'all hungry?" Miss Grace asked.

"Yes, we are," Peso smiled. "You know I came for a plate. Where's Timah?"

"I sent her to the store a little while ago. She should be back any minute. Let me make these plates for y'all."

Minutes Later

Hitta pulled up to Kaiser Park just as Timah was exiting her car. He hopped out of his Ferrari and walked over to her. He quickly took the bags from her hands. "Still a gentleman," Timah said with a smile.

"You know I don't change much." Hitta led the way inside of the park to the cookout. He walked straight over to Miss Grace and gave her a bear hug. "Auntie Grace, how are you?"

"I'm fine, handsome. It's so good to see you. I hope you are staying out of trouble," she replied.

"Of course I am," Hitta smiled.

"Your partner in crime is sitting over there on the bench with his lady. When are you gonna settle down? You still with Ashley?"

"Yeah, me and her still holding on tight. I ain't ready to jump the broom yet," he claimed.

"What the hell are you waiting for? You don't find women like Ashley every day."

"Mommy, I have to break up this little reunion real quick. Amir and I have something important to discuss." Timah grabbed Hitta by the arm and led the way to where Peso and Princess were sitting. Peso introduced Princess to Timah. The two of them shared a hug, and Timah got straight to the point. "Can I speak in front of her?"

"For sure." Peso nodded approvingly.

"You two have been my friends since forever. I love you two like I love my own brother. We family," she said sincerely. "Matt is alive. That's why I asked y'all to meet with me," she admitted. "Don't talk, just hear me out, y'all, please. Amir, you shot Matt, then Matt shot you, and a whole war started. This war has innocent people stuck in the middle. Tyler got shot, and I got kidnapped and damn near tortured. Does an innocent person need to die for this shit to stop?" She looked both of them in the eyes before she continued. "The day Detective Brown was murdered, Matt told me that he was meeting up with y'all, so when he almost didn't make it home to me, I knew one of you guys shot him. It was probably you, Peso. I say that because you looked more disappointed when I said he survived. You always did wear your emotions on ya sleeve," she weakly chuckled. "I am not here to judge either of you. I love you both, and I love my husband. Y'all were all best friends. Rico has to be turning over in his grave right now, watching you guys tryna kill each other." Timah now had tears falling from her eyes. "Matt has partial memory loss from being in a coma. He doesn't remember the beef that you guys had. This beef needs to stop. I'm begging you guys."

Both Hitta and Peso knew that Timah wouldn't play foul, but something still didn't seem right to them. "Amir, you woke Matt up from his coma," Timah claimed.

"How the hell did I do that?" Hitta asked, confused.

"That day you came to Jamie's mansion to speak with him and Peto is the day that Matt woke up. Exactly two minutes after you left, he came out of the coma. It was like he felt your presence. Ever since he's been awake, all he does is ask about y'all. His exact words were, 'Why Hitta and Peso ain't come check me yet? They mad at me or something?' He misses y'all. This can be a fresh start for all of us to leave the past in the past. I could have died the night Shoota, Heat, and that little crazy one kidnapped me after Peso got shot. Please dead this for me, Rico, and Relo," she begged.

"I don't know, Timah," Peso finally spoke. Timah ignored him and turned to Hitta.

"Amir, this is your beef. Tyler is involved because of his loyalty to you. This nigga just won five Grammy awards and is about to get married. It's time for y'all to really live. Don't let the streets claim y'all. Amir, remember when we were ten years old, and you told me that you would do anything to protect me?"

Hitta just nodded as a tear fell freely down his cheek. He loved Timah like his sister and to know how much she had been through behind his beef with Matt Murda really hurt him.

"I never known you to go back on your word. By ending this war with Matt, you are protecting me because I will die for Matt, so any day I can get hit in the crossfire. You ain't just saving me. You are saving Tyler, who is ya best friend. God knows he riding with you to the wheels fall off. Set him free, set us free."

"Sis, don't make me regret this," Hitta said reluctantly.

"I promise you won't, Amir. You and Ty are like brothers to me. Y'all always protected me since we were kids. I just want to bring our family back together, no more bloodshed. There goes his car right there." She motioned toward the blood red Maserati Ghibli that was parked in back of Peso's Rolls Royce. "I'mma go get him," Timah said before walking off.

Peso looked to Hitta, who seemed to be in deep thought. "You sure about this?" he asked. Peso knew Hitta wasn't the type to dead a beef. He left no score unsettled. He'd been this way since a teenager.

"Yeah, bro. To be honest with you, I been wanted to end this, but then you got shot. Timah is right tho. Let's just call it even and leave this shit in the past. Rico and Relo can't be happy with none of us right now," Hitta replied.

About five minutes later, Timah returned with Matt Murda on her arm. He had a huge Kool-Aid smile on his face as he locked eyes with his two old friends. Matt Murda grabbed Hitta and bear hugged him then did the same to Peso. "My fuckin brother. What's poppin? I don't know what I did to have y'all moving the way y'all been moving, but I apologize." This was something Matt Murda never did. His arrogance kept him from giving someone a simple apology when he was wrong, even if it was the people he loved. The only one he gave that satisfaction to was his wife, Timah, but today, he was giving it to his guys. "We all know if one of y'all was in a coma, I would have been there when y'all woke up. You niggas ain't even pull up on me since I been back," he said sadly, looking at two of his closest friends. "The Murda man is back," he added with a goofy smile.

"A lot has changed since you been in that coma, big bro. Niggas done leveled up crazy. I was touring. Truthfully, I'm just finding out about you being in a coma," Peso told him, which wasn't really a lie. Truth was, Peso thought he was dead, but he would never admit that now that the family was back together. "I'm happy to have you back tho, gangsta."

"Most definitely," Hitta chimed in.

"Trust and believe, I'm happy to be back. Peso, I'm proud of you. That's on my gangsta. Everything you ever said you was gonna do, you did it. Like you really won Grammys and everything, shit," Matt Murda said with a smile.

Peso introduced Matt Murda to Princess before Timah pulled her away, so the old friends could catch up.

CHAPTER 30

Lucci's funeral was packed. Everyone had come out to say their farewells to the little homie. You had people there from all walks of life. You had teachers, cops, gangbangers, drug dealers, scammers, young ladies, older ladies, the list went on. Lucci was someone who everybody loved.

The funeral home was so overcrowded that some people had to stand outside. Sadness filled the air. There wasn't a dry face in attendance, and everyone had teary eyes.

Reem hated funerals, but he couldn't let Lucci be sent home without paying his respects. His legs felt heavy as he slowly walked down the aisle to view Lucci's body. When he finally made it up to the casket, he sadly looked down. "I'm so sorry, lil homie," he whispered. "That was supposed to be me that day. I stood on business and knocked Doggy off," he added.

Lucci was being sent away in style. A white Tom Ford suit fit his body perfectly. The red tie matched the red and white Tom Ford shoes on his feet. On his wrist sat Reem's eighteen karat gold Rolex with the red face. The casket was pearl white with gold trimming. All of this was paid for by Reem. "I wish I never let you drive that day. I swear I wish I could have told you no, but the smile on ya face was priceless when I told you to hop in the driver's seat. I put in pain behind losing you, baby bro, so you can finally rest in peace." Reem took off his matching Cuban link chain and bracelet. "You always said you wanted my Cuban," he smiled weakly and placed them both in the casket. He bent down and kissed Lucci's forehead. "Goodbye, lil homie. I love you," were his final words.

MEANWHILE IN SEA-RISE Apartment Complex

It had been exactly two days since Flee and Fresh paid Lexi's ransom. Flee hadn't been home since. He was still a little crushed from her leaving him, so he didn't want to face her. He wouldn't even be in his apartment right now if he didn't need to be there. He'd just finished picking up a bunch of money from his workers, and he had to separate Hitta's cut from his own. Hitta would be meeting him there in less than an hour.

Flee greeted Fresh and Manny before heading to his bedroom. He didn't even acknowledge Lexi. He stepped inside of his room and closed the door behind him. Minutes later, there was a light knock at the door. "It's open." He turned around to see Lexi walking in.

"Flee, can we talk?" she asked.

"I thought you only spoke in letter," he replied dryly. "But speak ya peace tho," he added.

Lexi walked to the closet and grabbed a medium sized brown bag from Bloomingdales. "This is the money you put up to get me and my son back. Thank you for coming for me." She sat the bag at his feet.

"Good looking," he said without even looking up at her.

"Why are you being so dry with me? I'm trying to talk like adults."

"Leaving a note wasn't no adult shit, Lex. I think it's a lil too late for whatever you tryna do."

"Flee, I didn't have a choice," she claimed.

"Every day we wake up, we have a choice. You chose to go back to ya son's father."

"Manny's dad blackmailed me. I never wanted to leave with that nigga. I would never just up and leave Fresh. That nigga knows my biggest secret and was using it against me. I killed Swift's uncle because he tried to rob and rape me. He helped me get rid of the body, but I'm the one who shot him," she admitted.

"That's no excuse, Lex. You should have told me, and we could have handled the situation accordingly. You decided to keep that shit from me. So, like I said, you made your choice. We don't really have anything to rap about. All you had to do was talk to me, Ma," he said sadly.

"I know I fucked up, Flee, but I was afraid. I thought I was doing the right thing. I thought I was protecting you by leaving you out of it. I'm so sorry. I will never keep anything from you ever again. You have my word. I promise no more secrets, Papi. Please forgive me because I already forgave you."

"Forgave me for what?" he asked, confused.

"For having sex with my sister. Fresh would never keep anything from me. She already told me everything. I understand tho, so can we put all of this shit behind us?"

Flee just shook his head. He couldn't believe that Fresh had told on them, but he admired the loyalty.

"Yeah, we can," he submitted.

Hitta rang the doorbell to Flee's apartment. Fresh got up and answered the door. "How can I help you?" she asked in a feisty tone.

"You can help me by moving out the way." He squeezed past her and entered the apartment. "Yo, Flee!" Hitta called out.

"Damn, this nigga fine," Fresh mumbled to herself as she eyed Hitta.

"Nigga, pull up. Since when you move like a stranger in my crib?" Flee entered the living room.

"Ever since you got security." He looked to Fresh.

"I ain't no security, nigga," Fresh yelled out playfully.

The two of them entered Flee's bedroom. "Lex, let me holla at bro real quick," he dismissed her. Once she stepped out, Flee closed the door. "Damn, nigga, you got two bitches now? I see you learned a thing or two from ya boy," Hitta teased.

"Nah, big homie. That's my lady and her little sister. They heavy in that scamming loop. You still be getting the credit card info?"

"Yeah, my white boy just gave me mad new shit. You wanna pass it to them?"

"Yeah, we should. They gonna do the right thing with it. My bitch and her team is on point with that shit. Let's get down to business tho," Flee said while going under his bed and pulling out a Gucci suitcase. He unzipped it, and Hitta smiled in approval when he saw all the rubber band stacks of hundred-dollar bills. "That's $570,000 for the last three thousand bricks I had left. A nigga did good numbers off those last ones." Flee smiled while rubbing his hands together.

"Nigga, you always do good numbers," Hitta replied.

"Indeed, I do. You know me, bro. I just be tryna get rid of

that shit super quick. I was hitting a lot of people at $250 a brick. That last three thousand tho, I hit the ground," he chuckled. "I moved one thousand of them at $250 a pop, another thousand at $275, and the last thousand, I moved them for $300 a pop. I made $255,000, all profit. I know you be frontin a nigga the motherload, but I'm tryna put some cheese up with you to throw something on top of what you already fronting me. How that sound?" he asked.

Hitta looked at his protégé and smiled. He was truly proud of what he and Peso had molded Flee to become. Flee had been around them since he was eight years old and had been soaking game up ever since they all chose the streets. "That sounds like a plan. You a boss, and you wanna make boss moves. Ain't nothing wrong with that. From now on, I'mma give you bricks at $120 a pop."

"Say less. I'mma put $100,000 on top of this $255,000 I got right here."

"Bet. Just hold the bread for me. Tonight, we gon turn up. You coming with me and Peso to Swagger B's album release party. We gon take care of this money first thing in the morning. Today is our day off. Get fresh and I'mma come scoop you in a few hours."

CHAPTER 31

Peso stepped inside of The 40/40 Club. He was looking clean as always. As promised, he allowed Princess to be his stylist for the event. He was sporting a sky-blue Chanel vest, which had four big, square pockets, two on each side. The pockets were each a different color. The top two were pink and yellow, while the bottom two were white and sky blue. His ripped white jeans were Amiri denim. A yellow Chanel belt held them up. The colorful Chanel scarf tied around his head matched his vest and colorful, high-top, suede Chanel sneakers. Several Cuban links and gold rope chains hung from his neck, iced-out pinky rings were on each hand, and a bust down Rolex SkyDweller was on his left wrist.

Princess was on his arm, looking like eye candy. The colorful Chanel bodysuit fit her body like a glove. She rocked the same colors as Peso. Her oversized Chanel shades and huge Chanel bag gave her the look of a basketball wife, but Presidential Peso didn't dribble a ball.

The two of them elegantly strutted through the crowded club and headed straight for the V.I.P. section where Swagger

B sat with his entourage. His new hit single, *Bustdown*, which featured Peso, bled through the speakers. Swagger B shook Princess' hand and greeted Peso with a brotherly embrace. "What's poppin, my guy? I'm glad you showed up. Where's Hitta and the guys at?" he said, all smiles.

"You already know how we rock. I wouldn't have missed this. Hitta and the guys are on the way tho," Peso replied.

"Tell me you gon fuck the stage up with me tonight."

"We both know a function ain't a function if we don't burn down the stage together."

Peso took a seat, and Princess sat next to him. Everyone came out to show Swagger B some love —_rappers, super-models, Instagram models, actors, athletes. Everybody who was somebody was there. Just when Peso popped a bottle of Ace, Kat and Roxy Royal entered the V.I.P. section.

ONE HOUR Later

Hitta, Flee, and Santana entered the club just as Swagger B was performing his new hit single that featured Peso. The crowd went crazy as Peso stepped on the stage, spitting his verse.

"I jumped off a jet when I touched down/ already got a Rollie that's a bust down/ a hunnit bands for the Cuban just to bust it down/ niggas screw facing every time I come around/ risked my life for these jewels/ I'll die for 'em/ lost some homies, man, I wished I could of died with 'em/ real nigga so you know I had to ride for 'em/ money never been a thing so the drop's foreign/ youngin I do this, I'm ballin, I'm fly/ had fire work like the Fourth of July/ for times in jail when I wanted to die/ now I'm touching these bands and I feel so alive/ ball til I fall ball til I drop/ ball til my daughter straight cop me a yacht/ ball with my niggas who came from that block/ now we all see the jeweler to bust down them clocks."

The people in attendance all rapped along as Peso flowed.

After Swagger B and Peso's performance, Hitta and the guys walked over to the V.I.P. section. Swagger B greeted Hitta with a brotherly embrace. Then, he greeted Flee and Santana both with a pound and one arm hug. Hitta took a seat next to Peso and Princess. "Where is Ashley?" Princess asked. She and Ashley had become good friends since she'd been with Peso.

"She in Cali with Nautica for a movie shoot," Hitta said. His attention was stolen by someone on the other side of the club. He and the person locked eyes. "Pardon me. I'll be right back." Hitta got up from his seat and headed toward the restroom.

"Wassup, bro, everything good?" Peso asked.

"Yeah, everything is healthy. I just got some unfinished business to take care of," Hitta replied before walking off.

Hitta walked inside of the ladies' room and locked the door behind him. There stood Kat, looking beautiful as ever, in her open back, Prada mini dress. The two of them hadn't been face-to-face since Kat lied and told Rolex Rich that Hitta tried to date rape her. "I think you are in the wrong bathroom, Hitta," Kat smiled devilishly.

"Nah, I'm in the right spot," he replied while looking her up and down, admiring her beauty. Kat's beauty was intoxicating. She was like a drug, and Hitta was becoming weaker for her by the second.

"Why you lie on me, Kat?" He moved closer to her. He was close enough to kiss her. Instead, he quickly turned her around and bent her over the sink. As of now, Hitta owed Rolex Rich no loyalty, so he had every intention on fucking the shit out of Kat without regretting it. "We both know I ain't slip you no date rape drug to get this pussy," he said with the arrogance that Kat loved so much.

Kat turned back around to face Hitta. She looked him in the eyes before squatting down and unzipping his jeans. She pulled out his dick and stroked it up and down in her small hand, spitting on it before gladly slurping it into her mouth like a pro. Kat's mouth was so warm and wet that Hitta was ready to release his load already.

Hitta grabbed a handful of hair and started to slowly fuck her mouth. Not to be outdone, Kat started jerking, slurping, and sucking him harder. She looked up at Hitta. They locked eyes as she sucked him off, and it was driving him crazy. Kat deep throated him. "That dick taste good, don't it?" he asked.

"Yes, it does," she replied while popping his dick out of her mouth. She sucked and played with his balls for a few seconds before slurping his dick back into her mouth. She jerked him rapidly while sucking him. Hitta could feel himself about to explode and stopped her.

"Get up, Kat, and let me fill that pussy up." He pulled her up, turned her around, lifted her dress, slid her thong to the side, and in one swift motion, he entered her soaked and wet opening. Kat's pussy was so wet that her juices were dripping down her legs. Hitta gripped a handful of her hair and pounded her pussy from the back. "That's right, Hitta, kill this pussy!" she demanded.

Hitta had never felt a pussy so tight. Kat was throwing her ass back, matching his every stroke. "Fuck me harder, Daddy, please," she begged. Hitta pounded harder just like she asked.

"Damn."

"Daddy, this dick is so fucking good," she cried out as her body began to shake. Hitta continued to fuck her as she reached her first orgasm. "This my pussy now. You hear me?" he growled.

"Yes, Daddy, I hear you. This pussy is yours!"

BACK AT SWAGGER B's Album Release Party

Peso was sitting in VIP, having a good time, when Royalty Records artist, Bo-Money, approached him with Richie Rich by his side. "Presidential Peso, what's good, fam?" Bo-Money greeted him with a pound.

"Ain't shit. Talk about it," Peso replied.

"Wassup with me, you, and Richie doing a track? You know that feature is long overdue. We the hottest shit on the label, so it's only right."

"That ain't gon happen, Bo. I don't fuck with ya man. I'mma say this respectfully. Get boy from around me. I'm tryna enjoy my night with my family, and boy being so close is blowing mine. You got my number. You can hit me when you tryna work. Maybe me, you, and Swag could do something," Peso dismissed them.

"Pardon self. I ain't know," Bo-Money apologized before walking off. Richie Rich just cut his eyes at Peso as they exited the V.I.P. section.

"Aye, lil man," Peso called out to him. "Don't get yaself hurt tryna face fight. That fake gangsta shit you got going on ain't fooling nobody. I know you soft," Peso chuckled.

"What, nigga?" Richie Rich barked aggressively.

Both Flee and Santana stood up. "Chill, gang. We ain't gon disrespect Swag's function. Lil Richie ain't really tryna do nothing. Nigga salty cause he ain't have a hit since I been signed," Peso taunted.

"Peso, you might wanna slow ya roll before ya album gets pushed back," Richie shot back.

"Nah, pussy, you better slow ya roll before I buy into the label and demote you from that president spot. My money long enough to do it. Now burn it the fuck up before it gets ugly in here tonight."

Bo-Money grabbed Richie Rich by the arm. "Come on, homie. Let's go fuck with these hoes," he said, trying to lighten the mood.

Hitta returned just as they walked off. "Fuck that lil nigga wanted? An autograph?" he chuckled.

"Lil nigga was tryna get a feature. Fuck you been at tho?" Peso asked.

"I had to holla at Kat real quick."

Peso eyed his righthand man suspiciously. "You had to holla at Kat?"

"Long story, bro. We can kick it about that later tho. It's really kind of a long story, and I don't think this is the place for that, my brother," he answered with a smile. Peso just shook his head and smiled at Hitta's antics.

After several more drinks and pictures, Peso and the gang were all ready to go. Peso turned to Princess. "You tryna go to the strip club, my love?" he asked.

"Yeah, Daddy, let's go slap some ass," she smiled.

On the way out, Flee stopped to talk with Kayla, a beautiful R&B singer who was signed to Interscope records, and Peso stopped to holla at Swagger B. "Yo, beloved, we about to slide. I had a great time tho, my nigga."

"Good looking for poppin out for ya boy. What y'all about to get into tho? I know the night ain't over for y'all," Swagger B replied.

"We about to go fuck one of these strip clubs up. You and ya team should pop out."

"Which one y'all headed to?"

"Aces."

"Say less. I'll meet y'all there." Swagger B gave Peso some dap, and they departed ways.

MEANWHILE IN BROOKLYN

Shoota pulled up in front of a building in Crown Heights and double parked his Maserati. Music could be heard coming from the backyard, and the smell of barbequed food filled the air. Shoota grabbed his iPhone and placed a call. The caller picked up instantly. "Hey, you," she greeted.

"Wassup, love? I'm up front. Pop out," he said.

"Okay, I'm coming now," the caller replied and ended the call.

Minutes later, Lanie walked from the back of the building, looking sexy as hell. She still rocked the short Dej Loaf haircut that brought out her beautiful facial features. She was dripped in designer, just like she was on the first night Shoota met her. Today, Fendi was her designer of choice.

Shoota hopped out the driver's seat of his Maserati. He was no slouch himself. Today, he was rocking a white Givenchy fit and a fresh pair of Yeezys. A kilo worth of Cuban links bounced off of his chest. The two chains weighed five hundred grams apiece. One had an iced-out UGF pendant, and the other had an iced-out Jesus piece. On his left wrist was an eighteen-karat gold presidential Rolex.

He looked Lanie up and down. "Damn, you looking like a snack," he said with a smile. His comment caused her to blush.

"A snack?" She rolled her eyes playfully. "Nigga, I'm looking like the whole meal," she added while spinning around and giving him a look at everything. "Come on, let's go to the back." She took his hand and led the way to the backyard.

The backyard was crowded with people. Everyone seemed to be having a great time playing cards, dominoes, and dice, while other were dancing and kicking it. The weed could be smelled from blocks away. There was plenty of food and liquor for the guests. "Lanie, this ya boyfriend?" a cute woman, who appeared to be in her late thirties, asked when they entered the backyard.

"Nah, not yet, but he about to be," Lanie said boldly. She then turned to Shoota. "This is my Aunt Shay. Auntie Shay, this is my friend, Shoota," she introduced them.

Shoota reached out and shook her hand. "It's a pleasure to meet you," he said with respect.

"Likewise, are you hungry? We have plenty of food," she replied.

"Nah, I'm good for now, but before I leave, I will take a plate. Thank you."

Lanie took his hand, and they walked to a table where a few females were sitting. They were smoking, drinking, and making videos for Snapchat and Instagram. "Everybody, this is Shoota," Lanie said to her friends. Then, she looked to Shoota. "You already met Jazzy, Coco, and Star. These two beauties right here complete the crew. That's Lexi and Fresh."

"Wassup, ladies?" Shoota greeted the group of eye candy. They all greeted him with smiles.

"Where you from, light skin?" the one introduced as Fresh asked.

"I'm from Coney Island," Shoota answered.

"That's why you look so familiar. You Flee's man, right?"

"One hunnit percent. Where you know bro from?"

"That's my sister's little hunny."

"Hold up. You Presidential Peso's brother, right?" Lexi asked.

"Yeah, that's big bro," he chuckled. "Y'all over here tryna investigate me and shit. Where the roll up at? I'm tryna put some of this gas in the air."

CHAPTER 32

Same Night

Shoota was enjoying himself at the cookout. Lanie and her home girls were really good company. Lanie was sitting on Shoota's lap while her and her girls were gambling in a game of Spades. Shoota saw a familiar face over by the dice game. "Baby girl, get up for a second. I'll be right back," he leaned in and whispered in her ear.

"You tryna leave me? I already told you that you are mine for tonight, so don't go making plans," she whispered back at him. Lanie was a little tipsy, and she was feeling bold. "You giving me some dick tonight." She leaned in and kissed his neck.

"I'mma give you whatever you want tonight," he replied. "I ain't going nowhere, Ma. I see my old head over there by the dice game. I'm going to chop it up with him real quick," he added.

"Ya old head? Who you know over there?" Lanie screwed her face up.

"The old head, Block."

"Oh, that's my uncle. If you going to chop it up with him, then you valid. Where you know my uncle from tho?"

"You o'd nosy," Shoota laughed. "We was up top together tho. Now get up." He leaned in and kissed on her neck.

"Save that for later, Daddy," she replied and got up from his lap.

Shoota walked over to the dice game and approached Block. "What's the vibes, old head?" Shoota greeted him.

"Oh, shit. Shoota, what it is?" a surprised Block bear hugged him. He was really happy to see Shoota. The two of them had built quite a bond when they were on lock up together. "What you doing over here on these ends, man?" Block asked.

"My lady friend invited me. She told me that she's your niece."

"You must be talking about Lanie. Yeah, that's my baby girl right there. She's more like my daughter than my niece. You looking good tho, my nigga." He touched the chain on Shoota's neck. If this was anyone else, Shoota would feel disrespected, but Block was his people.

"This light right here, big bro. I know you over here tryna break these niggas' pockets, but I got something I need to holla at you about in private. Let's go talk in my car," Shoota suggested.

"Nigga, we don't gotta talk in no car. We can go in the crib. Pull up." Block led the way.

Minutes later, the two of them entered the apartment, and Block led the way to the living room. "Can I smoke in here?" Shoota asked.

"Hell yeah, nigga, light that shit," Block replied while walking to the kitchen. A minute later, he returned with a bottle of Hennessey and two cups. "Talk to me, baby boy," he said while taking a seat on the sofa. He poured both him and Shoota a cup.

"You still got a lane for that dog food (heroin)?"

"Yeah, that's always gon be my lane. I leave that scamming to y'all young niggas. I got a nice thing going outta town right now. Why? Wassup? You tryna get ya hands on something?"

Shoota lightly chuckled. "Nah, OG, I'm tryna put something in ya hands. Block, I got the best heroin around. It's a ten all over the land. Ain't no dope around fucking with mine, and my numbers are lovely," he claimed.

"You got the best heroin around?" Block asked in disbelief. "Miss me with that shit, nephew. Yo ass don't sell no dope. You fuck with those cards," he laughed.

"Nah, Unk, you got me fucked up." Shoota was laughing now also. "This is my lane. Have you ever heard of the Untouchable stamp?" he added.

"Yeah, that's the dope that's been slowing my money up," he admitted.

"Well, me and my niggas are the face behind that brand."

"People saying that's the best dope they had in about ten years. My shit is runner up behind that tho," Block claimed.

"Second place is the first loser, big bro. Come shop with ya boy. I'll take care of you." Shoota passed him the blunt.

"What you charging a gram?"

"I won't do you like that. This Untouchable shit is a brand, kinda like Pepsi. You can't buy it without the label," he smiled. "I sell them buy the bricks, but I have an unlimited supply."

"What's the tag on the bricks?" Block was trying his best to hide his excitement right now. Truth was, he was doing cartwheels on the inside. He had been trying to get his hands on this dope for the longest. Ever since the Untouchable stamp hit the market, Block's money had been slowing down. Even his out-of-town spots had been suffering because his competitors got their hands on this top-of-the-line heroin.

"I be charging $275 to $300 a brick, and shit be flying," Shoota claimed.

"Damn, that's expensive."

"This is expensive dope right here, big bro. I tell you what tho. Just give me $250 a brick, and I'll front you whatever you cop. How that sound?"

"Like music to my ears. I need five hundred bricks right now. I got cash on deck too. How soon can you get next to me?"

"Give me until tomorrow afternoon and I'll have everything ready for you. Just have the bread for the five hundred. Lock ya number in my phone," Shoota said while handing Block his iPhone.

Hours Later

After Swagger B's album release party, Peso, Princess, and the guys all hit up the strip club. Swagger B and his crew met them there, and they all had a blast. The time was now 4 a.m., and Peso was dropping Flee off at the crib. The Rolls Royce pulled into the parking lot of the complex. Flee stumbled out of the automobile. He was a little tipsy, but it was nothing too crazy. "You good, baby boy?" Peso asked.

"Bro drunk," Princess teased.

"Nah, I'm sturdy," Flee claimed. "Pass me my water," he added, knowing Princess was right. He really had too much to drink, but he held his liquor like a champ.

Peso handed him the bottle of water. Flee opened it and

quickly downed the whole bottle in one gulp. "Now I'm good. Y'all drive safe, big homie. UGF!" Flee tossed the bottle.

"Til my death," Peso saluted back. "Love you, my boy. Hit me in the a.m.," he added.

"Love you more, gang. Princess, later, sis."

"Later, Flee, be safe," she replied to Flee, who was already walking toward his building.

When Flee stepped off of the elevator, two plain clothed detectives rushed him with their guns brandished. One of them grabbed Flee and body slammed him. He quickly patted him down to make sure he wasn't carrying a weapon. These two men weren't regular detectives; both men were dirty cops who used to run with Detective Brown, the dirty cop who murdered Relo in cold blood. "Wassup with y'all niggas, man?" Flee shouted.

"Shut the fuck up!" Detective Green barked while pulling Flee up on his feet. The other detective, whose name was Taylor, went in Flee's pocket and pulled out his keys. He then tried to throw the handcuffs on Flee.

"Nah, you niggas ain't putting the cuffs on me. I know how y'all give it up already." Flee pushed Detective Taylor, and the other cop mushed his head into the wall. Out of pure reflex, Flee threw a punch that landed dead on his chin, knocking him down.

Detective Taylor smacked Flee with his gun repeatedly until he fell on the floor. Both detectives stomped on him before unlocking the door and dragging him into his apartment. Once inside, they closed and locked the door. Flee's face was covered in blood due to being pistol whipped. "Where the fuck is the money and dope at?" Taylor barked.

"I don't keep no money or dope here," Flee claimed.

SMACK! Detective Taylor smacked Flee in the face with

his gun again. "You think this shit is a game?" He grabbed Flee by the collar and pulled him back to his feet. "Don't make me tear up this nice little bachelor pad. Get me to it, Flee. We ain't come here to play games. You lucky we don't kill your little punk ass for what ya mans did to Brown." He turned to his partner. "Search the bedroom," he ordered.

Detective Green walked to the bedroom. The first thing he did was search the closet. After coming up emptyhanded, he looked under the bed. The two Gucci suitcases caught his eye. He quickly pulled them from under the bed one by one. He unzipped them, and a huge smile was plastered on his face when he saw that they were both filled with cash. There was a total of $825,000 there. That was the money that Flee had made from the last three thousand bricks of Untouchable that he had. $570,000 belonged to Hitta, and the other $255,000 was his.

Detective Green quickly zipped both suitcases up and rolled them into the living room. "Lying ass nigga talking about he don't keep nothing here. We done hit the jackpot. There wasn't no dope in there, but there was a whole lot of cash," Green chuckled. "Let's blow this joint," he added before heading for the door.

Detective Taylor brandished another gun from his waist and aimed it at Flee. *BOC! BOC! BOC!* He shot him three times. "Prince sends his love," he said before he grabbed the other suitcase and caught up to his partner, leaving Flee in his living room, bleeding out, with the door wide open.

Eleven Minutes Later

Lexi and Fresh stepped off of the elevator and walked toward Flee's apartment. When they saw that the door was wide open, they knew that something was wrong. Hesitantly, they entered the apartment and found Flee laid on the floor, bleeding out. Together, they ran over to him. "He's still breathing. Call the cops," Lexi cried. "Hang in there, Papi. It's gonna be okay, just keep fighting. Help is on the way," she added.

"Cops," Flee said weakly.

"Don't talk, Papi, just breathe. They are on the way."

"Tell Hitta cops did this," he managed to utter before passing out.

CHAPTER 33

Shoota was awakened by the sound of Lanie's phone ringing. He tapped her lightly. "Yo, ya phone been ringing like crazy. That may be important," he said to her while rolling out of the bed to check his own phone. The two of them had a great night together. Shoota would definitely be seeing her again. Not only did he dig her style, but he also really enjoyed the sex. Shoota was not one to keep a chick around, but Lanie may just have been a little lucky.

Lanie's phone rang again. This time, she lazily reached on her nightstand and grabbed it. She had a brief conversation with the caller then hung up. She looked to Shoota. "The Flee kid that fucks with my sis, Lexi, is in the hospital. They found him in his crib shot up."

Shoota quickly started getting dressed. Lanie got up and ran to the bathroom. While getting dressed, Shoota called Heat and Caine to tell them to meet him at the hospital. After speaking to them, he called Hitta and did the same.

Minutes later, Lanie exited the bathroom and quickly began getting dressed also. She threw on some Nike tights, a

Nike sports bra, and a pair of Air Max 270s. "It's an extra toothbrush and washcloth in there for you. Go brush ya jibs and wash ya face real quick. We taking your car or mine?" she asked.

"You coming with me?" Shoota asked.

"Yes, I am. Your friend was shot, and that friend happens to be my best friend's man. Being there for both of you is the right thing to do. She found him in his apartment bleeding out. That shit has probably traumatized her. Now go get ready, babe."

MEANWHILE AT ROYALTY Records

Peso was in the studio with Baby Buccs and Kiyanne. They were currently working on a joint mixtape that they were putting together. Peso was also putting together the finishing touches on a surprise album that he was about to drop. He was taking a huge risk right now because the album would be dropping without any promotion. It would be a package album, meaning he would be dropping two albums at once.

The sound of Peso's phone ringing interrupted his thoughts. Mariah's name popped up on the screen. He picked up instantly. "Wassup, baby momma?" he answered.

"Richie Rich and Bo-Money just put out a track dissing you. It's all over the internet. Tyler, you better show these niggas why you are who you are. I want a legendary response. Don't play with these clowns," Mariah said.

"Say less. I'mma check that shit out now tho. I'll hit you back in a minute." He ended the call.

Not even a minute later, his phone rang again. This time, it was Hitta calling. "What's the word, bro?" He picked up.

"Flee got hit last night. We all at Lutheran right now," Hitta informed him.

"I'm on my way right now," Peso replied then ended the call. He got up from his seat and looked to Kiyanne and Baby Buccs. "Listen, I have a family emergency. Y'all keep working. Don't slack just because I'mma be gone for a few. If shit doesn't sound right, y'all will be recording it all over," he said before walking out of the studio.

Thirty minutes later, Peso walked into Lutheran Medical Center. Being in this hospital brought back so many bad memories, but it reminded him that he was meant to be alive. It reminded him that he was on Earth for a reason. Each time Peso was shot, he was brought right here to this hospital.

This was also the hospital that so many of his friends died in due to gun violence.

Just when he located everyone in the waiting room, a doctor walked out and let them know that it was okay to go in and see Flee. Peso was still trying to figure out when Flee was shot because he just dropped him off last night after Swagger B's album release party.

When everyone made it to Flee's hospital room, Peso stopped the females. "Respectfully, ladies, let us go holla at lil bro real quick. We won't be long. The minute we are done, y'all can have him," he said.

"No problem," Lexi replied.

Peso, Hitta, Shoota, Heat, Gat, and Caine all entered the room. Flee looked a little banged up, but he was alive. That was all that really mattered to his crew. "Wassup, gang?" he greeted them weakly.

"How you feeling, baby boy?" Hitta asked.

"Like shit but the pain lets me know I'm alive," Flee replied.

"What the fuck happened, bro? I just dropped you off. I know you ain't go roaming the streets all drunk. You know better than that, Flee," Peso said.

"Hell no, nigga. When you and wifey dropped me off, I went upstairs, and the two dirty cop niggas, Taylor and Green, blitzed me. They jumped, robbed, and shot me. Those pigs caught me for a nice piece of change, but they were looking for dope tho," Flee explained. "They hit me three times. Twice in my chest and once in my shoulder. Prince sent them niggas at me," he added.

"Why the fuck would Prince do that? When we started beefing with the old nigga?" Hitta asked.

"When the nigga tried to call himself running down, trying to get in on what we building. I thought I parked that nigga tho," Flee replied with a hint of disappointment. He looked over to Hitta. "I'mma get the bread back to you, bro," he said.

"Fuck that money, bro. This shit comes with the game. I'm just happy you alive. Check this out tho. Shop is closed until further notice. It's officially war on Prince and everybody affiliated with him. Y'all take care of that, and I'mma take care of those dirty cops," Hitta said.

"Nah, big homie, don't take my glory away from me. I want those niggas bad, bro. We don't gotta shut down shop. Y'all left us the throne, so let me and my niggas handle this. Let us show y'all that the throne is in good hands. Just sit back and watch all the shit y'all taught us be put to use."

Hitta just smiled at Flee. "Spoken like a true Gorilla."

"Y'all got one shot to end this, or I'm coming back in the field to end it for y'all. Those old niggas never played fair. They always involving cops to do the dirty work for them. There is really no rules to the streets. Since when gangsters call on cops to put work in?" Peso said while shaking his head in disappointment. "Before we slide, we want y'all to know that the beef with Matt Murda is dead. Yes, he's alive. That story is for another day tho. Just know me, him, Hitta, and Timah had a nice sit down. Flee, rest up, and y'all niggas be safe. I love y'all."

Peso and Hitta exited the room. They approached the females. "Thank y'all for being patient. Y'all can do y'all now," Peso said to them.

As Peso and Hitta were walking off, Fresh called out to him and let him know about the diss track that Richie Rich and Bo-Money had put out. Peso just smiled and promised to handle the little rap beef accordingly.

Meanwhile at 225 Cadman Plaza East
The Federal Court Building

Rolex Rich sat in front of AUSA Tanya Greene along with his attorney, Lisa Mayes. After several attempts to get Rich to sit down and have a conversation, he had finally agreed. "Good afternoon, Mr. Royal. My name is Tanya Greene, and I'm the United States attorney," the lady introduced herself.

Tanya Greene was a thirty-four-year-old African American woman. She was a very good-looking woman with a perfect pair of breasts and a nice butt. "Let me cut straight to the chase with you." She pulled out a manilla envelope and removed a stack of pictures from them. She laid them across the table. All of the pictures were of Peso. "Do you know this young man right here?" she asked.

"Who doesn't know Presidential Peso? That young man is the hottest thing in hip hop," Rolex Rich replied with a hint of sarcasm.

"You can kill all the sarcastic shit, Mr. Royal." She rolled her eyes. "I'm asking do you know him outside of music."

"I don't know him at all. I only know of him. He's signed to my label, but I never met the kid. As you already know, my wife and son run the label. From what I know, the kid is legit. Why bring me down here to talk about a rapper?"

AUSA Tanya Greene didn't respond. She just removed the photos from the table and replaced them with another set. Only this time, Hitta was in all of the pictures. "I'm pretty sure you know this young man personally. The two of you built quite a bond while in Sing Sing Correctional Facility a few years ago."

"Okay, what's ya point? Making friends in prison isn't a crime."

"Mr. Royal, you are serving a six hundred twenty-four-month sentence, which is a fifty-two-year bid. If you are willing to help us bring Hitta down, along with his crime partner, Tyler Carter, I just may be able to ask the judge to resentence you," she claimed.

"I met the kid in jail, so how can I be any help to you?"

"Did he ever speak to you about the Murda Team?"

"Nah, I never heard of no Murda Team." Rolex Rich turned to his lawyer. "Lisa, I'm ready to go," he said while standing up from his seat.

"Mr. Royal, I'm aware of your newfound beef with Hitta. You can walk out of here if you want, but these young men are savages. They are coldblooded murderers. How long do you think this war will last before they murder your wife or one of you children? Your daughter, the poor thing, is sleeping with the enemy and doesn't even know it. I'm pretty sure Peso is just using her as a pawn, and she doesn't even know it. Fuck the street code, Rich. Real men are home taking care of their families. You always been a great businessman. That's how you became so successful. Just look at this as another business decision," AUSA Greene replied.

"I'm not at war with anyone. I really don't know what the hell you are talking about. Whoever you are getting your intel from needs to be fired because they played you, Ms. Greene," he chuckled. "I must admit, this trip was worth it. I always hear dudes come back from court and talk about how beautiful you are. I'm just glad I finally got to put a face with the name. You are by far one of the most beautiful women I ever met," he added.

"Do you think they will stand tall when asked about you?" she asked, ignoring his last comment. "One thing I do know is that once Hitta was released from prison, a bunch of people who were linked to you started turning up dead. I think you paid Hitta to kill those men for crossing you, but I'm willing to run off the theory that he was just proving his loyalty to you for changing his life.

"Think on it, Mr. Royal, but don't take too long." She smiled for the first time since the meeting began.

CHAPTER 34

Kaiser Park

Coney Island, Brooklyn

Six days ago, Peso dropped two diss tracks and recorded a video for each of them. Both songs had the internet in a frenzy. The first song titled *Stick Up* was a track aimed at Richie Rich and BoMoney. The second song was titled *King Me*, and on this track, he was dissing all of the hottest rappers in the game. He also dropped two albums on the same day, which currently held the number one and two spots on the Billboard 200. His album knocked Swagger B's album from number one to number three. The crazy thing was that Swagger B was the first one to call and congratulate him.

He also did four shows and shot three videos other than the ones for the diss tracks in the six-day time frame. Still after all of the hard work, Peso was still trying to coach his team of teenagers to a victory in the STARBURY Classic basketball tournament. Just last year in this same park, Peso was shot after coaching his team to a win. Some would call

Peso a fool for coming back, but under no circumstances would he let these boys down.

The park was packed. Everybody from all over Brooklyn was here today. Peso still had no security team, but he did have a bunch of killers around him, strapped with heavy handguns, that he trusted with his life.

Peso stood in a huddle, talking to his team, who had a seven-point lead. A young kid who played for another team approached Peso. The kid's name was Kenzo, and he was by far the best basketball player from Coney Island of his generation. Peso wanted the kid on his team, but he was already running with his high school basketball team. "Yo, Peso, what's good, big homie?" Kenzo greeted him with the UGF handshake.

"Wassup, my boy? You coming to hang with the winning team?" Peso teased.

"Nah, I'm only over here because my mom wanted me to give you her number."

"Okay, cool," Peso replied and handed the young man his phone. "Wassup with Baby Ghost?"

"He's around here somewhere. I saved it under Queen Savage." The young man handed the phone back to Peso. "I'mma let y'all get back to it," he added.

"Yo, don't go too far after the game. We gon shoot out to the city. I got the party bus. We got more than enough room, so snatch Baby Ghost up and a few of ya guys."

Once Kenzo walked off, Peso put his focus back on his team. On the opposite end of the court stood Peso's older cousin, Euro Carter, who was coaching the other team. Euro's stepson was the star player for the other team. The kid jumped like he was in the pros. Peso's team had possession of the ball. Zaya, Peso's star player, pushed the ball up the court. "Yo,

Zaya, pace yaself. We got the lead, lil bro. You can slow it down," Peso yelled out.

The kid reminded Peso of NBA superstar, Russell Westbrook, because he was so explosive. Zaya got the ball to the top of the key and dished the ball to a teammate who was cutting to the basket, and the kid laid it in. "Good pass, baby boy. Now play some defense," said Peso.

Messiah, Euro's stepson, got the ball down the court and pulled up a three pointer from thirty feet. *Swish!* The ball fell in, all net. "Get back, Messiah, move those feet," Euro called out. Just when the words left his mouth, Messiah came up with a steal. He quickly pushed the ball back down the court and did a windmill slam dunk. The crowd went crazy.

"Timeout, ref." Peso used his fourth timeout.

MEANWHILE

Hitta sat in the passenger's seat of Matt Murda's Maserati. He never thought he would live to see the day where the two of them would put their differences to the side. However, it did feel good to have his day one homie back on his side. "Aye, we should go see Gangsta this week," Hitta suggested.

"I'm with that," Matt Murda replied.

"You still be fucking with Gettz and Snow?" Hitta asked.

"I don't really fuck with them, but I got a line on them niggas because they be moving work for me. You know both of them niggas got gambling habits, so they be fucking money up on the regular. I haven't heard from them niggas in a few days. I feel like they ducking me cause they fucked some money up. Why? Wassup?"

"The lil bros is beefing with the old head, Prince, and you know them two niggas are his shooters. The bros don't want me getting involved. They wanna handle the beef themselves. They don't know about Gettz and Snow tho, so the old niggas have the upper hand. I'm tryna knock them niggas off to even the score for them."

"Say no more. We can get next to them niggas right now." Matt Murda quickly made a U-turn.

Twenty minutes later, they pulled up in front of a barbershop in Flatbush. When they stepped inside, all eyes were on them. As usual, the shop was very busy. Six barbers stood behind chairs, cutting hair, and several men sat around, waiting for an empty chair. The place had flat screen TVs with PlayStations hooked up to them. They even have a luxury pool table.

Matt Murda led the way to the back office with Hitta on his heels. He kicked the door open and brandished a huge Desert Eagle. Hitta followed up by pulling out his Glock 45. The two men caught Gettz by surprise. He jumped up from his chair and tried to go for his gun, but he was too late.

"I dare you to grab the gun, nigga," Matt Murda taunted him.

"Come on, Murda, you coming in my place of business, scaring the customers. I ain't know who the hell you was. I would never draw my pistol on you, bro," he claimed.

"Yeah, whatever, nigga. Where my money at?" Matt Murda asked. "And where that bitch ass nigga, Snow? He's been igging my calls for days. You niggas owe me 200K, and I'm here to collect. If y'all don't have my money, I will gladly take my payment in blood."

"Murda, you know we gon get that to you. It's just a lot of shit has been going on. We had a lil setback. The boys hit one of our traps. I can have Snow bring half of the paper, and we can get the other half to you in a few days. How that sound?"

"So, make that happen."

BACK IN KAISER Park

There was currently twenty-two seconds left in overtime, and Peso's squad was up by one point with possession of the ball. Zaya dribbled the ball up from half court, and his defender guarded him closely. Zaya quickly blew past him, and another defender stepped up to block him off. He did a pretty spin move and got straight to the basket. Messiah, a bigger defender, jumped up to block the layup, and Zaya dished a fancy pass to his teammate, who laid the ball in.

"Press! Press!" Peso shouted.

The other team inbounded the ball and got it into the hands of Messiah, who dribbled between a double team. He dished the ball to a teammate, who quickly dished it back to him. Messiah created space for himself then pulled a James Harden like step back jumper from three-point range with exactly four seconds left. The referee blew the whistle, and the ball fell in, all net. The game was now tied up. "Number six, foul on the play. One shot," the referee called out.

"Foul? Are you shitting me?" Peso ran over to the ref. He was livid right now. He really felt like the ref just cheated his team. He jumped in the ref's face and barked. Cameras were all on him, but he didn't even care in the moment. The referee blew the whistle again.

"Tech on the coach. The offense now gets two shots."

Peso was pissed, and it was written on his face. Messiah went to the free throw line and knocked down both shots. Euro's team won the game by two points.

. . .

BACK IN FLATBUSH

Hitta and Matt Murda stood inside of Gettz's office. They were waiting for his partner, Snow, to show up with the money that was owed to Matt Murda. "Yo, Gettz, get up. We gon go to ya crib and get my bread. I'm tired of waiting around. I have shit to do," Matt Murda said.

"He's on his way now, Murda," Gettz claimed.

"Nigga, fuck all that shit. Get ya bitch ass up." Matt Murda walked over and yanked him out of the chair. He followed up by smacking him with the butt of his gun. The blow sent Gettz to the ground. "Get ya punk ass up!" he barked.

Hitta stood in the cut, just smiling. It'd been a long time since he had seen Matt Murda in action. The two of them hadn't been on a mission together in years. Hitta had almost forgotten what it felt like.

Once Gettz was on his feet, Matt Murda grabbed him by the neck. "This is what we gon do, nigga. We gonna go to ya crib and get my cheese. Not the one a few blocks from here. We going to the crib out in Long Island," Matta Murda said.

Hearing him mention his Long Island hideout really had Gettz spooked because no one knew about that spot, not even Snow. "Don't look so shocked, nigga. I know the whereabouts of every nigga I do business with. Now, let's go."

Outside the barbershop, the three of them stood by Matt Murda's Maserati. Matt Murda popped the trunk. "Get in," he ordered.

"If y'all gon kill me, y'all can just do it now. I ain't getting in no trunk," Gettz said, trying to sound tough.

"That's fine with me," Hitta said and pulled out his Glock.

"Alright, I'mma get in. Just please don't kill me," Gettz pleaded and climbed inside of the trunk. Hitta just shook his head in disgust. He hated a killer who turned into a bitch when the gun was pointed at them. Gettz was responsible for a lot of dead bodies on the New York streets. He and Snow were very dangerous but seeing him today made Hitta wonder if the stories he'd heard were even true.

Once Gettz was secure in the trunk, both Hitta and Matt Murda hopped in the Maserati. Just when Matt Murda pulled out of the parking spot, gunshots rang out. He mashed on the gas just as bullets shattered the back window. The shots were coming from a black BMW, and the man hanging out of the passenger's window was none other than Gettz's crime partner, Snow.

Snow continued to fire recklessly at the Maserati. Not being one to run from a gun fight, Hitta fired back at the BMW. The Maserati drove for another three blocks with the BMW tailing. Hitta fired at the BMW while Matt Murda drove. An unmarked police car tried to cut the Maserati off. With no respect for the law, Hitta fired in their direction. Matt Murda pushed the pedal to the metal, and the chase was officially on.

SAME DAY

Peso's team lost by two points, but they still exited the park with their heads held up high. Peso stopped at the entrance to chop it up with Euro. "Good game, cuzzo. Ya lil man put on," Peso said while giving him dap.

"Yeah, lil man got game. He reminds me of me when I was his age. He still needs to improve in certain areas tho. As strong as he is, he shouldn't be struggling to get offensive rebounds," Euro replied just as Messiah approached.

"Dad, can I get a pic with you and Peso for my Instagram?" he asked.

"Why you wanna take a picture with the coach of the losing team?" Euro teased, and the three of them shared a laugh.

"Yo, Zaya, come get in this pic," Peso called out.

After a brief conversation with Euro and a few more pictures, Peso headed toward the party bus with his team. Euro and Messiah decided to roll with them. Peso stopped when he noticed two of his little homies. "Yo, Baby Ghost and Kenzo, pull up!" he called out.

The two teens walked to him, and he greeted both of them with the UGF handshake. "Peso, what's the word, big homie?" Baby Ghost greeted. He was a short kid with long braids that hung horizontally on his head. He was labeled a pretty boy to the young ladies, but to the streets, he was known as one of the youngest killers on the streets of Coney Island. Just like Baby Ghost, Kenzo had a reputation for letting his hammer go, but he was really known for being one of the best high school basketball players in the country. Peso had watched the two teens grow up, and he was very good friends with their mothers.

"Ain't shit, lil bro. What y'all got going on? We about to shoot to the city, then we gon head out to my mansion in Jersey Y'all should pull up," he suggested.

"I don't know, big homie. It ain't no females on that bus. I ain't really into no sausage fest," Baby Ghost replied, and the three of them rolled over in laughter.

"It's a bunch of room, nigga. That big ass bus holds like forty people. I know y'all got some young jawns that would be happy to roll with y'all. Hit them up and tell them y'all got a party bus. They can roll to the city, but they won't be coming with us to Jersey. Now, if you got a lil lady friend, who you deem as someone special to you, that's a different story. Ain't shit going on in the hood. Get away for a lil minute."

"Say less. We gon shoot out. I'mma hit my lil hunny and tell her to bring some friends for Zaya and them."

MEANWHILE

Matt Murda pulled up on a quiet block in the Brownsville section of Brooklyn. They had to shake the police, and they did. Matt Murda had always been super good behind the wheel. Both men hopped out of the Maserati, and Matt Murda popped the trunk. "Get the fuck out!" he barked while pulling Gettz from the trunk. Hitta already had his Glock brandished. "So, you tipped off ya man, huh? The punk ass nigga tried to come on some super nigga shit," he chuckled. "You thought y'all could take out a nigga like me? Don't trip tho cause if the cops ain't catch him, he will be meeting you in hell," he added and pulled his gun from his waist.

BOC! BOC! BOC! Hitta fired three shots and beat Matt Murda to the punch. Gettz's body collapsed to the pavement, and Matt Murda stood over him and pumped two more shots in him.

CHAPTER 35

Flee's Benz floated along Neptune Avenue. The sound of rapper Lil Durk's song, *500 Homicides,* bled through the speakers. He turned into the parking lot of the high-rise complex and parked his car. Flee hadn't been here in Coney Island since the night he was robbed and shot by the dirty cop. When he was released from the hospital, Lexi and Fresh already had a condo in downtown Brooklyn that was fully furnished for them.

In the back of the complex, where the basketball courts were located, everybody from the block was outside. He greeted all his members with the UGF handshake before hugging the ladies who were on the block. "Yo, Flee, let me scream at you real quick, bro," said Ready, an older dude from the hood.

"What's the word?" Flee replied, stepping off to the side to holla at him.

"I'mma get straight to the point, my nigga. You know I be down the way on 21st getting money with the homie, Thugga, the old head, Prince's nephew. I ain't know y'all was at war. Word around is you shot Prince," Ready said.

"You saying all that to say what?" Flee asked.

"The nigga ain't healthy. He fucked over real bad, so he can't really move around. I got word that he teamed up with the young niggas on 21st, and his niggas are supposed to be looking for you, so keep ya eyes open," he warned.

"You said ya man, Thugga, is family to Prince, right? Well, I'm tryna get next to that man," Flee said with a cold stare.

Sadness plastered Ready's face because Thugga was his little man, and he knew what Flee was asking him to do. "Come on, Flee. You know I can't get involved in that," he claimed.

"You already involved, Ready. You from back here. So, wassup?"

"Nah, Flee, I can't do that. Thugga is like family, bro."

"Like family, huh?" Flee chuckled. "Ready, let me explain something to you. Prince sent police at me, and them dirty cops almost took my life. So, anybody associated with Prince will get touched. Whoever ain't with me is against me. That's what I'm on right now. So, you fucking with my ops makes you an op. With that being said, you are no longer welcomed back here. I don't care if you from here. For all I know, you could be feeding them niggas info."

"Come on, Flee. You like family too, bro. You know I don't give it up like that. I put the block before everything. The same way I won't line him, I won't line you. I am neutral to the situation y'all have. I only put you on because I fuck with you heavy and watched you grow up. I could have never said nothing about what I heard. I got love for you, Flee."

"So, prove it. Get me next to that man or end up dead with

him. You have twenty-four hours to make a decision. In the meantime, you are not welcomed on my block, so burn it up, nigga. When you show me that you are one of us, then I will allow you to come back down here." Flee walked off, leaving Ready alone in his thoughts.

MEANWHILE

Shoota sat in the passenger's seat of a Dodge Charger. In the driver's seat was his old head, Block. "Yo, nephew, this shit is pain. Them dope heads loving that Untouchable," he said excitedly. "Niggas ain't have heroin this good in a very long time," he added while reaching under his seat to retrieve a Bloomingdales shopping bag. The bag contained $55,000 cold cash. "That's the fifty-five I had for you, nephew. My face is clean now. I ain't ready to re-up just yet. I just wanted to get you out the way by getting yours to you. I'll see you in like a day or two, so I can snatch some more."

"Say less, Unk. You got my number, just hit my line," Shoota replied, giving him dap. "Let me get up outta here. You drive safe, big fella," he added while exiting the Charger. The minute Shoota entered the building, he got a text message from Flee, telling him to meet the guys at the spot in the next building. Shoota made a U-turn and walked one building over.

Shoota walked inside of the trap and greeted everyone with the signature UGF handshake. "I'mma get right to the point, gang. As we already know, both Prince and Poe survived. I just got word that the old nigga teamed up with the 21st niggas, so we are on they line also. This ain't gon be some long, drawn-out war. We gon get these niggas out the way, so we can focus on this bag. The block is temporarily shut down. We are only gonna deal with our out the hood clients."

"What you mean, bro?" Caine asked. "We can't just shut our block down and feed other niggas' hoods. I know we got a lil situation, but we can down these niggas without stopping my money. I ain't got niggas from all over coming to cop bricks. I get most of my money in the trenches, bag for bag or bundle for bundle," he added with a hint of frustration. He was simply not used to getting money on this level. So, the thought of being taken out of his *glo* was killing him. Unlike the rest of the crew, Caine depended on the block money. He needed the dope fiends as bad as they needed him. Flee understood him, so he came up with a plan for Caine.

"This is what we gonna do," Flee said. "We gon round up some hittas to take care of the 21st niggas, and us five are gonna handle Prince and his circle. Once we knock Prince off, the war will be over cause once you hit the head, the body dies. Shit about to be super-hot for a minute. Y'all know murders bring the Feds, so we must catch niggas lacking outside of the hood." He turned to Caine. "Baby bro, don't trip. You still gon eat. I got a play for you that's gon have you sitting pretty for a while. You have my word," Flee promised.

MARLBORO PROJECTS

Reem sat on the hood of his Maserati. He and Sho-Tyme were here on the Crip side of the projects. However, they were as comfortable as they would be on their turf. The two of them ping ponged a blunt back-and-forth as they waited for Wiz.

The day of Lucci's funeral, a lot of bangers pulled up from the Crip community to come pay their respects. That right there was what made Reem agree to have a lil sit down with them.

Wiz and two other Crip members approached them. One went by the name of T-Top, and he was a short, chubby dude who rocked a Mohawk cut. The other man was Monster, a legendary OG Crip in New York. He was about 6'3" and two hundred eighty pounds solid muscle. His baby face gave him the look of an oversized teen instead of the ruthless killer that he was. Monster was respected on the entire east coast; he even got love in Cali from both Crips and Bloods. He was much older than Reem, but in the streets, gangsta always respected gangsta. So, the two of them had a mutual respect.

"What's poppin, fellas?" Reem greeted them all with a pound, and Sho-Tyme did the same.

"Ain't much, cuz, everything blue," Monster replied humbly.

"Nah, my nigga, everything is green," Reem smiled. "Y'all wanted to chop it up. Well, we here. Let's talk money, skrap." He rubbed his hands together. Monster smiled also.

"That's what I like to hear. Listen, Reem, I'm tryna open up a line with y'all. That dope y'all got is some eighties shit. These projects ain't seen nothing like this since 09 when that Black Rose stamp was out. We ain't coming with our mouths open and hands out. We are here to do good business with cash on deck. All you gotta do is set ya price," Monster said.

"$260 a brick," Reem replied. Monster chuckled at his response.

"$260 a brick? That's insane, cuz, but we ain't here to cop no bricks. I ain't no D-league player. I need raw dope, whole keys of it. I got three hunnit and sixty racks to spend right now," he claimed.

Reem stood there, unfazed by the number. A year or two

ago, that price probably would have moved him, but these days, $360,000 wasn't what it used to be to Reem. That was small change to him in this date and time. "Listen, my nigga, my product comes stamped with a label, just like Hershey. We all know Hershey is not selling you a candy bar without a wrapper on it because it's a brand. The three hunnit ain't really no money to me these days. I leveled up," Reem said with a little bit of arrogance.

"I can see that," Monster smiled. "Check this out tho. It's ya show, so we gon play by ya rules. $260 a brick is a little high tho. Reem, bring that number down a little bit, and you have my word you will be seeing me on a weekly basis," he claimed.

"Two sixty, no debating."

"Come on, Reem. Niggas who spending short paper are getting a better number than that. I know we play for different teams, but real is universal, my nigga. The only color that matters is green.

"Me and the locs run through bullshit dope with ease, so imagine what we gon do with that shit you got. We gon make you a lot of money in a short period of time. With your work and our manpower, we can do some things, some real big things." Monster rubbed his hands together with a smile.

"$220, take it or leave it."

"That's still a little too high, but we gon fuck with you. All I ask is that you don't do any business with any other Crips on this side. If they wanna get next to you, they have to go through us. Deal?" Monster reached his hand out, and Reem gladly accepted it.

CHAPTER 36

The time was now 4:15 a.m., and Hitta was rolling out of the bed. Ashley and Nautica both laid there, sleeping peacefully. Later today, the three of them were leaving for a trip to Ibiza, a Spanish island in the Mediterranean Sea fifty miles off the coast of Spain.

Never in a million years did Hitta ever think he would be in a relationship with two women who actually knew about each other. He smiled to himself as he stared at the two beautiful women in his bed. The sight of them was a good one.

Hitta grabbed a blunt out of the ashtray and sparked it up before exiting the room. He walked to the balcony and took a seat. After unlocking the screen to his iPhone, he went to his recent calls and FaceTimed Peso. After ringing for a few seconds, Peso's face popped up on the screen. Hitta could hear music playing in the background. "What's the word, gang?" Peso greeted.

"Ain't shit. I seen you called me, so I was just tapping back in," Hitta replied.

"Don't trip, my boy. I wasn't calling for nothing. I was

just checking on you. What you fucking with tho?" Peso asked.

"Ain't shit. I'm about to go link Unk in a minute, so we can pass out the jerseys for the summer league team," Hitta said, speaking in code. He was referring to the shipment of heroin that he needed to distribute. "Them niggas balling in the league, bro. Euro is the leading scorer. He came off the bench and put up some historic numbers. I'mma give him some more playing time. I got a nice bag for you too. Shit kinda heavy, bro," he chuckled. "Where you at right now?"

"I'm in the studio with Kiyanne, Baby Buccs, and a few of the guys. We at Lee shit. I ain't been to Royalty since I dropped the double album. We officially independent, and I got both of the top spots on the Billboard," he bragged.

"That's wassup, my boy. How many albums you sold so far?" Hitta asked.

"They both platinum already. And I'm killing them on the streaming tip too. Both projects been streamed over ten million times. Niggas making history, bro."

"I'm super proud of you, bro, no bullshit. I'mma pull up on you after I take care of the team. We can smoke something before I catch my flight."

"Copy, just hit my line. Love you, bro."

"Love you more, my nigga," Hitta replied before ending the call.

THIRTY MINUTES Later

Hitta left his condo dressed in a FedEx uniform. Today, he didn't drive any of his cars. He hopped in an Uber. Twenty minutes later, he was exiting the Uber in front of the McDonald's on Fulton Street in downtown Brooklyn. He entered the McDonald's and saw his uncle, Nick, sitting in the corner, eating his breakfast. This was their routine every time a shipment had to be distributed.

Nick, also known as Rich Nick, was Hitta's mom's younger brother. He was a major player back in his day, but a twelve-year Fed bid slowed him down. These days, Nick was just known for being the chemist. He was the one who turned up the volume on the product. He cut the heroin with an unknown product and got it bagged up into bricks. Hitta paid him a hefty fee for his services.

Nick was currently employed by FedEx, but he made way more working with Hitta. Hitta took a seat across from him. "Uncle Nick, what's the word?" Hitta greeted him with a fist bump. Nick chewed his McGriddle and took a sip of his orange juice before he replied.

"Ain't much, nephew, just tryna live."

"How we looking?"

"The same way we always look," Nick smiled. "You know I don't half step. Each package has the receivers name on it and a fake address. 50,000 bricks all bagged up and ready to be passed out. You ready to make these drops?"

"Hell yeah. Let's get to it." Hitta got up from his seat, and Nick did the same. Together, they headed outside and walked to where Nick had the FedEx truck parked.

SEVERAL HOURS Later

Peso had just spent the night in the studio. He had a very productive session with Kiyanne and Baby Buccs. After dropping Kiyanne off, him and Baby Buccs headed to Kings Plaza Mall in Brooklyn. Mya had called, telling him that her phone was broken, so he was here at the T-Mobile store trying to get her a new iPhone.

"Good morning, love." Peso approached the counter. For the first time, the young lady who was working the register looked up. Her eyes widened when she saw Peso. She thought her eyes were playing tricks on her.

"Oh, my God, it's really you," she said, not able to hide her excitement. "It's really you!" she shouted.

"Calm down, love. I'm tryna be low right now. It's been a real long night. I still didn't get any sleep, and I'm too tired to be stuck here signing autographs all day," he smiled.

The young lady excitedly jumped up and down like a kid who had to use the bathroom. "I'm so sorry, but I'm a big fan. Hold on, let me get myself together," she said before taking a deep breath. "Okay, I'm ready now. How can I help you?"

"My daughter broke her phone, and I cannot go home without a new one for her," he explained. "Just let me get ya newest iPhone with the most gigs," he added.

"Are you a T-Mobile carrier?"

"Yes, I am, but I'm not tryna go through all of that right now. I'll pay full price for the phone."

"No problem. I'll be right back," the young lady replied and walked to the back.

Peso looked around the store for Baby Buccs but didn't see him. He then walked to the entrance and peeked outside, only to find Baby Buccs recording a live Instagram video. A crowd was quickly beginning to form. Peso just shook his head and smiled.

Just as Peso walked back to the register, the young lady returned from the back with an iPhone in her hand. "How much?" Peso asked.

"You said it's for your baby girl, right?"

"Yeah," he replied.

"So, it's free. I will take care of it. I am the manager. All I want from you is your autograph and a picture." She handed him the T-Mobile bag with the phone inside of it. "If that's not too much to ask for," she added.

"Nah, not at all. What do you want signed?"

"You can sign my shirt," she replied while handing him a permanent marker.

After signing her shirt, Peso took a few selfies with the young lady. "Thank you so much, Peso. This is really like a dream come true," she beamed.

"Nah, love, thank you," he smiled. "This was clutch right here. To show my gratitude, I'll make sure to get you some tickets and backstage passes to my next show for you and ya peoples."

"How will you get them to me?"

"I know where you work," he chuckled. "Tag me in the picture too, so I can repost it and get you some more followers."

When Peso exited the T-Mobile store, Baby Buccs had a huge crowd of people surrounding him. When the people noticed Peso, a crowd started to form around him. Baby Buccs was loving every second of this. He still hadn't gotten used to his newfound celebrity status. "Yo, baby bro, you tryna have some fun?" Peso called out.

"Hell yeah, big homie, what you got in mind?" Baby Buccs replied.

"Just follow my lead." Peso took off running. Baby Buccs took off behind him, and the crowd followed.

MEANWHILE

After distributing all of the heroin, Hitta was now sitting in the living room of Flee's new condo along with Shoota. Stacks on stacks of one-hundred-dollar bills were piled up on the glass table that sat in the middle of them. "Yo, big homie, that's the chicken I owe you from the loss we took. Every dollar is here, not a cent short," Flee said.

"Nigga, I told you don't stress that. Losses are part of the game. I'm just grateful that you're alive. I'm glad to see you been saving ya coins tho. You prolly got a bigger bag than me right now," Hitta said with a smile. Truth was, he was quite impressed with Flee.

"Nah, big homie, I got to tuck at least five Ms to catch up to you," Flee replied modestly.

"I ain't up like that," Hitta claimed. The smile plastered across his face indicated that he may not be telling the truth. "Check this out tho, gang." He looked to both Flee and Shoota. "I'm about to patch y'all niggas all the way in. I only be giving y'all work in bricks because I be having my uncle work his magic on the raw dope we getting. We got some fire, but my uncle is who turns that fire into that Untouchable. Whatever he's using makes it more potent, and it stretches it. I pay good money for his services tho," he explained. "From this moment forward, I'mma be giving y'all whole kilos at 50K a joint. They going for no less than 60K all over the land, so y'all getting a head start. I'mma introduce y'all to my uncle. He charges me 10K for each kilo he has to chef up, so I'mma make sure it's the same price for y'all. When dealing with outsiders, never serve them the shit you got fixed up unless they buying bricks. If they want the Untouchable brand, they will have to buy the shit stamped," he added.

Just when Hitta finished his sentence, the door opened, and Lexi, Fresh, and Lanie walked in. "Oh, boy, the pretty boy gangster is here," Fresh said playfully, rolling her eyes at Hitta.

"Yo, Flee, if I would of knew ya bodyguard was gonna be here, I would of came with a bigger strap," Hitta joked.

"You ain't the only one with a glizzy, nigga." She playfully mushed him.

Lanie sat on Shoota's lap and hugged his neck. "Y'all go in the back for a minute. Let us handle this shit real quick," Flee said to Lexi. What impressed both Hitta and Shoota was that the females were not fazed by all the money that sat in front of them. If Flee was correct about the money not being a dollar short, there was over a half of million in front of them. This let Hitta know that they were used to being around big money.

"Nah, gang, they cool. These the two that saved ya life, so that means they family. You share a crib with them, so that means they can be trusted. Besides, I got some business I wanna run by them also," Hitta said, shifting his attention to the ladies. "I know y'all be fucking with the pieces (credit cards). I don't know what type of numbers y'all doing, but I got the sauce. I'm talking real back card BINS," he claimed.

"What they going for?" Lanie asked

"I'm willing to break bread with y'all for a seventy/thirty split. Y'all take seventy percent and just hit me with thirty. I ain't a greedy nigga. One hand wash the other, and both count the money," he winked.

"I thought it was both hands wash the face," Fresh laughed.

"Baby girl, I don't need help washing my face, but better believe, I'mma need help counting all these racks we about to make," he replied, and they all shared a laugh.

Lanie instantly got back into business mode. "Let us see

what ya sauce hitting like before we make any agreements. Deal?" She reached her hand out. Lanie was the alpha-female of the group. She was the one who taught Lexi and Fresh the fraud game.

"Deal." Hitta accepted her terms. "I gotta cut out, gang. I got a flight to catch. I just wanted to situate y'all before I left the country. Shoota, I'mma fax you one hundred dumps for the ladies as a test run." He then turned to Lanie. "When my pieces hit, I just want the Richard Millie with the Cuban link band. It gotta be bust down tho. If my pieces don't hit, I got twenty bands for all of y'all." He flashed his trademark smile and headed out of the condo.

CHAPTER 37

Peso walked inside of Royalty Records like he owned the building. He was cordial with everyone as he strolled to Kat's office. He had no beef with the label; he was simply just trying to spread his wings and build his own empire.

Kat's office door was already open, so Peso just walked inside. Kat, Roxy, and another female were sitting down, having girl chat, he assumed. "Ladies," Peso said, greeting the group.

"Peso, how are you?" Kat asked. "Congrats on your double album. They are both platinum, and you are holding the top spots on the Billboard. It feels good to be back up there, doesn't it?" she added.

"Back up there?" Peso chuckled. "I haven't left the charts since you signed me. I see you haven't been watching this beautiful movie that has been playing before your eyes," he replied with arrogance.

"You are so damn cocky. I see why my daughter is crazy for you," Kat smiled.

Peso glanced over to Roxy, who was blushing, then looked back at Kat. "Wassup tho? Why you called me over here?" he asked.

"Peso, you just announced in front of the world that your label is no longer an imprint of Royalty Records, but that isn't quite true," she claimed.

Peso was now confused. "What you mean that's not true? I gave you three albums —three number one albums at that —and I won Grammys. I honored my end of the deal."

"Well, according to these documents, you still owe me one more album. There is a clause in your contract that says at least one of your albums must be cleared by the board. Yes, you have full creative control over your music, so you control all releases, but not for your first album."

"My first album was cleared, Kat. What the fuck are you talking about?" Peso was becoming more pissed off by the minute. Kat fumbled through some documents on her desk. Once she found what she was looking for, she handed them to Peso. As he read, she further explained.

"Those papers in your hands show you that your first album was never cleared. Everybody signed but me."

Peso saw that her claims were true and became even more pissed. He just shook his head. "What do you want from me, Katrina?" he asked.

"Peso, you know that this label is built on family. Through good and bad family, it's still family. With that being said, we don't want you to leave our family, Peso."

"Family?" Peso laughed in her face as if she was Bozo the clown. "That family shit went out the window when you did that foul shit to Hitta. Bitch, you must be crazy if you think I'm staying on this label."

Kat looked over to Roxy. "You two let me and Peso chat real quick."

Once Roxy and her friend were gone, Kat continued to speak. "Tyler Carter, you are family whether you like it or not. My beautiful daughter is having your child," she claimed. The statement caught Peso off guard, and it was written on his face. "You should have wrapped it up. Check this out, Peso. I will sign this paper right now if you re-sign with us. I will give you fifty million upfront, and you will no longer be an imprint under Royalty. You will be my partner. Royalty will put up the money for your label's production, marketing, and everything else. First Class will handle distribution like they been doing. My company will be taking all of the risk," she added.

"And if I say no?"

"Then you owe me another album and your fiancée finds out that my daughter is pregnant and about you and Tia Savage," Kat grinned. "Roxy will have an abortion today if you just sign the contract. Don't be so stubborn. We'll make this all disappear. All you have to do is just sign the new contract."

"Sounds like you just tryna sell ya grandbaby," Peso chuckled lightly. "I'm no deadbeat nor do I support abortions, but let me think on this, Kat," he added.

"Well, you have forty-eight hours to let me know your answer, or this shit will be all over TMZ by the morning. Let me tell you something. If your bitch ever put hands on my daughter again, I will have her killed. This meeting is now concluded." She dismissed him with a smile. Peso was livid right now, but he kept his cool and headed for the door. "Peso!" she called out.

"What, Katrina?"

"Tell Hitta to call me. It's imperative."

Two Hours Later

Peso returned to his mansion and found Mya riding around on her hoverboard. "Daddy!" She cheerfully jumped off and ran over to him. She jumped in his arms with the biggest smile. Peso hugged her tightly.

"Hey, pretty girl." He kissed her forehead.

"Did you get my phone?" she asked.

"Yes, I did," he replied while handing her the T-Mobile bag.

"You are the best dad in the whole world," she said before happily running off.

Peso took the spiral staircase up to his bedroom. He found Princess sitting on the bed with her MacBook in front of her.

"Hey, Queen," he greeted her with a kiss on the lips.

"Hey, King," she replied with a smile. "You ready for more kids?" she asked.

Hearing her mention kids instantly made him think that Kat had already leaked the news about Roxy being pregnant.

"Babe, I'm talking to you," she said, snapping Peso out of his thoughts.

"I'm ready if you want one," he replied, not sounding too convincing.

"Ty, I'm pregnant," she said. Peso smiled, but she could sense that something was off. "King, what's wrong? I feel like you have something to say, but you holding it in."

"Nothing is wrong, P," he lied.

"If you are not ready, it's okay. I don't want you feeling like I'm trying to trap you," she said sadly.

"Princess, you are about to be my wife, so I'm already trapped," he replied while stripping down to his boxer briefs. "Til death do us part, Queen," he added.

"So, talk to me, Ty. What's wrong? You don't seem happy about me having your child."

Peso sat down on the bed. He moved closer to her and stroked her cheek with his hand. "P, I'm ready for you to have my child. You don't have to second guess that."

"But?"

"What you mean?"

"You still not telling me something. What's wrong?"

Peso let out a deep sigh. "P, Roxy is pregnant also," he admitted.

"When did you find this out?" she asked.

"Right before I came home, Kat called me in to her office, trying to blackmail me into signing a new contract with Royalty. I was going to tell you as soon as I walked in, but you hit me with the good news about you being pregnant, and I didn't want to steal your joy," he said sincerely.

"It would have been nice to have this moment to myself, but I will not let this kill my joy," she replied and just stared at him.

"What, Queen?" he asked.

"Roxy Royal tho?" She burst out laughing. "You really smashed the supermodel, Roxy Royal. That had to be on ya bucket list. I can't even be mad at you. Shawdy is a bad bitch. At least you ain't go out there and get some cruddy ass bitch pregnant," she added. Peso was trying his hardest not to smile because he didn't want Princess to flip out. "Nigga, you can try and hide that smile all you want," she teased. "You can't hide the redness on ya cheeks tho. You blushing ass nigga," she said while cracking up. "You really that nigga, Daddy, no cap. Now tell me about this Kat bitch trying to blackmail you."

"Ain't nothing I can't handle. But to make a long story short, I'm basically still signed to Royalty even tho I gave them three albums because at least one album had to be cleared by the board upon my release," he explained. "She was saying that if I re-sign with Royalty, she would have Roxy get an abortion on the low, so you wouldn't find out."

"Do you wanna stay on that label?"

"To be honest, my situation is good at Royalty. I'm not getting jerked or nothing. I'm one of the rappers who are actually making real money off my music. I own my masters; I make great numbers off of my albums sales. The contract ain't bad at all. I just want my own situation, feel me?"

"Yeah, I feel you. Remember the night we were up late, and you had me doing research for you on record labels and stuff?"

"Yeah, that may have been the night I got you pregnant," he smiled, and Princess just cut her eyes at him before hitting him with a pillow.

"You always playing, Daddy. I'm trying to be serious right now," Princess playfully whined.

"I was being serious, but I'mma chill."

"Well, that night, I did some digging on Royalty Records and found out that ever since Rolex Rich has been locked up, the company went public. Royalty Records is a publicly traded company, which means that they have shareholders. The Royal family only owns sixty-eight percent of the company. The other thirty-two percent was split between three other investors," she said then put her attention to her MacBook. "I saved this just in case you ever needed it. It says here that a man name James Flint bought out the other shareholders. Find a way to get his stake in the company and you become an owner of the label. I just gave you the keys, now use them, King. Oh, yeah, get on social media and let the world know that Roxy is having ya baby. Beat them to the punch, so there is nothing hanging over us."

CHAPTER 38

The time was 10 p.m., and the projects were packed like it was daytime. People of all ages were out enjoying this beautiful summer night like it was daytime. Shoota and several members of the UGF from his age bracket and younger were standing by the flagpole in the middle of the projects, popping bottles, passing blunts, popping pills, and sipping Lean. "Yo, I'm hungry as shit right now," said Mula. He was a funny looking, brown skinned dude who was always dressed in designer. He wasn't part of the immediate circle, but he was a day one comrade. Mula wasn't into drug dealing or playing with guns. His lane was fraud. Mula was a scammer.

"That's a fact, gang. Let's go to Wendy's," Shoota suggested.

"Nah, let's go to Mickey D's," said Baby Ghost, a younger UGF member.

"Bro, Wendy's got better burgers," Harlem said.

"This nigga trippin. Ain't nothing like a Big Mac," Mula shot back.

"All y'all niggas tweakin. Ain't no burger like the Big

AZZ burger from the corner store," Caine said, and everybody rolled over in laughter. "Y'all niggas laughing. I'm dead ass tho."

"Let's just go to the chicken spot and then head to the rides. Kia just text me and said shit litty down there," Heat suggested.

"That sounds like a plan," Shoota said. "We not driving. We taking the Ave. Grab the glizzy out the trash can," he added.

They were seven deep heading down the way. Mula was playing music from his Bluetooth speaker that was hooked up to his phone. G-Herbo and Lil Bibby's track, *Kill Shit,* bled through the speaker. They all rapped along as they walked.

When they made it to 31st and Mermaid Avenue, they were met by a group of females. "Yo, Shoota, look at Tati. You better go get ya old thang back," Caine said. The young ladies greeted them all with hugs. Shoota pulled a chick named Tati into his embrace.

"Where ya pretty ass going?" he asked.

"My sister said the rides are poppin right now, so we headed down there. What you getting into? I missed you, punk," she replied.

"We headed that way too, but the way this Ave looking, we might not even make it down there. I missed you too tho. You with me for the night."

Meanwhile

Reem was standing on the corner of 28th and Mermaid in front of the chicken spot. He had his homie, Young World, with him, and the two of them were sipping Hennessy out of ice cups and kicking it with a few honeys from around the way. "Reem, you taking me home with you?" one of the females asked.

"Home?" he chuckled. "You tryna get us both killed. You know my lady is not having that," he added.

Reem looked up and saw a group of people walking in their direction but on the opposite side of the street. He also noticed a black SUV parked by the corner store. "Yo, World, be on point. That black truck just parked by the store, but ain't nobody get out," he informed his comrade.

Shoota was walking in the back of the crowd, talking to Tati. They all approached the corner store. "Yo, Shoota!" he heard someone call his name. Shoota looked across the street and saw Reem waving him over.

"Yo, I'm going across the street real quick to holla at the bro," he informed the guys.

As he crossed the street, something told him to look back. The moment he turned around, the doors of the SUV flew open, and two men jumped out with guns brandished. One gunman raised his firearm. *BOC! BOC!* Two shots went off, both missing Shoota by an inch. He stood in shock for about a half second before pulling his gun from his waist. Another series of shots went off.

Reem and Young World both began to fire in the direction of the gunmen who'd jumped out of the SUV. Shoota upped his cannon and fired three shots while backpedaling toward the sidewalk.

The second Shoota turned around to take off running, his body cringed as a slug ripped through his shoulder. "Agghh!" he grunted in agony. Just as he made it to the sidewalk, another slug hit him in the back of his head. The impact sent him crashing down on the pavement. Reem quickly pulled

Shoota behind the nearest car for safety. Young World fired more shots to cover him.

That was all Shoota saw before blacking out.

Hours Later
Lutheran Medical Center

There were so many sad faces in the hospital waiting room. Peso walked in with Princess on his arm. All eyes were on him as he entered. The place was packed with young UGF members and female friends of Shoota. There wasn't a dry face in sight. Peso could feel the sadness in the air, but he didn't think the worst. He was a firm believer of what you thought actually became reality, so his only thoughts right now were that his little brother was alive.

Heat was pacing back-and-forth like a madman as Caine sat in the corner with his face in his hands. Heat quickly walked over to Peso and Princess. "What the fuck happened, bro?" Peso asked.

"We was on the Ave heading to the rides, and shots started going off out of nowhere, bro," Heat said with tears in his eyes. "You know I would die for Shoota, bro. That's my brother too." He began to sob uncontrollably. Peso knew how close Heat and his brother were, so he knew the pain he felt right now was identical to his. Peso hugged Heat. "Bro is gonna be alright," he said.

"Family for Tymel Carter," a doctor called out.

Peso quickly walked over to the doctor with Heat and Caine on his heels. "We are Tymel's family. He's our brother. How is he doing, Doc?" Peso asked.

"Tymel is a very strong young man. I must say he has a very hard head," the doctor smiled. "The bullet didn't do any damage there, but the shoulder is pretty banged up from the shot he took there. We successfully removed the bullet. Tymel is going to be okay; he just needs to rest."

MEANWHILE IN BINGHAMTON, New York

Breeze sat parked on Pine Street in front of one of his many trap houses. He was on his way to one of the many parties going on tonight, but a call from Rocko, one of his many clients, had him on standby.

Breeze wouldn't normally wait this long, but Rocko ordered one thousand bricks. Just when Breeze pulled out his phone to call him, Rocko tapped on the passenger's side window. Breeze unlocked the door, and Rocko hopped in. "What's goodie, my guy?" Breeze greeted him with a pound before reaching in the back to grab the shopping bag filled with heroin he had for Rocko.

"Ain't shit, boy. On my momma tho, my phone ain't stop ringing since I got my hands on this shit," Rocko said with a big Kool-Aid smile on his face.

The sound of Breeze's phone ringing caused him to fumble in his pocket for it. Rocko used this to his advantage and swiftly brandished his 9-millimeter. Breeze looked up in shock when he saw the barrel of the gun in his face. The dark hole suddenly lit up with a red glare. *BOC!* Breeze put his hand up in an attempt to cover his face. The bullet landed in his forearm. Breeze leaned forward and tried to grab the gun, but Rocko fired again. Breeze opened the driver's door and fell out of the car. He quickly attempted to crawl away. Rocko grabbed the shopping bag with the dope before running over to Breeze and shooting him two more times.

CHAPTER 39

A Week Later

Peso entered the huge upper Manhattan building and took the elevator to the 23rd floor. In his hand was a small legal binder that contained some important documents. He stepped off of the elevator and approached the secretary's desk. "Good afternoon, my name is Tyler Carter, and I'm here to see Mr. James Flint."

"I know who you are," the lady said with a smile before picking up the phone and placing a call to her boss. Minutes later, James Flint stepped out of the back office. He was a short, muscular, white man with a bald head.

"Mr. Carter, good afternoon," he greeted Peso with a firm handshake. "You can follow me to my office," he added while leading the way.

Peso followed him into a huge office. The place was decorated well. He could tell that the man had class. "Would you like a drink, Mr. Carter?" Mr. Flint offered while walking over to the mini bar.

"No thanks. I rather just get down to my reason for being here —if that's okay with you," Peso replied.

"That's fine. I'm all ears."

"I want your thirty-two percent of Royalty Records."

Mr. Flint downed his shot of whiskey. "That's not happening, kid. So, if that's why you are here, you can see yourself out. I am sorry. You just wasted your time."

"I don't waste time, sir," Peso said with a smile. "I was willing to buy your share of the company, but since I don't like the way you spoke to me, I am going to just take your share for free," he added while fumbling through the legal binder in his hand. He pulled out a small stack of pictures and handed them to Mr. Flint, who looked through them with a shocked expression.

Thanks to Peso's old friend, who was a private investigator, he was able to get some dirt on Mr. Flint in a matter of days.

In the photos, Mr. Flint and another powerful label owner named Dru Lovell were quite cozy together. Both men had been hiding their true sexualities. They had been having a down low homosexual relationship for quite some time now. The only problem was that both men were married with families. "My cameraman is better than TMZ, right?" Peso teased. "It's cool, Jay. I can make these photos go away. Just sign over your thirty-two percent of Royalty. You have many successful businesses. I already had my lawyer draw up a contract," he added while pulling some documents from the binder along with a pen.

"Is this your only copy?" Mr. Flint asked in defeat.

"Yes, it is," Peso lied with a straight face. Truth was, he kept a copy to have dirt on Dru Lovell in case he needed to use it in the future. James Flint sadly signed the documents and pushed the papers back in front of Peso.

ONE HOUR Later

Peso walked into Kat's office, all smiles. As always, Kat was looking stunning. "Peso, you're late. I have a meeting in about an hour. I'm sorry about what happened to your brother. Is he okay?" she said sincerely.

"Yeah, he's okay. Thanks. I know you got a meeting in a few, so I'mma skip the small talk. I came here to inform you that I now own thirty-two percent of Royalty Records. Mr. James Flint no longer wanted to be a part of the hip hop culture," Peso said with a smile. "Katrina, you can sign that paper that states my first album was cleared, or I will burn this label down."

"You are not serious," she said in disbelief.

"I'm very serious, just give Mr. Flint a call and he will fill in the blanks. I don't owe any explanations. I will see you at the next board meeting tho. Enjoy ya day, love," he said and made his exit.

By the time Peso made it home, it was 6 p.m. He entered the living room and found Shoota playing *NBA 2K*. Peso greeted him with a brotherly embrace. "How you feeling, big homie?" he asked.

"I'm just ready to slide on the niggas who did this," Shoota replied.

"Slow down, killer. That was a close call. You need to be sitting here counting ya blessings. You took a head shot, baby boy. You could have been off the count."

Shoota's facial expression instantly turned sour. "Nigga, do you hear yaself?" he asked in disgust. "I just got hit in my head, and you in front of me talking this bullshit. All that work you put in behind niggas in them streets, and you wanna stand down when I get hit. Nigga, I'm ya blood!" He raised his voice a little.

"Shoota, you almost lost ya life because you wanna still be in the hood, walking the Ave like we some regular ass niggas. Look around you, nigga. We fucking rich. You can be anywhere in the world, and you still wanna be playing the block. We got a lot to lose."

"You really turning into one of these industry niggas. I don't even know you no more. Where the fuck is my brother at?" Shoota said while trying to get up from the sofa. A sharp pain instantly shot through his shoulder and stopped him.

"You don't gotta get up, killer. I'll leave since you in ya feelings," Peso said while walking away.

"It's crazy how you turn up for everybody but me." Shoota shook his head.

His comment got Peso to stop dead in his tracks. "You forgot what happened the last time you got shot, Tymel? I damn near murdered an entire block by myself. I was on the run for murders, knocking niggas down for you, nigga. But I don't brag on it because that's what I'm supposed to do. You on some real bitch shit." Peso walked away.

MEANWHILE

"We ain't taking no shorts. Him and his bitch is off the count," Heat said from the driver's seat.

"I'm with whatever," said his young hitter, Baby Ghost, who was sitting in the passenger's seat. Baby Ghost was a wild teen who was still in high school. Even though he was young, this was not the first time he would lay something down. He clutched the Glock in his hand and smiled. Murder really gave him a rush.

A bright set of lights illuminated the dark block. They could see the huge grill of the Rolls Royce from down the block, and both men cocked back their firearms in anticipation. They had been lamping on this townhouse for hours, waiting for a man named Suge to show up.

Suge was the older brother of Prince. Knocking him off would really put the UGF up on the scoreboard. Heat had his eyes glued to the Rolls Royce as it slowly cruised by and pulled into the driveway of the townhouse. A young lady hopped out of the passenger's seat. "That's not his bitch; that's his daughter. I go to school with shawdy," Baby Ghost informed his comrade.

"Say less. We gon let her go inside, then we gon off boy," Heat replied.

The minute the girl was out of sight, Heat pulled the gorilla mask down over his face, and Baby Ghost did the same. The driver's door of the Rolls Royce opened, and Suge got out just as Heat and Baby Ghost were exiting the car. Suge saw two masked men and reached for his gun. *BOC! BOC!* Heat squeezed off two rounds, both shells hitting their mark. *BLOCKA! BLOCKA! BLOCKA!* Not to be outdone, Baby Ghost let off a series of shots, knocking Suge off of his feet. The minute his body hit the ground, both men stood over him and emptied the clips to their firearms, silencing him for good.

CHAPTER 40

Ibiza

After dinner and a nice walk on the beach, Hitta returned to the villa with his two ladies. For the past three days, they had been enjoying each other's company without any interruptions. All three of them had their phones on do not disturb. Hitta sat between Ashley's legs in front of the fireplace. He was inhaling the potent weed smoke while she played in his hair. Ashley was dressed in some sexy lingerie; her oiled skin gave her a glow. Both Hitta and Ashley stared at Nautica, admiring her beauty. She was dressed in some sexy lingerie also. "What?" Nautica asked with a smile.

"You are so fucking sexy," Ashley replied.

"Thank you," Nautica blushed.

"I gotta be the luckiest man alive right now," Hitta finally spoke. "At times, this be a lil hard to take in. Pause," he chuckled. "How many niggas get this lucky? I'm in Ibiza with two of the most beautiful women in the world. You ladies are truly a dream come true," he added while getting up from in between Ashley's legs. He walked over and grabbed the bottle of D'USSÉ from the glass table. He held the bottle out for both of them to tap, then he opened it and poured some on the floor for his fallen comrades. Then, he poured each of them a glass. "Nauti," he said, calling her by the nickname he'd given her. "Ash and I been through some shit together over the years. Baby girl had my back in every situation. She's been down for me since we were kids. Her loyalty has been proven on many occasions and vice versa. Ashely will do anything for me including kill, die, and get on the stand and lie. If you are not willing to do the same for us, then we can't be a family. We can just enjoy this trip, have fun, and enjoy this good vibe, then when we get back, we can go our separate ways with no hard feelings," he said, looking Nautica in her eyes. She matched his stare without blinking.

"I'm all in, Amir," she said then looked to Ashley. "I'm all in, Ash, one hundred percent," she added.

"So, let's make a toast." Hitta held up his glass.

"To us." Ashley touched glasses with Hitta.

"To us." Nautica did the same.

"To us," Hitta repeated, and they all threw back their shots.

Nautica stared at Ashley while she stared at Hitta. One thing Nautica loved about Ashley was her undying love and loyalty to Hitta. It was like every time she looked at him, she was doing it for the first time. The look bled love. It was like Ashley worshipped Hitta.

Hitta pulled Ashley in his arms and kissed her passionately. Nautica watched as she poured herself another shot. The two of them locked lips like this was their last kiss. Nautica downed her shot and joined the action.

. . .

MEANWHILE IN CONEY ISLAND

Caine cruised the streets in his brand-new Mercedes-Benz G63 G-wagon. It was triple black with red rims and tinted windows. There would be no more stunting from the passenger's seat for him. He pulled up on 36th and Neptune Avenue, in front of the corner store, just as Flee and Gat were exiting. They both smiled when they saw Caine hop out of the SUV. "That's what the fuck I'm talking about, bro," Flee said with a huge smile on his face. "This is pretty," he added while greeting Caine with the UGF handshake.

"This shit sexy as fuck, but ya ass too little to be jumping out this big ass truck, nigga," Gat teased. "Why you cop this big shit?" he added.

"Same reason I keep a big ass gun, nigga. It makes me feel taller," Caine replied, and they all shared a laugh. "Y'all spoke to Shoota?" he asked.

"Yeah, he at Peso's crib laying low, getting the rest he needs," Flee replied.

Caine's iPhone vibrated and caught all of their attention. He picked up instantly. "What's the vibes?" he answered. The caller was rambling so fast that he could barely understand what he was saying. "Slow down, nigga. You said who is at the barbershop?" Caine asked and let the caller repeat the name. "Say less, I'm on my way now." He ended the call and looked up to Flee and Gat. "The old head, Goon, is at the barbershop on 32nd and Mermaid.," he informed.

"So, let's go bump this nigga," Gat replied, walking toward the G-Wagon.

Minutes later, Caine pulled the G-Wagon in front of the corner store on 32nd and Mermaid. He grabbed his blue steel .38 and tucked it in his waistband before hopping out of the SUV. Gat followed, and Flee hopped in the driver's seat. The barbershop was located around the corner from the store. "Caine!" a female voice called out to him. He turned around and saw Raven, his childhood love. She had a few friends with her. The young ladies walked inside of the store while she talked to Caine. "Wassup, big head?" She hugged him.

"Nothing much, staying out of the way. When you gon let me take you out? You know I miss your company," he said smoothly.

Caine looked up and saw Goon exiting the barbershop. "Yo, baby girl, go in the store. Shit is about to get nasty, I'mma call you later. I promise," he said while walking toward Goon.

BOC! BOC! BOC! Gat walked up to Goon and shot him three times at point blank range. His huge body collapsed to the ground. Caine trotted over to him and put a bullet in his head, leaving him dead on the sidewalk.

CHAPTER 41

Two Weeks Later

Hitta sped through the streets with the expertise of a NASCAR driver. He was not speeding for any reason in particular besides the fact that the brand-new car that he was driving was an Aston Martin Vantage. It was a gift from Nautica.

As Hitta cruised down Surf Avenue, he spotted Detective Greene get inside of a Chevy Impala and pull off. Hitta instantly followed the dirty cop, who was responsible for what happened to Flee. He pulled his phone out and placed a call to Flee, who picked up on the second ring. "Yo, what's the word, big homie?" Flee greeted.

"Where you at right now, gang?" Hitta asked in an excited tone.

"I just got off the Belt Parkway. Why? Wassup?"

"Remember that shit that happened at ya crib? I got one of these niggas right now. I been tailing boy for a few minutes. I'm on Surf. He just pulled into the parking lot of the little school," Hitta informed him.

"What school, bro?" Flee asked.

"288. He parked the car but didn't get out. Get to me asap, Flee. We got this nigga," he said with anticipation. "I'm parked across the street by the bus stop. If you come down 25th and take Surf, you gonna see me. I'm in the Aston Martin."

"Say less, I'm on my way now," Flee replied before ending the call.

Meanwhile

Flee turned down 25th Street until he was on Surf Avenue. He parked his Benz directly in front of P.S. 288. Hitta's brand new Aston Martin pulled up beside him. Flee jumped out of his Benz and hopped in. The smell of good weed and fresh leather filled the air. "This shit is nice, big homie." Flee admired the car's interior.

"Good looking, baby boy," Hitta smiled. "You grippy, right?" he asked.

"You know I wouldn't come to a party without my knock." He pulled the Glock .45 with a converter switch from his waist and placed it on his lap.

Just when Hitta made the right on Surf Avenue, Detective Greene was pulling out of the parking lot. "We gon follow him. That's the Impala right there." Hitta pointed out. "We ain't gon whack this nigga yet. I know he gon fuck around and lead us to a bag," he added while sparking the blunt that he had in the ashtray.

"Say no more," Flee replied while firmly gripping the Glock. Revenge was so close that he could taste it.

Hitta looked at the gun in Flee's lap and smiled. "That shit sexy, bro. The switch makes it a fully automatic, right?" he asked.

"Facts, bro. This shit shoot like a baby machine gun," Flee chuckled. "I got a lil plug on these shits. I picked up a few of them. I got one for you," he added.

"Say less. You know I need that."

Detective Greene made a couple of unexpected turns, and like a true pro, Hitta was on his tail without being noticed. He kept a nice distance, so he wouldn't alarm him. The detective led them to the Sunset Park section of Brooklyn, which was right outside of Coney Island. He parked the Chevy Impala in front of a small building and hopped out. Hitta parked about a half block away from him, but they had a perfect view of the building the dirty cop just went in.

Minutes later, Detective Greene exited the building, carrying a military duffle bag. He tossed it into the backseat of the Impala then headed back inside of the building and came out with another one. "Yo, Flee, you see that shit, bro?" Hitta asked. "That gotta be money in that duffle bag. That shit can fit a body in there," he added.

"That shit might be some bricks," Flee replied.

"I got ten bands that it's cash in that bag," Hitta offered a bet.

"I got ten bands that it's drugs in the bag," Flee challenged.

"That's a bet. Now, let's go find out. We on this nigga," Hitta said and hopped out of the car. He headed toward the building with Flee on his heels. It was drizzling lightly, so they didn't look out of place with hoodies on their heads. Both men had their guns brandished as they walked toward the dirty cop. Flee upped his Glock and let off a series of shots. Several shots hit the dirty cop and sent his body crashing into the Impala. Hitta fired two shots from his Keltek, giving the dirty cop no chance to survive. Hitta then pulled one of the huge military duffle bags from the backseat of the Impala, and Flee grabbed the second one.

As the two of them were making their getaway, a series of gunshots sounded off, and bullets flew in their direction. Detective Taylor, another dirty cop, who was Greene's partner, was firing two cannons from the building entrance. Hitta spun around and fired back at the dirty cop.

Detective Taylor ducked low. Once the gunshots stopped, he jumped down the flight of stairs, ran in the middle of the street, and fired some more shots. A bullet crashed into the duffle bag, causing Flee to drop it.

Flee turned and fired back at the cop, his shots forcing him to take cover behind the nearest car. Flee and Hitta were a few feet away from the Aston Martin. "Keep pulling that bag, Flee. We almost there," Hitta said to Flee, who looked like he was about to let go of the bag.

BOOM! BOOM! Detective Taylor fired, and one of the shells crashed into Hitta's rib cage, nearly knocking the wind out of him. He let go of the huge duffle bag and fell to the pavement, landing on his back pockets. *BOC! BOC!* Hitta fired two more shots out of desperation to put a few feet in between him and the detective. Flee fired a series of shots to protect Hitta; his shots forced Detective Taylor to roll under a car.

This gave Flee a few seconds to run and help Hitta, who was back on his feet backpedaling, still dragging the huge bag. "Come on, big bro." Flee helped Hitta with the bag. Together, they made it to the Aston Martin with both bags.

. . .

Meanwhile in Brownsville. Brooklyn

Peso pulled up in front of the funeral home in a bullet-proof, matte-black Mercedes Benz G63 AMG Wagon, which sat on twenty-four-inch AMG wheels. The G-Wagon looked more like an army truck than a luxury SUV.

Peso was here today accompanied by his best friend, Crystal, who flew in early this morning for the funeral. Nothing in the world could have convinced them to miss Ms. Vida's homegoing.

Inside of the funeral parlor, sadness filled the air. There wasn't a dry eye in sight. The love these people had for Ms. Vida was quite evident. This lady was like an aunt to everyone in the projects. She was known for her wild card games, great cooking, and after hour drinks. She was also the aunt to Peso's first love, Kendra.

Peso used the column in the aisle as a shield. He was trying to hide his face to avoid attention. For the past few minutes, he'd been tempted to walk up to the coffin and say goodbye, but he couldn't bring himself to do so. Instead, he just looked on from a distance, holding a single white rose in his hand. "Come on, best friend. Let's go say goodbye to Auntie." Crystal took him by the hand, and the two of them walked up to the coffin together.

Peso looked at a peaceful Ms. Vida and smiled. He knew that she wouldn't want anyone to be sad about her passing. Always being the life of the party, she would rather the people she loved to celebrate her life instead of sitting around in tears. He leaned in and planted a kiss on her forehead. "Sleep well, beautiful," he whispered before placing the single white rose in the casket.

On the walk out, Peso's attention was captured by Kendra. The two of them locked eyes for what felt like eternity. The sight of this woman made Peso's heartbeat increase. She was still as beautiful as he remembered.

When Peso and Crystal made it outside, he heard a soft voice call from behind him. "Light!" the person called out. Only three people in the entire world called him this, and those three people were Kendra, her mom, and Aunt Vida. He turned around with a smile on his face. He locked eyes with his first love.

"Wassup, slim?" He hugged her tightly.

When he let her go, he just looked her up and down. Kendra Allen was definitely candy for the eyes. She was naturally beautiful with a pair of green eyes that were identical to Peso's. She was very petite but somehow curvy at the same time. Kendra looked like Jada Pinkett-Smith in her old days.

Seeing Kendra on Instagram and seeing her in person was totally different. To Peso, she was much more beautiful in person. Those pictures didn't do her any justice. He gently stroked her face with his hand. "How you been, slim?" he asked.

"I'm living life. No complaints," she smiled. "I see you are living too. I'm so proud of you, Light," she added sincerely. Kendra turned to Crystal, who was standing off to the side in her phone. "Well, hello to you too, bitch," she said jokingly. Crystal walked over and hugged her tightly.

"Hey, KK," she smiled. "I know y'all having a lil moment, and I didn't want to spoil it. Look at my boy, K. He can't keep his eyes off of you," Crystal teased. Her comment caused Kendra to blush.

"Knock it off, Crystal," Peso smiled then gave Kendra his undivided attention again. "You still so fucking bad, K," he said, and the compliment got Kendra to blush some more.

"Boy, you better quit. Ain't you about to be married?" she replied.

"Yeah. She's a good woman."

"You are a good man. She's lucky."

"Nah, I'm the lucky one. You talking about me but look at that rock on your finger." He lifted her hand to get a better look at her engagement ring. The diamond was huge. "You went and got you a producer, huh?"

"City is a good guy. He makes me happy," she claimed.

As Kendra was speaking, a slim, brown skinned dude walked up from behind and wrapped his arms around her waist. "Babe, this is Peso," Kendra introduced.

"City," the man said while reaching his hand out to Peso. "I heard a lot about you, King," he added.

"All good things I hope," Peso replied.

"This girl and her family loves you more than they love me," City said jokingly. "On the real tho, Peso, it's a pleasure to finally meet you. Hopefully in the near future, we could do something together. I'm working on my album. It would be dope to get you on there."

"We can make that happen." Peso shifted his attention back to Kendra. "It was good seeing you again, slim. Maybe we can all do lunch before I go on tour," he said.

"Sure, we can. You still got my number, just hit me." She gave him a hug and planted a kiss on his cheek before walking away. When there was a nice distance between them, Kendra looked back at him and smiled.

Hours Later

Hitta stood in the living room of Flee's condo. He was pulling off his sweater and the paper-thin bulletproof vest.

Lexi, Fresh, and Lanie were all sitting around the minibar, having drinks.

Fresh was lowkey watching Hitta's every move as he stood in front of the mirror shirtless, looking at the bruise on his rib cage. "Good thing you had that body armor on, big homie, cause that shit would have really damaged you," Flee said while looking at the huge black and blue bruise.

"Facts, ya boy could have been off the count," Hitta replied then turned to the ladies. "Y'all not gon pass none of that bud?" he added.

Fresh reached out to hand him a blunt, and Hitta walked over and gladly accepted it. "Good looking, shawdy," he thanked her.

"Anything for you, husband," Fresh flirted while taking her hands and running them all over Hitta's shirtless upper body. She took her time to view every piece of art on his body. His tattoos told a story; they were like a soundtrack to his life.

"These tats and scars make you sexier. I will kiss all over them." She was now running her fingers across his scars. "You super handsome, super tatted, super light skin, ya bag super up, and you super fly. You are really my type of nigga," Fresh admitted.

Lexi and Lanie both rolled over in laughter. Fresh had always been the outspoken one in the crew, but today, she was really in her bag. "What the fuck y'all hoes laughing at?" Fresh joked with a smile.

"Fresh, you better chill before I give ya lil sexy ass what you looking for," Hitta replied.

"Oh, my God, please do."

Lanie's phone rang, and she instantly picked up. It was Shoota calling her. He asked to speak to Flee, so Lanie passed

Flee the phone. Flee spoke to Shoota briefly then passed it to Hitta, who spoke for a minute and gave Lanie back her phone. "Bro bored. We gon shoot out to Jersey and have a family meeting. Peso wants everybody to pull up," Flee informed them.

MEANWHILE

Reem sped through the Brooklyn streets in a Dodge Challenger SRT. This was his lowkey ride. Nobody knew he owned this besides his lady. Earlier today, Reem's girlfriend called crying. She was crying so hard that he could barely make out what she was saying. However, he did understand when she said the cops were looking for him. The minute he hung up with her, he started getting back-to-back calls from the homies, letting him know that his spots were getting rushed, and his team was getting locked up.

Reem parked the car and quickly walked to one of the buildings in the projects. He took the stairs to the third floor and entered one of the many apartments with a key. As always, no one was home when he entered. Running straight to the backroom, Reem pulled out a pocketknife and cut open the mattress. He was now removing plastic Ziplocs stuffed with neat stacks of cash. Once all the money was out of the mattress, he grabbed a duffle bag from the closet and filled it up with the money. His vibrating iPhone caught his attention. He pulled it from his pocket and saw that he had a message from Peso, telling him about the family meeting he was having at the mansion.

Reem quickly texted back and told him that he was on his way.

After zipping up the duffle bag, Reem headed out of the

apartment. He took the stairs all the way to the bottom floor and exited the building. He quickly walked three buildings over and headed up to April's apartment. April opened the door with a smile plastered on her face. "I'm sorry for poppin' up unannounced, but I have a lil situation and need ya help," he said.

"Boy, stop acting like a stranger and come in," she replied while stepping to the side, so he could enter. Reem walked straight to the bedroom, and she followed. "Hold up, nigga. How you know I ain't got a man back here?" she said jokingly.

"I ain't on nothing. Boy would have to know that I'm family. On the real tho, police been hitting my spots all day. Shit is messy right now. They on my line," he explained.

"Well, you can stay here as long as you need to."

"That won't be good for either of us," he said while eyeing her up and down. The look he gave her caused April's thong to instantly become moist.

"Why you say that?" she asked.

"It's already hard to just chill with you. Spending nights here would be torture," he admitted.

"Don't make me blush."

"All jokes aside tho, in this bag right here is over a half a million in cash. If they catch me, just get me the best lawyer that money can buy. Okay?" Reem looked at her and saw a look of sadness. He gently grabbed her face with both hands. "Don't look like that. Everything will be alright. No matter where I am, you will be taken care of. That's my word," he promised.

"Why can't you just run? I will run with you," April said seriously. She meant every word. Hearing her say this touched Reem's heart because his lady was talking about leaving if he went back to jail, and April was standing here telling him that they could run together.

For the first time, Reem really looked at her, not as his little homie's mom but as a woman. Standing here without makeup, she was extremely beautiful. All-natural beauty. Reem pulled her into his arms and kissed her lips. To his surprise, she kissed him back. After about a minute of locking lips, Reem pulled away. "My bad, April. I'm tripping," he said softly. "Like I said, hold this bag down for me. I will check in once I'm situated," he promised.

CHAPTER 42

Same Night

Peso's New Jersey mansion was filled with guests. Nothing major was going on. He and Princess just decided to invite some close friends and family over. Peso sat on the foot of his bed in deep thought. Princess entered the bedroom and walked over to him. She took a seat in his lap and planted a kiss on his lips. "What's wrong, King?" she asked while running her hands over his waves.

"Nothing, Queen, just thinking," he replied.

"Well, it looks like you are thinking pretty hard. No pressure. When you are ready to talk, I am ready to listen." She kissed him again before getting up from his lap.

"Do you think I've been moving funny? Like, have I changed since we've known each other?" he asked as she walked toward the walk-in closet. His question got her to stop and face him.

"You are the same man that I fell in love with. There are no changes that I can see," she replied.

"Shoota told me I'm getting soft," he chuckled.

"He's upset. Don't stress that."

"That nigga is more than upset. I never heard him talk to me the way he did a lil while ago. I never seen that look in his eyes before. He expects me to be on some cowboy shit like I used to be on back in the day, but I have way more to lose now. He just doesn't get it," he vented.

"He gets it, babe. He is just being a little brother. He's in his feelings right now. Shoota will come around. We don't need tension amongst the family, so I'm gonna entertain our guests while you go make things right with our brother."

MEANWHILE

When Hitta pulled into Peso's driveway, there were already a bunch of cars there. You could hear the music blasting from the inside. It looked more like a party than a family gathering. Hitta and Flee hopped out of the Aston Martin, and the ladies hopped out of the Benz.

Princess was standing in the doorway of the mansion, looking fashionable as always, dressed in her designer fit. She looked at Lexi, Fresh, and Lanie with a smile. "You three bitches are gorgeous," she said, smiling.

"And so are you, bitch," Fresh replied. "You must be Princess," she added.

"I am," Princess replied.

"I'm Fresh, this is my sister, Lexi, and this is our ride or die bitch, Lanie," Fresh introduced. After introductions and hugs, Princess led the ladies inside of the beautiful mansion.

PESO STOOD in front of the full-length mirror in his bedroom, just staring at himself. "I am a king. Everything I touch prospers and succeeds. Blessings are chasing me down," he said his affirmations. Right now, Peso was dressed in a white Dior button down that he only buttoned halfway, revealing the art on his chest and neck, a white pair of Dior chinos, which were being held up by a Dior belt, and on his feet was a white and silver pair of Dior low top sneakers. Several Cuban links sat on his neck. He took a sip from the bottle of D'USSÉ in his hand.

KNOCK! KNOCK! KNOCK!

There was a knock at his door. "Come in," he called out. Crystal and Hitta both entered the bedroom. "My two best friends," he said with a smile. "What's the word?"

"Check you out, looking all handsome on ya casual shit," Crystal complimented while rubbing his face.

"Thank you, lovely," Peso blushed.

"Ain't shit, bro. Another day, another dollar. You know the vibes. Pass that bottle tho, nigga." Hitta reached his hand out for the bottle, and Peso passed it to him. "Tell me you got some money counters in here, gang."

"Nigga, my name Peso. Why wouldn't I have money counters in here? Nigga, I am money," he chuckled.

"Yeah, talk that shit, best friend," Crystal chimed in.

"They in my office tho."

"Well, let's chop it up in ya office then. I got some shit to fill you in on anyway."

TWENTY MINUTES Later

Peso sat behind his desk with his feet up. He was puffing on a Backwood that was stuffed with London Poundcake, an exotic strand of weed. Hitta and Flee had stacks of one-hundred-dollar bills all over the office. They were feeding them to the money counter. Shoota stood in the corner of the office; he was next to Flee. He was giving them the play by play on when he got shot. "Shit got nasty," Shoota explained. "Niggas started flockin out of nowhere. I sent a few shots back tho, but the homie, Reem, saved my life. He popped out like Rambo." Shoota was telling the story with a spark in his eyes, the same spark Peso used to have when he was putting in work, the same spark Hitta had to this day when he smelled gun smoke. Shoota moved around all animated like he was never even shot.

"Baby boy, you alive. That's all that matters," Peso cut him off.

"Of course you would say that. This money and rap shit turning you soft," Shoota shot back.

"Everybody in this room knows I've been rich way before I signed any deal," Peso chuckled. "Everybody in this room also knows that there is nothing soft about me. I probably got the highest body count in the room, and I'm in a room full of niggas with plenty bodies. I put in enough work to last a life-time. I am just smarter than I was years ago," he added.

"Hold up. What the fuck is going on right now?" Hitta interjected.

"Big bro turning into one of these rap niggas," Shoota claimed. "Nigga been on some soft shit."

"Soft don't run in my blood. You should know that, Shoota, cause you're a little *me*," Peso replied.

"Fuck you, nigga!" Shoota barked. "I get shot, and you wanna stand down all of a sudden. You ain't my fucking brother."

"Shoota, chill the fuck out," Flee spoke up.

"Ain't no chill, Flee. Let him get that black shit off his heart now. If he don't, it will become dangerous in the long run. Let him air it all out," Peso said.

"Man, fuck all the talking. I'm off this." Shoota tried to leave, but Flee stopped him.

"Gang, you ain't leaving until we figure this shit out. You of all people know when we have a problem in this family, we get it all off our chest in one sit down. We ain't letting shit linger," Flee said.

"Ain't nothing to figure out," Shoota replied.

"Fuck you mean ain't nothing to figure out? We brothers." Hitta shot him a deadly look.

"Brothers?" Shoota said, full of sarcasm. "This nigga ain't my brother. My brother would've murdered a whole block for touching me. This nigga is just some Grammy winning rapper now."

Shoota didn't know it, but his words just stabbed Peso in the heart. Sadness was plastered on Peso's face. A lone tear dripped down his cheek. He let it fall freely. "So, that's how you feel? You not a baby no more, Shoota. I can't hold ya hand and take you outside no more. You in the field; you kill niggas. Getting shot is what happens when you choose the field. Trust me, nigga, I know. I've been shot on many different occasions. It's sad how the one nigga who is supposed to be happy for me is the same nigga who wants me to self-destruct. So, it's fuck me, huh? Fuck my daughter? Fuck my dreams? Fuck the baby that my fiancée is carrying right now too, huh?" Peso vented. "You want me to risk all this shit that I worked so hard to obtain for *us*! Not me, baby boy, *us*! I don't do this shit for me, Tymel. I do this shit for all of us. You want me to throw it all away cause you out there doing a bunch of shit that you no longer have to do? Look around, Tymel. We rich. None of us gotta be in them streets. You niggas are one of the biggest reasons I go so fuckin hard, bro. I am tired of losing niggas to the trenches. I'm the way out for all of us nigga." He looked his little brother in the eyes. "You think me and Hitta put in all that work out there for us to die in them streets?" Peso unbuttoned his Dior shirt and peeled it off. "Look at our life story, Shoota. This ink and these scars tell our story, baby boy. Look how much we lost; ninety percent of my tats are rest in peace portraits. I am tired of losing my niggas to the trenches." Peso grabbed his shirt and exited the room.

Two Hours Later

It was twenty minutes past midnight, and the game room in Peso's mansion was packed with family and friends. A huge dice game was taking place.

Leeky was one of Peso and Hitta's closest friends; he was part of the inner circle. Leeky was heavy in the fraud game. He was into cracking cards, checks, and money wires. At the moment, he had the bank in the dice game. He'd been on a roll for the past hour; he hadn't rolled anything less than a four. Leeky was drenched in sweat, with a big blunt dangling from his mouth, while he shook the dice up in his right hand. "It's eighty bands ($80,000) in it. All bets down," Leeky said.

"I got a dub ($20,000)." Hitta dropped two stacks of money on the floor. Everyone else who was playing followed up until the bank was stopped. Even Lanie placed a $10,000 bet.

Leeky shook the dice and let them go. He rolled a 4-5-6, which was Cee-Lo, an automatic win. "I ain't cutting the bank. It's a buck-sixty ($160,000) in it," he said while kicking all the money he just won with the stacks he already had on the floor. "What y'all got? Talk to me?" he added with a smile.

"I got the stop," Peso said while dropping a Dior duffle bag filled with bankrolls at his feet. Leeky just smiled.

"You ain't saying nothing but a word, fly guy," he said while shaking the dice up. He blew on the dice before letting them go. He rolled a 1-1-5, so his point was 5.

Peso picked up the dice and shook them up. He blew on the dice then let them go. He rolled a 4-5-6.

"Cee-Lo, nigga. I got bank," Peso said while picking the dice back up.

"Say less. What's in the bank?" Leeky asked.

Peso picked the duffle bag up and poured all the money on the floor. "That's a million cash right there. Everybody bets good," he replied with a smile.

CHAPTER 43

Days Later

Several labels had been contacting Peso ever since he announced his independence. They had all been sending emails, trying to partner with him. After many hours of thinking on his next move, Peso had finally made his mind up. He would remain independent and seek a distribution partnership. When he got the call from New Era Distribution, he was all for sitting down and meeting with them.

Peso, along with Hitta, walked into the office of Jon Rubin, owner of New Era, and negotiated a partnership. Peso turned Luxury Music Group into a multi-media company. New Era agreed to give Peso a two hundred-million-dollar advance. The company would now be distributed through New Era, who would get twenty percent of all earnings.

Jon Rubin was seeking a bigger percentage, but due to Peso's success as an artist and the overnight success of his artists, Peso was able to get Mr. Rubin to dance to his beat.

Peso and Hitta cruised through the Brooklyn streets in Peso's snow-white Rolls Royce Wraith. Hitta had copped

Peso this beauty for his birthday. The minute he laid eyes on this automobile, he was in love. "Bro, we really just landed a two hundred-million-dollar deal. This shit doesn't even feel real right now. I really manifested this, bro. The law of attraction is really real, my nigga," Peso said. He was so excited that he couldn't hide it if he wanted to.

"Truth be told, I didn't understand shit y'all were saying in there. But I understood two hundred million loud and clear," Hitta laughed. "I let you handle all that shit cause I know you really ain't just a rapper, bro. You really studied the game. Look how you just inked us that deal without a lawyer present. Regular rappers ain't doing that. We used to tease you back in the day when you would be studying and reading all those damn books. Now look, bro. All that shit done paid off. I'm super proud of you, Peso, no funny shit," he added.

Peso's iPhone vibrated and interrupted their conversation. "Yo, who this?" Peso answered even though he didn't recognize the phone number.

"Peso, this is Amina. Breeze got shot. He's hit up pretty bad," she informed him.

"Where is he now?"

"Still in the hospital."

"Send the addy. Me and Hitta on our way."

MEANWHILE

Shoota was riding shotgun in Lanie's Porsche. The two of them had been spending a lot of quality time together. Shoota should be resting right now, but he begged Lanie to come and get him. He needed to get out of the house for a few. Lil Durks' *Glock Up* boomed through the speakers.

"Tymel, put ya phone away, nigga. Ya eyes been glued to

that screen since I picked you up. That's very rude." Lanie rolled her eyes.

"I ain't talking to nobody, La. I'm reading something," he replied truthfully. Still, Lanie reached over and tried to snatch his phone. "La, chill before you kill us or get us pulled over," he chuckled.

"Glad you think I'm a fucking joke," she replied with an attitude. Truth was, Shoota really wasn't entertaining any females. He was actually reading an article that had gone viral. The article was about UGF members in the Bronx being indicted. Shoota instantly sent a text to Santana, so he could make sure his comrade was good. "I really can't believe this nigga right now," Lanie said to herself. "I'm really a bad bitch. I don't have to deal with this shit," she continued.

"La, stop acting like that. I'm reading an article. A bunch of the guys got indicted, so I'm checking in with everybody to make sure they on point," he said.

"Fuck you, Tymel."

TWENTY MINUTES Later
Pristine Jewelers, NYC
Shoota and Lanie entered the jewelry store. Shoota was there to buy a little something for Peso. He felt like shit for some of the things he said the other night.

Celine bookbag in hand, Shoota approached Elliot, the jeweler. He had over two hundred grand in this bag. His eyes settled on a two-tone, rose gold Patek Philippe. "Yo, E, what's this right here?" Shoota pointed to the luxury watch.

"Shoota, my friend, how are you?" Elliot greeted.

"Everything is healthy. Talk to me tho. What kind of watch is this?"

"This right here just came in two days ago." Elliot grabbed the watch from the glass. "This is an eighteen karat, rose-gold Patek Phillipe Nautilus. It has a eighteen karat bracelet; the fixed bezel has a custom diamond dial with luminous hands and index hour markers. The minute markers are around the outer rim," Elliot explained. "Should I keep going?"

"Nah, I get the picture," Shoota smiled.

"One thing I can say to you is the diamonds in this watch are the highest clarity, so it gives the watch an unbeatable shine."

"I want it." Shoota unzipped the bookbag, but Lanie stopped him.

"I got it, babe," she said then looked to Elliot. "Those Rolex diamonds in that Sky Dweller?" she asked.

"Absolutely," Elliot smiled.

"We want both watches. Bag them up for us," Lanie said and pulled a Black card from her purse. The card was a clone, but it worked just like the actual card.

MEANWHILE

Flee pulled into the parking lot of Burger King. Lexi occupied the passenger's seat. As always, she was looking beautiful. Today, she was hiding her face behind some oversized Chanel shades.

Flee hopped out of his Mercedes and walked inside of the fast-food spot. He wasn't here to purchase a meal. He was here to meet a client. He ordered a number two then walked to the restroom. A minute later, a man wearing a Burger King uniform entered. "Flee, what's shaking?" the man greeted with a smile.

"Another day, another dollar. You know the vibes," Flee replied.

Flee and this man went way back. His name was Chavo, and he was the father of Flee's younger brother. He was from the Bushwick section of Brooklyn. After a small Fed bid, Chavo was back on the streets doing what he did best, and that was selling heroin. The whole Burger King gig was a front for his federal probation. Chavo was actually the owner of this fast-food joint. "Tell me something good," Chavo said while rubbing his hands together.

"The ball is back rolling, but I'mma be running shit a lil different," Flee explained. "I'm only bringing you in this deep because you family. I still got the bricks on deck, but I know you wanna get back to ya regular flo, so I got whole birds for you if you interested," he added.

"Say word?" Chavo asked in a high-pitched voice. Flee could see the spark in his eyes. "What a bird going for?" he asked.

"For you, 65K."

"Tell me you on deck right now."

"Yeah, it's one call away, my nigga. I ain't doing no talking on phones, so I pulled up on you in person. It's way too much shit going on right now in the streets. Place ya order right now, and I'll get to you asap," he claimed.

"I need three. It's the same work, right?"

"Yeah, same work, but it's not Untouchable. I pay the chemist to do a little dance on it for it to be that Untouchable," Flee explained.

"Flee, my clients want Untouchable," Chavo said, clearly disappointed.

"Untouchable is a brand, bro. You can only buy that with

the label on it. Meaning, I'm only doing that by bricks. The dope is still a ten, my nigga."

"Can you front me some bricks on top of the birds I'mma cop?"

"That won't be a problem. Just text me when you off, and I'll pull up." Flee exited the bathroom.

One hour later, Flee parked his Benz in front of the corner store on 36th and Neptune Avenue. He and Lexi both exited the car at the same time. It was a beautiful day, so everyone was out enjoying the sun.

When they made it to the back of the complex where the basketball court was located, he was surprised by Santana being there. Flee approached his comrade and greeted him with the UGF handshake. "What's the vibes, ape?" Santana said.

"Ain't shit, bro. What you doing on these ends?"

"You know this my second home. Shit messy on my side right now, gang. A big ass indictment went down, so I've been lowkey over here," he admitted.

"Say less. If you gonna be over here laying low, I gotta get you a building key just in case you have to get low. Let's walk to the front real quick."

When they made it to the front of the complex, Heat and Caine pulled up on dirt bikes. Flee's iPhone vibrated. It was a FaceTime call from Peso. Flee answered the call instantly. "Yo, what's the vibes, big bro?"

"Shootout at the mansion tonight, round up the dawgs. Me and Hitta drove out to Binghamton to check on Breeze. He's hit up pretty bad, but he's gonna pull through. Have every-body on deck at 11 p.m.," Peso said. The minute those words left his mouth, two unmarked police cars pulled up. Detective Taylor jumped out with three other detectives on his heels.

Flee didn't waste any time. He just took off running at full speed. He made it to the small building and used his key to enter. He then sprinted down the long hallway that led him to the other building. He took the stairs up to the fifth floor and watched the detectives from the balcony. He called Lexi, who picked up on the first ring. "Papi, you okay?" she asked.

"Yeah, I'm straight. Go get the car and meet me by 33rd and Neptune where the bus stop is at. I'm in the building walking toward the exit now. This shit gon bring me directly to the bus stop. Hurry up, love," he said then ended the call.

11 P.M. Peso's Mansion

The backyard area of the mansion was filled with Peso's most trusted comrades. Princess, Ashley, Nautica, Lexi, Lanie, and Fresh were there also. The grill was on, and cold drinks were being served.

Weed smoke filled the air —not any regular weed, exotic shit only. This wasn't a regular crowd of people. This was the Untouchable Gorilla family.

Princess started tapping her glass with a spoon to get everyone's attention. "Thank you, Queen." Peso kissed her.

"You're welcome, King," she blushed. Anytime he referred to her as queen, it gave her butterflies and made her blush.

Peso stood up and took another drag from the blunt in his hand. He then passed it to Flee, who sat directly on his left side. "First and foremost, thank you all for showing up here tonight. If you got an invite to be here, that means you are family," Peso said just as his cousin, Euro, entered the back-yard with a beautiful woman on his arm.

"I see y'all started without me," he said to Peso.

"I see you still never on time for shit," Peso teased while greeting his cousin with the UGF handshake and a bear hug. "For those of y'all who never met the legend, this is my cousin, Euro. The lovely lady on his arm is his fianceé, Chanel," Peso introduced.

After all of the introductions, Shoota stood up. "Aye, big bro, can I get the floor for a minute?" Shoota asked.

"Do ya thang, baby boy," Peso replied. Shoota looked him dead in the eyes.

"Peso, I apologize for the way I spoke to you the other day. Truth was, I was in my feelings, and I was being selfish. Real shit, I was dumb. I stepped outside my gangsta and let my feeling control my actions, something you and Hitta taught me to never do. I guess I was just being a little brother. At some point, we all may outgrow this street shit. I just never thought I'd see the day you weren't terrorizing the streets anymore. I ain't mean it when I said you getting soft, bro. You just getting smarter, and I have no choice but to respect that. Presidential Peso, you are a legend in the streets, but I want ya legacy to be so much more than some street shit. Keep leveling up, my brother. I know I ain't just speaking for me when I say you are one of the realest niggas to ever walk this earth. Here is a lil something to show my love." Shoota reached in Lanie's purse and pulled out a huge jewelry box. He handed it to his brother.

Peso opened it instantly. A huge smile was plastered across his face when he saw the bust down Patek Phillipe. "Good looking, baby boy." Peso hugged his little brother.

Fresh stood up with a Rolex jewelry box in her hand. "Bro, if you don't mind, can I get a minute?" She looked to Peso.

"Do ya thang, sis," he smiled, still looking at his new

watch. Peso had a crazy watch collection, but this timepiece here was his new favorite. Fresh walked over to Hitta.

"Here, you bum ass nigga," she joked. "We couldn't get the watch you requested but take this one until we find it."

"So, that mean my pieces hit?" Hitta smiled with arrogance. "Thanks tho, ladies."

Peso downed the cup of yak in his hand before speaking. "Like I said a few minutes ago, thank you all for pulling up. If you are here, that means myself or one of my closest friends trust you one hundred percent." He gave everyone a once over then continued. "Things have just changed for us all in these past couple of years. The level up has been challenging but look at us. We look damn good," he grinned. Hitta reached out and passed him a blunt. Peso gladly accepted it and took a few good pulls before continuing. "Yeah, we took some losses, but this one big win is so fucking beautiful. The sky is the limit for us, my brothers and sisters. It's nothing but kings and queens in here. There is way more to life than the hood. Stop putting limits on the things we can do. I want my story to be so unreal that people in the hood think it's a myth," he chuckled. "I'm laughing, but I'm dead serious. Luxury Music is officially independent. We ain't just a label no more; we a multi-media company. Shit about to be bigger than ever. Crazy thing is, shit is playing out the same way I always seen it playing out in my head.

"A nigga gonna be putting out merch, movies, documentaries, video games, books. Who knows, I may just get into fashion. All this shit is for us, not just me, *us*. I got jobs for whoever want them. Me and Hitta just signed a deal for $200 million with New Era Distribution. I'm about to change the game. Things only gonna get bigger for us. The level up doesn't stop here. I may own a basketball team in the next few years. I just want my family on top with me. The UGF ain't like no other organization. We are really a family. The universe put me and Hitta in a position to change lives, and we putting y'all in the same position. Not a mouth in this family goes unfed. Look around. It's about a half billion sitting here in this backyard," he said, and everyone looked around at each other in approval. "With that being said, I am not letting anybody destroy what took me and Hitta's blood, sweat, and tears to build. Some of y'all may not know all the shit me and bro had to go through to get where we are today. Niggas done lost a lot of people along the way. Niggas had to put in a lot of pain along the way. We came way too far to turn back.

"Look at all the apes that just got indicted for the dope. Nigga, that shit so good it's killing people. That dope taking niggas off the count," he chuckled. "Real shit tho, I'mma say this one time and one time only. Keep that drug shit away from me. I'm sure all of y'all got some change tucked away. Lil bro buying me Pateks and shit." He got a laugh out of everyone. "What's the sense of being rich if we can't enjoy the fruits of our labor? There is so much legal shit we can do to stay rich and create more money. I'm tryna build generational wealth. I'm trying to make sure our kids' kids are great. Dope ain't the only way to eat." Peso looked down at his iPhone and shook his head. "Someone just sent me another article. Sixty-four apes in Staten Island just got indicted on drug charges. Look at all these overdoses. This right here is what I'm talking about. I don't want no parts of this. We ain't make it out of the trenches just to go back every day and sit around. The world is so much bigger than New York City. Look what's going on. Niggas getting locked up every single day. Sooner or later, the Feds gon start knocking. Fall back from the drug shit, move whatever y'all got left, and take a break. These baddies right here," he pointed to Lexi and the crew, "they got the swipe game on lock. You niggas can learn a lot from them. I don't care what y'all do, just stay away from the dope for a minute please," he begged. "Most of y'all already know Crystal and Tamara. Both of them were in the Navy; now they work for the label. All that aqua-woman shit is over," he teased.

"Fuck you, nigga." Crystal playfully gave him the finger.

"On some real shit tho, there are a lot of spots open. All of y'all here know music. I got spots open in my camp, plenty of spots. Look at Mariah. She's the hottest manager out right now. All her artists got number one records. Y'all can do the same. I love y'all, man. I swear I do. There is nothing I wouldn't do for y'all. Let's just continue to level up. I already spoke my peace. If y'all don't have nothing to say, we can just kick back and enjoy our family."

Minutes later, Peso was standing at the grill, flipping the chicken over, when Hitta approached him. "Yo, bro, I got something I need to tell you," Hitta said.

"What's the vibes, my brother?"

"I fucked Kat," Hitta admitted. "Before you go in on me, just hear me out. I never wanted to cross that line, but shawdy was doing too much. She was begging for it. I even caught her trying to lace my drink one day. Never did I ever make an advance toward her. She always came for me," he claimed.

"I already knew you hit that, my nigga," Peso smiled. "Just wanted to see how long it was gonna take you to tell me. I'm glad you finally got it out," he added.

"I just ain't wanna be judged," Hitta admitted.

"When have you ever known me to be judgmental? Hitta, you are my best friend. You know damn near all my secrets and vice versa. Where you are right now, I been there before, bro. You know that. Out of everybody in the crew, I always had the hardest time keeping my dick in my pants. The same way Kat was off limits, so was Goldie when I fucked her. Truth is, we men, my boy. Shit happens. I love you no matter what, nigga. Who knows? If I wasn't fucking Roxy, I prolly would of fucked Kat too," he said, and both of them shared a laugh.

The two of them kicked it for a few more minutes before Peso called over Reem, Caine, and Santana. When they approached, he got straight to the point. "I called y'all three over here because all of y'all are on the run. Reem and Santana, y'all got drug beefs. That shit can be handled," Peso said and turned to Caine. "Baby boy, you got a more serious issue. Them people looking for you for a body. The nigga you slumped daughter or niece picked you out. I'm sure we can let our money talk. I will never ask a man to turn himself in, but I am letting you niggas know I am with y'all one hundred percent."

CHAPTER 44

Two Weeks Later
Bro-Day in Coney Island

Today was Bro-Day, a Coney Island holiday. People from all over came out to show love. Everyone was having a great time. This was the hood, but it looked more like a star-studded event. There were all types of people in attendance. There today, you had rappers, NBA stars, WNBA stars, street stars, gang stars, glam stars, social media stars, Instagram models, real models, and a bunch of hood rats blending in with the models.

The entire Mermaid Avenue was blocked off. It was really lit out there right now. Peso and his entourage were in attendance. He and Hitta stood there in a parking lot on 25th Street and Mermaid Avenue. They were surrounded by several NBA stars from Coney Island.

All types of luxury automobiles were sitting around, looking clean. This particular section looked more like a car show. People were crowding around, trying to get a picture.

Today, Peso had backed out his Rolls Royce Wraith, Hitta

came in his Aston Martin Vantage, Flee pulled up in his drop head Mercedes SLSS0, Shoota was in a brand-new drop head Ferrari 458 Spider, Heat was in a drop head Mercedes Benz SLS Roadster, Caine pulled up in his Mercedes GWagon, and Santana went all out and pulled up in his orange Lamborghini LP 550-2 Gallardo Spyder. All of the ball players came in Bentleys and Rolls Royces.

Newz, who was Peso's cameraman, had been following the crew all day, getting footage. He was kind of making a documentary of the day; this very second was no different. Weed smoke was thick in the air, plenty of bottles were being popped, and the women were out looking good. This actually looked like a scene from one of Peso's rap videos. "Aye, Peso, you mind if I get some footage for my YouTube channel?" a cameraman by the name of Mack White asked. He was a popular cameraman from around the way. He shot all the videos for the up-and-coming New York rappers.

"Enjoy life, baby boy. Do what works for you," Peso said, inhaling the weed smoke. "You wanna know some real shit tho?" Peso said to Mack White and his camera. "We all come from the trenches. Every single one of us is trench babies. I remember playing ball with these niggas in the center back in the day. Now, these niggas all in the NBA, doing big shit. We manifested this shit. Every nigga here talked about being exactly where they at right now many years ago," he added. Mack White had his camera on Peso and the guys. Today, Peso's fit was light. He wasn't heavy on designer like he usually was. Today, he kept it simple with a custom Palm Angels track suit with no shirt under the jacket and a pair of Air Max TNs. However, his jewelry was loud. Peso brought the cooler out today. Several bust down Cuban links with custom pieces hung from his neck.

Several bust down Cuban links and Cartier bracelets sat on his right wrist, a bust down Patek Phillipe was on his left wrist, two carats were in each ear, and two huge rings were on each hand. "It's a blessing for all of us to be here right now. We all niggas who really made it from the bottom. Take a good look around. Fuck the drip and all the extra shit. Look at all the big boys niggas got out right now. Every whip here is paid for." He pointed to the cars, and Mack White and Newz both rotated the camera around to give the viewers a good look at all of the luxury automobiles. "Coney Island niggas stunt different. Yo, Flee, y'all pull up real quick," he called out.

Flee approached along with Shoota, Caine, Gat, and Heat. "Look at my young niggas. They each got a lead role in this movie," Peso grinned. "They don't rap or play ball; these niggas right here stunt for a living. Look at all that water on my niggas. Good quality diamonds hit different. We ain't into blurry stones, only water. Ain't a watch here under eighty racks," he bragged.

Everyone began flashing their watches in the camera. "Big packs too." Caine took the Goyard bookbag from his back. He opened it, and it was filled with rubber banded stacks of money. The bookbag had at least 100K inside.

"I told you. They stunt for a living," Peso said with a smile. "They may not rap or hoop, but they stars. Believe that. Ain't a broke nigga in this family," he added.

A cherry red Lamborghini LP 610-4 Huracan coupe pulled up and stole everyone's attention. Matt Murda hopped out looking like money. "This another legend. Told y'all my niggas stunt for a living. The big homie brought the Lamb out."

. . .

THIRTY MINUTES Later

Flee and the guys stood not too far from where Peso and the others were standing. A bunch of young ladies surrounded them. "Yo, ain't that Isis over there?" Caine whispered to Flee and Shoota, who looked in the girl's direction.

"Hell yeah, that's her," Flee replied.

"Say less. I'm about to bump that op ass bitch," Caine scowled.

"Not here, gang. It's way too many people," Flee reminded him.

"Respectfully, big bro, our brother is dead because that op ass bitch lined him. Shawdy is outta here tonight. I got it. Nobody gonna even see where the shot came from. This one is for Dolla," he replied and blended in with the crowd.

Caine moved through the crowd of people like a trained hitman. The basketball game that was going on had everyone's attention. Caine got directly behind the girl. He tightly clutched the Glock in his pocket. *BOC!* He aimed and fired without even removing the gun from his pocket. The girl's body hit the pavement, and everybody took off running and screaming. No one even saw where the shot came from. Caine just sneakily blended in with the crowd again.

CHAPTER 45

Months Later

The Coney Island streets had been quiet ever since Bro-Day. Even the war with Prince had died down. Rumor had it that the old head fled down south after the death of his main man and enforcer, Goon. With things a little less tense, Flee had been able to sit back and focus on business.

Flee and Shoota were the golden boys of the UGF's heroin operation. The two of them were copping kilos and paying Hitta's uncle to put his special touch to it. They just asked that he turned the volume down on the dope to decrease the number of overdoses.

However, the UGF still had the purest heroin in the entire state of New York. With over eighty members of the UGF incarcerated for drug charges, Flee and Shoota's clientele increased drastically. The two of them flooded all five boroughs with the Untouchable brand of heroin, and the mecca of their dope trade was right there in Coney Island. There hadn't been this much dope traffic in years. The Murda Team was the last to do it this major on the dope tip.

Flee finally had his turn. He was the plug, just like he always wanted to be. After he and Hitta scored the three million dollars in cash from the lick they caught on the dirty cops, one would think he would have slowed down. Truth was that the lick gave him a rush. The more money he touched, the harder he went.

Detective Taylor and several dirty cops from his crew had been lurking around, looking for Flee and Hitta, so he was very strategic on how he moved. Flee walked through the parking lot of the complex with his hand tucked in the pocket of his Pelle Pelle leather jacket, clutching a compact 9mm. A group of young kids approached Flee, asking for dollars. G-Baby, the ringleader of these young men, was past the dollar phase. "Big homie, let me get $10," he said to Flee.

"What ya bad ass need $10 for?" Flee asked with a smile.

"I'm hungry," G-Baby lied with a smile on his face. He knew that Flee knew he was lying, but everybody loved G-Baby in the hood. No one ever denied this kid.

"Nigga, ya lil bad ass ain't hungry. You tryna buy some weed," Flee chuckled while pulling a hundred-dollar bill from his bankroll and handing it to the young kid. "Split that up between ya crew. When one eat, you all eat. I know you gonna go buy some weed, but make sure y'all eat some food too, lil homies."

"Yo, Flee, watch out!" one of the young boys screamed.

Flee turned around just in time to see Detective Taylor creeping up on him with a gun brandished. Flee didn't waste any time. He upped his compact 9mm and fired. Another series of shots rang off. They were coming from a huge .44 in another detective's hand. Flee ducked behind one of the many cars in the parking lot. He peeked his head up and fired in the direction of the dirty cops. One of his bullets struck Detective Taylor in the chest.

The sound of gunshots were now replaced by police sirens. Flee took off running out of the parking lot, only to be cut off by a bunch of plain clothed detectives. They all had guns brandished. "Freeze! Put the gun down!" one of the many cops ordered.

"Fuck!" Flee said to himself as he surrendered.

MEANWHILE

Shoota sat inside of Chipotle in Kings Plaza Shopping Center. Sitting down across from him was his old head, Block. A large Game Stop bag sat under the table at Shoota's feet. Inside of the bag was three kilos of heroin stuffed in the PlayStation box. In the chair next to Block was a Footlocker bag with $195,000 cash inside of it. "Damn, Unk, slow down," Shoota clowned Block, who was eating like he hadn't ate in years. Block took a few more scoops then sipped his soda.

"All that ripping and running got me hungry as shit," Block chuckled. "What's goodie tho? My people love this shit," he beamed. "But they miss that Untouchable dearly," he added while playfully making a sad face.

"Unk, you asked for birds, and you got them. If you want Untouchable, then you have to buy that brick by brick. That shit is a brand, big fella. We ain't moving it without the label on it. You family, so if you want the Untouchable, I will bring the number down on the bricks for you. I have way more room than I had before," Shoota admitted.

"What's the number?" Block asked. He had a huge smile plastered across his face now.

"For you, $190 per joint, no debating."

"Say less, nephew. Just have five thousand of them ready for me in about forty-eight hours."

SAME NIGHT

Hitta and Matt Murda had just come from visiting their comrade, Gangsta, in Elmira Correction Facility. Matt Murda was beat from the long drive there, so he sat in the passenger's seat, asleep. Hitta was behind the wheel now, and he smoked a blunt as he drove.

It was 9 p.m. when they reached the city. Hitta pulled up in front of a nice house in Queens. "Yo, Murda, I'll be right back," he said to Matt Murda before exiting the car.

"Hurry up, Bloody," Matt Murda replied while wiping the sleep from his eyes.

"I gotchu, gang. I'm only gonna be a minute." Hitta walked to the front door of the house.

He approached the front door and rang the bell. About two minutes later, the door opened, and there stood a beautiful chocolate colored female. This was Vonna, and she was the best friend of Hitta's sister. She was extremely close to Hitta also due to the fact that all of them grew up together. But she and Hitta had their own bond that only Peso knew about. The two of them had been fucking since they were teenagers. She saw Hitta, and her face lit up. "Amir!" She happily jumped into his arms. He bear hugged her tightly and kissed her on the neck. "Boy, you better quit." Vonna playfully mushed him.

"You know I miss you, V. When you gonna let me taste that shit one more time?" he said smoothly.

"Nigga, you have two women. Is that not enough for you?" Vonna teased with a smile.

"Here you go." Hitta shook his head. "Wassup tho? I got your text and pulled up as soon as I could. Why Mommy tripping?"

"Ain't nobody tripping, muthafucka!" Ms. Val, Vonna's mom, playfully barked from the living room.

"Hey, Momma Val. I ain't even know you was here." Hitta walked past Vonna and hugged her mom.

"Damn, you smell good, boy," she smiled. "Amir, you know I love you like my own son," she said while getting up from the sofa. Ms. Val was wearing a t-shirt that barely covered her huge ass. She was pretty enough to give women half her age a run for their money. She didn't at all look her forty-four years of age.

"I love you too, Ms. Val," Hitta said to her.

"I know you do, now follow me." She led the way up to the attic. Hitta already knew what this was about. Ms. Val had found what Vonna had been holding for him in her home.

The two of them could barely fit in the attic. The place was filled from wall to wall with bills wrapped in plastic. The money was stacked all over the attic. "Amir, my house ain't no damn stash spot, boy. This has to go."

Hitta didn't mean any disrespect by stashing his money there. It was just that money had been coming in so fast that he didn't even know what to do with all of it. This money here was all small bills —ones, fives, tens, and twenties. So, even though it was a lot of money, it looked like way more than it was.

"You know I wasn't trying to be disrespectful. I would never play myself like that. It's just I have nowhere to put it, and I don't trust too many people. Check this out tho. The holidays are right around the corner. You and Vonna can split the money. That's my early gift to the two of you. I gotta run. I love you, ladies." He kissed both of them on the cheek and headed out of the attic.

Meanwhile

Peso entered his mansion and dropped his bags on the floor. The long flight had him jetlagged. He'd just returned from London where he did four shows for four million. Thanksgiving was two weeks away, so he made sure that his schedule was clear for the next three weeks for family time.

At this current moment, the mansion was filled with kids. A lot of Peso's little cousins and godchildren were there to keep Mya's company. When she asked to have a sleepover, Peso didn't think she meant calling the whole family over. There was at least twenty kids running around.

Peso's little cousin, Shay, noticed that he'd just walked through the door. Instantly, she ran over to him. "Hey, fave," she smiled while jumping in his arms. Peso was by far her favorite person in the world, so fave was what she called him. Peso picked her up as if she was still a little girl and spun her around. Shay was now seventeen, but Peso still treated her as if she was a little girl. This was, by far, his favorite little cousin.

"Wassup, lil momma? When you get here?" he asked.

Princess walked up just as Peso was putting her down. "Little girl, don't be hugging on my man like he belongs to you." She playfully pushed Shay, who had the biggest Kool-Aid smile on her face.

"Fave, tell her to leave me alone," Shay whined like a baby.

"Cut her some slack, Queen," Peso said to his lady while pulling her into his arms and kissing her on the lips.

"Oh, so you taking her side?" Princess playfully rolled her eyes.

"Queen, you know this is my baby right here," Peso said while wrapping his arm around Shay's shoulder. Shay taunted Princess by sticking her tongue out. Princess gave Shay the middle finger and walked away. When she made it to the spiral stairwell, she turned around. "Blame ya fave cause you will not be getting any tonight." Princess smiled before strutting up the stairs. Both Peso and Shay laughed at her antics.

"I so love her for you, fave. Princess is really the one," Shay told him.

"Yeah, that's my love right there. Now where is my other love? I don't see her running around here," he asked, referring to Mya.

"She's in the movie theater with Auntie Pat, my mom, and the rest of them bad ass kids. They were watching some new kids' movie. Mike and them are here too. They in the gym playing ball," Shay informed him.

Peso peeked his head in his home theater. Everyone was so into the movie that they didn't even notice his presence. Instead of disturbing them, he just walked to his indoor gym and got one of his little cousins to carry his suitcases into the master bedroom. After grabbing an apple juice from the refrigerator, Peso headed up to his bedroom.

When he entered his bedroom, Princess was sitting on the bed, Indian style, with a bunch of books in front of her. "What you doing, Ma?" He plopped on the bed and placed his head on her thigh.

"I started doing my online classes. I'm honestly thinking about being a teacher, babe. How do you feel about that? And get out of our bed in your street clothes." Princess playfully pushed him.

Peso got up from the bed and walked over to where his suitcases were. He opened one of them and pulled out a huge gift box. He then walked back over to the bed and handed it to Princess. "That's for you, love, and to answer your question, I think that would be dope. You gonna be the sexiest teacher on the planet." He leaned in and kissed her again. "You know how I feel about you working tho. I rather you just be a boss and run ya cosmetic company, but you have to do things that really make you happy. I know how much you love kids, so you being able to connect with kids on the daily would be dope. I'm here to support your journey the same way you support mine," he added.

"That's why I love you so much, Ty," she replied.

"I'mma go take a shower real quick," he said and headed for the bathroom.

Twenty minutes later, Peso walked back into his bedroom wrapped in a towel. "King, how did you know I wanted this bag?" Princess asked. She was talking about the new Chanel bag he'd just gotten her. That was what was in the gift box. She jumped off of the bed and hugged him. Princess was just about to order the bag for herself, but thanks to Peso, she could keep her money.

"Honestly, I didn't know you wanted it, but I do know ya style. I know what you like, so when I laid eyes on the bag, I thought of you. We both know how much you love your bags," he smiled.

Peso held Princess in his arms and stared into her eyes. He did this a lot; he really would stare at this woman all day if he could. "You are so beautiful," he complimented, meaning every word. His comment caused her to blush.

"Thank you, handsome." She kissed his lips. With no makeup and her hair in a simple ponytail, Princess was still drop dead gorgeous. Her beauty could never be denied. The pregnancy was giving her a glow. To Peso, she was even more beautiful.

"Daddy, I'm horny," Princess said softly. "Can I have it?" She stroked his dick through the towel.

"Since when you gotta ask for what's yours?" Peso replied while kissing her neck. Princess squatted down, but Peso pulled her back up. "Nah, Queen, let me take care of you first," he said while quickly pulling down the Nike tights that she had on. He laid her down on the bed.

Princess instantly began to rub her pussy. She was soaking wet. "I missed you so much, Daddy. Look how wet my pussy is right now." She now had two fingers slowly going in and out of her pussy. Peso licked up and down her crease slowly. Right now, he was teasing her. "Sssssss!" she moaned while arching her back a little and palming the back of his head. In a swift motion, Peso's lips locked on her clit as he slid two fingers in and out of her box. "Oh, my God. Yes, Daddy, eat that shit." She opened her legs wider. Peso gripped them and pushed her knees to her chest.

He was attacking her clit while fingering her full speed. "You gon cum for me, Ma?" he asked while softly blowing on her clit. This drove her crazy every time.

"Yes, Daddy, I'mma cum for you," she moaned while playing with her nipples. Princess' body began to shake. "Fuck, fuck, fuck!" she screamed while locking her legs around his neck and cumming all over his face.

Peso came up and kissed her lips. Princess then started to lick her juices from his lips and face. Slowly, Peso entered his lady and began to slow stroke. Princess was so wet that her pussy was making noises. "You hear that pussy talking to me, Ma?" He started to pick up the pace.

"Yes, Daddy. I hear that pussy talking to you," she moaned. "Daddy, I wanna ride it. Please let me ride it." she begged.

Once Peso was on his back, Princess climbed on top of him and lowered herself on his dick. She wasn't a lazy lover who rode the dick on her knees. Princess rode his dick with her feet planted on the mattress. Peso gripped both of her huge ass cheeks as she planted her hands on his chest and bounced up and down. Minutes later, Princess was cumming again, but this time, Peso came with her.

RIKERS ISLAND, Days Later

After a couple of days in Central Booking, Flee was shipped to O.B.C.C., also known as OH BOY. This was one of the most dangerous buildings on the whole Rikers Island. Flee stepped into the crowded bullpen. A look of anger was plastered on his face. He hated that he was back in jail. The judge set his bail at one million dollars. He knew for a fact that the guys wouldn't let him sit. Bail would be posted the second he made a call. He was more worried about parole dropping a hold on him. The fact that he shot a cop was more than enough for his parole officer to violate him.

Flee took a corner and looked around the crowded cell. He immediately spotted Caine sitting on the bench with his face in his hands. He knew it was Caine from the tattoos and swagger. "Gorilla on deck!" Flee saluted.

"Better show some respect," Caine replied, lifting his head. A huge smile was plastered on his face when he saw Flee, who greeted him with the UGF handshake.

All eyes were on the two of them at the moment. The tension between the Bloods and the UGF was very thick in the building. The Bloods in the bullpen watched Flee and Caine with a vicious eye, but no one said anything to them. "What they got you for, bro?" Caine asked.

"I boomed that cop nigga, Taylor. The nigga tried to catch me lackin. I got booked with the hammer on the scene and all that. The judge set my bail at a mill," Flee explained.

"They got me for a man down. That nut ass judge denied my bail, so I'm in jail mode right now. I'm super tight cause I'mma miss Hitta's party. I know that shit gon be a movie."

"Listen up!" A C.O. approached the gate of the bullpen. "If you hear ya name, step up. Kenny Jones, Sean Blackwell, Kevin Caine, and John Edwards."

"That's me, gang. Hold ya head. Big UGF!" Caine saluted.

"Til my death," Flee replied.

MEANWHILE IN CONEY ISLAND

Hitta pulled into the parking lot of Gravesend Houses. Fresh was sitting in the passenger's seat of his Ferrari. She was the person who'd called him and told him about the incident that happened with Flee.

Shoota and a few other UGF members stood there at the flagpole. Hitta greeted them all with the UGF handshake. "What the fuck happened with Flee? And where Caine at? I been calling his lil crazy ass for two days," Hitta said.

"Caine and Flee both got booked, bro. Shit is wocky right now," Shoota replied.

"Wasn't Caine supposed to be with Peso, laying low?" Hitta asked.

"He was, but he popped out for his lil sister's birthday and got knocked. He seen the judge already, and they denied his bail. That shit with Flee is a whole nother story tho. Lil G-Baby seen the whole shit," Shoota further explained.

"Yo, G-Baby, come here!" Hitta called out.

G-Baby rode over to the flagpole on his scooter. A smile spread across his face when he saw Hitta. "Wassup, big homie?" he greeted Hitta.

"Nah, you the big homie," Hitta replied, giving him dap.

"He's so cute," Fresh said while pinching his cheek.

"Since I'm cute, give me your number," G-Baby said to Fresh.

"You are too young for me, handsome. But when you turn eighteen, you are all mine," Fresh said and hugged him. G-Baby was blushing now. He loved when he got attention from the older chicks.

"G-Baby, take a walk with me." Hitta turned to Fresh. "Come on, shawdy, walk with us."

"My name ain't shawdy, nigga," Fresh replied playfully, rolling her eyes.

"You been going to school, G-Baby?" Hitta asked.

"Yeah, but I hate school, man," G-Baby replied sadly.

"Why you hate school?"

"Because I don't be having fresh clothes like the rest of the kids my age."

"Don't worry about that no more. I'mma make sure you fresh for school. I need you to do something for me tho."

"You need me to put some work in, big homie?" G-Baby said, forming his finger like a gun.

"Nah, lil homie. I just need you to finish school," Hitta replied.

G-Baby was a good kid, who came from a single parent

home. His mom had way more kids than she could afford, so they suffered by being teased by other kids for not having the latest clothes and sneakers. "That's easy because I already get good grades," G-Baby claimed.

"That's wassup cause if you gonna be my lil partner one day, I need you to be smart. I need one more thing from you, lil homie. I need to know what happened with Flee and that cop. The guys told me you were right there."

G-Baby pulled out his cellphone, went through the videos, and then handed it to Hitta. After watching the video about three times, Hitta sent it to his phone. "This gonna help Flee out, lil homie. Thank you," Hitta said while pulling a huge bankroll from his pocket and handing it to GBaby. "This should be more than enough for you to get you fresh. Make sure you look out for your brothers and sisters."

CHAPTER 46

Days Later

Peso had just finished booking the club for Hitta's surprise birthday party. Ashley and Nautica were in charge of hiring all of the bottle girls and strippers. Peso's iPhone vibrated and stole his attention. He answered the FaceTime call. "Wassup, brother?" Ashley's face popped up on the screen.

"Same shit, different day. The club is booked," Peso replied.

"Good, cause me and Nauti hired all the bottle girls and dancers. We are trying to get a few people to perform. Do you have anybody in mind?"

"I'll hit Jeezy and a few other good niggas I fuck wit. You know bro love the Snowman. Everybody gon pop out to show Hitta love tho, so getting people to perform will be easy. I was able to get the gorilla too."

"So, you were dead serious about this gorilla thing?"

"Ash, you of all people know Hitta is gonna wild the fuck out when he sees the gorilla in the spot. That shit is gonna make his day. Bro fuck around and try to slap box that shit,"

Peso chuckled. "Shit gon be epic. We gonna do it bigger than Big Meech did for his birthday. When y'all coming back to New York?" he asked.

"Nauti has two more days of filming, so we hopping on the flight after that."

"Say less. Be safe and make sure you hit me when y'all land," Peso said and ended the call with Ashley.

Peso hopped in his Rolls Royce and headed to the studio. He had to meet up with Baby Buccs. After a one-hour drive, Peso entered the studio. Baby Buccs was already there, laying down some tracks. In the studio with him was an up-and-coming artist who went by the name of Quelly Bands. Just like Baby Buccs, the kid went hard.

Baby Buccs exited the booth and greeted Peso with some dap. "What you think, big homie?" he asked Peso.

"Good track, but I think you could have went a lil harder. It's okay to step out of your normal sometimes, bro. Don't be scared to think outside of the box and be more creative. You can do things different and still be you. I wanna play something for you when you done."

"You can play it now," Baby Buccs replied.

"Yo, Lee, play that track I sent you earlier," Peso said to his engineer. About a minute later, a beat dropped. Baby Buccs and Quelly Bands had never heard anything like this before.

"This beat is fire. Who made this, Twizzy?" Quelly Bands asked.

"Nah, my nigga, that's all me," Peso said with a smile. "Y'all tryna fuck with this?"

"Hell yeah," Quelly said and slapped fives with Baby Buccs. This was a big moment for Quelly. He had a chance to get on a track with one of the biggest names in the game right now, and he most definitely planned to show out.

MEANWHILE IN CALIFORNIA

Hitta walked through the doors of Nautica's luxury apartment and found her and Ashley in the kitchen, frying chicken and making waffles from scratch. Both of them were dressed in wife beaters and boy shorts. He greeted both of his women with a kiss on their lips. "I came home just in time," Hitta smiled while grabbing a piece of chicken from the pan.

"Wash your hands," both women said at the same time. Hitta just shook his head and smiled while putting his hands up as if he was surrendering. "I gotta catch my flight back to New York in six hours. We staying in or heading out?"

"Bae, why don't you just leave with us?" Ashley asked.

All of their attention was stolen by the sound of someone fumbling with the doorknob. Hitta lowkey brandished his gun and put it behind his back. Nautica walked to the door and opened it.

Standing on the other side was Raymond Royal, her ex. He was trying to use a key that no longer worked. "As you can see, I changed my locks. Like why pop up if we haven't talked in months?" Nautica said while rolling her eyes.

"C'mon, Nautica. Don't be like that, babe. I just wanna come home," Ray pleaded.

"This is not your home, Ray, and I am not your babe. You can get your things and leave, so that way I don't have to worry about you coming back." She stepped to the side and let him in. Ray stepped in and saw Hitta and Ashley. Him and Hitta locked eyes, and he then looked to Ashley and shook his head. "So, this what we doing? You really doing this?" Ray asked.

"Nauti, I see you and Ray have some unfinished business y'all need to discuss," Hitta said before turning to Ashley. "Get dressed, Ma. We gon give these two some privacy."

"Why do you two have to leave? This is our home. He's gonna get his things and get the fuck out," Nautica said. She was ready to cry. She didn't want this to mess up what she was building with Hitta and Ashley.

"Love, it seems like he needs some closure. Me and Ash gon step out for a few and let you two chop it up for a minute, so y'all can come to an understanding on what it is. If we come back in twenty minutes and boy is still in your face, then that means you chose him over us, and we will be out your way," he said while heading toward the door. "Ash, hurry up please," he called out.

"I'm coming." Ashley walked back into the living room dressed in some Nike tights and a Nike sports bra. "I'm ready, bae," she said.

Hitta looked to Nautica. "Twenty minutes, Nauti," he said while opening the door.

"All I need is five. He doesn't have much shit here," Nautica replied.

THE FOLLOWING DAY

The time was now 9:32 a.m. Hitta and Peso sat outside of Great Meadow Correction Facility, also known as Comstock. Today was the day their day one comrade was set to be released after doing a six-year bid for attempted murder.

At exactly 9:40, Capo came strolling out of the maximum-security prison. He was dressed in a Kenzo sweatsuit and a pair of Balenciaga runners. The six years he had spent behind the wall had done his body justice. Capo had always been in shape, but now, he looked like an action figure. His long hair was pulled back into two braids, and his shape up was crispy. Capo was a spitting image of the rapper, Jim Jones.

He saw his two closest friends sitting on the hood of a 2016 Bentley and ran over to them. "My brothers," he said while bear hugging them both.

"Welcome home, big bro," Peso said, all smiles.

"Good looking, gang. I missed y'all niggas, man, and Peso, I'm super proud of you. You really did everything you said you were gonna do." He then turned to Hitta. "I'm proud of you too, my nigga. Y'all niggas is living legends. This is how y'all doing it?" Capo eyed the Bentley.

"Nah, gang, that's how we doing it. Welcome to the level up, my nigga. The only way to go from here is the top, no homo," Hitta replied. "Let's get from in front of this jail."

THE FINAL CHAPTER

January 3, 2016

Tonight was the big night. The night of Hitta's surprise party was finally here. Club Lust was packed. Everybody who was somebody showed up to show Hitta some love. You had rappers, trappers, ball players, actors, models, radio personalities, Instagram models, gangsters, drug dealers, scammers, chicken heads, classy women, and so much more.

Peso had Hitta thinking the party was an event for the label. He had no idea what was in store for him tonight. Hitta walked inside of the packed strip club with both Ashley and Nautica on his arms.

They were both looking as beautiful as always. Tonight, Hitta was dressed in a white and silver Fendi fit with a pair of high top Fendi sneakers. He was not at all calm with his jewelry tonight. Hitta had enough drip on to feed a small town for months.

The first thing Hitta noticed when he walked inside of the club was the gorilla that was caged up in the middle of the club. He had never seen anything like this in his young life.

"Oh, shit, the man of the hour is here. Everybody say happy birthday to my man, Hitta!" the DJ announced. "Y'all better get them umbrellas out now cause Hitta and the UGF are about to make it thunderstorm in this bitch."

A group of bottle girls were walking in line, carrying cases of liquor, champagne, and a bunch of sparklers. The happy birthday signs let Hitta know that this party was for him. The club owner approached. "Happy birthday, Hitta. I came to personally escort you and your ladies to your V.I.P. section. Peso and the family are already there waiting for you."

When Hitta made it to his V.I.P. section, he was greeted by all of his closest comrades. Peso approached and hugged his righthand man. "Happy 25th, gang. The world is ours, my nigga."

"Thank you, my brother. Words can't express how grateful I am. You ain't have to do all this for me, bro. You know I'm a simple please, my nigga," Hitta smiled.

"Yes, the fuck I did —_well, we did. Ashley and Nauti helped me plan all of this. You deserve this shit, bro. This is for all the birthdays that we spent in the box, kicking the cell door down," Peso replied. "Look around, Hitta, this is us. We changed the lives of all the people we loved. We lost some to the system and lost others to the graveyard, but the ones who we were able to save, we did that. We painted the perfect picture. It's other stars in here, but our niggas are shining the brightest. Our team stole the show, real UGF shit. Look at what we created, bro. We doing it bigger than B.M.F. Meech had tigers; we got a fucking gorilla in the middle of the club. Who really running the jungle?"

Hitta looked around at all of his comrades with a smile. He nodded his head in approval. There was a lot of money in this section. "Yo, bro, I'm ready to make a movie," he said to Peso, who just smiled.

"I was waiting for you to say the words. I came with a mil in cash. Five hundred racks for you and five hundred racks for me. The money guns are on deck also. We making some strippers rich tonight," Peso replied.

"I couldn't ask for a better birthday," Hitta said.

"It only gets better. Stay right here," Peso said and walked over to Princess and Mariah. "Let me get the final gift," he said to Princess, who dug in her oversized Birkin bag and pulled out a custom-made jewelry box. She handed it to Peso, who walked back over to Hitta.

Flee, Shoota, and Reem were now standing there with Hitta. One of their young niggas was taking a picture of them. Peso hopped in the final picture then handed Hitta the jewelry box. "Open it, bro. They only made one of these, and you got it," he smiled.

Hitta almost fainted when he saw the exotic see-through Richard Millie timepiece. The watch was a one of one. Hitta already had a Richard Millie with a white band on his left wrist, so he put the one of one on his right wrist. "That's 1.5 on ya wrist, my nigga. You really the trillest." Peso threw one arm around him. "It's your quarter year, my brother. A lot of our brothers ain't make it this far, but you did. Let's go turn up," Peso smiled.

"Say that. Fuck this V.I.P. shit. I'm tryna mingle with the people. Where the money guns at?" Hitta replied with a smile.

TWENTY MINUTES Later

Lexi and her crew came out to show Hitta some love. They would not have missed this party for anything in the world. In such a short amount of time, the UGF had become their family. Every immediate member had embraced them with nothing but love from the start.

Fresh approached Hitta and hugged him tight. "Happy Birthday, Papi." She kissed his cheek.

"Thank you, baby girl. I ain't gon lie. You got a nigga ready to rip that fit off you, Ma," Hitta flirted.

"I would love that," Fresh replied while biting her bottom lip.

Hitta looked her up-and-down with a smile. So many things were running through his head right now. The Fendi bodysuit that Fresh had on fit her body perfectly. It looked like someone had painted it on her. "You gon be my gift tonight, Fresh?" he asked.

"I'll be your gift forever." She winked at him before walking off.

"That lil bitch is bad," Hitta said to himself as he watched her walk away.

Minutes later, Fresh returned with Lexi and Lanie at her side. She held a Richard Millie jewelry box in her hand, and Lanie held a big red jewelry box in hers. "Go first, sis," Lanie said to Fresh.

Fresh opened the box, and Hitta smiled when he laid eyes on the eighteen-karat gold Richard Millie with the Cuban link band. "Y'all really found it tho." He nodded his head in approval.

"That ain't it tho, bro. Happy birthday," Lexi said while Lanie opened her jewelry box, revealing a yellow- gold bust down Cuban link choker. The huge pendant said "HITTA." The high-quality stones danced all through the pendant.

"Let me put it on you, so you can add it to your drip," Fresh said.

. . .

MEANWHILE IN MDC-BROOKLYN

Rolex Rich laid back on his bunk. All of his attention was on the screen of the contraband iPhone in his hand. He was currently watching live footage from Hitta's birthday party. Rich had to admit that the young man knew how to stunt.

Today was not only Hitta's birthday, but it was Rich's birthday also. He wouldn't be at the club tonight, but after the midnight count, he would be having his way with the lady C.O. who worked overnight. Rolex Rich took a pull from the blunt that he was smoking. "These niggas really know how to ball," he said to himself. Rich had never seen anything like this in his life. Hitta's birthday party would go down in history. The UGF was the first to outdo BMF. There was literally money everywhere, piles of money at that.

A knock on the cell door stole the attention of Rich. Quickly, he tucked the iPhone under his pillow and got up from his bunk. "Who is it?" he asked while uncovering the cell window.

"I got something for you," a lady C.O. said and slid an envelope under the door before walking off.

Rolex Rich quickly opened the envelope. It contained a birthday card, some pictures, and a short letter. He read the letter first:

MAY this message find you in the greatest stages of health in all aspects. Happy birthday, old man! Did you look at the pics yet? These pics are proof that I stayed solid and never made an advance toward ya bitch. It was her who made advances toward me. Shawdy even tried to lace my drink. Every message between me and her is now in your face. You should be mad at your wife, not me. But anyway, you are officially an op now, so I will enjoy that pussy every chance I get. Sleep well, big fella!

Respectfully,

Mr. Untouchable Himself...

ROLEX RICH PUT the letter down and looked through the pictures. Hitta was telling the truth the whole time. Rich just shook his head in frustration because he had made a move that he could never take back. His next move was a foul one, but what was done was done.

BACK AT CLUB Lust

Hitta was onstage having a blast at this very moment. Clubbing wasn't really his thing, but tonight, he was the life of the party. A bottle of Ace in one hand and a money gun in the other, Hitta did his little dance.

Ashley and Nautica were both on the stage with him, shooting money from their guns at the strippers. Out of nowhere, the music stopped, and a bunch of armed agents swarmed the strip club. "FBI! Everybody down now!" There were at least one hundred agents present. They cuffed Hitta and read him his rights. He was being arrested for the murder of ex-police commissioner, Jay Kelly. When he was escorted out of the club, the media had a field day taking pictures.

HOURS Later

What started out as a wonderful night had ended in disaster. The Feds had locked up Hitta, and both Reem and Santana were booked on state charges.

Flee pulled into the parking garage of his building. He parked his Mercedes and headed for the elevator. As he pressed the button, he noticed Detective Taylor standing beside him with a .9mm Sig Sauer brandished. He took a step closer to Flee. "We can do this the easy way, or we can do this the hard way, but I want my fucking money!" he barked while stepping a little closer to Flee. That was a big mistake because Flee quickly grabbed his gun. The two of them were now in a tussling match. Flee threw a wild haymaker with his left and connected to the cop's jaw. The blow caused him to lose grip of his gun, which fell to the ground. Quickly, Detective Taylor recovered the gun. Flee grabbed him again, and they began to scuffle.

BOOM! A gunshot sounded off, and Detective Taylor slowly dropped the gun and fell to the ground, holding his chest. Flee picked up the gun and began pacing back-and-forth. His mind was racing because he was almost caught slipping. He kept asking himself how this dirty cop got his new location. He didn't know what to do right now, so he pulled out his phone and called Peso.

"Yo, bro," Peso answered on the first ring.

"Big bro, I think I fucked up," Flee said, talking very fast. "I shot Taylor again. I came home, and the nigga was waiting for me in my building," he explained.

"Flee, slow down. You are talking way too fast, bro. Take a deep breath and breathe;" Peso attempted to calm him down. "Now talk to me, baby boy."

"I came home, and the nigga was here waiting for me. He had his gun drawn, and I grabbed it. We tussled, and the gun went off," Flee explained.

"Fuck, Flee!" Peso said. He couldn't believe what he'd just heard. "Where you at?"

"In the parking garage of my building."

"That nigga next to you?"

"Yeah. He ain't got a vest on, so he just laying here bleeding out. I'm not sure if anyone heard the shot, but it's definitely cameras in here," Flee said.

"This is gonna sound crazy, baby bro, but I need you to trust me. Flee, you know I would never tell you anything wrong. You did good, Flee. It was either you or that dirty cop. I expect you to pick yourself over him every time. You have to call the boys tho, bro."

"Call the boys?" Flee questioned in disbelief.

"Yeah, nigga, call the boys. Flee, this is the same cop who shot you. The nigga is currently suspended behind some shit that had to do with you. The fact that he was in ya building, waiting for you, makes him one hundred percent out of bounds. The nigga isn't supposed to be anywhere near you. You strapped?" Peso asked.

"Nah, I took his gun."

"Say less. Hang up with me and call the boys. This will make that pending case go away. I'm behind you all the way, bro. Call them now. The lawyer will be on his way to you in a minute."

"Copy." Flee ended the call and dialed 911.

TO BE CONTINUED...

Assisted Publishing Packages

BASIC PACKAGE

$699

Editing

Cover Design

Formatting

UPGRADED PACKAGE

$1,000

Typing

Editing

Cover Design

Formatting

ADVANCE PACKAGE

$1,400

Typing

Editing

Cover Design

Formatting

Copyright registration

Proofreading

Upload book to Amazon

LDP SUPREME PACKAGE

$1,700

Typing

Editing

Cover Design

Formatting

Copyright registration

Proofreading

Set up Amazon account

Upload book to Amazon

Advertise on LDP, Amazon and Facebook Page

Submission Guidelines

Submit the first three chapters of your completed manuscript to ldpsubmissions@gmail.com. In the subject line add Your Book's Title. The manuscript must be in a Word Doc file and sent as an attachment. Document should be in Times New Roman, double spaced, and in size 12 font. Also, provide your synopsis and full contact information. If sending multiple submissions, they must each be in a separate email.

Have a story but no way to send it electronically? You can still submit to LDP/Ca$h Presents. Send in the first three chapters, written or typed, of your completed manuscript to:

LDP: Submissions Dept
P.O. Box 944
Stockbridge, GA 30281-9998

DO NOT send original manuscript. Must be a duplicate. Provide your synopsis and a cover letter containing your full contact information.

Thanks for considering LDP and Ca$h Presents.

NEW RELEASES

BLOODLINE OF A SAVAGE 1&2
THESE VICIOUS STREETS 1&2
RELENTLESS GOON
RELENTLESS GOON 2
BY PRINCE A. TAUHID

THE BUTTERFLY MAFIA 1-3
BY FUMIYA PAYNE

A THUG'S STREET PRINCESS 1&2
BY MEESHA

CITY OF SMOKE 2
BY MOLOTTI

STEPPERS 1,2&3
THE REAL BADDIES OF CHI-RAQ
BY KING RIO

THE LANE 1&2
BY KEN-KEN SPENCE

THUG OF SPADES 1&2
LOVE IN THE TRENCHES 2
CORNER BOYS
BY COREY ROBINSON

TIL DEATH 3
BY ARYANNA

THE BIRTH OF A GANGSTER 4
BY DELMONT PLAYER

PRODUCT OF THE STREETS 1&2
BY DEMOND "MONEY" ANDERSON

NO TIME FOR ERROR
BY KEESE

MONEY HUNGRY DEMONS
BY TRANAY ADAMS

STANDING ON HER BUSINESS 2
BY DG SANTANA

TENDER
BY KHUFU

HUB CITY MENACE
BY JAQUILLE M. WHITE

COUNTDOWN TO A KILLA
CLOCK'S TICKING
BY LO-LIFE

FO'EVA ROLLIN'
BY ASSA RAYMOND BAKER

THUG OF SPADES 3
BY COREY ROBINSON

THE PLUG'S RUTHLESS DAUGHTER 2

BY TONY DANIELS

DYING FOR LIKES
KILLING AIN'T A GAME
BY ARYANNA

GET IT IN SLUGS
BY B STALL

BLOODY MONEY BAGS
VIOLENT LOVE
BY KINGPEN

KILLA CREW
WHAT'S MINE IS YOURS
BY ARYANNA

GUNS DOWN, BOTTOMS UP 2
BY LO-LIFE

MONEY HUNGRY DEMONS 3
BY TRANAY ADAMS

CONFESSIONS OF A DOPEBOY
BY NICHOLAS LOCK

THUG OF SPADES 3
BY COREY ROBINSON

THE LEVEL UP 2
BY LUXURY KING

Coming Soon from Lock Down Publications/Ca$h Presents

IF YOU CROSS ME ONCE 6
ANGEL V
By Anthony Fields

IMMA DIE BOUT MINE 5
By Aryanna

A THUGS STREET PRINCESS 3
By Meesha

PRODUCT OF THE STREETS 3
By Demond Money Anderson

CORNER BOYS 2
By Corey Robinson

THE MURDER QUEENS 6&7
By Michael Gallon

CITY OF SMOKE 3
By Molotti

CONFESSIONS OF A DOPE BOY
By Nicholas Lock

THA TAKEOVER
By Keith Chandler

BETRAYAL OF A G 2

By Ray Vinci

CRIME BOSS
By Playa Ray

Available Now

RESTRAINING ORDER 1 & 2
By CA$H & Coffee

LOVE KNOWS NO BOUNDARIES 1-3
By Coffee

RAISED AS A GOON I, II, III & IV
BRED BY THE SLUMS I, II, III
BLAST FOR ME I & II
ROTTEN TO THE CORE I II III
A BRONX TALE I, II, III
DUFFLE BAG CARTEL I II III IV V VI
HEARTLESS GOON I II III IV V
A SAVAGE DOPEBOY I II
DRUG LORDS I II III
CUTTHROAT MAFIA I II
KING OF THE TRENCHES
By Ghost

LAY IT DOWN I & II
LAST OF A DYING BREED I II
BLOOD STAINS OF A SHOTTA I & II III
By Jamaica

LOYAL TO THE GAME I II III

LIFE OF SIN I, II III
By TJ & Jelissa

IF LOVING HIM IS WRONG…I & II
LOVE ME EVEN WHEN IT HURTS I II III
By Jelissa

PUSH IT TO THE LIMIT
By Bre' Hayes

BLOODY COMMAS I & II
SKI MASK CARTEL I, II & III
KING OF NEW YORK I II, III IV V
RISE TO POWER I II III
COKE KINGS I II III IV V
BORN HEARTLESS I II III IV
KING OF THE TRAP I II
By T.J. Edwards

WHEN THE STREETS CLAP BACK I & II III
THE HEART OF A SAVAGE I II III IV
MONEY MAFIA I II
LOYAL TO THE SOIL I II III
By Jibril Williams

A DISTINGUISHED THUG STOLE MY HEART I II & III
LOVE SHOULDN'T HURT I II III IV
RENEGADE BOYS 1-4
PAID IN KARMA 1-3
SAVAGE STORMS 1-3
AN UNFORESEEN LOVE 1-3
BABY, I'M WINTERTIME COLD 1-3

A THUG'S STREET PRINCESS 1&2
By Meesha

A GANGSTER'S CODE 1-3
A GANGSTER'S SYN 1-3
THE SAVAGE LIFE 1-3
CHAINED TO THE STREETS 1-3
BLOOD ON THE MONEY 1-3
A GANGSTA'S PAIN 1-3
BEAUTIFUL LIES AND UGLY TRUTHS
CHURCH IN THESE STREETS
By J-Blunt

CUM FOR ME 1-8
An LDP Erotica Collaboration

BLOOD OF A BOSS 1-5
SHADOWS OF THE GAME
TRAP BASTARD
By Askari

THE STREETS BLEED MURDER 1-3
THE HEART OF A GANGSTA 1-3
By Jerry Jackson

WHEN A GOOD GIRL GOES BAD
By Adrienne

THE COST OF LOYALTY 1-3
By Kweli

BRIDE OF A HUSTLA 1-3

THE FETTI GIRLS 1-3
CORRUPTED BY A GANGSTA 1-4
BLINDED BY HIS LOVE
THE PRICE YOU PAY FOR LOVE 1-3
DOPE GIRL MAGIC 1-3
By Destiny Skai

A KINGPIN'S AMBITION
A KINGPIN'S AMBITION II
I MURDER FOR THE DOUGH
By Ambitious

TRUE SAVAGE 1-7
DOPE BOY MAGIC 1-3
MIDNIGHT CARTEL 1-3
CITY OF KINGZ 1&2
NIGHTMARE ON SILENT AVE
THE PLUG OF LIL MEXICO 1&2
CLASSIC CITY
By Chris Green

A GANGSTER'S REVENGE 1-4
THE BOSS MAN'S DAUGHTERS 1-5
A SAVAGE LOVE 1&2
BAE BELONGS TO ME 1&2
A HUSTLER'S DECEIT 1-3
WHAT BAD BITCHES DO 1-3
SOUL OF A MONSTER 1-3
KILL ZONE
A DOPE BOY'S QUEEN 1-3
TIL DEATH 1-3
IMMA DIE BOUT MINE 1-4

By Aryanna

A DOPEBOY'S PRAYER
By Eddie "Wolf" Lee

THE KING CARTEL 1-3
By Frank Gresham

THESE NIGGAS AIN'T LOYAL 1-3
By Nikki Tee

GANGSTA SHYT 1-3
By CATO

THE ULTIMATE BETRAYAL
By Phoenix

BOSS'N UP 1-3
By Royal Nicole

I LOVE YOU TO DEATH
By Destiny J

I RIDE FOR MY HITTA
I STILL RIDE FOR MY HITTA
By Misty Holt

LOVE & CHASIN' PAPER
By Qay Crockett

TO DIE IN VAIN
SINS OF A HUSTLA

By ASAD

BROOKLYN HUSTLAZ
By Boogsy Morina

BROOKLYN ON LOCK 1 & 2
By Sonovia

GANGSTA CITY
By Teddy Duke

A DRUG KING AND HIS DIAMOND 1-3
A DOPEMAN'S RICHES
HER MAN, MINE'S TOO 1&2
CASH MONEY HO'S
THE WIFEY I USED TO BE 1&2
PRETTY GIRLS DO NASTY THINGS
By Nicole Goosby

LIPSTICK KILLAH 1-3
CRIME OF PASSION 1-3
FRIEND OR FOE 1-3
By Mimi

TRAPHOUSE KING 1-3
KINGPIN KILLAZ 1-3
STREET KINGS 1&2
PAID IN BLOOD 1&2
CARTEL KILLAZ 1-3
DOPE GODS 1&2
By Hood Rich

THE STREETS ARE CALLING
By Duquie Wilson

STEADY MOBBN' 1-3
THE STREETS STAINED MY SOUL 1-3
By Marcellus Allen

WHO SHOT YA 1-3
SON OF A DOPE FIEND 1-4
HEAVEN GOT A GHETTO 1&2
SKI MASK MONEY 1&2
By Renta

GORILLAZ IN THE BAY 1-4
TEARS OF A GANGSTA 1/&2
3X KRAZY 1&2
STRAIGHT BEAST MODE 1&2
By DE'KARI

TRIGGADALE 1-3
MURDA WAS THE CASE 1-3
By Elijah R. Freeman

SLAUGHTER GANG 1-3
RUTHLESS HEART 1-3
By Willie Slaughter

GOD BLESS THE TRAPPERS 1-3
THESE SCANDALOUS STREETS 1-3
FEAR MY GANGSTA 1-5
THESE STREETS DON'T LOVE NOBODY 1-2
BURY ME A G 1-5

A GANGSTA'S EMPIRE 1-4
THE DOPEMAN'S BODYGAURD 1&2
THE REALEST KILLAZ 1-3
THE LAST OF THE OGS 1-3
By Tranay Adams

MARRIED TO A BOSS 1-3
By Destiny Skai & Chris Green

KINGZ OF THE GAME 1-7
CRIME BOSS 1-3
By Playa Ray

FUK SHYT
By Blakk Diamond

DON'T F#CK WITH MY HEART 1&2
By Linnea

ADDICTED TO THE DRAMA 1-3
IN THE ARM OF HIS BOSS
By Jamila

LOYALTY AIN'T PROMISED 1&2
By Keith Williams

YAYO 1-4
A SHOOTER'S AMBITION 1&2
BRED IN THE GAME
By S. Allen

TRAP GOD 1-3

RICH $AVAGE 1-3
MONEY IN THE GRAVE 1-3
CARTEL MONEY
By Martell Troublesome Bolden

FOREVER GANGSTA 1&2
GLOCKS ON SATIN SHEETS 1&2
By Adrian Dulan

TOE TAGZ 1-4
LEVELS TO THIS SHYT 1&2
IT'S JUST ME AND YOU
By Ah'Million

KINGPIN DREAMS 1-3
RAN OFF ON DA PLUG
By Paper Boi Rari

THE STREETS MADE ME 1-3
By Larry D. Wright

CONFESSIONS OF A GANGSTA 1-4
CONFESSIONS OF A JACKBOY 1-3
CONFESSIONS OF A HITMAN
By Nicholas Lock

I'M NOTHING WITHOUT HIS LOVE
SINS OF A THUG
TO THE THUG I LOVED BEFORE
A GANGSTA SAVED XMAS
IN A HUSTLER I TRUST
By Monet Dragun

QUIET MONEY 1-3
THUG LIFE 1-3
EXTENDED CLIP 1&2
A GANGSTA'S PARADISE
By Trai'Quan

CAUGHT UP IN THE LIFE 1-3
THE STREETS NEVER LET GO 1-3
By Robert Baptiste

NEW TO THE GAME 1-3
MONEY, MURDER & MEMORIES 1-3
By Malik D. Rice

CREAM 2-3
THE STREETS WILL TALK
By Yolanda Moore

THE STREETS WILL NEVER CLOSE 1-3
By K'ajji

LIFE OF A SAVAGE 1-4
A GANGSTA'S QUR'AN 1-4
MURDA SEASON 1-3
GANGLAND CARTEL 1-3
CHI'RAQ GANGSTAS 1-4
KILLERS ON ELM STREET 1-3
JACK BOYZ N DA BRONX 1-3
A DOPEBOY'S DREAM 1-3
JACK BOYS VS DOPE BOYS 1-3
COKE GIRLZ
COKE BOYS

SOSA GANG 1&2
BRONX SAVAGES
BODYMORE KINGPINS
BLOOD OF A GOON
By Romell Tukes

CONCRETE KILLA 1-3
VICIOUS LOYALTY 1-3
By Kingpen

THE ULTIMATE SACRIFICE 1-6
KHADIFI
IF YOU CROSS ME ONCE 1-3
ANGEL 1-4
IN THE BLINK OF AN EYE
By Anthony Fields

THE LIFE OF A HOOD STAR
By Ca$h & Rashia Wilson

NIGHTMARES OF A HUSTLA 1-3
BLOOD AND GAMES 1&2
By King Dream

GHOST MOB
By Stilloan Robinson

HARD AND RUTHLESS 1&2
MOB TOWN 251
THE BILLIONAIRE BENTLEYS 1-3
REAL G'S MOVE IN SILENCE
By Von Diesel

MOB TIES 1-7
SOUL OF A HUSTLER, HEART OF A KILLER 1-3
GORILLAZ IN THE TRENCHES
By SayNoMore

BODYMORE MURDERLAND 1-3
THE BIRTH OF A GANGSTER 1-4
By Delmont Player

FOR THE LOVE OF A BOSS 1&2
By C. D. Blue

KILLA KOUNTY 1-5
By Khufu

MOBBED UP 1-4
THE BRICK MAN 1-5
THE COCAINE PRINCESS 1-10
STEPPERS 1-3
SUPER GREMLIN 1-4
By King Rio

MONEY GAME 1&2
By Smoove Dolla

A GANGSTA'S KARMA 1-4
By FLAME

KING OF THE TRENCHES 1-3
By GHOST & TRANAY ADAMS

QUEEN OF THE ZOO 1&2

Coming Soon

By Black Migo

GRIMEY WAYS 1-3
BETRAYAL OF A G
By Ray Vinci

XMAS WITH AN ATL SHOOTER
By Ca$h & Destiny Skai

KING KILLA 1&2
By Vincent "Vitto" Holloway

BETRAYAL OF A THUG 1&2
By Fre$h

THE MURDER QUEENS 1-5
By Michael Gallon

FOR THE LOVE OF BLOOD 1-4
By Jamel Mitchell

HOOD CONSIGLIERE 1&2
NO TIME FOR ERROR
By Keese

PROTÉGÉ OF A LEGEND 1&2
LOVE IN THE TRENCHES 1&2
By Corey Robinson

THE PLUG'S RUTHLESS DAUGHTER
By Tony Daniels

BORN IN THE GRAVE 1-3
CRIME PAYS
By Self Made Tay

MOAN IN MY MOUTH
By XTASY

TORN BETWEEN A GANGSTER AND A GENTLEMAN
By J-BLUNT & Miss Kim

LOYALTY IS EVERYTHING 1-3
CITY OF SMOKE 1&2
By Molotti

HERE TODAY GONE TOMORROW 1&2
By Fly Rock

WOMEN LIE MEN LIE 1-4
FIFTY SHADES OF SNOW 1-3
STACK BEFORE YOU SPLURGE
GIRLS FALL LIKE DOMINOES
NAÏVE TO THE STREETS
By ROY MILLIGAN

PILLOW PRINCESS
By S. Hawkins

THE BUTTERFLY MAFIA 1-3
SALUTE MY SAVAGERY 1&2
By Fumiya Payne

THE LANE 1&2

Coming Soon

By Ken-Ken Spence

THE PUSSY TRAP 1-5
By Nene Capri

DIRTY DNA
By Blaque

SANCTIFIED AND HORNY
by XTASY

BOOKS BY LDP'S CEO, CA$H

TRUST IN NO MAN

TRUST IN NO MAN 2

TRUST IN NO MAN 3

BONDED BY BLOOD

SHORTY GOT A THUG

THUGS CRY

THUGS CRY 2

THUGS CRY 3

TRUST NO BITCH

TRUST NO BITCH 2

TRUST NO BITCH 3

TIL MY CASKET DROPS

RESTRAINING ORDER

RESTRAINING ORDER 2

IN LOVE WITH A CONVICT

LIFE OF A HOOD STAR

XMAS WITH AN ATL SHOOTER